AUGUST RECESS

ALEXANDRA KLEIN

For anyone summoning the courage to start over.

1

INDEPENDENCE & FIREWORKS

A haze hung in the low light, clinging to the brick and weathered millwork, a filmy scrim between me and everyone else in the bar. I tried to locate the smokers, then remembered no one had been allowed to smoke in a DC bar for almost twenty years. That was half my lifetime ago, long enough that my vision had become incompatible with dimly lit places meant for twentysomethings.

I blinked as if it would clear my eyes, then noticed the open patio door. Not cigarette smoke, then, but a fine mist of gunpowder smoke from the Fourth of July fireworks riding in on the humid air. A heavy oak countertop stretched the length of the narrow room, covered in glassware, patrons clustered about. I sat at the end. A basket of beer-battered chicken wings wafted past on a tray, the smell a welcome break from the fug of stale Guinness.

I could feel my straightened brown hair going poofy as the swampy night crept in and tried to tamp down the frizz. I crossed and uncrossed my bare legs, martini glass perched in my fingertips, going for an effortless look. But my thighs smothered the barstool the way cookie dough spreads across a hot baking sheet. What I'd thought was a cute skirt now seemed ambitious. The regrettable red on my fingertips had seemed sexy at the time too.

Before I could pull my pose together, Dylan returned from the bathroom. He was in his mid-forties, tall, blondish, and built. He carried himself with the swagger of a fraternity president, snarky graphic T-shirt and flip-flops adding to the youthful, carefree aura. Back in college, I would've felt lucky to capture that blue-green gaze. I even did now, as he slid onto the barstool beside me.

"There you are." I smiled. "I was starting to wonder if you'd died in there."

"Ah, yeah, I ran into some people I know." He grinned, rubbing the back of his neck, and claimed an IPA as it appeared before him. He nodded at my glass. "Looks like you already got another."

I glanced at my mostly full dirty martini. "No, this is the same one."

For a split second, he looked surprised. "Oh! That's cool. I like to savor a good drink too. I'm not just a beer-chugger."

He raised his glass and took a gulp. "How's the martini?"

"Pretty standard," I said, shrugging, though it was more like subpar.

"Yeah, cocktails aren't really their jam here. You're better off with something on tap."

"I'll keep that in mind for my next one." I twirled my glass stem, sensing a lull. "How'd you pick this place anyway?"

A brogue from behind the bar answered me before Dylan could. "It's where he lures *all* the pretty girls on a first date!"

Dylan lit up, leaning over the bar to fake punch the arm of a bartender swabbing out a pint glass with a mildewed towel. "Awww, that's my *boy!* Natalie, this is Colin. Colin, Natalie."

"Natalie. Pretty name." Colin cocked his head in Dylan's direction. "What're you doin' gettin' mixed up with this degenerate?"

I was unprepared for the interruption. "We connected online about a month ago—"

"Natalie found me on social," Dylan cut me off. "She slid into my DMs." He gave Colin a wink and a nod.

I felt compelled to explain. "We know a couple of the same people."

"Who *doesn't* know Dylan?" Colin asked grandly as Dylan shrugged in less than humble agreement. "So, what are you two kids up to tonight?"

"Finishing your shitty martini and then taking this party elsewhere," Dylan called back as he turned toward me. "I was thinking we'd head up the street. My building has a pretty amazing rooftop. I can make us something there. It'll be a little more … comfortable."

It wasn't what I was expecting, but it would be a less distracting place to ask Dylan some of the questions I'd accumulated over weeks of cyberstalking him.

I slugged the rest of my drink. Tito's and olive brine stung the back of my throat. I brushed away a drip at the corner of my mouth with a forearm, hoping he didn't notice. "Let's go!" I rasped.

Dylan led me by the hand past clusters of bargoers. A musclebound meathead rolled up, slapping Dylan a dude's handshake. His biceps burst from his short, rolled sleeves like Popeye after a can of spinach. "Hey bro! Been a while. How you been?"

"Greg, my man! I've been outta pocket. Gotta get back into that CrossFit life."

"Yeah, man! I just put together a sick WOD. Hit me up!" Greg pounded Dylan's fist and shot me the *hey random girl* side-eye.

Greg returned to his posse, and we made it another few paces before two very thirsty twentysomethings in microskirts leaned way back on their bar stools, blocking Dylan's path with a curtain of dangling hair.

"Dy-*lannn* …" the blonde crooned. Dylan dropped my hand to rub the back of his neck. She smacked him playfully with her menu. "You *owe* me!"

He played along, "Owe you?!"

"Yes," she insisted, her cleavage about to split her leather tube top. "For our *bet* last week!"

Dylan ran a hand through his hair. "You mean the one I won?"

"*DYLAN!*" Her eyes widened beneath layers of smoky eyeshadow as he fired double finger guns at her. She smacked him again with the menu, this time harder.

They continued to play-argue. It was Dylan's scene, and I was clearly an extra, not even worthy of an introduction. Before meeting him in person for the first time tonight, I imagined he'd be more subdued, maybe even a little nervous. More like me. The two people we shared in our lives were beginning to seem like all we had in common.

I was still considering whether to be offended that he didn't introduce me to this cast of characters on his curtain call to the door when we finally made it outside. I took another step and nearly face-planted over the tented sidewalk sign whose rainbow chalk letters promised "Thursday Night Karaoke" on one side and "$15 Fishbowls" on the other. I felt like a guppy, flopping out of my own vodka fishbowl into the street.

"Whoa, Nellie!" Dylan laughed, catching me by the arm. "Don't make me beat that guy up for you." He jutted his chin toward the offending sign, eyes laughing.

For a moment, it felt nice to be caught. To be saved from myself. I recovered my strappy heel and some dignity before following Dylan up 16th Street.

He pointed to the other side of the street. "You ever been to that park over there? That's Meridian Hill. My great-great-grandfather was encamped there during the Civil War."

"Oh?" This was actually interesting. "Which side was he on?"

He slowed and parted his hands with a dramatic *swoosh,* as though it really helped paint the scene. "I dunno, their tents were like … all over the place."

"No … I mean, which side of the Civil War was he on?"

Dylan made an abrupt about-face. I nearly bumped into him. "The *Union,* of course."

He said it as if I were stupid. We resumed walking uphill in silence, and I tried to recover the conversation, pointing up at the tall ginkgoes lining the street. "Were these trees here back then too?"

"I dunno. I'm not, like, a botanicalist, or whatever." The look on his face said *bored now.* Chalking it up to the IPAs he guzzled at the bar, plus whatever else he drank before I got there, I decided to press on.

"I'm pretty sure these are ginkgoes. When I used to live here, I loved how they'd turn a vibrant yellow in the fall. You know, the Colonials even called them 'the maidenhair tree,' because the cascade of yellow leaves looks like a woman's head of hair."

I glanced over to see if that got any interest. His phone was to his ear, listening to a voicemail.

"All I know about these trees," he finally said, having, I suppose, decided to deal with the message later, "is that they dump shit-stank berries on the sidewalk that are impossible not to step on."

"Oh …" I started to say, "I remember—"

He didn't pause. "They got all over my suede Bruno Maglis, and I had to throw them out. They reeked like third-world asshole."

I didn't know what was more off-putting: imagining the smell of "third-world asshole" or the guy who was enough of a first-world one to say that.

A few blocks up the street, my feet were throbbing, old bunions freshly outraged between my sandal straps. Our walk ended at the stately pair of double doors to a building with the year 1918 chiseled into a slab of stone. We entered a palatial marble lobby flanked by two rows of pillars. Piano music rippled from hidden speakers, out of sync with the metronome of my heels.

At the end of the lobby was a beautifully preserved and now automated birdcage elevator. Dylan slid the door back and I filed in after him, pressed together in the tight space as he hit the button marked "R."

The rooftop lived up to Dylan's "pretty amazing" billing. Magical, even. Beneath a coffered fourteen-foot ceiling was an expansive space arranged with mid-century modern seating, exposed brick walls on three sides. There was a bar, empty but inviting. The fourth wall was a wide glass curtain that put all of downtown on display. The Washington Monument glowed as the centerpiece, still wearing wisps of post-fireworks shroud. A large glass door led to a terrace that would've suited a luxury hotel.

Dylan left to fetch drinks from his place, leaving me to pick a spot to sit. I kicked off my heels and nestled my petite frame into one of the plush indoor sofas. I tried to smooth my long, frizzy hair with my palms. Definitely better to admire the view from the air conditioning.

Reappearing with bottles and glasses, Dylan bustled behind the bar like he knew what he was doing. Then he brought over two of what he presented as "America's Oldest Cocktail, the Sazerac." You could hear the capital letters.

Sazerac? Who makes a Sazerac these days? I thought, taking the outstretched rocks glass. Then again, what did I know? I had only just learned about Aperol Spritzes.

"Sooo …" I struggled with where to start. "How long have you lived here?"

"Several years," he said, taking a seat in a tufted leather armchair across from the sofa I'd curled up on.

That was interesting. "Oh, so … you *both* lived here … while you were still married."

"Uh, yeah," he answered, mildly annoyed. "So, how do you like it?"

"Like it?" I asked, sitting up. "Your rooftop?"

The slow return of his smile stalled out. "No. The drink."

I sipped, holding back a grimace. Rye was not my thing. I pressed my lips together thoughtfully. "It's strong."

He relaxed into the armchair. "Since I can tell you like a good cocktail, I figured I'd make you something to wash down that dirty martini swill." Then he leaned forward on manspread knees, face illuminated by the tea lights on the glass coffee table between us as I sipped again. This time I braced for it.

"So how long has it been since," I ventured, "I mean, how long have you been here on your own? Like, when did Victoria …?"

He swigged his Sazerac. "That's old news, Mama. Old news, old Dylan. But *this* delicious little number is an old classic with a new twist."

He held up the crystal glass by its base as if showcasing it on QVC. The tea lights twinkled through its facets. "See, my buddy Dan-O and I were at The Jefferson last week. You know the bar, Quill?"

He paused, so I nodded as if I knew. "Well, we go there a lot as part of what I call our 'Fancy Man Bar Tour.' The bartender, Trinity, made these for us as a new test cocktail. She was like, 'Try this,' and Dan-O and I were like, 'Fuck, that's amazing. What is it? Is that Peychaud's?' And she was like, 'Yes, but can you taste the secret ingredient?'"

Dylan paused again, as if expecting me to call out *"Chartreuse! It's chartreuse, you savvy bastard!"* so I nodded back at him like it was on the tip of my tongue.

He was happy to help me out. "Pastis. You're tasting *Pastis*, right? I thought you might say Pernod. I figured I'd recreate it for us tonight. Pairs great with a charcuterie board. Not that I have any charcuterie." He sat back in his chair, contented.

"I love charcuterie. Is that a staple on your—what did you call it? Fancy Man Bar Tour? Or was it something you typically had at home, with Victoria?"

He sized me up for a moment, along with my transparent attempt to redirect. "I'd rather try a new flavor profile tonight."

He came and sat beside me on the couch. I was getting a little frustrated. He wasn't talking about the drink. Or the charcuterie. And he *definitely* wasn't interested in talking about Victoria.

He leaned toward me and I leaned away. "So, you're kind of a culinary aficionado! Caleb always prided himself on that too. He'd tell me about all these client dinners they'd go on."

Dylan held up a hand as if to snatch the words from my mouth. "I don't know that your ex-husband is exactly a *culinary aficionado.*"

"Husband," I said quietly.

"What?" I couldn't tell if he was surprised or just couldn't hear me.

"He's still my husband," I said a little louder.

Disgust and pity flickered across his face. "Not to toot my own horn or anything, but it takes more than a comped meal at Del Frisco's and a bottle of Lafite-Rothschild to make an *aficionado* out of some wannabe media suit."

I wasn't about to comment. Dylan leaned in with a conspiratorial grin. "Have you been to Pascual yet? I think they're getting a Michelin star."

I inched backward. "Not yet, but it's on my bucket list to eat at a Michelin 5-star."

His smile went sideways. "That *would* be an event, especially since Michelin stars only go up to three."

Ouch. Stupid, stupid ...

I let a nervous laugh escape. "Just shows how much *I* get out these days ..."

He gave a wan, polite little smile. Clearly, the whole idea of meeting him was a huge mistake. Maybe I could still land a direct hit with the right question.

"So you've told me all about growing up in New York, and how you got to DC, and pieces of the last twenty years. But you never actually said how you found out."

"Found out that Pascual is getting a Michelin star?" Dylan asked, preparing to preen again.

"No, I mean about the affair. About Victoria and, you know, Caleb." I took a little sip of Sazerac, feeling my heart pound *thump thump thump.*

His good humor melted, eyes chilly. "You know, Natalie, when you messaged about meeting up, I thought you wanted to have a fun night."

I wondered if it was too late to smush his waxy face back into its broadcast grin. "Well ... yeah, of course. I'm having lots of fun. Aren't you?"

He crossed his arms. "Not particularly, no."

I realized I was wringing my hands. I also realized I didn't care. "Look, I know what happened with Caleb and Victoria is probably ancient history to you, but I only just found out in March. There's still so much I don't know."

He didn't blink. "And *that's* how you want to spend the rest of the night? Having me rehash those details?"

I looked away. When I had imagined this conversation, even before I'd tracked Dylan down online, I'd envisioned a man eager to answer my questions and deliver everything he knew about our shared plight. I did not expect that asking about it would put me at odds with the person who should—or so I'd thought—be my most enthusiastic sympathizer. I'd thought maybe I'd end up with a new shoulder to cry on, some encouragement that I was still beautiful and worthy and, "Wow, how crazy was Caleb to leave *you*?" Some reassurance that I would get through this stronger than before. None of that seemed to be in the cards, but I needed to hear Dylan's story regardless.

I drew a deep breath and directed my words at a tiny potted succulent beside the tea lights. "I've reconstructed the timeline in my mind so many times: What I was doing. What I *thought* Caleb was doing. The reality Caleb was actually doing *your wife*—then coming back home to me from the news station day after day. *For a year.*"

I took a nauseated pause. "So I'm sorry, I couldn't help but wonder. How'd you find out?"

Dylan looked like he was trying to decide what to say next, or possibly just inventorying his dwindling empathy.

He closed his eyes and let out a sigh. "I went through Victoria's phone. That's how I found out. How I confirmed it."

I sat up in misplaced excitement. "Oh? What made you look? Did something happen that tipped you off?"

Dylan rolled his eyes and stretched out on the sofa, pulled a vape from his pocket and took a long pull. "I got a weird vibe at that *Party Lines* anniversary dinner. Then I started noticing other stuff. I looked at her texts—nothing. But her browser history … she'd been touring apartments across from the news station."

He took a gulp of his drink. "Anyway. Let's talk about you."

"Wait, wait! You can't just leave it like that," I protested. "Your wife was acting suspicious and secretly looking at apartments across from work. Were you confused? Or did you realize Victoria was setting up a love nest with her boss?"

Dylan's nostrils flared and his grip on the glass tightened. "Of course, I'm not some stupid beta cuck!"

"What did you do when you realized it?" I couldn't keep myself from interrupting.

The vein in his forehead bulged. "What do you *think* I did? I confronted her as soon as I could. She was literally in a towel coming out of the shower. She didn't deny it. So I told her to get out. Which is funny, because this was her place first."

Dylan drained his glass. I was a little frightened by the outburst, but after months on a diet of bare bones and stale details, I felt high on the new information. Caleb barely told me he was leaving me before he walked out the door. I'd had to piece the rest together on my own. This was a new insight into my waking nightmare.

Dylan got up to fix himself another drink.

"So this was when last year? Right before they got the apartment?" My question was met by clinking and clanking from behind the bar. "Or, I guess, *she* got the apartment, and Caleb just … visited her there during work …"

Dylan said nothing while I probed the worst chapter of my life from this new vantage point. When he returned to his seat, he leaned in, but not to bemoan the marital injustice we shared. Now, inches apart, his eyes bored into mine, unapologetic. A shot of electricity jolted up my spine that left my face hot and the back of my skull tingling.

His voice was low, liquored up, and tightly wound. "I don't want to waste this view on my ex-wife. I don't want to waste another night thinking about your piece of shit husband and how he and Victoria had a whole secret work romance. I've moved on with my life. I'm interested in things that make me happy. What makes *you* happy, Natalie? What made you happy before that asshole?"

It was like Bugs Bunny had dropped a cartoon bell over me and hit it with a hammer. My whole body vibrated, but my tongue was tied. A stranger was asking me this, when I'd forgotten to ask myself: *What makes you happy, Natalie?*

My answer was almost a whisper. "The truth is, Dylan, I don't know how to answer that. I've been with Caleb so long—"

He waved a hand. "I get it, Natalie, I was with Victoria a long time too. She became my whole life. But she's not anymore, and I'm doing just fine. You need to grab hold of what's left of yourself and *move forward*. And personally, I've found the best way to get over someone is to get on top of someone else."

I felt my eyes go wide.

"This is our chance, Natalie. Our chance to get the last laugh. Your chance to get the closure you obviously never got."

He had me pegged about the closure thing. But this was not how I'd wanted to get it.

"I feel like we don't even know each other …" I scooted back on the couch, searching for anything else to focus on.

"Well," he asked, palms facing impatiently upward, "what would you like to know?"

"Well, no. I mean, you've done a good job of telling me who *you* are."

"Okay, then. What about you? What's your 'thing'?"

"My 'thing'?" I asked.

"Yeah, like, what do you like to do?"

"I don't know if it's that simple, Dylan."

"Jesus *Christ*, Natalie. This doesn't have to be so hard!" He threw up his hands. "You don't have *one* thing you can say you like to do?"

"Interior design?" I squeaked. The response surprised even me. "I mean, I *used* to be an interior designer. At a studio in Georgetown."

I took a breath. Apparently he wasn't about to interrupt me again. "I loved it. I was really good at it. I even got to work on a couple high-profile projects for the Obama Administration."

"Oh, interesting," he lied, stretching his arm across the back of the couch behind me.

"But then Caleb and I got married a few years later …" I continued, "And all I wanted at that point was to work on the fixer-upper we'd bought in the suburbs."

Dylan eyed my jugular like it was his next meal and moved in to murmur in my ear. "You don't get this skyline view in the suburbs …"

The closeness was alien. Only Caleb had ever been that deep in my personal space. I realized I missed it, feeling someone so near.

This was the man my husband's lover had been married to while she was busy seducing my husband. In a way, what Dylan had said about taking something back from Victoria was very appealing. She had taken so much from me.

"Yes," I conceded, "I forgot how much I loved the DC skyline. I can't believe it's been over fifteen years since I lived here. I feel like the math can't be right."

But the math was right. I remembered each one of those years, lined up like nesting dolls, taken apart one by one, shrinking smaller and smaller into the distance.

Dylan's other hand advanced to my knee. I halted it with a question. "Did you and Victoria ever want kids?"

"What? No." He shook his head, confused. "I dunno, maybe I'll have kids someday. What's the difference?"

I looked back out over the skyline. "Caleb and I wanted kids for the longest time."

Dylan snorted. "You mean the guy who couldn't keep his dick in his pants was having trouble getting you pregnant? That's a riot."

I cringed at the comment, but more so at the truth. I looked down at my lap, throat tightening. "Caleb wasn't the problem."

"Ohhhh," said Dylan, tilting back his head as though he'd just unraveled a great mystery. He gave me a shoulder rub that was probably meant to be consoling. "Bet you feel like you dodged a bullet now, eh?"

"What?" I clipped.

"Aren't you relieved that you didn't have kids with him?"

"We did," I said. "We have a son."

"Ohhh, that's right, I forgot. You're a mom. Good thing you got a babysitter tonight though, Mama," he said, leering.

"He's actually at camp," I said, putting my drink between my mouth and his.

The arm that lay along the backrest tightened around me. "Oh yeah? So you don't have to get back home tonight then?"

I gulped my drink. "Actually, it *is* getting late. I should probably—"

"Aw, c'mon, hang awhile. No work, no kid for the summer … sounds like you got some free time to fill." His roots were starting to show in the form of an alcohol-induced New York accent.

I bristled. "I keep plenty busy."

"Oh yeah?" he challenged. "With what?"

"Lots of stuff," I fumbled. The reality was that my days were mostly filled with switching from big screen to little screen and back again. But what was I supposed to say? For years, Caleb had tried encouraging me to take on projects, part-time jobs, pastimes that never got off the ground, but the truth was I never really tried. I didn't have it in me. I slowly let everything go, eventually including my husband.

Dylan was silent for a change, letting me twist in the wind. I couldn't find a single thing to say about what was keeping me busy these days or even these past few years. And it felt pathetic. Hot tears trickled down the valley between my cheek and nose. Before I could stand up to walk away and pull myself together, Dylan's arm pulled me and my bleary face against his T-shirt. Realizing he was attempting to comfort me, not smother me, I stopped resisting.

Please don't say anything, Dylan, I thought. *Please don't say anything.* And he didn't.

We stayed like that for a moment. Then he drew my face up to his own, breath steady and warm, emanating spice and bitters. My own breath caught in my chest. I'd been skirting the moment, but now our noses nearly touched.

Part of me wanted to struggle free, but I didn't. This physical contact, this unexpected thrill, sent me swirling in a whirlpool of helplessness and uncertainty, down into the blue-green abyss of Dylan's Ken doll eyes. He brought his mouth to mine, hot and wet and strange and electrifying. He ran a hand through my hair, the other at my waist. The hairs on my arms stood at attention.

Maybe I want this.

I clung to Dylan like a life raft, pressed my mouth against his neck, tasted the salt on his skin from the hot July day turned muggy District night. I yearned for something tender, something nurturing, for someone to cradle and caress me in muscular arms that could just as easily crush me. I wanted the promise that I could be loved, that it was all going to be okay.

His weight collapsed onto me, almost knocking the wind out of my chest. His mouth connected to mine in deep, aggressive throbs. He uprooted my tank top, pulling it up over my lacy pushup bra and racing heart. His hands roamed to my breasts, then he peeled off his

T-shirt, revealing a hard, hairless chest. My fingertips brushed against it, surveying Martian territory, not yet ready to land. I felt hurried and a step behind.

Dylan's hands slid up my thighs and under my skirt. I jolted upright. He shimmied down between my legs.

"You want to feel better, don't you?" he asked, looking up at me. "You want closure?"

My fingertips pressed his chin back. "I need a second."

He released the elastic band of my underwear with a puzzled look. I wanted to give in, to shake this feeling. But it felt like trying to use an arm that had fallen asleep.

I sat up, drawing my legs together and pulling my top back on. For a moment, his expression read *are you kidding me?* He got up to fix himself another drink.

I peered out at the skyline again, slid my heels back on and gathered my purse. Dylan returned, fresh drink already down to half full.

My words were barely audible. "I think," I said softly, "I think I'd better get going."

"Yeah." He took a long hard swallow of his drink and smacked his tongue on the roof of his mouth without looking at me. "That's probably a good idea."

2

VISITING DAY

I was utterly lost. The highway was more than an hour behind me, and my navigation app was useless with little to no cell service. I was winging it through the winding roads of the Poconos en route to my son Aiden's sleepaway camp.

It was Visiting Day, the midway point of my summer vacation from parenting. The day that, aside from one phone call from him and a multitude of online photos from the camp, I would get to see my kid. He would show off his creations from woodworking and robotics and tell rambling stories that were almost as hard to follow as his handwritten letters.

A flicker of cell service let a call through. My best friend Dana's photo lit up my screen, glossy magenta lips puckered into a kiss.

I answered tensely. "Hi, I'm still trying to find the camp."

"Oh my God, you haven't gotten there yet? I've been trying to call you to make sure you got there okay, but it just kept going to voicemail."

"Yeah, tell me about it. My nav is all fucked up too, because I keep losing service. Hence why I'm still trying to find the camp."

"But this is, like, your third year visiting him," Dana blurted.

"Yeah." I gripped the steering wheel tighter. "But Caleb always drove. I never actually paid attention. I never thought I'd have to do this drive alone!"

"Okay, gimme a sec." Dana's tone clicked into helper mode. "I can look up directions to get you there, as long as we don't lose the call."

I glanced down at the dashboard clock. It was five past ten already. I'd lost any hope of being the first one to reach his bunk. The camp had to be around here somewhere.

Through a patchy connection, I relayed my coordinates to Dana, who began navigating me toward the entrance, step by step.

"I *have* to show up for Aiden," I moaned to Dana, bumping down what seemed an interminable byway. I had phoned it in too many times when it came to Aiden. Caleb had reminded me of it the day he moved out, punctuating it with a door slam.

"You *are* showing up," she reassured me, "you're almost there. Just keep your eyes peeled and your nerves cool."

Keeping my nerves cool sounded great but seemed far from today's reality. I felt like one of those old lottery machines on the local news, a thousand ping-pong balls ricocheting around inside me, each with some troubling question printed on it as they popped up into the display, one after the next.

"What if he brings Victoria?"

Dana was calm. "So what if he does? Nothing you can't handle."

"What if everyone thinks Victoria is Aiden's *mother?*" I hunched over the steering wheel, straining to see the next road sign.

"They're not going to, because you'll be right there beside him as he introduces you to all his friends and all the counselors," Dana replied evenly.

"I just don't want Caleb to make it awkward …"

"You can only control you." Dana had an answer for everything. "No matter what Caleb does or what he throws at you, you have the choice of how you react to it."

"Have you been, like, listening to Mel Robbins or something? Studying Buddhism?" I snarked, scanning for street signs.

"Hardy-har. I *am* listening to a good audio book, but seriously,

Natalie, you have more leverage in this situation than you think. You're Aiden's *mother*. Own it. Stop demoting yourself."

At that moment, it was as if the clouds parted. Sun shone on the sign. Camp Wunita—the Lenni Lenape word for "one who is able," or so camp lore told.

"Oh my God! I'm here!" I crowed, cutting the wheel hard and flying up tracks laid earlier that morning by two hundred other families.

"Hooray!! We did it! Go have an amazing visit!" Dana cheered, voice crackling in and out as I careened into the grass lot.

A college-aged parking attendant scrolling his phone startled upright in his chair. He jumped to his feet as I approached, motioning at my car with an orange traffic baton.

"Just keep going all the way down, ma'am! Yup, I'll help you out." He guided me past row after row of squarely parked luxury vehicles, following me to a muddy puddle that encompassed the last few open spots. The branches of a giant evergreen swept the gravel dust from my rear window as I backed in.

I sprang out of the car, an oversized bag with a gift for Aiden swinging from my shoulder, the scent of grass and cedar filling my lungs. My burst of enthusiasm was short-lived as my flip-flops thwacked the giant mud patch, flicking sticky, dark brown spatter up the back of my legs and onto my white shorts. I froze. Mud sucked at my feet.

"Ohhh, ma'am!" the parking attendant sighed sympathetically, orange traffic baton flaccid at his side. My nostrils flared. *Of course. Of fucking course.* I stared straight ahead, pursed my lips and freed myself from the mud, determined not to sink into the Pit of Despair. Not today. Aiden was waiting for me.

- -

A cavalcade of family members had already been turned loose on the campgrounds. The initial brouhaha of bear hugs, happy tears, and shrieks of reunion had subsided into uncoordinated milling about. I crossed the empty green Welcome Lawn and speed-walked up the wooded path to the cabins, catching snippets of joyful conversations. I beelined past the freshly stained cedar siding of Cabins 1, 3, and 5, pressing on toward Aiden.

Trotting up the steps to Cabin 11, I yanked open the flimsy screen door, glancing left and right in search of him. Two or three other campers' families watched them tearing open care packages of candy, books, and toys with such squeals of delight you'd think the kids had been in juvie, not summer camp with all the trimmings.

I ducked in toward the left side bunks and spotted Aiden. He was displaying his artwork, taped to the wall of the top-corner bunk, talking a mile a minute at Caleb and Victoria. Mixed in with his drawings were several photos of the two of us I'd sent up with him on the bus. Then my stomach knotted when I noticed the ones of him, Caleb and Victoria: playing soccer, eating ice cream sundaes, fishing in the neighborhood lake, sporting silly dress-up clothes, carving a pumpk—

A pumpkin? That was just last October! Wait a minute. How many of these memories were made before I even knew what was going on between Caleb and Victoria?

I had been standing there unnoticed a beat too long when the trio finally looked up at me. Caleb stood tall, trim and sporty in what was probably an expensive new outfit, leaning on the bunk bed frame where Aiden was perched. Victoria, a slim, athletic woman in her late thirties, sat facing them on the bottom bunk on the opposing wall. Her slender legs curled behind her in a white tennis skirt and an aquamarine tank top that accentuated her tan. Her golden, beachy hair fluttered in the cross-ventilated cabin.

"Mom! What took you so long?" He jumped down from his bed and threw his arms around my waist. I hugged him back tight, letting the oversized bag fall off my shoulder and onto the dusty floor.

"I am *so* excited to see you!" I told him, squatting down. "I got you something." I pulled out a folded sherpa blanket from the bag, tied up with a fabric bow. The blanket had tones of blue-gray-black plaid on one side and creamy fleece on the other.

I untied the bundle and wrapped it around him, giving him a snuggle. "You are going to be snug as bug in a rug in this blanket on chilly nights!"

"Thanks, Mom!" he shouted, tossing the blanket on his bed. "Did you see what Daddy and Victoria got me?"

I looked up at Caleb towering above me, hands jammed into his shorts pockets. His square jaw was set, his posture rigid. I stood up. He didn't bother with a hello.

Aiden ran up to get something from Victoria, still seated on the bottom bunk. All sets of eyes were on me now, as Aiden ran back over with the dark velvet pouch Victoria produced.

"You have to be really careful with it," Aiden told me, probably parroting his father. Reaching into the pouch, he pulled out an exquisite, fossilized tusk that fit neatly in his palm. It was flecked with cobalt and polished to a smooth finish. He placed it in my hand.

I turned it over a few times, not sure what to say. Aiden hastily took it back from me to flick open a small half-moon blade nestled within the tusk. I was startled.

"It's an *ulu*!" Aiden sang. "It's an ancient knife from Alaska, and the handle is, like, thousands of years old. Daddy and Victoria just got back from vacation and brought it for me."

I had many thoughts swirling in my head, the first of which was, *Are you two fucking crazy, getting a ten-year-old a switchblade?* but I only managed a "Wow … okay …"

"We'll supervise him," Victoria offered, unfurling her tan legs. "It's not a fighting knife. It's for traditional Alaskan meal prep. Cuts veggies, skins animals. Easy stuff. We'll only use it for cooking together."

I stiffened, wishing she'd stop talking to me. What words was she even saying? 'Skins animals?? 'When we cook together?' Did I enter a parallel universe even worse than the one I was in?

My mouth hung slightly open, brow furrowed. "Yeah, Mom, it's totally safe," Aiden chirped.

Victoria continued talking, relaxed, her lip gloss sparkly, "I know Caleb got his first knife at Aiden's age." She glanced up at him affectionately. "It's made by a native Alaskan artisan. The handle is from a fossilized walrus tusk."

Aiden pressed the blade back into its handle, returned the knife to its pouch, then handed it to Victoria for safekeeping.

Caleb slung one arm around Victoria and the other around Aiden. "Well, kiddo, I think we better get over to the woodworking shop to check out that shelf you made. We can bring it back and hang it up in your new room."

I watched, anesthetized, as the trio headed for the door. I willed my limbs to move, to function normally, like I was trying to run in a dream.

I followed them outside on the porch, where we were greeted by one of Aiden's counselors, a skinny, chipper college kid with a shock of copper hair sporting a green Camp Wunita T-shirt.

"This is Colby!" Aiden explained.

"Great to meet you, Colby," said Caleb, resting his hand on the counselor's shoulder. "I'm Caleb and this is Victoria. We heard about you in Aiden's letters."

"I heard a lot about you guys too," Colby told them in prototypical camp counselor fashion. "I finally get to meet Aiden's parents!"

He glanced at me, unsure of the relation. I exited my nightmare with a limbic kick, hand shooting forward for an awkward handshake. I introduced myself loud enough for all to hear. "Hi! I'm Aiden's mom."

"Well, uh … hi, Aiden's mom. It's great to meet you. Aiden is an amazing kid. I know he can't wait to show you everything he's been up to the past few weeks."

I forced a smile. My face felt hot, even in the temperate mountain air. I was jittery and itchy, sure that mosquitos were feasting on my exposed flesh. I just had to get through this day. Two more hours until lunch. I descended the porch steps ahead of the others, eager to break free of this scene as I tried to recall which way the woodworking shop was.

"Oh, Mom!" I heard Aiden gasp from behind me, "What happened to your shorts?" He giggled.

I twisted to look at my backside, reminded of the parking lot mud patch.

"Yeah, Natalie. Jesus Christ," Caleb smirked as Victoria rubbed his shoulders. "I hope you brought a change of clothes. You look like the aftermath of that ice cream mix-up for the lactose-free kid last year."

- -

If I'd had a tail, it would've been tucked between my legs. My approach to this whole visit was to stay in the periphery whenever possible. Certainly I had encouraging words for Aiden. I mirrored his excitement when he showed us what he was making in woodworking or robotics or what water sports they played on the lake, but I was not about to compete for his attention against the dynamic duo of Caleb and Victoria.

They barely paid me notice, and in truth, I was kind of relieved. It was as if two separate visits with Aiden were happening in parallel, overlaid atop each other like sheets of tracing paper. With Dana's words echoing in my head that it was *my* choice how I reacted to them, I convinced myself that "separately civil" was the best of all possible outcomes, if Caleb and I had to be together in front of Aiden. Rather than vie for Aiden's affection, I stood back as the natural momentum of Team Victoria took center stage, telling myself *you can't lose the power struggle if you never compete.*

After Aiden showed off for us on the spiral water slide, he and Colby the counselor raced Caleb and Victoria in a tandem kayak paddle. Caleb and Victoria won, of course. Then Aiden suggested the four of us head up the hill to the pickleball court.

"Mom, you can be my partner against Dad and Victoria."

I looked at him, surprised. "Why don't you guys go ahead? I didn't bring the right footwear." I gestured down at my mud-crusted flip-flops.

"What if you take them off? We could play barefoot pickleball!" Aiden exclaimed, excited by his own idea.

"That's a good way to roll an ankle, buddy," Caleb warned, redirecting him toward the court. "And then you'd be injured before soccer starts."

Aiden nodded, but he was disappointed.

"I'll watch you guys play from here," I said, taking a seat at a picnic bench under the shade of a huge oak tree.

Victoria and Aiden teamed up against Caleb, tapping the bright plastic ball back and forth over the net.

"Dad," Aiden panted, "when did you get so good at this?"

"I have to keep up with Victoria!" Caleb replied, mid-swing. "We play with a group of friends a couple times a week."

"Your dad is so competitive, Aiden," Victoria said, popping back a perfect dink to Caleb. "He loves to win!"

I scowled. *And now he has a winner for a partner.*

A voice came from behind me, "Natalie! Oh, it's you!" I spun around to see Tricia Melman trotting over from the woodworking shop across the field, juggling at least three creations her son Max had made.

"How are you?" she gushed. "How's your summer going?"

"Tricia, hi!" I cooed, coating myself in a sugary, social shell. "I'm good, how are you? What have you guys been up to?"

"Oh, my God; it's been a whirlwind. Jeff and I just got back from Greece—*incredible!*" Tricia's facial expressions made up for her hands being too full to gesture. "We were worried it might be too much with putting the house on the market, but the timing worked out *perfectly.* Now we're just getting the new house set up before Max and Aubrey come home."

I smiled politely.

"Take pity on me," Tricia went on, crouching as if to tell me a secret. "Jeff's been working double time since he started at the new firm. I've barely seen him! I have ten million boxes to unpack in three weeks, and I'm still holding paint samples to walls." Tricia's eyes grew big with overwhelm, as if she'd been asked to broker peace in the Middle East.

"Ugh, that's a lot," I played along, though I had once redesigned the entire Office of Management and Budget suite in the Eisenhower building in less time.

"What about you? What have you and Caleb been up to?" Tricia looked over at the pickleball game in progress. "Who's that?" she asked with a thrust of her chin.

"That," I replied carefully, "is Victoria."

Tricia's eyes bore into me, and I began to construct an explanation. I got no further than "Caleb and I" before a wave of comprehension washed over her face. She dropped Max's woodworking on the picnic bench and rested what was intended as a sympathetic hand over my shoulder.

"I am so sorry," she whispered. "I wasn't aware. *How* are you holding up?"

I felt like all the air had been let out of me.

Was the situation so transparent that even Tricia could read it that fast? How did she know I didn't end it with Caleb? Or that we hadn't simply had a "conscious uncoupling," and Caleb happened to re-couple first? Or that maybe I'd re-coupled too, but simply had the common decency not to bring a new other half to Visiting Day?

"It's all very amicable," I lied through a smile. "Aiden's doing great. It's all for the best."

"So, are you sharing custody, or how does that work?" Tricia pried.

I took a breath. "We actually haven't brought lawyers into it yet. But yes, we've been sharing time. Caleb is renting a place in the neighborhood, so it's easy to switch off and take Aiden to school and soccer and whatnot."

"Ugh, that must be so hard for you, not seeing Aiden every day." Then her brows climbed as high as the Botox would allow. "But what a silver lining! Half the time, you can do whatever you want! Sometimes Jeff and I joke that we should get divorced just for the benefits of shared custody."

She cracked herself up, then stopped herself short, putting a hand on my arm. "Have you been dating? Are you on the swipies? Oh my God, I'd love to know what *that* feels like! We didn't even have social media when Jeff and I met. Please tell me you've had endless smoldering nights with hot, single Washingtonian men."

My thoughts flashed back to Dylan and my stomach lurched. "Oh, it's been an adventure, all right."

Tricia looked like she was stroking out from vicarious pleasure. "You are so lucky."

With a squeeze of my arm, she collected Max's woodworking projects, destined for display in her extravagant new home in Westchester. She whisked herself away, and I wished for a moment she'd take me with her.

- -

The PA system crackled. It seemed that the family obstacle course competition would begin shortly, followed by lunch served on the Welcome Lawn. Aiden, Caleb, and Victoria put down their pickleball paddles. I stood up.

"Mom, are you going to do the obstacle course with me?" Aiden asked.

"I'm still stuck in these flip-flops," I reminded him.

Caleb swooped in. "Victoria will do it with you, bud. You guys are gonna kick butt!"

"I'm so fast on this course, Dad! You have to see me. I run up the warp wall like *whooosh!*" Aiden struck the pose of an Olympic sprinter.

Victoria put her arm around Aiden as he prattled his way down the hill. Caleb hung behind to walk beside me. The unexpected attention released butterflies in my stomach, like a high schooler getting noticed by her crush for the first time. My nervous system hadn't yet learned that any interest from Caleb, at this point, was frankly going to suck.

"I need to talk to you about Aiden's soccer," he said matter-of-factly. "Tryouts for the feeder system that takes them all the way through high school varsity are happening a couple weeks after he gets home from camp. He's going to need to practice hard to get up to speed again and make the team. I don't want him distracted going back and forth between houses, or worse, getting to tryouts late because you forgot to check the shared calendar."

"What makes you think I can't get him to practice on time?" I shot back.

"Only the last two times he didn't get to practice at all." Caleb's voice was cold. "Because you forgot."

"I don't know what you're talking about," I said reflexively, although of course I did.

"C'mon, Natalie. You couldn't even get *here* on time!"

I felt my sweaty palms balling into fists. I grasped for something to defend myself with. "There's no cell service up here! I would've been here on time if—"

Caleb stopped and looked me straight in the eye, a patronizing look on his face. "Please. I'm asking you nicely, in the interest of our son. Just make this easy and do what's right."

"What exactly are you asking me, Caleb?"

"I'm asking that when Aiden gets home from camp, you let him stay with me and Victoria for a while to minimize disruption as much as possible."

I stared at him, not saying what I was thinking. *Disruption? You mean the disruption you caused by having an affair with your director of advertising under my nose, leading a double life, then telling me about it as an afterthought, once you'd already decided to abandon me? That kind of disruption?* Instead, I steadied my voice, trying to choose my reaction wisely.

"When exactly did you have Victoria carve pumpkins with Aiden? Where was I? I didn't even *know* yet, Caleb!"

"Oh Natalie." Caleb let his crossed arms fall to his sides. "Where *were* you? Where you *always* were, wasting the day on the couch! Sitting out another adventure with your son and husband. Procrastinating on everything you didn't feel like doing until it overwhelmed you, then taking the path of least resistance or having me do it for you."

I choked on tears, enraged, as Caleb landed the blows I seemed to be begging for.

He lowered his voice and pinched the bridge of his nose, head tilted to the sky as though staving off a nosebleed. "Listen, just think about it. Think about what's best for our son." He paused as if he had more to say, then turned on his heel and jogged after Victoria and Aiden.

I watched as he caught up, playfully startling Aiden and throwing him into the air as Victoria acted out a rescue. Aiden's giggles floated up the hill, as the scene shrank into the distance. I could only observe, a ghost replaying my past life.

- -

I skipped the obstacle course and staked out a lunch table well before the Welcome Lawn had officially opened. I needed space away from all the happy families, including the one that used to be my own. What gall Caleb had, phasing me out of my own son's life. Replacing me, even while we were still living together, with his ... his *Fembot*.

I mean, maybe Caleb was right about making a more stable living arrangement for Aiden. But when was I supposed to see Aiden if he stayed at Caleb's? How long would this be for? Until school starts? Longer? Would Caleb make it hard for me to see him? Act like I was some unstable drug addict or something and allow only short, supervised visits? I wanted what was best for Aiden. Of course I did. I just didn't want that to mean playing a bit part in his life.

At the same time, Tricia Melman's comment jangled in my head: *What a silver lining! You can do whatever you want.*

"Whatever I want" had, thus far, mostly been lying around all day, scrolling social media and eating sleeves of Chips Ahoy. At least until I got the wine-fueled notion to stalk Victoria's ex-husband and arrange an investigation-slash-commiseration rendezvous. *That* had certainly gone well.

Anxiety twisted my stomach. If I let Aiden stay with Caleb for the rest of the summer, what would I do with all that time alone? Would I ever get Aiden back? Did I want to? I felt disgusted with myself for even wondering. Fortunately, I was interrupted by a stream of hungry families noisily arriving at the Welcome Lawn. Aiden rode in on Caleb's shoulders holding a trophy above his head.

"These two winners just *crushed* everyone on the obstacle course. None of the other kids and parents stood a chance," Caleb proclaimed.

"Mom, where should we put the trophy? Can we make space on the shelf in my room?"

"I was thinking," Caleb answered, "that we bring it back to our place. You can keep it on the shelf you just made, and you and Victoria can enjoy it together."

Caleb looked at me as if daring me to contradict him. "In fact, to make it easier for you and Mommy, with soccer tryouts coming up, how about you'll stay at our place until school starts, so you don't have to switch back and forth between houses? You'll still see Mommy. We were all thinking it'll just be easier this way."

The hell we were. He'd yanked the rug out from under me, and I had no idea how to regain my footing.

Aiden looked at me, eyes wide. "Can I, Mom? Victoria is helping me work on my stepover. She used to play soccer in high school."

The unconflicted question gutted me. Apparently, everyone had made up their mind without me. I managed to move my head in a nodding motion like a marionette, unable to look at Caleb.

"Thanks, Mom!" Aiden wrapped his arms around me in an appreciative squeeze, then pulled away before I could hug him back. "We'll still go to Lorenzo's for pizza on Mondays, though. Right?"

Caleb answered for me yet again. "We'll see what the soccer schedule looks like, but of course, you can get pizza with Mommy whenever you like, if you don't have somewhere else to be. Or maybe she'll make her Lazy Lasagna for you." That last bit was just for me. Despite my having "countless hours at home with nothing to do," as Caleb complained for years, I had never become an enthusiastic cook.

"Speaking of pizza," Victoria interceded, "it looks like they've put the food out. Aiden, are you hungry?"

"Starving!" he said, and the dream-paralysis feeling swept over me again. The whole world was whirling, yet I couldn't move, couldn't do a thing about it. I felt my hands clenching, frustration building in me like fizz in a shaken bottle, and I didn't want the cork to pop.

I stood up. "Aiden? I think … I think I'm going to get on the road."

He turned around and walked toward me. "What? Aren't you hungry, Mom?"

"I ate a protein bar from my purse a little while ago. It filled me up. It's a long way back, so I think I'll get a jump on the traffic, as long as you don't mind." I faked a smile.

"But you're gonna miss archery. After lunch."

I squatted down beside him. "I know, honey, but you'll do great. Daddy will send me a video. I'm not really one for bows and arrows."

"Okay," he gave in, and squeezed me tight in a big hug, leaving a little boy kiss on my cheek. "Love you, Mom!"

I squeezed him to me, the bag that had held my gift now flat against my side. "I love you too, kiddo," I exhaled. "I'll see you when you get off the bus in a few weeks. Enjoy Color War! I'll be looking for you in all the pictures."

Best to say goodbye on a high note. Aiden's disappointment in my leaving early at least gave a glimmer of hope that I still mattered. I spent my last reserves of energy on a happy farewell face before turning to walk back to the parking lot.

Sheltered by the anonymity of my car, I slumped onto the steering wheel in a tempest of tears.

3

BY DESIGN

Nero had the right idea. Dana's imperial Sphynx stretched out on his back, bathed in sunlight, cradled by a plush corner of couch. His outstretched paw tapped a hanging tendril from the philodendron overhead, which looked like it had suffered the same claw before.

I never considered myself a cat person and struggled to find Dana's bald, wrinkly gremlin endearing. But I could respect, even envy, the total lack of fucks Nero gave for anything outside of his own comfort and delight.

Dana reemerged from the kitchen carrying two sparkling highball glasses with floating berries and sprigs of rosemary. Her idea of a "lazy Sunday" was trying new TikTok recipes, sprucing up her California-inspired farmhouse, working out compulsively, and fitting in a French lesson on the app she used whenever her other constant productive whatevers afforded a five-minute interval.

"Voilà, ma chérie! Deux boissons pour nous!" Dana sing-songed *en français.* She danced around the furniture on her way to where I sat across from Nero's side of the sectional. Dana's caramel hair was piled atop her head in an elegant, messy bun, complimenting her well-coordinated athleisure outfit. Her ankles still sported color-coordinated

weights from the "quick butt workout" she'd been doing before I arrived.

She set down my beverage on a coaster on her pristine, minimalist coffee table. The vaulted room was full of morning sunshine made even brighter by cream-toned upholstery, white oak, and brushed bronze. A tracery of scent filled the space, fresh lilies, amber and vetiver, seeming to mingle with the low-fi playlist Dana had going in the background.

Dana plopped down on the couch. Nero cast a wrinkled scowl in our direction and moved on to some other sunbeam.

"So where are Andrew and the kids today?" I asked, relaxing into an absence of commotion not typical of Dana's house.

"He's shuttling them all over creation for lacrosse and field hockey, and then they're having a late lunch with his mother. I'm all yours today." Dana wore a big smile.

"Perfect timing after yesterday," I said, picking up my glass. "The only thing that could've gone worse was if I had a car accident on the way home."

Dana scootched toward me. "You were so courageous! That was hard. *Extremely* hard. And you handled it with strength and grace."

"And mud all up my legs and ass."

"You didn't tell me about that part."

"It's not even worth telling, by comparison." I sighed. "Would you believe Aiden has pictures next to his bed of him with Caleb and Victoria from last fall? Like, when was Aiden introduced to her, anyway?"

"You're not serious."

"I am serious. Still stunned even. I spent half the car ride home trying to think if Aiden had ever mentioned her. Like, had he ever come home and said something like, 'I met Daddy's work friend. She was really nice. We ate ice cream and played soccer at the park'? I keep trying to figure it out."

Dana sipped her drink thoughtfully. "Well, how often were Caleb and Aiden going out without you?"

A guilty feeling crept over me. How often *did* they go out without me? Caleb had always been an engaged dad, taking Aiden to the endless professional ball games and other events that were part of the scenery for the founder and publisher of a top online political news magazine like *Party Lines*. And I encouraged these father-son outings. It gave me a break for a few hours to sprawl out on the couch and watch trash TV, unbothered. This, I was pretty sure, was something Dana would never have had the desire to do.

"I suppose enough," I understated. "I guess it would have been easy for Caleb to introduce Victoria to Aiden. All he'd have to tell him is 'Victoria is a work friend,' and Aiden wouldn't have thought anything of it."

"Good Lord." Dana un-Velcroed her ankle weights and drew her legs up into a crisscross, patting me on the arm. "Well, no use spinning your wheels over it now, honey. Just keep moving forward."

"Yeah." I made a face. "The bigger issue is what am I going to do about Caleb asking to take Aiden full-time through the end of the summer?"

"*What?*" Dana's head spun around, messy bun flopping.

"Caleb wants Aiden to stay with him and Victoria for a while when he gets back from camp. Like through soccer tryouts or something. I don't know how I feel about that." I bit my lip.

"Does Aiden know yet?"

"Yeah, he was all about it. Caleb took me aside yesterday. We had a huge blowup. He said it was best for Aiden, and I dunno. As smug as he is, he may be right."

Dana left a pregnant pause. "What do *you* want to happen when Aiden gets home?" she finally asked.

I took a breath and shifted position on the cushions, pulling a pillow to my chest like a shield. "I dunno. If Aiden is excited about staying with Caleb, then I guess, I mean, I might even be a little relieved? Is that horrible to say? Am I a horrible mother?"

"You are *not* a horrible mother. You are a woman who had her life turned upside down a short while ago and could use a little time for self-care and the headspace to make a plan for where you want your life to go from here." Dana always had a way of snapping me out of catastrophizing. It was probably one of the qualities that made her so successful at starting her own real estate brokerage and basically winning everything at life.

I exhaled. "It's probably better that I don't fight Caleb on it. He would be extremely difficult if I tried to renege now. And what for? Aiden seems to be right at home with them. Besides, it'll spare me from effing up anything else that Caleb would love to punish me for."

"*And,*" Dana added, "it'll give you time to focus on yourself. To manifest the New Natalie."

"Yeah, the New Natalie." I rolled my eyes.

"I'm serious. You're overdue for an overhaul."

I slouched down behind the pillow. "If only it were as simple as redecorating."

"Yeah, well, why *not* think of it that way? Why don't you take on a new project? You'll have gobs of time now, with Aiden taken care of."

"A new project? Like in my house? Probably not the best time for that kind of expense. I have no idea what's happening with my financial situation, and—I don't have to remind you—I have no job. Why don't I just join you at a spin class once in a while?"

Dana gave me a long-suffering look. "We both stopped holding out hope for that a while ago. And even if you did, spin hardly fills the other twenty-three hours of the day."

"Do I need to fill all twenty-three?" I taunted her.

"Shut up. You know what I mean. You need something substantive. You need an *ikigai.*"

"I had an *icky guy* two weekends ago. One you warned me not to even contact."

"That's not what I mean!" Dana's messy bun bounced atop her head while staying impossibly intact. "*Ikigai* is Japanese. For 'purpose.' All the Blue Zones have it. You know, people living to one hundred with passion and meaning."

"And socialized medicine."

Dana shook her head. "No, you'd be surprised. There's even a Blue Zone here in the U.S. in Loma Linda."

"You love California," I said, attempting to shift the conversation.

She looked wistful. "Yeah, I really hope Benny goes there for college."

"Would you move?"

She caught on, giving me a look. "This isn't about me, Natalie. *You* need a purpose. And what better purpose than one of your best talents: interior design and decorating!"

I narrowed my eyes at her. "I'm beginning to get the sense you have something very specific in mind."

"What? Me? No!" Then she shot me a goofy smile. "Ok, maybe. I mean, what if an opportunity came along? Like, a *perfect* opportunity? Like the kind out of a movie?"

"Go on …" I braced for an outrageous scheme, something only someone like Dana would act on.

"Remember I'd told you about this deal I was brokering downtown for a VIP? The gorgeous brick townhouse in Capitol Hill?" Dana loved to tease a reveal.

"Yeah …"

"Well, the deal is done; they close next week … and since the buyer needs light interior design and full decorating services … I gave him your contact as my personal designer!"

Dana's expression said *"ta-daaah!"* Mine said *"what the fuck is wrong with you?"* I hadn't designed or decorated so much as a backyard shed in over a decade.

"Are they going to call me?"

She looked mildly offended. "I'd be shocked if they didn't. It was a personal recommendation."

"What were you *thinking*? I'm going to look like a total fool when I tell them—"

"You will *not!*" Dana held up her pointer finger, staring me down. "*I* would look like the fool if you backed out now and, I'm sorry, it's just too late. You're going to have to do this."

Dana stood up and pretended to busy herself re-draping a knit throw over a new accent chair. I'd meant to tell her I liked it, but now I was too flustered to say so.

In the silence, I found my shock making room for a flutter of anticipation. It wasn't like I didn't know how to redesign a house or decorate it. I'd done much bigger projects before. I just didn't have the recent resumé for it. Or a firm I belonged to. Or a website. But the need for all those things had apparently been bulldozed by Dana, who had already secured the client. A high-profile one at that.

Dana fluffed one of her boho pillows. She was going to make me ask. "Okay. Who is this client, anyway?"

Her smile was eager. "You know that JFK Junior-looking freshman congressman that's been all over the news?"

"I try not to 'news' too hard these days. You know. Caleb's wheelhouse."

She took out her phone and tapped in a quick search, then held it up to my nose. I had to lean back to get a good look.

"*Him.*" Dana said, with an audible full stop.

The pixelated image showed a square-jawed, smiling, dark-haired man in a well-fitted T-shirt and joggers who appeared to be shopping in the NoMa neighborhood of DC. He did, in fact, have modern day overtones of JFK Jr., but no Carolyn Bessette in tow.

I read the headline aloud: "Hot biscuit, Rep. Oliver Thames (RI-1) spotted shopping at Union Market." I looked up. "Dana, this is hardly news."

"Exactly why I thought you might have read it. But you're missing the point."

She took the phone back, pulled up an official congressional head-shot, and shoved it back in my face. "This guy is the it-man of politics right now. Everyone wants a piece of him. And you're getting him and his staff handed to you on a silver platter with a golden opportunity to jumpstart your career again. Even with half the Old Natalie mojo on this job, the referrals will flow down Capitol Hill like manna from heaven."

The hairs on the back of my neck stood up. Dana had a way of making everything sound predestined and fabulous. I was still thinking "hard pass," but I couldn't help but feel a little swept up.

"I wouldn't even know where to begin," I said, but we both knew I only half meant it.

A satisfied smile spread across Dana's face. "Already got you covered. It's a total rehab job that's mostly complete. House flipper gutted it and made it, like—wow. But they left some of the finishes, fixtures, and finer details to the new owner to personalize it. That's where you'll pick up. I'll send you the plats and photos of each room from multiple angles. That should get you started before they call. Could be as early as tomorrow, who knows? His team moves pretty fast. Very sharp. I think you'll like working with them. I'm not sure how involved Congressman Thames is going to be in the details, but I wouldn't be surprised if you got some face time with him. I met him briefly on a walkthrough, and he seems very invested in this becoming his homebase-away-from-home. I'm told he spends a lot of time back in his district in Rhode Island."

The more Dana talked, the more the panic set in. "Dana! I am *not* doing this. I will not embarrass myself in front of a public figure. No thanks."

Dana wasn't having it. "You need to jump in the deep end already, Natalie!"

"Or you're going to push me?"

"Yup. You've got your swimmies on!" She looked delighted with herself, almost devious. "Which means I'm here for anything you need. Or if you get freaked out. I have every faith in your talents, no matter how much time has gone by since you've used them. All you need is the nerve to show up, and the rest will come back to you naturally. Like riding a bike."

Sure, I thought, *like riding a bike. Down Pennsylvania Avenue at rush hour. With no brakes.*

I didn't come here for a fight, and seeing as neither of us were backing down, I changed the subject.

Dana just smiled.

4

———————

ANSWERING THE CALL

I was absolutely *not* taking this job, but Dana didn't hesitate to send me the files anyway. By the end of the day, curiosity prompted me to open them. What could it hurt? That harmless look somehow turned into poring over the plats and photos, which bled into catching up on new home design trends.

I was on my third cup of adaptogen mushroom coffee—a "wellness gift" from Dana—and I was almost getting inspired. The next day, I found myself breaking away from daily tasks to quickly sketch out ideas that popped into my head.

Later that night, out of sheer boredom, I ended up many clicks deep in online recon about Congressman Thames. I was looking for clues about his personal style beyond the footnote Dana had jotted, quoting Thames's Chief of Staff: "beset by '80s bachelor pad style. Please help." It had me imagining black leather upholstery, gold finishes, geometric wall art, and a zebra-print rug, maybe a giant aquarium or a glass block dividing wall. I shuddered. But everything I was seeing of the congressman's very public life suggested his taste wasn't as tragic as his right-hand man would have us believe. Thames seemed to have a boyishly charming, magnetic way about him, the reasons for the whole "Camelot" comparison becoming even more apparent as I researched. "The room where it happens" seemed to be any room Oliver Thames happened to be in. He also wasn't hard on the eyes.

Snuggled up in bed in the glow of my laptop, I muttered aloud, "He *is* a biscuit."

--

When the call from the congressman's office came on Tuesday, I already felt ridiculously read in for a project I had no intention of taking on. But telling myself for two days that I was "only curious" made any pre-work low-stakes enough that I wound up getting it all done before I could even procrastinate doing it. Leave it to Dana to know me that well.

My phone rang. "Hello?"

"Hi, is this Natalie Espinosa?" a young woman on the other end asked. How like Dana to have given them my maiden name.

"Yes, speaking." I probably should have answered the unknown 202 number with a more professional greeting than "hello?"

"This is Maryam Abadi, from Congressman Thames's office. The Dana Krist Brokerage referred you as someone who could help the congressman with interior design and decorating for his new town-home on Capitol Hill."

This is it, Natalie. Are you in or out?

"We were wondering if you'd be available for a preliminary consultation and proposal after the closing this Friday, since the congressman will already be at the property. Would ten a.m. work for you?"

Considering my only plans were to (maybe) go to the grocery store?

"Hmm … this Friday… hold on, let me just check my schedule …" I muted my phone and took a deep breath. I *had* already done the prep. Saying yes would save face with these people *and* prevent a fight with Dana. It also sounded kind of fun to be part of a political celebrity's personal life for a hot second.

I unmuted the phone. "Yes, well, I can move a couple appointments, so ten should work fine."

"Great! We're looking forward to it. Let me give you the house address."

"No need," I said reassuringly. "Ms. Krist already provided it."

I hung up feeling exhilarated for the first time in a while.

Damn you, Dana. I smiled, shaking my head. Then I flipped open my laptop. Time for some finishing touches.

- -

On Friday morning, I kicked into gear, blew out my hair, shaped up my nails and applied a fresh coat of quick-dry nail polish. Then I put on a light gray skirt suit that I used to wear when I worked in Georgetown.

In spite of the outfit being fifteen years old, the style still flattered, though it hugged my curves a lot closer than it used to. Or maybe it was just hard to remember what real clothes felt like after a decade plus in sweatpants and freebie Washington sports team T-shirts. The barely healed foot blisters from my walk with Dylan squealed as I stuffed them back into a pair of pleather pumps.

How had I possibly worn outfits like this five days a week walking all around the District?

They say that the entire body's atoms are replaced every seven years. By that math, the girl who wore this outfit was a full two iterations of me ago.

The lookbook I'd compiled, layouts, drawings, product photos, and so on objectively had a lot to like about it. I obsessively rehearsed every possible question the congressman and his team could ask me about each page, flow-charting the scenarios that could play out. But as I made my way down the sidewalk off East Capitol, my legs felt gelatinous, my underarms dampening my silk shell. I wished my blazer had come with a maxi pad stapled under each armpit to contain the liquid anxiety.

Then, catching a glimpse of myself in a car window, I almost took a stutter step. The woman I saw reflected there gave no indication of what I was feeling inside. She looked professional, confident, even sexy. I'd forgotten what I'd looked like as a career woman. And what I used to feel like.

I lingered a moment, smoothing my skirt and checking a couple of angles. My hair was up in a tidy pencil bun, held fast by my lucky engraved silver pen. I didn't just look the part, I *was* the part. I had done my homework. There was no need to be nervous. It was like I used to tell my colleagues before a big pitch meeting: *Clients want to consult us, not quiz us. They're looking to us as the experts.*

Whatever I'd been feeling moments ago had melted in the DC summer morning heat. I strode up the new black metal steps of the congressman's red brick townhouse and rapped the knocker against the heavy wood door.

A statuesque, ebony-complected man in his mid-fifties drew it open. He stood there posing like an underwear model, taut skin, glossy bald head, and high cheekbones in a tan summer suit with a bright dress shirt and matching pocket square.

"You must be Natalie. I'm Channing Cartwright, Congressman Thames's Chief of Staff. Come on in. They're finishing up the paperwork down the street at the title office."

The front door led directly into the unfurnished, open plan space I now knew well from the files. I loved that the house flipper had faithfully restored the historic Victorian facade but had given the interior a full contemporary overhaul. It felt spacious and new, accented by the most charming features of the original house.

The first floor was a bright, airy space with a two-story ceiling. They'd kept the original wood-burning fireplace. It led back into a large kitchen with a generous center island and a backsplash of creamy white subway tile. A floating staircase and exposed brick wall rose from the entryway to the second-floor landing, outlined by a cable railing running the width of the house.

I envisioned the second-floor guest rooms and shared bathroom just beyond, which I had seen in the pictures. Then there would be another staircase leading up to the third floor, now a massive loft of a primary bedroom centered around a Palladian window whose central panel stretched from floor to ceiling, set in exposed brick. The bedroom adjoined a spacious bathroom behind a sliding door. It featured a newly renovated walk-in glass shower and a restored, claw-foot tub perfect for soaking nineteenth-century debutantes. I knew every inch from studying the plans and photos. Below where we stood, there'd be the partially finished basement, the majority taken up by where the study would be, plus another full bath. There was space for a wine cellar and a small gym off the study, both of which I'd sketched.

"Will anyone else be joining us?" I asked, my voice bouncing off bare walls and hardwood floors. The space smelled of fresh sawdust and epoxy.

"Let's get started, just us, and he may pop in later," Channing suggested.

I opened my portfolio on the speckled terrazzo kitchen island, mentally assessing whether four or five counter-height stools would work best.

"I took the liberty of putting together a lookbook as a starting point for the congressman," I explained. "It takes a modern, but enduring approach to furnishing the space that should complement the bold finishes and contemporary updates from the reno. Of course, I want to leave room for the congressman's personal taste."

"Please don't." Channing held up a hand in protest. "That would only ruin it. The congressman is—"

Now it was my turn to interrupt. "Beset by '80s bachelor pad style?"

Channing's well-groomed eyebrows skipped upward.

"Did I … mention that to someone already?" he asked coyly.

I realized who I actually needed to win over. Apparently the congressman delegated his aesthetic sensibilities to Channing, perhaps to his own benefit.

Channing and I began the walkthrough. Back in the living room, I presented the corresponding lookbook pages for Channing to eyeball and painted the picture, trying to bring it to life. My hands became a

TV weathercaster's, standing against a green screen gesturing at invisible things.

Channing stroked his clean-shaven chin, glancing down at the page, then up at the room as I spoke. I tried to read his expressions, his body language, offering alternatives to get a feel for his tastes. Channing didn't say much, which I wasn't sure how to read, but I pressed on. He gave a couple nods of approval and once ventured to build upon my thoughts, but otherwise he was either playing his cards close to the vest, or he was the most dramatically silent gay man I had ever encountered in the industry.

Moving downstairs to the basement, I outlined a modern but functional space that considered the inherent publicness of this home office in the making. I assumed Channing would provide more input here, but he let me go on with how we could maximize natural lighting despite being below grade and give the illusion of a larger space with mirror placement and armless chairs. With all the hard surfaces, well-chosen area rugs would be key for noise reduction.

I asked whether the congressman had any wall art he intended to hang or personal items I should work into the room's décor.

Channing could not resist. "Not if I can help it."

I laughed and winked. "Well then ... wanna take it to the bedroom?"

"You move fast, Natalie Espinosa," Channing teased, taking to the stairs. "Be gentle with me. If there's a low-profile platform bed in your book, I might not be able to contain myself."

Up in the bedroom loft, I couldn't help but feel like I was winning Channing over. At one point he even admitted that he loved something, tapping a picture that was a particular favorite of mine. "You subdued this color palette and made it accessible again. I thought mustard would never come back."

By the time we'd reviewed the whole lookbook, Channing had warmed up considerably and was beginning to treat me as a colleague, not as someone auditioning for the role. "The key with Oliver," he began, giving me an abrupt field promotion to first-name basis with the congressman, "is making him think it's *his* vision. He's going to come up with his own *ideas*, but you just need to steer him toward the light and make him think it was his idea all along."

Footsteps on the staircase made us turn. A voice echoed up with playful authority as a dark head crested the landing. "Is that how I *actually* got elected? Channing, you puppet master, I don't pay you enough."

With that, Congressman Oliver Thames emerged from the stairs to join us face to face. I was taken aback, though I couldn't have said why. I had certainly seen my share of pictures of the man. But no picture could convey the presence he commanded when he walked into a room.

I already knew from my research that he was forty-six years old, though he gracefully straddled the line between refined and youthful, so it could have been hard to peg. His wavy, dark locks had been tousled by the breeze on his walk over from the title office. There was a sprinkling of gray salt in his sideburns. He wore blue suit pants, closely tailored over long, athletic legs, but wore no tie with his checkered button-down shirt. In fact, the top two buttons were undone, giving a distracting hint of defined chest. He smiled playfully, a row of white teeth deepening his tan. The smile arced up to pale, glass-green eyes whose corners crinkled with humor and kindness.

The room felt warm all of a sudden. My peripheral vision seemed a little blurry. A demi-god was floating my way, eyes and smile locked on me.

Snapping my mouth closed, I looked down at my portfolio to break the spell.

"You must be Natalie," the congressman said, casually confident. In one hand he held a paper cup of coffee on which some barista had gotten his name wrong. The black marker read "Gulliver." He shook my hand without breaking eye contact and, in a split second, I finally understood what people I'd met who'd known Bill Clinton meant when they said he was positively captivating, regardless of which party you belonged to. You just instantly wanted to be next to him.

I shook the congressman's hand firmly. His palm and fingers were a bit rough, like he was an avid sailor or enjoyed sports and outdoorsy things, but it was also warm and gentle. While it had certainly been a long time since I had been doing much shaking hands with business associates, it felt like we were suspended there in space and time for a moment, our eyes fixed, palms pressed together, two galaxies spiraling toward collision.

Before I could do something awkward, Channing spoke up. "Let's get back to that comment you just made about not paying me enough."

The congressman released my hand with an amused chuckle. "Aren't I already paying you the max salary the federal pay scale allows?"

"Yes, but I'm convinced taxpayers would bipartisanly agree that funding Hugo's and my annual retreat to Palm Springs would be federal dollars well spent."

Then Channing's eyes narrowed. He pointed at the misspelling on the coffee cup.

"Because of all my travels," "Gulliver" joked.

"They've admitted to doing that on purpose," Channing said, "just so people will post it on social media. We should really work that into your campaign somehow."

The congressman turned back to me, sending a zing up my spine. "I take it that if Channing is priming you on how to manipulate my decisions, he's already signed the contract?"

I cleared my throat. "I have an estimate drawn up here, but this was just the preliminary meeting. If you'd like to make any changes, I can incorporate them and get you something final to sign."

"May I?" he asked, gesturing at the open lookbook. I handed it to him, meeting his twinkling green eyes. I could've sworn he smiled.

He flipped through the book and reviewed the estimate for what felt like an eternity. He furrowed his brow and nodded, glancing up at me periodically, as if about to ask me something.

After the fourth time, he finally did. "Is that pen really holding up your hair?"

"Sorry?"

Now he was staring at my updo, hand hovering in the air between us as if poised to pop a bubble. "Like, do you have a bunch of secret pins in there, or is that silver pen the only thing holding it all together?"

I reached up and pulled out the pen, giving my head a little shake as my tresses fell past my shoulders. "No tricks," I grinned.

For a fleeting moment, he wore the awe and delight of a boy who just had a quarter pulled out of his ear. It made me feel bold. "No tricks in there either." I glanced down at the estimate and handed him the pen. Dana would be proud.

His expression stretched into a grin and he met my gaze, flaying back a few layers I wasn't aware had accumulated. Then he looked down at the estimate again, studious and focused. I managed not to bite my lip.

"I like it!" he finally exclaimed, scrawling his signature on the line and snapping the portfolio shut. "A couple details I want to work with you on, but nothing that should change the paperwork here. Channing can coordinate next steps with you. Let's put a time on the calendar next week to get started. I want this done before we're back from August recess, if we can help it. My schedule blows up after that."

"*I* will be handling this," Channing pushed in, "as you are in the throes of reelection and must attend to untold other responsibilities these coming weeks."

I was sure that was true. I also guessed Channing's real motivation was to keep the congressman out of as many design decisions as possible.

"What do you look like on Monday?" Channing already had his phone out, calendar app open. I fumbled to get mine out of my purse with the hand not holding the portfolio. I scrolled the blank lines of my calendar to Monday and booked a time with Channing, who offered to walk me out.

"I'm interested to see a few options for the layout of the study," Channing said as we descended two flights of stairs to the entryway.

"Yes, well, the built-in shelving poses some limitations, but also some unique opportunities," I explained. Then leather-soled feet came drumming down the floating staircase after us, and I turned in time to hear the congressman calling my name. He caught up to us at the bottom of the steps.

"I meant to show you this," he said to me, producing a small, hand-made wooden shadow box. "It's something that should live in the house, probably in my study, but it's not just a knickknack. It's actually kind of a focal point for me."

What could have such importance to him? I wondered, eyes glued to the box. *Is it a Purple Heart or a Bronze Star? An old picture of his parents or relatives long gone? Maybe a 45-carat, flawless stone, like a Thames family version of the Hope Diamond?*

He turned it toward me, then lifted it closer to my face so I could peer in. There, tied down by simple twine on each of its five points, was—

"A starfish?" I was intrigued.

"I'll allow it," Channing chimed in with a referee's raised index finger, "only because I have a soft spot for the story and a conflicted affinity for the color salmon."

I looked up at the congressman, whose face had lit up at being given permission.

"Someone gave it to me a long time ago. And they told me about a mother and son who were walking along the beach one day. They discovered the beach was completely covered in starfish"—he broke for a moment—"Maybe you've heard the story already?"

I shook my head, so he continued.

"Well, the tide had receded, and tens of thousands of starfish were lying there, helpless, succumbing to their fate upon the shore."

My brows knit together, picturing those poor creatures drying out in the sand. He went on, "So the boy starts picking up the starfish and throwing them back into the sea, one by one. The mother watches him for a while and says, 'Son, you can't possibly save them all. It'll hardly make any difference.'"

"And the son pauses for a moment, looking defeated. Then he picks up another starfish and launches it back into the sea." The congressman pantomimed the boy's act of kindness. "And the boy turns to his mother and says, 'It made a difference to that one.'"

The line struck me for some reason. I choked up a little. I thought the story was over, but he continued.

"Well, the mother considers her son's words and starts picking up starfish and throwing them back. They keep at it, and as other people pass by, they see what's happening and pitch in. Before long, they had a whole team of people helping to save the starfish."

"And did they save them all?" I asked, hopefully.

"I don't know," he shrugged. "Save one, save some, save tens of thousands. It always makes more of a difference than if no one tries doing anything at all."

"Well, we know *that* one didn't make it." Channing burst our bubble without even trying, eyes locked on his phone screen. When he looked up, his expression was pointed. "Pastor Thames, if Sunday School is out, I just got an email that's going to knock you into next week. Can I see you in the *future study* for a moment?"

The congressman looked concerned.

"Natalie," Channing turned to me, "I want to finish our conversation before you go, but we have something *time-sensitive* to chat about. Grab yourself a bottle of water from the fridge and bond with that starfish. We'll be right back." I reached out to take the shadow box from the congressman. For a microscopic moment we held the starfish together, then he and Channing hurried down the basement steps.

I took a seat on the bay window ledge at the front of the living room, turning the starfish over in my hands. I could catch snippets of their conversation downstairs, names I didn't recognize and phrases I had no context for. Their work seemed so glamorous. I wondered if they appreciated that, or if even the most high-profile conflicts felt like standard work annoyances to them. Friends used to tell me how "glamorous" interior design and decorating was. Little did they know it came with all the same bullshit of their own desk jobs.

Then there was the congressman—or Oliver, as Channing casually referred to him. I wondered how much involvement Channing would let him have in our creative meetings. I certainly wouldn't mind the direct connection, though it could mean having to gently steer the congressm—er, Oliver away from troublesome, outdated tastes.

Something about just being in the room with Oliver felt enlivening. Even that starfish story had me hanging on every word. I'd have to be careful, I could tell. The last thing I needed was to get attached to a client. I'd seen former colleagues blur the lines of professionalism, even start falling for their client, and it only ever ended badly. It's all fun and games until someone takes a misstep. Then somebody gets hurt. Or fired.

I could hear Oliver and Channing returning to the main floor.

"Thanks for waiting, Natalie," Oliver said as I stood. He placed a hand on my shoulder and my stomach sprung into my throat. Once more, the crinkled corners of his eyes authenticated his smile. "You're gonna love working with Channing. And if I'm lucky, he'll let me work with you too."

"I'm looking forward to seeing a lot more of you both." I hoped the cool, professional smile would disguise my excitement.

Oliver wrapped an arm around Channing in a sideways hug. "And to think this guy was worried you didn't have a website."

"Due diligence is my job," Channing said primly. A fizz of embarrassment rushed through my bloodstream.

"The website is something I'm working on," I fibbed, feeling compelled to explain. "I'd taken some time off. For my son. But now he's old enough that I'm back to business."

"Son? Really? How old?" Oliver asked, reaching into his pocket to pull out a crumpled packet of Big League Chew. I did a double take at the bubble gum. They still made that stuff?

"Ten," I replied, "but going on twenty."

Oliver gave a knowing laugh. "I'm sure he keeps you on your toes."

"He does. You'd think I was a ballerina."

Oliver chuckled, eyes sparkling. A weird feeling seized me, like we'd had this exchange in another life.

"Do you have kids too?" I asked, taking a step closer.

"Nah," he said, looking down as he mashed soft green shreds of

Swingin' Sour Apple together. "But I remember that age well. Especially the 'going on twenty' part. Much to my mother's annoyance."

Oliver popped the wad of gum in his mouth, chomping as he spoke, "You know, Natalie, I really commend you for getting back into the workforce after raising a child. So many Americans have to make impossible choices between starting a family and exiting their career."

"Yeah," I said, "I'm thankful I had the luxury of taking the full-time mom role for a while."

"Exactly. Some people don't have that option. That's why my team and I worked on a bill that finally passed this year, to improve the standard for parental and family leave. Remember HR-143, Channing?"

Channing nodded. Oliver went on. "Everyone deserves time to be a parent or care for a loved one without fear of losing their job. Corporate America and federal law need to do more to retain talent from all walks of life and personal circumstances, rather than watching them exit the workforce when faced with an impossible ultimatum."

"Okay, Second Chance Whisperer," Channing cut in, "that's your stump speech quota for the day. You have a meeting."

Oliver looked at his watch. "You're right, I have to head out. I'll leave you two to schedule next steps." With a thumbs up and an enchanting smile, he was out the door.

"I promise you, Natalie," Channing said as the door closed behind the congressman, "I will minimize his involvement so we can get through this project on schedule."

I smiled to myself. Oliver's little policy talks wouldn't be the worst addition to this project. Minus the gum chewing. I was actually feeling a little inspired.

A few points of detail later, Channing accompanied me out to the brick sidewalk and gave me his cell number and a copy of the house key. "Oliver and I have to be up in his district and all over the place these next few weeks," he said, "but I'll be here to meet you Monday."

I placed the key inside the leather pocket of my laptop bag along with the shadow box and headed down the street to my sunbaked car.

I rolled down the windows and blasted the A/C, beads of sweat trickling between my back and the scorching car seat.

My bag was unzipped on the passenger seat, and I could see the edge of the shadow box out of the corner of my eye. Channing had called Oliver the "Second Chance Whisperer." Obviously, he had policy opinions on that. And here I was getting a second chance at my career. Was I Oliver's charity case? Had it really been Dana's personal referral and my performance today that made him ready to sign the contract? Or had Channing raised objections behind closed doors about the chasm in my work history and my lack of a business footprint, and Oliver saw it as an opportunity to put his money where his megaphone was?

The thought gnawed at me, but there was no way to know. The only thing to do was to prove I was the right choice for the job.

5

SERVED

I opened the door to my neighborhood coffee shop and was greeted by a whoosh of cool air and the aroma of freshly ground espresso beans. The morning was already hot and muggy, but movement and being outdoors tended to fire my creativity, so I'd decided to walk for the first time in a while.

I placed my order and nabbed the corner window seat, a voyeur's delight in the busy shop. A frazzled woman in a suit and flats with too many things in her hands was attempting to check out. She had a five-year-old clinging to her leg and a toddler off on some miniature expedition across the shop. The mother crouched down to convince the five-year-old to choose one of the ready-made boxes of healthy snacks, while the toddler discovered a display of ceramic mugs.

"Anastasia, you have to pick *something*," the mother raised her voice as a queue of coffee-dependent patrons formed behind her. "Mommy is going to be late for work, and you have to eat breakfast before you go to daycare."

Across the shop, a kindhearted customer coaxed a mug out of the toddler's hands and placed it back on the shelf, averting impending breakage.

I recalled all too well how exasperating those moments of motherhood were, and I'd only had one child, not two.

The mother's power struggle with her daughter concluded predictably in a public display of whining and wailing that would only end with bribery and sugar. The mother walked over toward an empty armchair beside my table to await her iced Americano and a rainbow-colored unicorn shake for Mommy's Little Tyrant.

As the mother double-knotted her toddler's shoelaces, five-year-old Anastasia sat in the armchair, prim as a princess on her oversized throne. She was content to tap on the iPad her mother pulled out of a diaper bag, as though hysterics weren't a mere sixty seconds in the past.

Meanwhile, the toddler sneezed out a glob of snot and tasted it with her bottom lip. The mother scrambled to find a napkin, and I reflexively handed her a stack.

"Thanks," she said without looking up, catching the snot glob before it could get wiped on her skirt.

"I've been there," I reassured. "It gets easier." I didn't know what made me say it, besides feeling obligated to say something.

The mom let out a clipped laugh. "Sure. In like eighteen years or so."

She had a point. I knew it didn't get easier *per se*, just the same amount of hard in different ways. When all the nose- and ass-wiping and shoe-tying finally relents, the schoolwork-helping and shuttling around to sports and activities kicks in, on top of all the feeding, nurturing and cleaning up, and I still wasn't out of the woods on those yet myself.

Then, as the more self-sufficient years arrived, at long last, you'd be left staring into the void that was once entirely occupied by motherhood. It was the same as the way a baby held your belly hostage, pushing your other organs to the side, feeding off you as their host, taxing your body to what felt like its breaking point, until they decided they were ready to vacate. Or, as in my case, were induced to.

"At least you'll get a break at work." I regretted saying it as soon as it left my mouth.

The mother paused, still crouched at the feet of her child. For the first time, she looked up. She let the look linger for a moment. "Lady, I don't even get a break *on* my break."

Collecting herself, her children, and their overpriced beverages, she bustled all of them out the door. My good mood was properly wrecked.

The barista brought my mocha. I'd known Caitlyn since she was little older than Princess Tantrum. Now she was in college.

"Did you know that lady?" Caitlyn asked.

"No," I said, looking out the window after her. "I was just trying to help."

"She's come in here before. I hope for her sake she doesn't have any more kids."

"Yup," I said taking the mug, "kids in any number are a lot."

Caitlyn glanced around. "I don't think I'm gonna do it. Have kids, I mean."

"Well, Caitlyn," I said, stirring my finger through the foam, then placing it in my mouth and sucking with a pop, "the good news is that's entirely up to you. In most states."

Caitlyn smiled, a hand on her hip. "I don't know if my mom told you, but I studied abroad last semester in Rome. I think I'm gonna get a visa and move there for a while to really focus on my writing."

No shortage of coffeehouses and starving writers in Italy! I was tempted to say. But seeing as I was already zero for one today with winning friends and influencing people, I opted instead for, "That's exciting, Caitlyn. It sounds like you know exactly what you want out of life. Now you just need to make it happen."

Caitlyn basked in my hollow words of encouragement, returning behind the bar to doodle more foam art into coffee cups. Her whole story remained unwritten. I wondered what she'd do when the world rushed in, but I was the last person who should be giving her advice. If that was what she wanted, I should probably introduce her to Dana.

As if on cue, the door jangled open and Dana sauntered in, spotted me, then headed to the counter to place her order. A few minutes later, she was sitting beside me with an iced herbal tea.

"No adaptogen coffee today?" I asked with a smirk.

"This is just social rehydration. I had my dose of mushroom coffee before barre class."

"No sunrise workout for me," I admitted, "but I did walk here."

"You walked!" Dana pantomimed applause.

"I walked!" I cheesed back.

"To the New Natalie," Dana toasted me, raising her disposable cup. I raised mine back.

Dana wasted no time. "I want to hear all about yesterday. Was he there?"

"He was," I taunted, knowing she was eager for details.

"And what did you think? Prince Charming?"

I sipped my mocha and spilled the tea. "Yes. More than I expected, even. Like, he's handsome in pictures and all, but then he walks into the room and I dunno, I mean, I had to stop myself from staring."

Dana grasped my knee. "Did he talk to you a lot?"

"Yeah, a decent amount. He actually told me a story about a starfish he's got in a shadow box. He wants it placed in his study somewhere."

Dana looked confused. "A starfish? Like a real one? Some family significance or something?"

"Something like that," I replied, unsure if I wanted to share the detail. I didn't know whether I wanted to let her in on my insecurities either. Dana would either pooh-pooh them or ask a million exhausting questions about exactly what Oliver had said to rule out the possibility that I was a pity hire.

"I mostly met with his Chief of Staff, Channing. He had his walls up at first, but then I think we hit it off." I left out the part where Oliver mentioned Channing's initial skepticism about my credentials.

Dana rattled the ice in her tea with the straw. "Okay, and then?"

"And then ... he signed the paperwork. I go back Monday to get started."

Dana swept me up in an enormous hug. "I'm so excited for you! Congratulations! Fantastic work locking that contract up. You're going to hit it out of the park."

At that moment, the door clanged open. A brusque guy in chinos and a short-sleeved button-down searched the shop. His eyes landed on me, of all people, then approached our table. "Natalie Weir?"

"Yes?" I looked at the man, then at Dana, then back at the man, who was producing a large manila envelope from a messenger bag.

"You've been served." He smacked the envelope on the table. Then, as abruptly as he entered, he was gone.

There was a long, silent moment. "Holy shit," Dana finally said. "Couldn't Caleb have just mailed you the divorce papers?"

I cupped my mocha with both hands, staring at the envelope. I bit my lower lip. "He did."

"*What?*" Dana gasped. "He already sent these to you?"

I didn't move, still watching the envelope.

"Natalie, when? Caleb filed for divorce, and you didn't tell me?"

"It was a while ago," I admitted, picking at my cuticle. "I wasn't ready to sign the return receipt."

Dana gawked at me, then shimmied closer on the window seat, wrapping her arm around me with a squeeze and resting her head on my shoulder. I knew she was trying to be supportive, but I took no comfort in it. Somewhere deep in my denial I knew this day was coming. Caleb had threatened it weeks ago. With everything going on, I had almost forgotten.

"Oh, Natalie." Dana seemed hesitant, which was unusual. "I know you've *really* been going through it. I can't even imagine what it must feel like to walk in your shoes every day. But I'm so, so excited for you with this townhouse project, and so proud of how you've tackled it, even though I know I kind of forced your hand. I'm finally seeing glimmers of your original self come back, though, with New Natalie. It brings me—and I hope you—great joy."

Dana picked her head up from my shoulder and looked at me. I was still lost in the swirls of my mocha. She tried to make eye contact.

"The reality is I've been worried about you. For a while now, not just since Caleb left. Years ago, you had drifted to this scary, isolated place, where I felt like breaking through to you was only an illusion. Like I never really could, no matter how many times I had you over for dinner or we had heart-to-hearts over drinks. I could tell you weren't all right. There were some unsettling things. Like what you just said about just not dealing with the divorce papers."

I felt offended. "What do you mean?" What about me wasn't all right?"

"Like when I'd come over and the cleaners had repositioned little things all over the place. I mean, as cleaners tend to do, of course. But then you'd just leave them like that."

"*That's* 'unsettling'? I was just keeping an open mind. Other people have good ideas sometimes."

Dana scowled. "'*Other people have good ideas sometimes*'? The only idea cleaners have is, 'Oh, shit! Where was this before I dusted it?' Natalie, you are an interior designer and decorator. You have educated opinions on where everything belongs. And it was like that part of you had dried up and fallen off. I was scared to say anything. I saw how you even shut out Caleb when he'd try to motivate you—"

"*Caleb*," I sneered, pulling away from her, "was only interested in getting out of the house so he could romance his director of advertising."

"You know that's not true. Not in the beginning. He wanted to see you happy. He was trying to help. He tried to motivate you and get your marriage back on track."

I refused to make eye contact with Dana. I did not want to have this conversation, but she kept on going. "I'm not condoning what he did later, Natalie, and I'm not saying he had all the answers to make you happy. But he *was* trying for a long time, and we were both concerned."

I pressed my lips into a thin line. "Oh, yeah? Did you have little clandestine conferences about my mental health too?"

"No!" Dana shook her head emphatically. "I mean yes, it did come up a couple times, but it wasn't premeditated. We weren't sneaking around behind your back to talk about it. We didn't know what to do!"

Dana folded a leg under her on the window seat, urging me to look at her. "Natalie, when I met you, you were this bundle of exuberance, working on fixing up your new house. We had that whole real estate and interiors thing in common. You were fun and funny and liked to drink mezcal margaritas, which was the clincher for me. As far as I'm concerned, *that* was the original Natalie."

I could feel the intensity of Dana's gaze but said nothing.

"Then you were all about getting pregnant, and I think that took some of your focus away from the things you loved. You quit work. Then when you found out having children was going to be a lot harder than you'd thought, possibly not an option at all, I know that crushed you. You lost your sparkle and started to clam up."

I had really heard enough. "You have *no idea* how stressful that was," I whisper-yelled. "*You* already had Benny and Sophie. *I* spent two years trying to get pregnant, then another two getting injected with hormones on schedule like a dairy cow. I had to have my eggs retrieved and put in a petri dish over and over, because I couldn't fulfill one of the most basic biological functions of being female. And even with the help of the entire medical community, it still almost didn't work."

"Honey, I know. *I know*. I never had to experience what you went through. But it was never lost on me how hard that was."

Dana rubbed my arm, and I yanked it away. "And it wasn't exactly sexy times for me and Caleb while they were trying to Frankenstein my lazy ovary. That was some of the least sexy I'd ever felt. Until I finally did get pregnant, of course. Talk about not feeling attractive."

"No one feels sexy during pregnancy, Natalie. If some influencer told you that, she's lying."

Dana was trying to calm me down, but I was just getting revved up. "I told myself, 'It's only forty weeks; you can get through this,' even when it got harder and harder, and I could barely even sleep by the end. It was horrible. I was losing my mind. I just wanted Aiden out."

Dana nodded vigorously. "I know. By the end, we *all* just want them to get the fuck out."

"Then it was like every last bit of energy I had went into pushing him out. And once he wasn't inside me anymore, I felt like Humpty-Dumpty. They stitched me up and sent me home with a newborn, who was even more needy out in the world than he was in the womb. Caleb could barely get any real time off of work. And you know my mother couldn't stay long. She had to get back home to take care of Dad in that final year."

Dana had stopped bobbing her head up and down, sadness settling across her face. I wondered if she was thinking back to ten years ago, when she was stressed out and overcommitted between building a business and parenting two little kids of her own. She knew I was having a hard time. She'd always made it a point to hang out at least once a week. She even referred me to her therapist multiple times. I never took her up on that.

"I'm so sorry," she whispered. "I've only recently realized you had a clear case of postpartum. And I think it metastasized into full-on depression as Aiden got older."

And everyone eventually just got used to it. The realization hit like a frying pan across the face. "Well, it's definitely good to know you and Caleb were talking about me while I became a shell of my former self."

I didn't know exactly what I wished Dana had done or not done. For that matter, the same went for Caleb. I knew they'd noticed. I knew they'd cared. They'd brought up their concerns and attempted to share helpful ideas on multiple occasions. They referred me to—sometimes begged me to enlist—professional help. But I still couldn't help but feel abandoned and disappointed, while simultaneously also feeling like I'd earned every single crappy bit of it.

I stood abruptly, jamming my laptop, the Thames portfolio, and the divorce papers into my bag. "I have a lot of work to do."

"Natalie, please don't leave like this," Dana pleaded.

"I have to prep for my meeting with Channing. I'll see you around." I yanked open the coffee shop door, stepped into a wall of sticky August heat, and wished I had driven.

6

VOTE OF CONFIDENCE

I spent the weekend in a sort of defiant capitulation. Just as I had started to pick myself up off the floor, the divorce papers came smashing down upon me. But unlike so many times before, the more I lay around feeling sorry for myself, the more anxious it made me. Even after hiding the manila envelope and stopping my mental replay of my argument with Dana, I couldn't shake the feeling that I was supposed to be *doing* something.

By Sunday night, Oliver's starfish beckoned me from behind its glass. I didn't feel like working, but I also didn't feel like distracting myself anymore. I pulled out the Thames portfolio and flipped through.

My designs, while beautiful and contemporary, suddenly felt impersonal. A project like this needed a special touch to make it unmistakably Oliver's home, something that would set me apart as the perfect choice of designer. Especially if I harbored doubts that my own merit got me the job.

But I knew so little about him beyond what was public knowledge. And Channing's disdain for adding elements of Oliver's personal taste glowed like a warning light in my mind.

I clapped the portfolio shut and began Googling aimlessly,

searching among already purple links for new information, fresh insight into the man in the house. What would endear my design concepts to him and all who surrounded him? What, what, what? Even though just getting the chance felt unearned, this was my chance to earn it.

By midnight, I found myself wading through dense legislation he'd co-sponsored, mostly championing the underdog in David-and-Goliath-type policy wars. I had a pretty good idea what he stood for. But how to translate that justice-seeking character into design elements and interior decor?

Exhausted and dissatisfied, I fell asleep, dreaming surreal fragments of encounters with Dana and Caleb and Oliver.

- -

As I climbed the steps to the townhouse on Monday, my insecurities needled me. My attempts to calm my own nerves became more like reprimands: *He signed the contract, Natalie. You're overthinking it. It's going to be another chummy meeting with Channing, who you already know is on board with your ideas. So there.*

I hit the knocker against the wooden door three times.

It swung open. But this time, there was no Channing in a summer suit to greet me. Oliver smiled back at me in pressed linen pants and a dark blue button-down. His tie was loosened and sleeves rolled up to his elbows, as if someone had asked him to fix a leak under the sink, chop down an oak tree, or perform CPR on a fellow Metro rider between Eastern Market and Capitol South on his lunch break.

"Hey, Natalie, great to see you again. Come on in."

My heart felt like a carnival hammer had sent it soaring up my throat to the bell at the top of my head, but I managed to say hello.

Oliver closed the door behind us. "Judging by your expression, you were expecting Channing. He had to put out a fire with a fundraiser we have coming up. With some reticence he allowed me to take his place."

I smiled, trying to find my stride. "I can imagine. I get the sense there are some things Channing thinks are best handled by Channing."

"And that is why he's my Chief of Staff." Oliver smiled, leading me toward the kitchen. "Would you like something to drink? We just put in the Nespresso."

"Water works great for me, thanks." The last thing my jitters needed was espresso.

Oliver emerged from the pantry with a bottle of water and slid it across the island. "To be honest, I'm glad my schedule opened up. I don't have a lot of time, but hopefully we can still make it productive. I'd typically be up in Rhode Island talking to constituents all August recess. But I'm here now, so I'm glad I can focus on the house and make it special. I've been renting a furnished condo in NoMa since I took office. Buying this place was overdue."

"I thought Channing said you're up for reelection in a few months?"

"Every two years," he said with a smile.

"But what if?" I blurted, then stopped myself.

"What if I don't get reelected?"

I nodded.

He swung around the island and came up beside me, leaning back against the countertop, his hip nearly touching mine. "If I *don't* get reelected, though they're telling me there's little doubt I will? Well, I still plan to keep a foothold here in the District. Consult on law and policy. Maybe start my own think tank."

He shrugged, but it was soft. I could feel the warmth of his body.

"That's a good reason to get a house here then." I gave a bashful grin and took a step back to maintain a professional distance. "Anyway, I'm glad I've got you here today, since I need to learn more about your style if I'm going to incorporate it into the house. There's only so much about you I can pick up from what's online."

"What's online, eh? Stalking me now, are you?" he teased.

"Just trying to spark some ideas," I said, but my laugh was nervous.

"I know. I'm just messin' with ya," he broke into a playful grin and nudged me with his elbow. Heat flashed into my cheeks at the unexpected contact. I hoped it didn't show.

"Hey, I have an idea," he said, "I'll tell you something about me, something you won't find online anywhere, if you tell me something about you first."

"Me? What do I have to do with anything?"

"I think it's only fair, don't you?" I couldn't tell if he was still playing or serious. "You already got all this research on me, and you're going to ask me a bunch of personal questions to learn my 'style.'"

"Not *that* personal," I mumbled. "I mean, I'm just an interiors person, not a psychoanalyst."

"So? I'd like to know a little more about the person I'm opening up to."

He looked at me expectantly. I waited a beat. "Well?" he urged.

"Well, what?" I asked, smoothing my hair behind my ears.

"Tell me about a room you decorated that you really loved. It'll put me in the right frame of mind," he suggested.

I took a deep breath. Okay. I could play along. "My freshman dorm room."

His eyebrows shot up and he smiled. "Your dorm? Really? Tell me more."

"Well," I said, focus drifting as I envisioned my old room, "I think the reason I loved it so much was because it was my first time really decorating my own space. I had left home and had this sudden taste of adulthood, and everything ahead of me was endless possibility."

I glanced back at him to make sure I hadn't taken the assignment too seriously, but Oliver, for whatever reason, was completely dialed in. "What did it look like? Or what was your favorite part about it?"

"The lights," I replied with a wistful smile. "I bought tropical, multicolored string lights that had glowing tiki heads on each bulb. My roommate and I hung them back-and-forth across the ceiling. We made that room into a tiny oasis. We had a blowup palm tree, coconut glasses with swirly straws, a piña colada-scented diffuser, the works."

"Piña colada diffuser?" Oliver's tourmaline eyes glimmered. "I bet it smelled like heaven. You'd never have gotten me out of there. My roommate loved to leave his wet sneakers lying around. We could've used a good diffuser."

I bet they could've. "Thankfully, my taste in decor has matured since then."

"Aww, man, are you telling me a blowup palm tree isn't in my near future?" he teased, leaning sideways into me.

"It was definitely a vibe. And a moment in time I'll never forget."

Oliver's attitude was infectious, but we had work to do. "Your turn. But instead of a room you already lived in, tell me about the most perfect one you can dream up."

He looked thoughtful as he wiggled the knot in his tie lower and lower, then pulled it off over his head. The scent of the renovated room's newness still hung in the air like a promise. He untied his tie, folded it neatly, and tucked it into his pants pocket.

"I'm not even sure where to start. I'd be better at this if I could look at something. It's hard for me to picture something out of thin air, but I'm good at recognizing what I like."

An idea occurred to me. "Okay, let's make it more tangible. There's a shop I like on Mass Ave., a couple blocks from here. You can point out what catches your eye, and that should help me understand enough to start designing."

He clapped his hands, relieved. "Great. We'll take it on the road. I don't have anything for us to sit on here anyway."

The humid morning air was infused with the smell of freshly cut grass as we trotted down the porch steps. A mower droned in the distance.

Oliver's stride was long and confident but not hurried. His eyes found mine now and again as I led the way to the shop. The jitters I'd felt earlier had dissipated. This was my show now. "Okay, let's start with a broad brush. When you walk into the house, what do you want to feel?"

"My keys in my hand," he said without thinking. "I have a terrible habit of leaving them swinging in the door. Channing will murder me if I do that again. Or possibly, as he says, the person letting themself in off the street will." Maybe this was his way of guarding himself, joking to avoid thinking about his emotions?

"I've got a workaround for that, as it happens. They make some sleek electronic locks now. Codes, not keys." He looked interested, like he hadn't known it was an option. I made a mental note to add some options to the list. "But what I'm really getting at is how you'd describe what you want to feel when you're in a place out of the public eye and able to let your hair down. Or take your tie off, as it were."

He rubbed his face. "Relief. A respite from the outside world. When I walk into my house, I want to feel an immediate sense of calm and orderliness."

For a second I thought about pulling out my phone to take notes, but something told me I wouldn't forget these details. "Calm and orderly can take a lot of forms. What do you see in your mind's eye when you enter the house? What about it stands out?"

"Books." He pressed his lips together and gazed thoughtfully into the middle distance. "Subdued colors. Leather. Warm lighting in the evening. Soothing music."

I jumped on that cue. "Music, that's interesting. What kind of music are you listening to? Or if the room were a sheet of music, what would it be?"

Our strides had synced, stepping to the same beat. He tilted his head toward the sky, enunciated each word as he let them out into the atmosphere: "Slow, bass-heavy jazz. Have you ever heard 'Introduction to Naked Soul,' by Michael Brecker? Or a soundtrack from an old noir film?" he asked, eyes alight.

"Sure," I said, catching the gist. "That's very helpful, actually. You have a knack for setting a mood."

"What's some of your favorite jazz?" he asked, slowing his pace.

"My favorite jazz?" I repeated, looking behind me and trying to match his pace again.

"Yeah, jazz. There's noir jazz, dark jazz, bluesy jazz, free jazz, acid jazz ... the widely detested *smooth jazz* ..." He stretched out the words as if expecting a reaction, but I didn't have one.

He stopped, putting a hand on my shoulder with a mock-dramatic whisper. "Natalie, it's ok, you can tell me: are you a closeted Kenny G fan?"

I blushed and started walking again. "I don't actually listen to a lot of jazz, but I totally get what you're going for."

"Don't listen to *jazz?!*" he wailed from behind me, like I'd just admitted to not stopping at stop signs. "Oh, man! You're missing out."

He jogged a few steps to catch up with me as I walked up to the shop. "And here we are." I smiled with relief. "I know you're on a timeline."

I yanked open the glass door, and we walked into the distinct scent of tea tree oil and varnish. The place was a cluttered mess, but also a treasure trove. I had loved it ages ago and had, during my first drive to the townhouse, been thrilled to see they'd managed to stay in business.

I turned to Oliver. "Why don't we take a spin through here, and you point out pieces you like? It doesn't have to be something you want to put in the house, necessarily, just something that appeals to you and why."

He gave me an amused smile, then spun around, hands on his hips, deciding which obstructed sightline of bits and bobs to explore first.

He set off down a cluttered aisle flanked by upholstered chairs and wooden end tables, pausing in front of a large, yellowed globe, giving it a spin.

He halted the globe with an index finger and glanced down at the spot, "You ever been to Morocco, Natalie?"

"I have not," I admitted. He could've spun that globe many more times and likely never landed somewhere I'd been.

"Do you like avocados?" he asked hopefully.

"I'm a big fan of avocados," I said, holding back from asking what Morocco and avocados had to do with designing his house.

"In Morocco," he continued, "they make the most delicious avocado milkshake. It's called ZaaZaa. It's really simple—just avocado blended with camel's milk and honey, usually. Moroccans enjoy it as a post-Ramadan treat, but sometimes I make them at home as a quick breakfast. I mean, with whole milk, not camel's—"

"What about this over here? Since you're so musically inclined?" An old record player, one of those 1950s monsters with a hinged lid that masqueraded as a console table, had caught my eye.

"Oh wow, it's like one my parents had." He touched a knob and the speaker buzzed. I was surprised it was plugged in. I turned to ask him whether he could envision something like it in his living room, but he'd crouched down to look at a shelf of old records.

"Can I play something for you?" he asked, excitedly pulling out an album he recognized.

"Umm, sure?" I checked my watch. Our time was flying by, and I still hadn't gotten much insight into his tastes.

He pulled the vinyl from its sleeve and dropped it on the record player. He carefully positioned the needle and set it free, sax and piano notes hurtling through the single speaker.

Oliver turned up the volume. His whole body conducted the music, as I bobbed my head along to the beat.

"Do you love this?" He almost had to shout over the song.

"I'm learning to!" It wasn't that I didn't like jazz, I just never listened to it much before, beyond maybe the soundtrack to *A Charlie Brown Christmas.*

"*That's* not how you enjoy jazz!" he cried, coming over to take me by the hand and twirl me around. The overture quite literally took my breath away. It wasn't just the spinning, but this sudden, intimate moment with a handsome near-stranger who also made legislative decisions for the free world in his working hours.

We weren't pressed together or anything—it was more like how the groom would dance with the flower girl to an up-tempo song at a wedding. But it was fun and irreverent and certainly more than I'd bargained for. I was dancing to "Giant Steps" in the middle of a funky furniture shop, and I let myself get swept away a bit.

"*This* is how you enjoy jazz, Natalie!" Oliver said over the music, dipping me backward.

I certainly was enjoying it, I even managed to forget for a moment that he was my client, not to mention my only ticket to rekindling a long-dormant career.

Then he stopped, reaching into his pants pocket to pull out his phone. He yanked the needle off the record. "Gimme a sec, I gotta take this."

It was an abrupt return to Earth as he stepped away, telling whomever it was, "Speak to me."

I scolded myself for letting us get sidetracked. How were we ever going to accomplish anything useful today? But as I waited for him to finish the call, I began to wonder if I had gotten more useful information out of this meeting than I gave myself credit for.

Treated to a taste of Oliver's stream of consciousness, I kept trying to steer him back to concrete questions. The man was letting me peer through the window to his soul, and I kept insisting he take me through the front door. Okay, so maybe he wasn't going to pick out an antique accent chair or have detailed thoughts on dominant and complementary color schemes. But maybe I already had what I needed. At least for now.

Oliver reemerged a couple minutes later, scrolling through his phone's music library, already out of congressman mode and back to being an animated hobbyist. "Sorry about that. You wanna hear more Coltrane, or should I put on something contemporary, like Kamasi Washington or Esperanza Spalding? Oh! I have to play 'Dream State' for you!"

"I know you're limited on time today," I said, moving it back toward the professional. "I want to make sure I've gotten all your thoughts on design for the house. Just to recap, you mentioned calm orderliness and black-and-white detective movies."

"Noir," he interjected without looking up.

"Sure, okay, noir. A distinction without a difference."

"Are you kidding?" He looked at me in disbelief. "A noir, while it *could* be a detective movie, doesn't necessitate a murder plot."

Was there no tangent he couldn't get on? I suppressed an eyeroll.

"I guess that depends on whether your house keys are swinging in the door or not." I laughed, waiting for him to join me, but he didn't. "Oh, c'mon! What noir doesn't involve a murder?"

"*A Streetcar Named Desire. The Birds. Vertigo. The Lady Vanishes…*" He rattled off movie titles without even having to think about it.

I threw up my hands. "Alright, you win. You'd like me to create a non-murdery noir space with a sullen jazz playlist fit for a femme fatale to pitch herself off a balcony to."

He thought about it for a second. "I'm not much into suicide-inducing environments either. Maybe we can reflect that in the color palette." Then he broke into melodic laughter.

He stepped toward me, close enough now that I could smell sandalwood, musk, and warm notes of moss, his aftershave mingling with his contrarian, know-it-all vibe. He wore a soft half-smile. "In all seriousness though, I think you get it."

A funny tingle pulsed through me. I straightened, rediscovering my authority. "Yes, I believe so," I told him. "You have clear nostalgia for an earlier era and would probably appreciate a space that evoked a sort of timeless, worldly glamour with touches of vintage, functional beauty, like this old record player. You want someplace welcoming but sophisticated, where you can think clearly, sheltered from the chaos coming at you from outside."

A quiet look of satisfaction spread across his face as he nodded, then cleared his throat. "Yes, that's exactly what I'd like to create. It sounds like you appreciate a space to think clearly, yourself. Do you work out of a home office?"

I pictured my cluttered desk at home. Besides being the temporary spot I'd set down his starfish, it was mostly covered in unopened junk mail, old catalogs, and an assortment of magazines I told myself I was going to read one day. I nodded.

"I'm sure it's challenging to have to share your workspace with the rest of your family," Oliver said. "My staff feels like family—some of them with no boundaries—but at least they go home at the end of the day. And I'm not responsible for making their lunch."

"Tell me about it," I said, "I could do with never having to make another SunButter sandwich the rest of my life."

"SunButter, eh? Sounds like you have unpaid interns too."

I laughed. His eyes crinkled up, probing mine, as he leaned back against a Victorian walnut armoire.

"I shouldn't complain. My son is at camp, so no lunches to make right now, and it's been almost uncomfortably quiet around the house."

"Well, I'm sure you and your husband deserve the break while you can get it."

I flinched. He noticed, expression turning sympathetic. "You must miss your son a lot. I don't have any kids, so that was probably an insensitive comment. Channing usually points those out to me."

"No, it's okay," I shook it off. "You'd be amazed how many parents look forward to the time off. When Aiden gets back from camp, he's actually going to be staying at my, uh, husband's for a while. So I'll have a longer break from sandwich-making than originally planned."

"Oh, I didn't realize you were separated."

I looked at the floor. "Yeah, I'm still getting used to it myself."

"Does that mean … it wasn't what you wanted?" He shifted his weight against the armoire.

"Well, I definitely didn't want the separation. And it wasn't my idea for Aiden to stay at Caleb's until school starts. That was kind of foisted on me in front of our son, and I felt obligated to go along with it. But, I don't know, it'll all work out I guess."

Oliver's brows knitted together. "Hmmm … Do you think your ex —Caleb, is it? Will he give you trouble over custody?"

The question surprised me. It was a thought I had been trying to push out of my mind since the camp argument. "I'm not actually sure yet. We had been sharing time with Aiden equally since Caleb moved out, but then …"

Oliver watched me patiently. Did I want to explain all this? I sighed and laid it bare. "Well, Caleb served me papers this past weekend, which caught me off guard. That was after he and I got in the argument about Aiden staying with him and his girlfriend for a while. Aiden already loves her. He was thrilled at the idea of staying with them."

Oliver's eyes were sympathetic. Or was it pity?

"Anyway," I said, abandoning my digression, "Caleb is pretty well-connected in DC. He started *Party Lines* and probably knows tons of lawyers and people of influence. So, I don't know. Should I be worried?"

Oliver took a slow, deep breath. "Worrying is not something I ever recommend. But lawyering up is. This is not a fight you want to be unprepared for, if he's already sent a process server after you."

My stomach knotted up as he continued, "Family law is neither predictable nor fair, Natalie. I've heard too many horror stories. The victor in these disputes may or may not be the wronged party. They *are* usually the most legally equipped party, though. If you care about how often and when you get to see your son, or what your financial situation will look like when the dust settles, I suggest you hire the best lawyer you can afford."

He put a hand on my shoulder. "I know someone who can help you," he said. "He's been a friend of mine since law school. He's barred in DC and Maryland—I think you live in Maryland, yes?"

I nodded. Oliver pulled out his own business card from his wallet and borrowed my silver pen to scrawl a contact on the back. "You don't have a paper clip, do you?"

I dug through my bag and retrieved the Thames Project portfolio, pulling the only paperclip I had off a magazine clipping of brass sconces. "Here. You can use this one."

"Thanks," he said, taking it and the portfolio itself from my hands. He clipped the card to the cover and handed it back. "Now every time you work on my house, you're going to be confronted by this until you give my friend Jake Cohen a call."

I took back the portfolio, bemused. I probably would have buried that card at the bottom of my purse, but he seemed to know better. And for my own good.

"Thank you," I said. I meant it. But for now, I wanted him to be our subject of conversation. "You definitely know how to set people up to follow through. Is this a tactic you use on the campaign trail?"

"You know, that's not a bad idea," he said. "Maybe we should mail everyone in my district a calendar with my face on it to stick to their fridge. And maybe each month features a picture representing a law we passed."

"You could put a big red circle around Election Day, lest anyone forget to head to the polls," I added.

"Let me worry about getting out the vote. *You* just make sure you put a big red circle on your own calendar when you set that initial meeting with Jake Cohen."

I winced. Oliver narrowed his eyes and studied me as though I were a museum exhibit under a pane of glass. The silence almost began to make me uncomfortable.

Finally, he spoke. "You know, for someone who impressed Channing and struck me as having this Wonder Woman energy, I'm beginning to see a dichotomy between your professional and personal life."

"Yeah, well …" I turned away, running my hand over the back of a pink velvet armchair as if admiring its bones. "Wonder Woman is a fictitious superhero from another planet. Nothing unrelatable or unattainable about that."

He made a pained face. I arched my eyebrows. What was it going to be now?

"Themyscira is not on another planet …" he said with a hate-to-clue-ya expression.

Ah, we were back to technicalities again. "Excuse me, *what?*"

"Where Wonder Woman is from. She's not from another planet, like you just said."

I narrowed my eyes as if trying to see through his facade. Was he serious, or was he fucking with me? Or was he *flirting* with me? "Aha, well, that might be, but in any case, I can see why the Amazons didn't want any men there."

"Fair point," he laughed, joining me beside the velvet armchair. "All joking aside though, I think you don't realize you have a Golden Lasso on your hip."

"Well," I deflected, "I'll be sure to loan it to my divorce attorney, whenever I finally get one."

Oliver started to say something, then looked down at the buzzing phone in his hand. "I'm sorry, gimme another sec. This should be a quick one."

This time he answered the call on speaker. "What's up?"

"Sir—" said a young voice on the other end.

"Maryam," he said in the tone of someone who'd said it twenty times before, "you can call me Oliver."

"Yessir. We have a problem with the interactive art installation you wanted at the gala."

"What's the problem?" he asked.

I could hear a flurry of background noise on the other end of the line.

"The artist informed us that it's not going to be ready in time," Maryam said anxiously.

"Not ready for the gala?" Oliver repeated, eyebrows rising.

"Precisely, sir."

"Oliver, please," he reminded her. "Hmmm… that's a real disappointment. Okay, well, I'm sure you're already seeing if there's anything he can do to speed along the creative process."

"Not a creative issue, sir. He says he's facing a technical setback," Maryam explained.

"Understood. Well. What are our backup options?"

"We still have the A.I. photobooth, the 360-degree action video, the table magician, the caricaturist, and the create-your-own popsicle station," she told him.

He nodded along as he spoke. "Okay, that's good… that's good. Well, hm. Let's see if we can get one of those—what are they called? BDSM stations?"

There was an awkward pause. "Sir??"

"You know. With soothing sounds and videos?"

"Ah. I believe the acronym you're reaching for, sir, is ASMR."

"Yes!" He gave a tiny fist-pump. "That one. The soothing stuff. People love that."

"I'm … just not sure it comes in *booth* format … sir?" Maryam fumbled.

A familiar, cheeky voice inserted itself at the other end of the line,

"Oliver, please do *not* put the letters *B-D-S-M* in that order outside the confines of your own home from now until the end of, oh, *any election cycle* you're participating in!"

"Your panic is unwarranted, Channing," Oliver soothed through a mischievous smile, steadying his gaze on me. "There are no reporters here. I'm in a vintage furniture shop with Natalie."

"You're still in that meeting? I seriously hope you're staying on task and not sending her on a wild goose chase for something bizarre." Channing sounded annoyed.

The congressman was enjoying himself. "Bizarre? Bizarre like what?" Oliver laughed.

"Like, I don't know, your adolescent fixation on superhero memorabilia?" Channing shot back.

Oliver's face lit up. "We were *just* talking about Wonder Woman!"

"You know, Channing," I chimed in, "with all this BDSM talk, if you need me to rewrite the contract to include reconfiguring the basement to support swings and chains…"

Channing sounded apoplectic. "Good Lord, Oliver! Am I on *speaker?*"

Oliver threw his head back in a silent laugh, like he and I were in on some hilarious prank phone call.

Channing was short. "Just try not to get impeached by the time I get back from Providence. And Maryam, look up 'ASMR event booths' and see if that's even a thing." The line went dead.

"Wow. A day in the life, huh?" I said, as Oliver pocketed his phone.

"Not as glamorous as you probably expected."

"I don't know," I approached him. "That fundraiser gala sounds pretty glamorous. I mean, a create-your-own popsicle station … that alone would get me to donate to your campaign, and I'm not even in your district. I don't even vote!"

"You don't what?" Oliver looked taken aback. Not listening to jazz had been one thing. This was evidently another.

I stuttered. "I mean, I vote. I have *voted*. You know what? Just pretend I didn't say that."

Oliver had left the building. Congressman Thames was back,

paternal and serious. "Natalie, voting is a fundamental right and responsibility that a lot of Americans take for granted, but the huge number of citizens around the world who are deprived of free and fair elections today is truly astonishing. Say what you will about the imperfections of the Electoral College or our winner-take-all system, or our two-party system that Washington himself warned against. But don't ever willingly give up the simplest, most universal way to impact people's lives, yours included, in meaningful ways."

"You're right," I surrendered, hands in the air, "I'll make it a point to vote in this election. I'll bring you my mail-in ballot. We can even fill it out together."

"We actually can't." His face was wooden. "Aside from showing you how to mark the box and place it in the return envelope, no one, especially not an elected official, is allowed to influence your vote."

I nodded seriously, regretting my hasty admission and this sudden left turn. I wondered how to lure back the other Oliver Thames, the one that relished jazz, old movies, and teasing everyone like an eighteen-year-old. "Indeed. Shall we get back to psychoanalyzing your music and film preferences and how that translates to design?"

He glanced at his watch. "Oh, geez … I wish I could. I've got to get back to the condo. My staff scheduled one of those shameless, hours-long call sessions to shore up support from big donors. I'm sorry we didn't get as far as I'm sure you'd hoped we would today."

My smile was gentle. "I actually came away with more than I expected."

He looked surprised to hear it as he chuckled, running a hand through his careless locks. Something in the way he looked at me sent a pulse of electricity up my spine and under my tongue. "Interesting!" he exclaimed. "Well, in that case, maybe next time you just hand me a Rorschach test, and the living room will decorate itself."

Again, I wondered if he was flirting. Possibly I'd just been out of the dating scene way too long to tell. Anyway, who was I kidding? He was probably trying to get on with his day so he could go give good phone to deep-pocketed donors.

Seeing us leaving, the clerk sitting near the door tried to insist on helping us, but we headed out into the midday heat. Mass Ave. bustled with traffic, so we ducked down a side street.

"This was good," Oliver said as we made our way back toward the townhouse. "I'm glad we checked that place out. You know, there are a couple pieces at an art gallery I'd like to show you next time. Don't tell Channing. I'd just like to get your take on them. It might shape what you're working on."

This was unexpected and exciting. "Sounds great. Which gallery?"

He did, in fact, look both ways before crossing the street. "Oh, I'm not sure you know it. It's gonna be a bit out of the way. Can you clear your Friday? It's going to take a while."

"Sure, I'm excited to see what you have in mind." It wasn't like I had much to move in my schedule, but I was wondering how far we possibly had to travel.

We had reached my car. "This is me. Good luck with your donors! Be sure to lecture them on how important voting is."

I smirked as he reached to open the door for me. "More like pandering for a piece of their generational wealth in exchange for political influence."

I looked up at him from the driver's seat. "You don't strike me as that kind of politician."

"All politicians are that kind of politician," he said with a wink. He began to close the door, then pulled it open again. "Oh, and Natalie, maybe wear sneakers and something comfortable Friday. There could be a lot of walking."

"Yes, Sir!" I pantomimed a salute and started my car.

"No 'sir,'" he insisted through that ribbon of white teeth. "Just Oliver."

7

***

SUITING UP

*O*liver knew what he was doing, I thought to myself, snapping the stiff business card paperclipped against my portfolio cover, *tick tick tick*. I'd rather it be facing front with his own contact information, but his chicken scratch of Jake Cohen's cell phone and email looked back.

Of course, Oliver was right. There would be no benefit to sticking my head in the sand any longer. Caleb was hell-bent on moving forward with the divorce and his life with Victoria. Based on recent events, Oliver wasn't wrong that Caleb could be posturing to take full custody of Aiden, too.

Mentally, I inventoried all the dirt Caleb could lay bare in court. Would he call out my parental missteps in front of a judge? Would he recite a litany of instances of my forgetfulness, or make a spectacle of my most vulnerable moments, when I was too emotionally spent to participate in family life? Would he paint a portrait of a depressed, incapable woman whose child would be better served in a home with two stable, successful, engaged parents who never forgot a soccer game, and who never made Aiden set his own alarm to wake himself up for school?

Caleb was far more prepared than I was, and certainly more motivated. He could pull out all the stops to get what he wanted and I wouldn't even see it coming. Oliver's words haunted me: *The victor in these disputes may or may not be the wronged party.* I knew it was true. Things wouldn't necessarily go my way. It wouldn't be the first time the family court system handed down an unfair judgment to a hapless but well-meaning victim.

I felt the impulse to dial Dana, then remembered I was mad at her. This was not a convenient time not to have my phone-a-friend option on what could literally be a million-dollar question. But I honestly wasn't ready to get her unvarnished opinion on what I should do either. Besides, I could already guess what it would be.

My restlessness finally drove me into the shoe closet. I slipped on my sneakers, tied back my hair, and went outside. I scampered down the back deck steps and took off jogging through the side gate. That pace only lasted to the end of the street before I lapsed into a walk, my lungs heaving and unsure what we were running from.

I pressed on, though, walking at a quickened clip, weaving my way into town. My heart forced blood through veins that thrummed in my temples, driven by an urge to break things, to burst through layer upon accumulated layer of what felt like the ash of some torched landscape, hardened into cement after rain.

The quaint stretch of businesses along Center Street bustled with life, and I blended into it. Arms swinging at my sides, I power-walked past the coffee shop, the bank, the chocolatier who somehow managed to pay the rent selling only tiny, outrageously priced confections. I passed the new boutique with the sign that read "Unexpected Things," then pivoted back.

A tailor's dummy in the window sported a chic, ivory silk blouse and ascot. A high-waisted, herringbone pencil skirt fell to mid-calf with a tasteful, asymmetrical slit up to the knee, fastened with a series of wooden buttons. I pulled the door open, hovering at the threshold for a moment before entering. I knew what to do now. It was time to suit up.

- -

I bounced a pointed leather mule on my foot, legs crossed in a new pencil skirt as I sat. The waiting room was a brightly lit, glass observation tank furnished with sturdy, well-upholstered chairs and a sofa. I couldn't quite pin down the scent in the room. I decided it smelled like wealth.

"Mr. Cohen will see you now," the pale blonde receptionist in a black mock turtleneck said through deadly red lips. I followed her down a long hallway to a corner office, where she knocked on double doors.

"Come in!" came an unassuming voice from inside.

The receptionist, who looked like she belonged in one of Oliver's noir *mise-en-scènes*, pushed open the door and let me in. In my head, a sultry sax melody played under a cliché male voice-over about her "faraway gaze" and how great her "gams" looked in that skirt. I almost cracked a smile, then switched back to the moment.

Jacob M. Cohen, Esquire was scrawling a note on a pad of legal paper, backlit by a panoramic view of downtown DC. His slight, hunched figure was dwarfed by his metal L-shaped desk, which was the definition of organized chaos: piles of papers, legal pads, books, magazines, a tablet, a phone, manila-foldered files in a tabletop cityscape of stacks and canyons. By contrast, the rest of the room was more like outer space, emptiness searching for gravity. I appeared to be somewhere in the Oort Cloud, not sure if he was aware of my presence. Then he put down his pen and looked up, dark, wiry beard pulling down the corners of his mouth. "Ms. Weir, I presume?"

I stepped forward into desk orbit. "Yes, Congressman Thames referred me to you personally."

"Oh, yes, Oliver. You'd mentioned that on the phone," he nodded, face still stony. "Come take a seat."

I settled into one of two matching polo green leather Chesterfield chairs, a gentle nod at old world style in an otherwise modern glass office. It struck me that I should have brought a notepad or tablet as he pushed his wireframe bifocals up the bridge of his nose.

"I reviewed the client information sheet you submitted online. Thank you. I understand that your husband, Caleb Weir, dispatched a process server to you last weekend after filing for absolute divorce earlier this summer and mailing you the complaint?"

"That's correct," I replied apprehensively, sitting very straight and still.

"So upon receiving the initial complaint, you chose to not acknowledge it?" It was a statement more than a question.

"That's also correct." I remained stiff, hands clasped in my lap, like a defendant at the bench.

"Was there any particular reason you chose to ignore this document the first time it arrived?" he asked.

I wasn't sure what to think. Was this an initial consultation, or a deposition? And how could someone like Oliver and this man, who had yet to even introduce himself, possibly inhabit the same solar system, let alone be old law school buddies?

"I wasn't prepared at the time to acknowledge it," I stammered, chin jutting forward.

"I see." He scribbled a note. "It would appear you are currently prepared to do so and are seeking to retain counsel for that express purpose?"

"That is correct, Mr. Cohen. May I ... I'm sorry, could we level set here a bit?"

"I was of the belief that that's what we were doing, Ms. Weir." He leaned forward with a neutral expression, elbows on his desk. His fingertips gently bounced against their counterparts on the other hand, like magnets of the same charge being forced together and repeatedly repelling each other.

I unclasped my hands. "Yes, of course. But if you'll permit me, I'd like to explain why I'm here, in my own words."

"Certainly, Ms. Weir. The floor is yours." He sat back in his massive leather rolling chair.

"Well, firstly, please call me Natalie. It's a pleasure to meet you, Mr. Cohen. Congressman Thames—Oliver—was emphatic that I reach out to you. I've been doing some work for him recently, which is how we met. We got to talking about my situation, which prompted his referral."

I paused, expecting an interjection from the bearded automat, but he continued listening.

"My husband Caleb and I have been married for sixteen years, and we have a ten-year-old son named Aiden. About a year and a half ago, Caleb started an affair at work, which only came to my attention this past March, the day he told me he was moving out. He's renting a place nearby with the woman he was having an affair with. She's his employee." I paused, expecting a reaction of some kind. There was no indication of intrigue.

"Caleb and I had been sharing time with our son up until he left for camp several weeks ago. But then, when we were visiting him there recently, Caleb told me he thought it would be better for Aiden if he stayed with him for a while. At first, I kind of said okay, but when I got back home, he served me those papers. Now I'm worried this is just the first step in him trying to claim sole custody." I could feel anxiety welling up in my throat. I waited.

"May I react now, Ms. Weir?" the lawyer asked.

"I cede the remainder of my time to you, Mr. Cohen," I joked, invoking Robert's Rules of Order.

He cracked a small smile at the reference. "First of all, Ms. Weir—"

"Please, call me Natalie."

"Natalie, then. First of all, Natalie, allow me to reassure you that, based exclusively on what you've told me so far, you haven't done anything that would jeopardize custody of your son. Maryland state law does not make light of separating a mother from her child. Unless you are a suspected drug addict or child abuser, or someone who is providing an unsafe environment for your son, it is unlikely Mr. Weir will succeed in obtaining sole custody, presuming that is his intent."

I let out a small sigh of relief. The authoritativeness of his emotionless words loosened the knot in my throat.

"That being said," Cohen continued, "since precedent between the two of you up to this point is that you and Mr. Weir share custody, a possible outcome to any mediation, arbitration or litigation—should we get to that point—could be one of equally shared custody, as you indicated you have already been doing. Are you amenable to half-and-half custody, or do you intend to fight for more?"

More? I took a breath. "I think a half-and-half situation would be my preference."

"You think, or you know?" he pressed.

"I don't want less than half," I affirmed, even though I was still unsure. What respectable mother would want less than half the time with her child?

"However," I ventured, "since Aiden seemed excited to stay with Caleb once he's back from camp, until school starts anyway, I'm fine with allowing it, as long as I can see him a couple times a week. I have quite a bit on my plate right now, so the timing works well."

Cohen relaxed in his chair and scribbled on the nearest legal pad. "We will draft official correspondence to Mr. Weir's counsel offering that generous concession and your willingness to take a cooperative approach in spite of Mr. Weir's transgressions. Is there anything else you'd like to discuss about your son before we move on to other foundational matters, like finances?"

I considered for a moment and shook my head. "My primary concern was how custody works."

"And your second concern should be that of child support. Fortunately, that is a standard calculation that will be determined by the inputs of Mr. Weir's earnings and your own."

"I have no earnings," I said flatly. "Well, I will have some. Very modest, part-time earnings from the contract work I'm doing for Congressman Thames. But other than that, I haven't worked in over fifteen years."

Cohen scrawled this down. "Mr. Weir, however, is a six-figure earner?"

"Yes, he founded the online magazine *Party Lines.* He's the publisher."

Cohen didn't look up. "That will work tremendously in your favor, Ms., I mean, Natalie. Based on Maryland precedent, the disparity in your incomes, between zero to what I presume to be mid- to high-six figures and for so many years, will give us substantial leverage on not only child support but the alimony front. Court determinations have been generous to women in similar financial circumstances, not just in the monthly sum itself but in duration of the alimony."

I blinked. I hadn't really given sufficient thought to my financial circumstances post-divorce. Caleb had handled all of that throughout our marriage, and we thankfully were never in a place of financial need. But it would only make sense that he'd be looking to shunt as much of his earnings and resources toward his new family. I had no idea what the law required after that.

"You've been married for sixteen years," Cohen continued, as if reading my mind. "Even after a few years of rehabilitative alimony to get you reemployed, if the disparity in your earnings and your husband's is still great enough, we've seen courts award alimony up to equal length of the marriage itself. This, of course, doesn't take into account the division of assets accumulated during the marriage. What is it you used to do for a living, and what have you begun doing now?"

"I was an interior designer and decorator," I said with a note of pride. "I'm doing contract work decorating Oliver's new townhouse. I'm not sure yet if this will be a one-off job or lead to others."

Cohen looked up from his notes and actually smiled. "Oliver bought a townhouse here? Good for him."

I appreciated the crack in his armor. "Oliver gave the impression that you two were close in law school. Did you spend much time together?"

Cohen lowered his pen and made eye contact. "I don't know that you get to spend much time doing anything besides studying and taking exams at Harvard."

It seemed a chilly response, but then his expression changed. "But I do credit Oliver with introducing me to my wife."

Finally! A trace of humanity in this personified encyclopedia of case law I was trusting with the most emotional matter of my life. "That sounds like an entertaining story."

"It is, but not one for today," he said, returning to notepad and formality. "Our time is limited, and we have much to cover."

Perhaps glimpsing the disappointment on my face, the lawyer put down his pen. "You've probably picked up, Ms. Weir, that I'm a straight-to-business kind of guy. Truth be told, I have a harder time with social graces that come more naturally to others."

"I wouldn't have thought that at all," I lied. "Especially with you being friends with Oliver."

"Oliver is my diametric opposite in that way." He chuckled lightly. "It's made him all the more successful. There's a lot to be said for charisma. I unfortunately don't happen to possess any, but that never stopped Oliver from taking me under his wing and coaxing me out with him once in a while. Less than he would have liked, I know."

"You're kidding!" I leaned forward in my chair. "I bet you have some good stories."

"Yes," he said, nodding and pulling his glasses off to clean them. "On what would become a fateful, inebriated night, Oliver convinced me to leave my studying behind and join him and some other students at the bar, and I am eternally grateful to him for that. Otherwise, he would never have overserved me and then sat me next to Imelda."

It was the closest thing to emotion I had seen out of him yet. Much to my surprise, he told the story, transporting us to a rag-tag pub in Cambridge, Massachusetts, two decades ago.

"She was a 1L at the time. Very shy. I wasn't the most outgoing guy myself, but being in Oliver's orbit gave just about anyone an instantaneous allure, and the liquid confidence helped. I invited Imelda to play what would amount to an embarrassing game of darts with me. Halfway through, we gave up and sat down to converse the night away. Every so often, I would catch Oliver out of the corner of my eye, cheering me on. The rest, as they say, is history."

A sense of satisfaction came over me, like I'd just jiggled open a stuck drawer. He was human after all. "Thank you," I said softly. "I like that story. And now I know something about you, too."

To my surprise, he smiled back. "Now, Ms. Weir—I mean Natalie. Where were we?"

"You know, Mr. Cohen, I think I'll be changing my last name back to Espinosa," I said, looking at my nails. "We'll be hearing Caleb's name quite enough in the coming months. If you're so inclined, you can call me by that name, if 'Natalie' doesn't roll off the tongue."

"Duly noted, Ms. Espinosa," he replied with a nod, returning his gaze to his notepad. "And thank you for your understanding. Let's dig in."

- -

I had just gotten home from the law office and changed into sweats when a text from Caleb sent me straight into palpitations. He had become such an infrequent communicator, especially with Aiden away at camp, that seeing his name pop up on my phone rattled me. I hated that he had that power over me.

It would be about Aiden. Caleb would only reach out if it were something he couldn't do without my cooperation. This time he wanted me to collect Aiden's soccer gear and a few other things that were left at my house and bring them over to his place before the camp bus returned our son on Sunday.

I'll just bring whatever he needs to the pickup spot when the bus drops him off, I texted back.

Aiden's already going to have a bunch of bags. It'll be an even bigger inconvenience. And if you show up late like you did on Visiting Day? Just drop it off here and make it easy on your son. You should have time between episodes of Too Hot to Handle.

I shook out my fists. I would normally have put off a task like this until the absolute last minute, but I wanted to get this over with. I stomped down the hall and began stuffing things into Aiden's school backpack. My cortisol spikes were not going to be at the mercy of a barrage of nastygrams until Caleb got his way, but it was still a demoralizing process. First, because I had trouble finding several things in the mess that was my son's room. I hadn't touched it since he'd left. Second, because there I was, at a time when I should be anticipating his return from camp, packing him up to give him away. I felt like an unfit mother.

By the time I had collected everything, my mascara had run, watercoloring my bottom eyelids.

Where do you want me to drop it? I texted Caleb.

Three dots appeared. *Just leave it on the front step.*

It was pouring out. *It'll get soaked.*

You're bringing it now? I could hear him whining.

Do you want it or not??

There was a long pause, then he responded with the side door code, instructing me to leave the bag in the mudroom. He'd unpack it when he got home from work.

Standing there in Aiden's room, his *real* room, in the house that Caleb and I had made into a home years ago, I looked down at my phone screen to read the door code to my husband's new home, which he had begrudgingly texted me. It took me a second to see it, but I couldn't unsee it once I did. Six digits, the day Caleb moved out of our house and into his new place with Victoria. A date they apparently commemorated every time they punched it in after work, every time they returned from a spirited pickleball round robin, and every time Aiden came home from school. I felt like I'd been punched in the stomach.

For as long as I could remember, our door code and password to almost everything had been the date Caleb and I met at our fraternity/sorority mixer. We had used it even before we got engaged. It had superseded all the dates since: our wedding anniversary, when we got our first apartment together, Aiden's birth.

Caleb and I had an infatuation-at-first-sight type of romance that had us memorializing that night, the same way that Jake did the night he met Imelda. Caleb had left our marital home, but I never thought to change the code to the door.

With a guttural scream I hurled my phone across Aiden's bedroom as hard as I could, into the shelf of bobbleheads from the countless Washington sports games Caleb had taken him to. Little men of plastic and resin, who I couldn't have picked out of a lineup, showered down upon Aiden's floor, a few in pieces.

How dare he? How fucking dare he?! The code my son would be

entering to get into his father's house—hell, the one he had *already* been using on his days back and forth—was the date Caleb marked as his new lease on life. The date Caleb emancipated himself from me and everything we had built together over twenty years.

I charged downstairs and flung my front door wide, fingers hovering over the keypad. I struggled to think up a new code. Aiden's birthday and my own would be too easy to guess. But every other date of significance in my mind had something to do with Caleb.

My fingers itched to type in *anything* else. But my memory failed me. I had nothing.

Defeated, I keyed in my mother's birthday. But it didn't make me feel any better. It only reminded me I'd forgotten to send her a birthday card the previous week.

– –

I pulled up in front of Caleb's house ready to get him out of my thoughts as fast as he had invaded them.

I threw my rain jacket hood over my head, stuffed Aiden's bag underneath the open front, and made a dash for the side door. I punched in the code with clenched teeth, and the door gave way. I slammed it shut. The house was dark and silent. I pulled the bag out from under my jacket, dripping onto a doormat that read "Doorbell broken. Yell DING-DONG really loud." I imagined Caleb, Aiden and Victoria cracking up together as they chose it.

I wondered where I should leave the bag. In one of the perfectly organized mudroom cubby holes? On the neat line of coat hooks? Or should I just drop it on the floor, the only thing out of place in this meticulous home? I stood there dripping a while longer, breathing in the fresh-laundry smells, and chose a coat hook, peering through the open mudroom doorway into a massive kitchen.

I would later tell myself it was the pull-down gooseneck sink faucet and matching fixtures that drew me into the house, just for a peek, crossing the boundary of where Caleb had pre-authorized me to set foot. But the stainless Thermador built-in fridge-freezer combo that I knew retailed for $16,000 was just the start of where I really lost my mind.

The house was fucking huge. How much money did this woman make? More importantly, how much did Caleb make? He paid her, after all. I had a vague idea what Caleb's salary was but realized when Jake Cohen asked that I hadn't gotten a recent number. Too bad, the lawyer had reflected, noting on his legal pad the need to contract a forensic accountant to get a good handle on what assets existed, how much money was coming in, and what expenses were going out. I had always left that stuff to Caleb and admittedly never had any interest in it when he tried to show me. But I'd be making up for lost time. Caleb was surely readying his affairs to be permanently separated from mine. My access to our joint accounts had a deadline.

In the sunken great room that flowed from the kitchen, a stone accent wall held a 70-inch television above a wood-burning fireplace flanked by two stone planters whose exotic climbing plants reached for the second story. There had to be enough seating in the room for twenty, all pulled together elegantly over a neutral-toned handwoven Berber rug and a gleaming, wide-planked wooden floor. Pictures of Caleb and Victoria were on display everywhere, as recently as what appeared to be their luxury Alaskan cruise. There were plenty of pictures with Aiden, too. The house felt as if they'd inhabited it happily for years.

I floated up the sweeping staircase in search of my son's room, passing a set of double doors that opened into a chalet-inspired primary suite. Tall French windows stretched up to the wood beam ceiling. The California King sat against the far wall, covered in an inviting ivory duvet. A wood-carved, topographical map hung in a triptych above the bed.

This is where my husband makes love to someone else.

Arriving at ground zero, I felt like one of Aiden's broken bobble-heads, head and pieces of limbs sailing in different directions. Both repulsed and compelled, I approached the bed and ran a hand along the fluffed duvet.

On the nightstand was a bottle of body lotion from a French brand

I had never heard of. The label looked small-batch and expensive. I squeezed a little into my palm, rubbed my hands together, and breathed in. A memory I had almost forgotten resurfaced on notes of smoke, earth, musk, and subtle florals. Caleb had attended an event at the Newseum, not long before it was sold to Hopkins, commemorating something or other about the history of political journalism. I hadn't been feeling great and decided to stay home last minute. But the scent on Caleb's pillow the next morning was distinctly *this* one, both masculine and feminine, powerful but not overpowering, subtle yet nuanced. I remembered wishing there was a scent search function online so I could identify and buy it.

That wouldn't be the only time I'd smell that scent. In fact, I'd even asked Caleb if he had a new aftershave or lotion he was using. But it was around that time that I'd stopped noticing it. Maybe I'd given away that I was catching on, before I even knew it myself. How could I have been so obtuse, I wondered now, hands held up to my face.

Another memory came on its heels, the very first time I'd laid eyes on Victoria. I had gotten roped into volunteering for one of Aiden's school field trips to the Building Museum. As the kids piled back onto the school bus to leave, and we volunteers headed back to our cars, I had the whim to pop into Caleb's office around the corner to surprise him. The receptionist took me back. Understandably confused, Caleb waved me in. Across from his desk sat a woman I'd never met. He introduced me to Victoria as if we'd met before. I was quite sure we hadn't.

Victoria extended her hand to shake mine, her sleek silhouette, chic bodycon houndstooth dress, and black thigh-high boots felt miles away from my mommy mishmash of pilled sweater from Loft and "fat jeans" with a stain that I told myself you couldn't see unless you really looked. I would later tell Caleb she reminded me of a younger, thinner version of myself. He awkwardly brushed it off. I'd thought about that encounter ever since Caleb admitted Victoria was the woman he was leaving me for. This woman lived up to her full potential, someone who could engage in industry conversation with my husband and stand toe-to-toe with him in a business he grew from nothing but gumption and a few useful connections.

I wandered down the hall in a fog, caught between past and painful present, peering into a guest room, then an office, then a hallway bathroom in search of Aiden's room. His *other* room. The one that wasn't at my house.

The low rumble of a garage door froze me in my tracks. Panic set in as the garage closed again. My eyes flashed from Aiden's closet to his bed. Was it better to hide behind the shower curtain in the guest bathroom? Now I could hear a downstairs door swinging open and Caleb's voice chatting casually with someone on the phone. Like someone in a movie, I wriggled face-down under Aiden's bed and prayed for a chance to flee.

"Yeah, well, it's looking all but certain for Compton to be her VP pick. No, no one's found any skeletons. Yeah … yeah … either way, it's gonna be a tight race. Says *who*? Says me and an off-the-record chat with Nate Silver! Heh. Really? Oh, I wish he *would*. I'd love to run *that* headline."

Caleb's voice floated up the stairs, growing louder and clearer, until I spied his perfectly buffed Italian leather shoes coming through the doorframe. I held my breath in terror, pressed against the floor as Aiden's bag landed with a thud on the mattress above.

"Well, we should grab lunch or something soon," Caleb said, slowly, ambling around the room. "I've got Aiden coming home next Sunday, and with the election news cycle ramping up, you know. … Yeah, things are going great. Ad revenue's way up. Victoria's been killing it. We just got back from Alaska … Yup, snowshoeing on glaciers, rock climbing, kayaking, watching humpbacks, all that shit. Trip of a lifetime. She's been amazing, and so good with Aiden. She's helping him with soccer. He just loves her."

A pause, then Caleb, cackling. "*That* has definitely been amazing as well. Let's just say my urologist told me I have the prostate of a twenty-five-year-old!"

Ew, uncalled for.

Another long pause where I watched his shoes and tried not to breathe. "Yeah … Speak of the devil, she was just here. … No, nothing like that. I had her bring over some of Aiden's things. … Yeah, it's movin' now. I got a process server to track her down last weekend, no more ignoring it. … Yeah, I know, that's the unfortunate thing, it's only the beginning. Let's see what kind of clown she hires. … Nah, I can't cut her off. Already asked my attorney. Wouldn't bode well with a judge."

Finally, Caleb wandered into the hall. "Listen, I just remembered I have to pick up a few things for Victoria at the store. She's making this spaghetti squash chicken piccata dish I love, but we're out of capers. … That's right, my man! Eatin' good, feelin' good! Beats Lazy Lasagna. But hey, talk to Kerrianne and see if she can put you on my calendar for Friday lunch. I want to hear all about Brinley going to UVA and the thing with your dad."

Caleb's voice descended the steps as he exchanged pleasantries with the man on the phone. Moments later, I heard the door to the mudroom slam and the garage door go up and down again.

"Jesus *Christ*!" I swore, shimmying out from under the bed, an errant dust bunny clinging to my arm. I couldn't have felt any lower. Aiden's alternate universe room wasn't that dissimilar from his room at my house, except much more orderly, even with his artwork and knickknacks.

He will keep making memories here, I conceded.

I was happy for my son that this transition was going well. Of course I was. I just wished it didn't feel like time with me was so easy for him to give up. I supposed my own gradual retreat over the years had acclimated him to my absence all too well.

I took a last look around, soaking in the atmosphere that was still uniquely Aiden, even if it existed in a world where I didn't belong. I glimpsed a picture frame on his nightstand, partially blocked by a stuffed animal. I picked it up. My heart leapt. Inside the frame were my son and me, side by side, hugging tight with big smiles, his right arm extended holding a painted turtle in his hand. Dana had snapped the photo at his reptile-themed birthday party a couple years earlier.

I swelled with joy. Not all was lost.

8

―――――

DIVINE PROVIDENCE

A nighttime torrent of summer rain had dried into a brilliant, dry Friday morning. The humidity that had hung heavy for days had been sucked out of the air, leaving behind a cloudless sky and neon yellow sun, a rare gift in a DC August. A spotless black SUV was already pulled up out front when I arrived at the townhouse. I couldn't help but feel excited. In spite of the odd conversational zigzags, the tantalizing process of unwrapping Oliver Thames had been on my mind.

He was sophisticated and educated—no surprise given that he was a congressman who'd gone to Harvard Law. He was handsome, too. It could've made him a total dick. Or one of those Frozen Chosen who occupy at least sixty-eight percent of the corner offices in the Federal government. But the man was also delightfully human—boyish, sometimes, but also fatherly, depending on the circumstance, and it fired me up and calmed me down at the same time. Twice now I had interacted with him, but the experiences were different. It felt like opening the doors to an Advent calendar, a new surprise each day. *The Unboxing of Oliver Thames,* I thought as I struck the bronze knocker to the front door to claim today's prize.

Channing opened the door with an air of impatience. He was obviously already having a day. "Natalie, dear, don't just stand there! The air conditioning and the moment are escaping us!"

He escorted me into cacophony, yelling into the basement. "*Oliver!* Get your refined behind up here!" The wine cellar and gym were being built out, the study subfloor installed. I saw that the crown molding in the living room, also part of the final finish work the house flippers had promised as a condition of sale, had been done already. As I snapped a quick picture, Oliver bounded up, taking the stairs two at a time.

"Oh, hey, Natalie," he greeted me with a carefree smile. "Right on time."

"I'm excited to show you what I've been working on," I said as I followed him into the kitchen.

"I didn't realize I gave you many details to work with!" he declared over the banging and sawing, grabbing a gooey, oversized chocolate chip cookie from a pastry box on the island.

"You definitely didn't make it easy."

Oliver strolled up beside me so he didn't have to shout above the noise. His breath grazed my ear. "But you *did* get to hear some jazz." The vibration of his voice elicited a tickle that wrapped around the back of my neck and went straight down my spine.

I followed him toward the stairs and away from the racket, chanting *client. client. client* in my head, the way a man might repeat the word "baseball" or "grandma" when trying not to prematurely—

"Come try this cookie," he said, breaking it in two, exposing craggy chocolate chunks. He popped an entire half in his mouth. "It's from that little French bakery on Penn." Crumb dust escaped from his mouth on the aromatic current of the word "Penn."

"I'm good for now," I told him. He shrugged and shoved the other half in his mouth.

We crossed the mezzanine balcony, where Oliver hung over the brushed bronze and aluminum cable railing to peer down into the living room. "I think you've got a better shot up here," he said.

"Huh?"

"Of the new molding," he pointed up.

I followed his finger. "Oh. Of course." I snapped another picture.

Oliver turned around. "We've got to spice up these two guest rooms," he nodded at them.

"Do you get a lot of overnight guests?" For some reason, it felt awkward to ask.

"I probably will if they hear I have all this space," he said, not seeming to notice. "Show me what you're thinking."

"Well," I said, "I feel like we should distinguish each guestroom with a bold color, like sapphire or emerald, but unify them with angular, brass finishes. It'd give a rich, 1930s feel but also make it easy to say, 'You're in the Green Room, Harry.'"

"Who's Harry?" he looked at me to ask. I could never tell if he was teasing or not.

"Or Belinda," I tossed back.

He raised an amused brow. "Belinda, you say?"

"Whatever your friends or … associates may be named."

"Are Harry and Belinda ghosts from when the house was built?" Oliver's whimsy curled my lips into a smile I tried to repress.

It only encouraged him. "*What if …* Harry is colorblind and winds up in Belinda's room? Or maybe she *sleepwalks* into Harry's room?"

I pushed aside my amusement. "Let's get back to—"

The congressman was undeterred. "*What if …* the conjoining bathroom—"

"Listen," I broke in, using my best Serious Business voice, "if you have distinct ideas about what these rooms should look like or the types of people you expect will stay in them, I'm happy to design to those specs. But you may be missing your calling as a romance novelist."

Again, I couldn't tell. Were we flirting? Or was he just a teenager trapped in the body of an elected official?

"I'm sorry, Natalie," Oliver said, laughter abating. "But I like Harry and Belinda. My actual guests would never be half as colorful. Please. Continue."

We took the stairs up to the third-story primary suite. The lofted space had been empty. Now there were two black vinyl beanbag chairs plopped beside one another, smack in front of the floor-to-ceiling Palladian window.

The '80s bachelor pad sensibilities make their debut! Just as Channing had warned me. A smirk tugged at the corners of my mouth.

I gestured at the beanbags. "What are *these* doing here?"

"Temporary seating," Oliver replied, plopping down in one and motioning me to the other. "I had them in the living room until Channing yelled at me to 'get these trip hazards out of here!' I figured we'd need something to sit on until the rest of the furniture came."

"When the *rest* of the furniture comes?" I asked, taking a mock-menacing step toward him and shaking my head. "You must mean when the *real* furniture comes. We're not keeping these in here."

"Oh?" He looked delighted.

"Absolutely not," I reprimanded, schoolteacher style. "The beanbag chair is the invertebrate of the furniture kingdom, suitable only for playrooms and stoners in dorms."

I took another step so I was casting a shadow over him sprawled on the vinyl. I pointed at the beanbag with one hand, the other on my hip. "That? Is a glorified dog bed."

Oliver's mouth formed an O of beguiled surprise. He loved it.

"Well, Ms. Haughty Designer, you may have strong opinions on the matter, but today I'm afraid you're sitting in a glorified dog bed too." He bowed his head and gestured to the amorphous black blob beside him, like a steward guiding his queen to her throne.

Satisfied, I took a seat beside him. He shimmied his beanbag closer. I pulled out my portfolio, and he noticed immediately what was missing.

"How'd it go with Jake?" he asked, motioning to the empty spot where he'd clipped the card.

I hadn't expected him to ask. Except of course he did. "Great, actually. He was a huge help. We've gotten started, and things are looking up."

Oliver clapped his hands together. "Fantastic! Jake will do right by you. You probably noticed he could be a little … *formal*. But his heart is true and he's super sharp."

"He took a bit of getting used to," I admitted, brushing a hair from my face, "but yes, I completely agree. I meant to thank you for connecting us."

"Ah, no thanks required," Oliver demurred. "Of course I wanted to help out a friend." He leaned over on his beanbag, close enough I could still catch the scent of cookie. "And by friend, I mean you. Last I checked, Jake needs no help getting business."

His comment and the feel of his breath left me tingling. His eyes lingered on my face until I had to look away, opening the portfolio.

Inside my head, the schoolteacher voice was back. This time I wasn't playing. *Stop, Natalie. Just stop right now. Do not become a cliché and get all twitterpated. He's a client, just like any other. Where is your professionalism?*

I started walking him through my sketches and clippings, laying out what he'd invoked in the furniture shop. He offered no digressions, following closely, buzzing with energy, validating how I'd translated his psyche onto the sketchpad.

As I finished sharing the last page in the portfolio, Oliver shifted forward in the beanbag chair to the *ssshht* of tiny little styrene pellets. Now his knees were grazing mine. Speaking of professionalism, where was *his*? Or was this just more of his very good-natured personality?

"You've really captured it, Natalie." The sincerity sent a flutter through me. "I love where this is headed."

He gave me another of those smiles I couldn't look away from, exhilarating and strictly off-limits. I felt myself melting. He didn't look away.

Channing's harried voice flew up the stairs, snatching us out of our trance. "They're waiting for you."

I wasn't sure who "they" were. The contractors? Campaign staff? Duty called, whoever it was. Oliver snapped back into congressman mode, already back on his feet.

A little dazed, I followed. Channing met us on the way out the door, where the black SUV waited. Channing opened the back door. I slid in, then Oliver sat beside me. Channing hesitated, still holding the door.

"Lemme see your shoes," he told me, pointing.

Baffled, I lifted my foot. I'd worn something comfortable as directed, tan leather with a low heel, cushy sole, and a broad, olive-green elastic strap over the arch.

"They'll have to do," Channing groused. "I hope they're as comfortable as they look."

I turned to Oliver. "What was that about?"

"*Pfffft!*" Oliver threw up his hands and made a face, then swiftly changed the subject. "So, Natalie, when did you start designing? You make it feel like you've done it for a lifetime."

I was still trying to figure out why Channing wanted to see my shoes, but I tried to answer. "I was always into art as a kid. I guess the real designing came when I decided to go to college for it."

"Oh, yeah? Where'd you go?" He rested his chin on his hand, elbow by the window.

"Maryland," I said, imagining it sounded pretty boring to a Brown and Harvard grad. "They had a good program, and I'd never been to the East Coast."

"Not an East Coast girl, eh?" he asked. "Whereabouts are you from?"

"Pismo Beach, California."

He quirked an eyebrow. "No kidding? You ever been to Morro Bay?"

"Of course," I said, bemused. "It's only about half an hour north of where I grew up. My dad used to take me to watch the elephant seals as a kid. I loved it. I still do."

"Same here!" Oliver's face lit up. "It's one of my favorite California spots. Totally underrated!"

"Completely!" I liked the thought of having a fellow elephant seal appreciator. "Did you vacation there a lot or something?"

He hesitated. "I was in Napa for a little while. Traveled down the coast to Santa Barbara and caught Morro Bay on the way. Then I hiked Sequoia on a visit to Paso Robles. Just incredible countryside."

"Huh, interesting. Napa, Santa Barbara, Paso Robles … was this a wine road trip? Are you a wine connoisseur?"

"Eh, I wouldn't say that," he looked out the window. "Just enough to be dangerous. California is such an ecologically diverse state. Parts of the coast even remind me of growing up in Rhode Island. Maybe that's why I love it so much."

"Oh, really? I've never been to New England." I wanted to hear more about his personal life.

"Never?" he asked, surprised. I shook my head. "You'll have to let me know what you think of it. I mean, when you get there. Anyway. You were saying how you came to Maryland, where you learned to hate beanbag chairs?"

I laughed. "I might've been a little harsh on you today. I have to be better about keeping my opinions to myself."

"Nonsense!" Oliver's expression was ardent. "You giving your true opinion is one of the most refreshing things about you."

I felt giddy at being praised for a quality that could easily go unappreciated.

"You've probably noticed I'm a bit of a think-it-say-it guy myself," he added. "It sometimes gets me in trouble."

"Exactly. Being that you're my client, I would definitely like to avoid getting myself in trouble. I'm glad I didn't overstep."

"Seriously, don't worry about it." He waved a hand to dismiss the thought. "I'm usually dealing with the exact opposite: sycophants. If I like something, they like it too. If I have a nuanced opinion, they're always interested and agreeable, but I never really know what they're thinking. Call me neurotic, but a lifetime of that can make you paranoid. You can't know if someone likes you for you, and you can't ever really know them either."

I nodded. It sounded exhausting.

"But you, Natalie, you're not afraid to show me who you are, and you push back on my bullshit. And my beanbag chairs." I felt heat rise into my cheeks and wondered just how red I was turning. "That's why

I keep Channing around too. It's a no-holds-barred stream of consciousness from that one. But one thing about him: he's infallibly honest."

"I have no doubt about that. Your antidote to the yes-men."

Oliver nodded slow and emphatic, running a hand through his hair. "You get it. But you were telling me about the start of your design career. What was that like? What inspired you?"

When most people asked me these types of questions, it either felt like an interview or an interrogation. When Oliver did, it felt like he actually wanted to know.

By the time the car pulled into its destination, it had begun to dawn on me that almost the entire conversation had been about me. But that realization was quickly eclipsed by a much bigger one: we were on the tarmac of Reagan National Airport, parked alongside a private jet.

"Is this the airport?" I peered in every direction like a meerkat peeking out of its hole. "Where *is* this art gallery, anyway?"

Oliver had already sprung out of the car. He reached a hand back in for me. I took it with hesitation and let him pull me up and out of the car. I could feel the blood drain from my face.

We are getting on this jet.

Oliver's boyish grin was back. "Natalie, I have a confession. I *may* have lied about the art gallery. I'm taking you on a little work trip."

On a plane. I hate planes. *Why did it have to be a plane?*

I hoped my panic wasn't obvious. Maybe it was. But maybe he was just being Congressman Thames again. "When we met last time, you mentioned that you don't vote. And I sense that's because you feel like you can't make a difference. And it bothered me, because someone like you is exactly the kind of person who could make a difference in so many people's lives. The thought of you giving away that power, well, just talking to you on the ride now, it convinced me even more that we should do this together."

"Do what?"

"Fly up to my district and start making a difference!" I had no idea what that meant. Oliver was already heading up the jet steps.

While I hated planes, it only took about two seconds for me to wonder if that was because I'd been flying commercial. This plane was a luxe living room that could fly, the kind of thing you'd see on a show about how the world's billionaires get around: glossy wood, soft cream-colored leather, warm lighting, gold accents, a tidily stocked bar complete with crystal glassware tucked into purpose-built shelves.

Oliver greeted the copilots by name, chatting as I took it all in. Two other staffers were already seated, completely absorbed in their phones, one scrolling endlessly, the other typing feverishly with both thumbs like the nuclear codes had been compromised. Both were young and well-dressed, smart, but less chic than casual. For that matter, Oliver was dressed down too, just khakis and a navy polo that accentuated his defined arms and upper body. Everyone wore what appeared to be fresh, unscuffed sneakers.

I took a seat on the sofa as the flight attendant took my drink order. I asked for a Diet Coke but felt like I might need an Alka-Seltzer or a gin and tonic. I had always been an anxious flyer, and the surprise didn't help.

Oliver sat down beside me as the crew pulled up the steps. "I imagine you have questions."

"That is the understatement of the year."

"Well, how much do you like walking?"

"About as much as I like flying, which isn't a lot."

Oliver thought for a second. "What about … trick-or-treating?"

"Oliver, with all due respect, where is this going? Or rather, where are *we* going?" I was clutching the armrest like the couch was about to turn into an ejector seat.

"We're going canvassing! Getting out the vote!" He said it like he was a kid about to go to Disneyland.

My mouth hung slightly open. "Canvassing? Like … door-knocking? For a cause?"

I inspected him for signs of goofball prankster, but the congressman seemed genuinely stoked. "Yup! I have a whole team of staff and volunteers who do this regularly, but I join them whenever I can fit it in. I feel more connected to the people that way. Keeps it real.

Keeps me grounded in who put me in office, who I work for and the things they care about."

My thoughts tumbled over themselves as Oliver continued into stump speech land: "In DC, it's easy to get sucked into ideological party wars that are so far removed from what citizens actually want and the values they hold. The people in my district, much like the rest of the country, want three main things. They want an economy that works for everyone. They want safe communities for their families. They also want accessible, affordable, high-quality healthcare. And a few other things, of course, but if I had to boil it down, those three are always top of their list. And so what we're gonna do today is a lot of listening to take the pulse of that, but also, we'll share some information and point people to resources to help them get the things they want."

I could see how he'd been elected so handily two years earlier. With a speech like that, off the cuff no less, he could've told me we were going door-to-door to sell vacuums and I would've let him wind me up and point me at the next front porch.

"So, no art gallery, just a little old-school campaigning?"

"Try it, you'll like it." He grinned, settling back in his seat and buckling up.

I followed his lead and buckled in too. "Okay, but you know I'm billing for this time, right?"

"You'd better be!" He tapped me gently with his elbow and my heart fluttered.

Pre-flight jitters, I told myself. Just the usual "anxfliety."

Cleared for takeoff, we sped down the runway. Whatever I had felt a moment earlier turned into pure adrenaline. My heart went from flutter to sledgehammer. Takeoff felt a lot faster in a small plane. We gained altitude, the headrush of G-force pressing down on me. I was buckled in safely. My hindbrain didn't care. I whimpered and reflexively grabbed Oliver's knee. He just chuckled, leaving my hand in place.

"You gonna be okay?" he asked over the roar of the engines.

I jerked my head up and down, white-knuckling his knee. In what was either a complete lack of situational awareness or a very kind gesture to distract me from the ascent, he blathered on about something or other that I hoped I wouldn't need to remember later.

When we finally leveled off, the flight attendant brought over our beverages. I downed the Diet Coke, both parched and aware that I must be emanating what Caleb always referred to as "fear breath." Oliver casually sipped a seltzer, slightly cloudy from a splash of grapefruit juice and adorned with a lime wedge.

My usual self would have spent the duration of the flight in some stage between vigilance and panic, but this chance to open the next door on the Oliver Thames advent calendar made me forget, at least a little, how high up we were in the sky. "Turnabout is fair play, Congressman. You asked me so much about myself on the way here, and yet I know so little about you."

"Fair enough," he said, grabbing a handful of snack mix from a nearby bowl. "What would you like to know?"

There were so many things I wanted to ask him, some of which were probably not exactly appropriate. I decided to keep it broad. "Where'd *you* grow up? What was growing up like for you? What drove you to get into public service?"

He crunched snack mix for a moment. "Well, I grew up in Rhode Island with my parents and sister, Madeleine."

"Madeleine?" I asked. "You mean your parents named both of you after fictional orphans?"

He paused to think. "Hmm! I guess they did!"

"A bold choice," I joked. "Are they still, ah, with us? Your parents?"

"Yes, thankfully. We weren't orphans, though we were raised by a series of nannies, so it could feel like that sometimes. There was no nanny Madeleine and I couldn't drive to her wit's end. But our cook, Maria—we called her Nonna—she was with our family for decades. We never tortured Nonna. We loved her. She was basically the closest thing we had to a typical grandmother growing up."

"Sounds like you were mostly raised by the help?" I realized that probably sounded off-putting.

He took a deep breath. "Yeah, you could say that." I thought I noticed a flicker of hurt behind his eyes, but if there was, it was short. "My parents were busy people, so there wasn't a lot of time for us. And now Maddy and I are the busy people. But she's become pretty close to Mom as an adult."

"And you?" I asked.

"I try to see them as much as my schedule allows. Major holidays, and every once and again I'll drop in on them."

I had to pull Oliver's not-very-typical childhood out of him question by question. Newport was only a backdrop. There was boarding school, frequent trips to Europe, and grand vacations to seemingly everywhere. Japan, the Galápagos, a safari in Botswana, and a Patagonia-to-Antarctica expedition that sounded like it qualified for *National Geographic*, all before adventure tourism was really a thing. He was better traveled by eighteen than most people would be in a lifetime.

"So you mean to tell me that when you spun that globe in the furniture shop the other day, your finger could have landed pretty much *anywhere,* and you'd have had some fun factoid to tell me about a visit there?"

"Well, not *anywhere,*" he deflected, sipping his seltzer. "It could've landed in the middle of the ocean. I'm not Magellan."

I laughed, then insisted, "But any *country.*"

"There are plenty of countries I haven't been to." He cast his eyes down modestly.

"Must you always be the consummate contrarian?" I asked, only half in jest.

He gave me a roguish look and extended his right hand at me. "Hi, I'm Oliver Thames. I don't think we've met. Politician, Constitutional law scholar, and consummate contrarian."

"And teenaged class clown for life," I added, pushing aside the handshake.

He laughed. "I can't help it! I was born this way."

I shook my head. "I seriously feel bad for all those nannies you burned through."

"So do I!" He swigged his seltzer.

"So, of all those countries, which was your favorite?" I asked, chewing an ice chip from my glass.

"Ah, geez, that's a tough one." He ran a hand through his hair. "They're all so different. What about you?"

I wiggled an index finger. "No, no. We're keeping it on you this time."

He shook his head. "You're a different breed, Natalie Espinosa. Given the opportunity, most people would rather talk about themselves."

"I don't have anything that interesting to share," I confessed.

"That's never stopped anybody else," he said over the rim of his glass.

Oliver had endless interesting things to say, but no desire to elaborate on his fairy-tale upbringing. Nor did he have a lot to say about his Ivy League education, world travels, or the fact that he spoke four languages, although he insisted it was only three because his Mandarin, he claimed, "wasn't so great." Give him a chance at policy or platitudes and he'd never shut up. But personal details? I had to tease out every thread.

I was really just getting warmed up when the plane began its initial descent into Providence. Turbulence shook us, but I crammed my fear down. I had finally steered this somewhat intractable conversation to a point where I felt comfortable asking about romantic relationships. I had been dying to know. But it never came up.

"And so all through school, was there ever anyone special? It seems unusual for a politician not to have gotten married." I hoped it didn't sound as intrusive as it felt.

"Boarding school didn't offer much opportunity to meet girls," Oliver replied.

"College? Law school?" I leaned in, as if he'd whisper some secret into a narrower space.

"Law school didn't leave a whole lot of free time either, unfortunately," he said coolly, recrossing his legs.

"Jake Cohen said the same thing. Is that a line they make you memorize at Harvard?" I thought Oliver would laugh, but he didn't, so

I forged on, "But even Jake Cohen met someone. His wife, in fact. And he tells me *you* were the one who made that possible."

That interested him. "Oh, Jake told you about that? It's very kind that he gives me the credit."

The details I wanted kept eluding me. Unraveling Oliver Thames was like untying a Gordian knot.

The flight attendant came through on her final pass. "Sir, I'll take your glass now," she murmured to Oliver.

He handed it over. "Thanks, Tammy. Could you please have Kylie pass up a section of today's list here, so we can take a look where we're going? Oh, and Efrain?" Oliver raised his voice, calling to the staffer a few seats away, "What did Shaheen have to say about the amendment?"

The interview was over.

- -

The drive out of T.F. Green International Airport did not afford the same privacy the ride into Reagan had. Before we even got off the plane, Oliver was surrounded by staffers issuing details about that morning's get-out-the-vote effort and the wording to an amendment to a major healthcare bill. I took a backseat both literally and figuratively.

The car pulled up at a park entrance in a working-class neighborhood. Oliver, staffers, and I walked up quietly behind a crowd of about twenty volunteers who were listening to a pair of campaign staff standing atop a picnic table. The field organizer briefed the volunteers on questions to ask, talking points to cover, and how to handle anticipated objections. They passed out lists of registered voters' addresses and reminded the volunteers that, as a standard safety measure, they needed to buddy up.

"Looks like you're stuck with me," Oliver whispered out the side of his mouth as the field organizer finished her announcements. He produced the list of addresses we'd be visiting—several pages long. I hoped that what I had assumed would be sensible footwear for walking around an art gallery would also hold up on this excursion.

Oliver excused himself briefly to cut through the crowd and make a parting rallying speech to the volunteers, who were surprised and excited by his unexpected appearance.

"Everyone, thank you for taking time out of your summer weekend to spend it getting out the vote!" Oliver announced from atop the picnic table. "There's no doubt—especially in the hot sun today—that this work is hard and tedious. You might get doors closed on you. You might face strong objections or even harsh criticisms. But it's your collective efforts in spite of it all that has enabled us to make a real difference in the lives of fellow Rhode Islanders and Americans these past two years. We couldn't have done it without you! So, without further ado, let's all get out there and knock some doors!"

When the whoops and applause subsided, buddies split off in all directions, including us.

"I'm surprised this neighborhood is in your district," I said as we left the park on our own.

"Oh? Why's that?" he asked, arms swinging, bounce in his step.

"This isn't exactly the land of nannies, boarding school, and weekend jaunts to Milan."

He nodded with a knowing smile. "Rhode Island's First District is diverse. I represent households from the Cliff Walk to the River Walk and up to Pawtucket—that's a very wide range of socioeconomic groups."

"You know, I don't think you ever mentioned what inspired you to go into public service," I said, returning the question he had asked me about design on the ride to the airport.

"Well," Oliver replied, scratching the back of his head, "coming from a place of privilege, but having someone close to me who definitely was not, seeing how he and his family and the people in their community struggled, I always felt a responsibility to them just as much as anyone in my family's inner circle."

This was fascinating. "How did a guy like you wind up close to someone from the proverbial other side of the tracks?"

Oliver glanced away. "Here's the street. I think the first door is just down a little way on the right."

I tried again. "So, you were saying … that guy whose family struggled …"

"Well," he finally said with a heave of his breath, "it was someone I only knew for a short while. But he meant a lot to me. I made the mistake of leaving at a time when he needed me most. Of course, I didn't realize then that that was the case. And by the time I did, well, it was too late."

"Too late?" I asked. "What do you mean? What happened? What was his name?"

"It was ages ago now," Oliver demurred. "But it made me realize that the root of some of our biggest problems as a society is how narrowly we as Americans tend to think about our own 'community.' Almost always what people mean by that is 'people who look and sound and live like us.' But a little further down the same street there are people having a hard time putting food on the table, or working multiple jobs, or aren't able to get a job at all. Or they or someone they love is suffering from a common health condition that wealthier people don't have to think twice about, because they have access to decent health care."

"Like your friend?"

"Exactly. Why do those people get left out so often? Why aren't they part of our 'community'? And why should 'communities' be so misshapen, so about socioeconomic sameness, instead of embracing the family one town over, whose only fault was not being born into the same advantages others of us get to enjoy? *That's* what got me inspired to go into public service. We talk a lot about the 'American dream,' Natalie, but this country is a woefully fractured one."

I had been waiting for him to run out of wind when we arrived at the first door. I was trying not to feel bothered that Oliver had taken a perfectly good opportunity to open up to me about something personal and used it for yet another speech. I wondered if it was too late to get him to tell me about his tragic mystery person. He seemed to be avoiding the topic for a reason. Sure, he had just told me a few hours earlier that he liked that I 'called him out on his bullshit,' but this seemed like sensitive ground.

"You wanna take this one, or should I?" Oliver teased, knocking on the front door.

"I'll watch you work your magic," I replied from a half step behind him.

A slender woman of about sixty answered, gray frizz framing her gaunt, lined face. "No soliciting!" her voice rasped in a Rhode Island accent where Rs were optional. "We can't afford anything anyway." She moved to close the door as quickly as she had opened it.

"Mrs. Brennen? Ruth?" Oliver's voice was gentle. She held the door slightly ajar.

"Who's askin'?"

"I'm Mrs. Brennen's congressman, Oliver Thames. I'm hoping to hear her thoughts on a couple issues going on in the community. I thought I could drop off information about her polling location for Election Day this November."

The woman eyed him suspiciously. "I'm Ruth Brennen."

"It's a pleasure to meet you, Mrs. Brennen." Oliver smiled. "I know the people of Pawtucket have been hit hard with rising prices these days, among other challenges. I'm visiting you and your neighbors today to ask you to bring me up to speed on your concerns. My goal is to make your voice heard back in Washington, so we can actually do something about these problems."

Mrs. Brennen straightened and opened the door fully. "Yeah, well, everything costs a damn fortune now. Can't hardly buy eggs or chicken and get outta Stop 'n' Shop for under a hundred dollars."

I listened to the rest of their exchange, captivated. Two seemingly opposite people, "just down the road" from one another, as Oliver would describe it, commiserating on inflation in the most personal terms.

In spite of his blessed beginnings, Oliver seemed to understand this woman and her troubles more like a social worker than a politician. It wasn't long before Oliver and Ruth—they were on a first-name basis now—got to talking about Ruth's husband Freddie's

COPD, and how he got laid off from his job. Ruth explained the run-around they were getting from their health insurance to cover his regular treatments, even though they'd been "payin' an arm an' a leg for that damn COBRA." By the end of their conversation, Ruth was patting Oliver's hand in her own, vowing to pray for him at St. Joe's on Sunday to help him break through the red tape in Washington. I was impressed.

Oliver and I walked back toward the street. "That was masterful."

"Empathy doesn't require mastery," he told me, "just caring enough to listen."

"If only every elected official embraced your mindset," I replied.

House after house, the reception was fairly consistent. Some constituents recognized Oliver right away, most did not.

By the time we were two-thirds through the list, he knocked on the next door, then stepped back. "You take this one."

I balked. "What? No, I'm not ready."

"Oh, you're ready," he said, smiling toward the approaching footfalls on the other side of the door. It swung open to reveal a very large man with a tuft of dark chest hair peeking out from his undershirt.

"Whadda ya want?"

I squeaked a nervous hello. This guy looked like he probably kept a Louisville Slugger right by the door. Oliver seemed totally unbothered, his silence now impelling me to speak.

"Ah, yes! Good afternoon … sir! We're visiting folks in the neighborhood today to make sure you know where your polling place is," I said, springing to life.

The unkempt man looked me up and down skeptically. "Yeah, the grammar school right around the corner." His flat, nasal accent emphasized an air of impatience.

"Yes! Exactly!" I exclaimed, hoping that if I was positive enough, maybe I'd remember some of what Oliver had been saying on the porches of the first umpteen houses. This was a lot harder than he made it look!

Oliver took pity and swooped in. "Mr. Drummond, my name's

Oliver. My buddy Natalie here bet me ten bucks that you already made up your mind on who you're voting for in November."

"Oh, yeah?" he asked, side-eyeing me. "What's it to ya?"

"We've been going door to door, campaigning for Congressman Thames to get reelected," Oliver continued with complete nonchalance, "and Natalie here thought we might be wasting your time."

"Depends who Congressman Thames is," the man replied.

Instead of introducing himself, Oliver looked expectantly in my direction and let the silence hang again until I filled it.

"Congressman Thames," I stammered, "has been working the past two years to bring back funding to this community to improve safety, increase job opportunities, and make quality healthcare more affordable and accessible."

Mr. Drummond looked over at Oliver, who nodded, then looked back at me again. "Those all sound like good things," Mr. Drummond agreed.

To my surprise, I felt encouraged. "You're right. They are. In fact, if you've seen and heard about less criminal activity in Pawtucket, it's because Congressman Thames has been working closely with local authorities to not just arrest people but take on a community policing approach that puts the power back in the hands of the people who live here. People like you. And he's been working with local schools and businesses to give kids better options after high school. Now more kids can get paid on-the-job training and placement in positions they're interested in, instead of resorting to crime."

"Oh yeah?" Mr. Drummond looked thoughtful. "I guess it has gotten a lot quieter the last year or so. Feels like less drugs on the street, less trouble."

"Are there other issues that are important to you that you'd want him to know about?" I asked, stepping closer.

"The firehouse," he said, nodding firmly. "Our boys over there could really use some bread to make repairs. I hear the roof is about ready to cave in, and they don't got no good furniture to sit in while they're waitin' for the next call. They're saving lives, but they're over there sittin' on ratty old chairs with duct tape holding the cushions together. They deserve better."

"They sure do," Oliver chimed in. "We'll talk to the mayor and see what we can do."

"You in tight with the congressman?" Mr. Drummond asked him, raising an eyebrow.

Oliver gave a wry smile. "I know him pretty well. They say I look just like him, anyway."

We finished the conversation with Mr. Drummond on a commitment from him that he'd make a plan to either get to his polling place Election Day or get his mail-in ballot in early. He said he usually didn't bother, but he would tell "the boys at the firehouse" about it and get everyone on board to mark a ballot this year "now that it matters."

Leaving Mr. Drummond's house, Oliver high fived me. "Natalie, that was fantastic! Did you *see* what you did there? Tremendous! You just got that man's vote. *And* his friends'." For a second I thought he might pick me up and spin me around.

I was caught up in it too. "I know! That was crazy! All of a sudden I knew what to say, and I really *cared*."

"You're a natural!" he exclaimed, throwing his arm around me in a side hug that had me walking on air. "This is what it's all about. This is us making steady progress, helping real people a few at a time." His arm stayed squeezed around my shoulder, head tilted ever so slightly up against mine.

A pair of canvassers came around the corner, and Oliver and I hastily broke apart like we'd gotten caught.

He called over to them, "How's it going, guys?"

They beamed back with thumbs up. "Going great, Congressman Thames! Had a few really good conversations today. Even got some commitments."

"Nice work, guys, keep it up!" Oliver cheered them as they headed up another walkway.

He pulled the creased address list from his back pocket and studied it. "Well, we managed to hit a good chunk of the houses, minus the ones who weren't home. Or hid from us." Then he looked up. "You're probably starving. Wanna grab a bite, and we'll head back to DC?"

Now that he mentioned it, I *was* starving. The last I'd eaten were some scrambled eggs around seven thirty that morning. Oliver called the car to pull around, while the rest of the team canvassed doggedly under the August sun.

"In the mood for anything specific?" he asked as we slid into the cool air-conditioned interior. "Any dietary restrictions?"

"Nope. I may start gnawing on my arm in a minute." I swiped a hand across my sweaty forehead.

He looked at me intently, then, to my surprise, pressed the backs of his hands gently to my cheeks. I couldn't breathe. "I think you caught a little sun."

All of a sudden, I was so flustered I wouldn't have been able to tell. "Yeah, well. I don't usually put on sunscreen to walk around an art gallery."

He looked genuinely apologetic. "I'm sorry, Natalie, I didn't even think about that. Let me make it up to you with lunch. I have the perfect place."

I nodded, less concerned about sunburn than what this day with him was doing to me on the inside.

The driver took us smoothly into downtown Providence. The historic Federal-style buildings and colonial homes we passed were the picture of urban New England charm. It evoked a lost era, full of hardship and hope, when the country was just coming into its own.

We pulled alongside a deli on Hudson Street. As we entered, we were greeted by the scent of freshly baked bread and a familial welcome from the heavyset, balding owner who emerged from behind the counter to give Oliver a bear hug and back slap. "Oliver! It's been too long. I know you been workin' hard for us in DC though."

"Eddie, you gotta open up a location on Capitol Hill! No one there makes Italian like you." Oliver turned to me, "This is the best Italian deli in town. If you want a hot sandwich, you gotta get the gabagool."

"The what?" I asked.

"The capicola."

"I'm sorry, are we speaking English?"

Oliver let out a breathy laugh and tried to explain. "Gabagool is capicola. Sicilian salami. Eddie puts it on marble rye with roasted red peppers, melts on some provolone. It's fantastic." I looked up at the menu board to note the combo was named "The Thames Street."

"No relation." He winked. "Just a street in Newport."

"Sure it is," I said, and ordered one.

A few minutes later we were stuffing our faces in the relative anonymity of a wobbly table for two, obscured from view from patrons buying a pound of egg salad or, since it was high summer, sampling the famous gagootz. We chatted about canvassing between bites. I was halfway through a sentence when he reached across the table and swept a fingertip against my cheek.

"Mustard," he said, wiping his hand on his paper napkin. "Eddie is generous with the condiments."

There he went again. Would he have done that with someone else? Or was it just for me? I sipped my soda, one leg tucked under me on the chair, the other swinging beneath the table. I wanted to box up the moment like a bit of leftover sandwich and take it home to savor.

"You never did say what happened to your friend, the one who inspired you to run for office," I ventured. It felt like the right time to ask.

Oliver didn't react.

"I mean, I don't want to keep bringing it up if it's a sore subject for you. It was just a cliffhanger."

His face tightened, and he rubbed his chin. "He died."

"Oh! I ... I'm so sorry."

"Me too," he mumbled, crumpling his empty sandwich wrapper. "It didn't have to be that way. I'm sorry. It's still hard to talk about. It was like losing a brother."

"Of course. It's always hard to talk about losing someone you loved." We sat for a moment in silence. "I lost my dad to Alzheimer's shortly after my son was born. His death wasn't even the hardest part. Losing his mind to the disease first was worse. They say with

Alzheimer's you die from the top down. By the time he finally passed, it was like he'd been long gone already."

"Wow, Jesus." Oliver wiped his frown with his napkin. "That had to be awful."

"Yeah. And I was stuck on the other side of the continent with a newborn. I didn't get as much time in that final year with him as I would have liked. Now I only have the memories."

"Like the elephant seals," Oliver remembered.

"Yes," I acknowledged, a smile edging onto my face. "One of many I take comfort in."

"My dad and I didn't spend as much time together as I would've wanted, but for totally different reasons," Oliver volunteered. I stopped slurping my Diet Dr Pepper so as to not miss any of this uncharacteristic sharing. "He and my mom were pretty isolated from each other for much of what I can remember. Then they finally split up while I was at boarding school. Not that I got much time with him before that either."

My thoughts flashed to my own son, and my impending divorce. "Was it your parents' divorce that put you off of marriage?"

"Who said I was put off of marriage?" he countered. "I said I didn't have *time*."

I gave him an incredulous look. "So you're secretly a hopeless romantic who just never had *time* to date someone all these years?" He said he liked it when I called him on his bullshit. I just hoped he hadn't changed his mind.

He crossed his arms. "I was in a couple relationships when I was younger. But unfortunately, or maybe fortunately for the work I'm doing, nothing ever stuck. As I'm sure you can relate, relationships demand a lot of both people. At this stage of my life, I'm always either in the spotlight or under a microscope, and that's not something most women want to sign up for. Those who do are usually in it for something besides love."

I wiggled my soda straw round in the cup. While everything he was saying was plausible, something just wasn't adding up. This was a man in his mid-forties—a very handsome, powerful, charismatic man from a wealthy family—who never had a romantic relationship of any significance he could point to? Or was he just glossing over it for some reason, like the death of his friend?

"Well … when was the last time you were in love?" I pressed him, slurping my way loudly to the bottom of the paper cup. Oliver stood up.

Oh shit. Had I crossed a line?

"Lemme get you a refill," he said, taking my cup and heading toward the soda machine.

I probably had. I considered the possibility of him having an illegitimate child from a torrid love affair, but the media would've uncovered something like that a long time ago, especially with his high-profile family.

Oliver dropped off my Diet Dr Pepper and told me he was going to take a peek at the pastries.

A teenaged girl poked her head out from the back kitchen area.

"*Oliver's* here?!" she shrieked like a boy band groupie. Tearing off her apron, she ran out to throw her arms around him.

Oliver greeted her like family. "Alexis! Wow! You are all grown up!" She basked in the attention.

"Oliver, look!" Alexis ran behind the counter, then emerged with a giant designer bag, strutting it down and up a black and white checked linoleum runway.

"*Giiiirrrrl!*" Oliver snapped his fingers, clearly channeling Channing. "Work it … *worrrrk it!* Slay all day!" This was a whole new side of Congressman Thames.

When their flamboyant scene ended, she asked him how long he was there for.

"I have to go back today, unfortunately. But maybe you could help me pick out something for the road?" he said, motioning to the glass case.

As Alexis selected her favorite treats from behind the counter, I wondered what was going on. Oliver clearly enjoyed the company of women. How had he not had any serious relationships? Or any that "stuck," as he put it? Like your tongue keeps finding the space from a lost tooth, I kept finding my way back to this gap in Oliver's résumé. He clearly didn't want to talk about it. Yet he *was* kind of painted by the media as a playboy, at least before taking office. I recalled pictures of him with models during Fashion Week a couple years ago.

Oliver sat down at the table, pulling me back into the present. He removed the red and white baker's twine from the plain white box Alexis had filled for him, reaching in for a mini cannoli. The tiny cylinder of dough and creamy filling was dusted in confectioner's sugar, each end dipped in the perfect number of minuscule chocolate chips.

"These are decadent," he said, pushing the box toward me and popping one in his mouth. "*Mmmmph!*" he closed his eyes, powdered sugar dusting his lips.

Maybe I had another card to play this round. "I didn't realize you were such a fashionista," I teased. He looked confused. "That whole runway scene there."

A look of comprehension came over him. "Oh, Alexis. She's been saving up for that bag since she was about as high as my hip."

"Liking fashion is nothing to be ashamed of! You know, those pictures of you at Fashion Week are all over the internet."

"I don't know if you've realized, Natalie," he said, enjoying another cannoli, "but the extent of my fashion sense is matching my dress shirt to my suit pants, and Channing tells me I don't always even get that right."

"So you were just there for the models then?" I shot him a wry grin.

He shrugged. "I was there for support."

"Support for who, your model girlfriends?"

"I wouldn't call them girlfriends," he said, busying himself in the pastry box.

"What would you call them then?" I knew I was pressing this well beyond professional boundaries.

He frowned. "Acquaintances. Friends of Channing." He dipped into the pastry box again.

A wild thought sideswiped me. What if, just like Channing, Oliver wasn't into women?

What if I've been misreading him the whole time? Could it account for why he kept avoiding the topic about dating and girlfriends? I gave my head a tilt and watched the dominoes fall. Was the nameless, "brother-like" friend who died—the one Oliver couldn't even bring himself to talk about—someone Oliver was *in love* with? What if all this time I'd been mistaking Oliver's interest in me for flirting, when he was simply a sweet, smart gay man doing the stereotypical gay man thing and befriending his interior decorator? *Oh, Natalie. You are such an idiot.*

"Not into cannoli?" Oliver's voice derailed my runaway train of thought.

"Are *you* into cannoli?" I blurted, overwhelmed by the picture coming into focus.

He tilted back in his chair and threw his arms wide, talking through the cannoli still in his mouth. "Obviously!"

"That's not what I mean."

He stared back, guileless. "I'm not sure I understand."

It all made perfect sense. Maybe he had to repress his sexuality to maintain standing within his family, then stayed closeted because it could hurt his electability.

"I mean …" I looked both ways, then whispered, "are you gay?"

"Am I *gay*?" he asked loudly. "Do I have to be to like cannoli?"

"No, are you gay and that's why you change the subject any time I've asked about past girlfriends?"

He went silent for a moment, looking at me perplexed.

When he spoke again, it was subdued. "I guess the real question, Natalie, is … why are my love interests such an urgent topic for you?"

My face flushed. Now it was my turn in the hot seat. I stuttered and stammered. Finally I gave up. "I'm just trying to understand who you are."

"Who I am?" He looked hurt. "I thought we were being pretty candid with each other these past couple weeks."

"Well, sure, but oh, I don't know. You have this outsized public persona, and you're all about helping the little guy. You get strangers to open up to you about their personal lives, myself included. And even though you're very talkative about certain things, on some personal topics you're just not. So I was only trying to ... I guess I was hoping you'd open up."

He sat there for a while, looking kind of disappointed while I sat there in agony.

Eventually he made eye contact again. "Well, Natalie, to answer your burning question: I'm not gay. I'm an ally, of course, if you couldn't already tell, but I do not identify as gay myself. I am, to my own detriment, quite boringly straight and, in addition, as cisgendered as they come. And I don't know what got into you all of a sudden, but if you're moonlighting as a gossip peddler for your ex-husband's political rag, or something like that, you can tell them to shove it up their ... inbox."

I gasped. "Jesus, no." I hadn't even thought about that.

This whole day had gone off the rails. I probably just destroyed weeks of rapport building with my only client, who owed me no explanations and had already overextended himself to me, and it was all my fault. "I am so, so sorry. I overstepped, I made assumptions, and ugh, no, I want zero, zilch, nothing to do with *Party Lines*. I'm just being nosey. And stupid."

Silence draped our table.

"Where's this all coming from then?" he finally asked.

"I don't know." I bit my lip. "I think maybe I have some trust issues to work through. You know, after everything that happened with Caleb."

"You mean him divorcing you?" He rested his elbows on the table, expression softening.

I stared at the pastry box. "No. More like the *reason* we're getting divorced," I told the pastry box, unable to make eye contact.

Oliver leaned back in his chair and crossed his arms, a hint of smirk playing at the corner of his mouth. "Ohhh. I get it now. Well, you know, you never actually told me *why* you're getting divorced, but

I didn't jump to the conclusion it was because you turned into a lesbian!"

I laughed out loud, in spite of still feeling like absolute garbage. He reached into the pastry box and held up yet another mini cannoli. "Well, Natalie, you know what Freud said. 'Sometimes a cannoli," he recited as he popped it into his mouth, "is just a cannoli.'"

- -

Oliver spent most of the flight home catching up on everything he'd missed that day, including breaking news about a senator who had the Office of Congressional Ethics hot on his tail. I enjoyed being a fly on the wall.

"Of course Compton released his statement late on a Friday," said Efrain, toggling between a phone screen, a laptop, a tablet, and a folio of papers.

"Yup," Oliver agreed, brows creased and eyes scanning the story, "forced admissions are best buried at the end of the news cycle."

My own attempt at a forced admission from Oliver was still squatting in my head, even though he seemed to have completely forgotten about it. Granted, the man had far more significant issues to worry about.

I'd really put my foot in it this time. This blossoming interplay between us—in whatever capacity—was so unexpected, yet something I had come to value more than I'd realized. The cannoli episode was proof I wasn't just starstruck, but actively crushing on my client. I'd been avoiding looking it in the eye because it made me feel bleak. Not only did it break every rule I had about professionalism, I also apparently had to pick a client miles out of my league. The conversation he was having, and the fact that we were on his private jet, were testament to our totally different worlds.

"Sir, we have the House Majority Leader pushing to meet tonight —" the other staffer announced from behind her phone screen.

"Have we heard back from Shaheen yet?" Oliver sounded strained. "Text Channing now. Have him lean on her for the 'yes.' I'm not talking to Johnson until Shaheen confirms." I hadn't met this version of Congressman Thames before—assertive under fire.

The flurry of details made me feel like I had a courtside seat to a sport I'd never watched, hearing the coaches call plays in the charged final moments of a game. I was rapt in the tension, but with no idea what was going on.

As the cabin prepared for landing, Oliver closed his laptop and turned to me. "So what did you think of Rhode Island? Especially since it was your first time to New England and all." A prankster's smirk betrayed his sincerity, and I recalled his comment in the car about having to tell him what I thought about his state "when I got there." Which he knew all along would be about an hour later.

I gave him a playful shove on the shoulder.

He leaned into the shove. "And what did you think of door-knocking?"

"It was definitely an experience," I said, bits of the day coming back to me. Especially that impromptu hug.

"Did it change your mind?" he asked eagerly.

"Change my mind about what?"

"About how one regular person can affect electoral outcomes and make a difference."

"You're not exactly a 'regular person.'"

His knee brushed mine. "But *you* are. And you got to see a whole team of regular people come together, mostly strangers, to reach other strangers with the same values and concerns. These people are more than the sum of their individual efforts. They're a movement."

"Yes, of course. Like your starfish story. It was inspirational. That moment with Mr. Drummond, too. I would've never expected that."

"That was all you!" His face lit up. "And didn't it feel amazing?"

"It did," I admitted.

"Did it change your mind on voting?"

"I definitely promise to vote again."

"It's not just about the voting itself," he said, making sure he was looking me in the eye. "It's about not feeling helpless. Not just letting things happen to you that you're not happy with. It's about feeling empowered to do something about it, no matter how big that mountain may be to climb. No matter how many forces are working against you."

"Oliver, listen, I believe in all those things you talked about with the people we met today. I really do. These people need you. Hell, this *country* needs you. I just don't know that they need *me*."

I watched his face fall. I tried to recover. "I mean, I wish I had more to offer. I can't exactly make a big donation. I also don't know that it's practical for me to fly up to Providence again to go door-knocking—or that I'd be any good at it. I would love to contribute to your campaign in some meaningful way though. Whatever that might be."

Oliver folded his hands quietly in his lap. "Well, I didn't bring you up here for the sake of the campaign, you know? I just thought it would be an inspirational environment for whatever personal hurdles you're facing. You don't have to be a person *in* power to *have* power, Natalie. I get the impression you sometimes forget that."

I could see how I gave him that impression, though it wasn't the one I wanted to leave him with. But the jet touched down, and he was swarmed by his people. I had to cram into the third row of the SUV next to one of the interns. A young adult novel slid out of her bag and onto my lap. I handed it back to her with a tired smile.

This tweenager reading vampire romance knows more inside baseball about Oliver's political life than I do. What am I even doing here?

We inched back through the District's clogged rush-hour bowels. Twice I thought I caught Oliver watching me in the rearview mirror. I looked away both times.

We made a pit stop at Capitol South to let out the staffers. As they climbed out, he called to me. "Wanna hop up here, so you're not stuck in steerage the rest of the way?"

I moved up and the car continued on to the townhouse. "You know, Natalie, you're in no way obligated, but if you feel like talking about anything troubling you, you can do that with me."

I half-laughed, brushing my hair from my face. "I'm really hoping the light fixtures we ordered arrive on time. I'd heard rumors about them going on back-order."

"That's not what I mean." He tilted his head. "I've seen the toll divorce takes on everyone involved. So if you ever want to talk, you know?"

The sentence trailed off. I nodded. I never *had* actually told him what happened between me and Caleb. I was still so embarrassed by it, I wasn't sure I was ready for him to see me like that. Especially since I'd been making such a great impression, between lunch and the plane. But I'd accused him of not being open with me, and he was opening a door.

I started to talk, but his phone buzzed in his pocket. I waited for him to answer. His gaze remained on me as the phone continued to vibrate.

"Do you need to get that?" I asked.

He reached in and clicked it over to voicemail. "Nope."

I waited a beat, then continued with what I'd started to say. "Well … for me, the beginning of the end of Caleb and I came out of nowhere. One Saturday morning in March—"

His phone immediately began buzzing again. His mouth scrunched into an asymmetrical line, then mouthed "sorry" to me as he pulled it out, looked at the caller, and answered. A brief but tense conversation followed, more inside baseball that meant nothing to me. He put the phone back in his pocket and apologized.

"It's okay," I said. "It sounds like things are pretty hectic for you right now. Probably they always are, in your position."

"And this is supposed to be the slow time of year." He shook his head ruefully. "But you were starting to tell me?"

Somehow the story didn't feel as dramatic now. "Really, it's stupidly simple. Basically, Caleb told me one morning that he was leaving me for someone else who turned out to be his director of advertising. He had already set up a whole separate life and pretty much let me know as a formality. Kind of like telling your employer you're quitting. He was even letting her spend time with our son. I was the last to know."

I let out a nervous laugh, but Oliver's expression reflected the pain I felt. "Wow," he said. "That is … brutal. I'm really sorry that happened to you, Natalie."

I pushed my hair behind my ears and swallowed my self-pity. "I guess the hardest part to come to terms with was how out of touch I was the whole time. Like, there were signs leading up to it. And every now and again I realize a new one. Too late, of course."

I shrugged, putting my hands on my knees. Oliver reached over and put his hand over one of mine. "Be kinder to yourself. It's one thing to grow from what you wish you'd done differently, but you can't grow if you're still beating yourself up over it."

His voice was so soft. A tear escaped out of the corner of my eye. It trickled down my cheek and paused there. Oliver reached out with his other thumb, smudging it away, his palm rounding into a cradle for my chin. I could neither breathe nor deny that something absolutely chemical was reacting in every cell of my body. Time stretched like bubble gum.

Then we were there, Channing waiting on the sidewalk, tapping his foot. Oliver pulled back his hand and the moment popped like a bubble.

Channing pulled open Oliver's door even before the car had come to a stop. "Don't even bother getting out, I just got off the phone with Shaheen. Johnson is waiting for us at Rayburn."

Oliver rubbed his eyes with a forefinger and a thumb still damp from my tear, then clapped his hands together as if hitting the restart button. "Okay! Let's do it."

"Natalie, I trust you had a memorable day?" Channing poked his head into the car to ask.

"More than memorable," I said, painting a smile on my face.

Oliver turned to me, casual. "You're a really good sport, Natalie. I know I threw a bunch of surprises at you today. I hope you felt like the trip was worthwhile."

"Definitely," I said quickly. "I learned some interesting things about both of us today."

I held his gaze, wondering if I'd hallucinated that flicker between us a minute ago. Then I realized everyone was just waiting for me to get out of the car. I let myself out. As Channing slid into my place, I thanked Oliver again. "It was eye-opening. Let me know if I can actually help out your campaign sometime."

The door closed and the car pulled away. Twenty feet further it stopped and Oliver's window lowered, smiling, sea-glass eyes glinting at me. "Natalie! I had an idea. Maybe you *can* help the campaign. Tell you Monday!"

The car took off into the gathering dusk. I stood in the middle of the street for a moment, shaking my head. "What just happened?" I asked aloud.

With no one to answer me, I retraced the steps to my car.

9

SOMETHING TO TALK ABOUT

*I*n an instant, my lifelong dread of Mondays had been turned on its head, but first I had a weekend to dither away.

Was I out of my mind to think we had some kind of—I wasn't sure what to call it—*moment* in the car? The electricity between us, even for that short spark in time, felt smoldering. But maybe it was just me. My intuition wasn't proving so reliable lately. Or maybe it was, and I was just second-guessing it. I drove myself mad with speculation as I soaked in the tub Friday night. I made it to eleven forty-five on Saturday morning before deciding I was either going to have to get some perspective on the matter or distract myself with something useful like organizing the basement. I bit the bullet and called Dana.

- -

I bounced my leg under the table, glancing out the window of the Center Street Bistro, rereading the menu.

I had been waiting for more than fifteen minutes. The server had politely offered to fetch me a basket of freshly baked bread. Thankfully, Dana reached the table before the bread did.

"Not to make you feel bad, but I botched my pedicure trying to get here on time." She pulled her tortoiseshell sunglasses up onto her head, pointing a freshly manicured finger down at two sets of toes still braced by foam separators. I nodded solemnly and told her I was glad to see her, which I was.

We ordered, but silence hung between us. It was my move. "I meant to call earlier," I offered.

Dana raised a brow and sipped her water.

"I mean, I should have reached out sooner." I looked out the window. "One time, I was even standing in your driveway, and I chickened out. I'm sorry. I let this go on way too long."

I looked back at Dana, whose raised brow was now accompanied by pursed lips. "Like, what the actual hell, Natalie? You iced me out. For what? All I've ever tried to do is help you."

"I know, I know!" I cried. Being told when you fucked up was miserable, especially when you felt so bad about it already. "You're completely right. You were trying to help me handle the divorce. I pushed you away because I wasn't ready to deal with it."

Dana's frosty expression began to thaw. "Thank you. I know that wasn't easy to say." And, as I said before, I know what you went through and continue to go through isn't easy either. That's why I want to be here for you. As a true friend, not just one who says what you want to hear all the time."

I nodded as my finger traced a path through the condensation on my water glass. "I appreciate that. I'm working on taking constructive criticism better. I'm realizing lately I probably have a few things I need to work on."

Dana sighed. "Why do you think I tried over and over to give you my therapist's number?"

I held up my hand. "One thing at a time, Dane. I just got a divorce attorney."

"Oh? You did?" Dana braced her enthusiasm with a cautious smile.

"He thinks I have a good case." My smile was cautious, too. "And he's like, the top family law attorney in the area, because he came as a referral from *you-know-who*."

She looked confused. "I don't know who."

I leaned in to whisper dramatically. "The congressman."

Dana's mouth fell open.

It took nearly two hours to catch Dana up on the past week. She gasped as I relayed the near-miss at Caleb's house, but she nearly fell out of her chair when the "art gallery outing" turned into a surprise flight to Rhode Island, followed by our private get-out-the-vote session.

"And now I'm driving myself crazy wondering what he meant by "helping his campaign," and if we actually shared some kind of, I dunno, affectionate glimmer? Before he got whisked away again."

"I'm not gonna lie, Nat, that is some crazy shit," Dana replied, swiping on lip balm. "You are really teetering on the boundary of—"

"What?" I asked defensively.

"Don't you think you two are getting a little … *familiar?*"

"Well … it crossed my mind," I sat back from the edge of my chair. "But I'm not the one prompting it."

She was matter of fact. "No, you're just the one who stands to sink a relaunched career before it gets off the ground again."

I looked down. The server dropped off the check as Dana and I sat waiting for someone to speak.

Finally Dana waved her hands as if clearing the air. "It's not like you've crossed the point of no return or anything. You know that. But word to the wise, you're better off parking those dreamy feelings if you want to be taken seriously in this town. Not a great look for your first time back in the saddle if you can't keep it professional. Besides, even if he's flirting, where do you honestly think it could ever go?"

I drew a difficult breath. Dana wasn't wrong. If it wasn't happening to me but some other woman, I wouldn't hesitate to tell her it'd only end in disappointment. I cracked a sarcastic smile. "You mean, in what world would a media darling congressman fall head over heels for a run-of-the-mill, middle-aged suburban mom?"

Dana's face softened as she snatched the check. "I'm not doubting it could happen, Natalie, but I'd worry about you if it did."

"What do you mean?"

"*Hello?*" Dana said, her sunglasses sliding. "You are literally getting divorced from the guy who runs *Party Lines*. Do you really want to be headed to the grocery store wondering if paparazzi are going to snap your picture in the parking lot on a day you haven't showered yet?"

"I don't think they'd find me that interesting," I countered, but the hypothetical shot a chill up my spine.

"Honey … you could be Oscar the Grouch crawling out of a garbage can, and that would only make you *more* interesting to the media. Do the math! The country's most eligible bachelor politician, who's been known to be a playboy, suddenly settles into a relationship with *a normal woman?* The media would never stop hounding you! If they can't show off how absolutely fabulous a woman is, and sometimes even if they can, they go after how pitifully inadequate she is, especially on the arm of a celebrity."

I fidgeted with my unused coffee spoon, my thoughts racing with this reframe. I wasn't even sure if Oliver's interest in me went any further than flirtation. If it was even that. He had been such a perfect distraction from the Caleb mess and my loneliness. But perhaps this was the reality check I needed.

"Yeah," I conceded, tossing my napkin on the table like the white flag of surrender. "You're right. I need to keep it strictly business from now on."

"Good!" she affirmed, and we stood to leave. "Trust me, you're saving yourself, and your image, a lot of drama."

Later, though, my thoughts drifted back to Oliver. He had a way of sweeping me up in such lively exchanges, even when I tried to keep it professional. And part of me really did love that it wasn't *all* business. It had to stay professional, and I planned for it to. Yet I began to worry that executing that plan might prove trickier than I thought.

- -

When Monday finally came, I was ready. I'd scheduled deliveries to the townhouse. There was loads to do. I arrived with punch list in hand and, thankfully, no sign of Oliver to distract me.

As the sunlight migrated from one side of the house to the other, I met with the carpenters finishing up the built-in shelving in the living room, checked in with the electrician installing the sconces, compared paint colors in the second floor guest rooms, and watched the tile guy complete the grouting on the subway tile in the primary suite's walk-in shower. In between, I accepted furniture deliveries, directing each piece to its respective rooms, generously tipping the sweating deliverymen for humping heavy things up so many flights of stairs in August. Then I'd jump back to my laptop, hunting down a few finishing touches, propelled by nervous energy and the gnawing expectation that a familiar face would breeze through the front door at any moment and break the productive flow.

When one finally did around five thirty, it wasn't the one I'd been expecting.

Channing pushed open the front door. He scooped up the mail that had fallen through the mail slot earlier. "Oh, Natalie, you're still here."

"Hey Channing," I said, hardly looking up from my laptop.

"You seem disappointed. Were you waiting for someone else?" Channing asked as he sifted through the mail.

"No, I met with everyone I needed to today, except the decorative tile guy, the guy in Lisbon. He stood me up on our call about the wine cellar. I'm chalking it up to the time difference. Don't worry, I'll get it rescheduled."

"Are you sure there wasn't a VIP—and by that I mean *Very Important Politician*—you were hoping would walk through that door?"

I sat up primly, refusing the bait. "Nope."

He smirked as he activated the Nespresso machine. "*Oliver* was just saying to me that the house is really coming along. I think we just have to sign off on the furniture choices for the bedroom."

He was trying to get a reaction, and I was trying not to give him one. "Mmm-hmmm. I was hoping to get some direction on the paint."

"Mmm *hmmm*," he returned, then nodded at the thick stack of paint chips beside me. "I see you brought your fan deck ..."

"Yup."

"Would you like me to narrow it down with you, and I'll bring them to Oliver?"

"He really should compare them on the wall."

"I can hold them up to the wall next time he's here," Channing replied.

I turned to face him. "No, I mean, they should be *painted* on the wall. They should be compared in different lights."

"Of course. Let's pick a few shades now, then, and you can get the samples up for me to show him on his next visit." Channing looked satisfied.

I had gotten used to not having an intermediary between Oliver and me. I was looking forward to our next moments together. Admittedly, it wasn't because I'd be showing off Pantone's Color of the Year. But I'd promised myself I'd keep my crush in check.

"Sure. I guess we can," I replied, harried.

"You sound uncertain," Channing tested.

"No, it's fine. I just don't know if that's what Oliver would want, since he talked about coming here to pick first."

Channing swished across the room to my side. "He's been tied up with this healthcare bill and the Conway ethics shitshow. Let's put up a few colors, and if he hates them all, we'll go back to the drawing board. Sound good?"

"Yeah. That's fine," I replied stiffly. "I mean, I just wanted to make sure the options were all colors he really wanted, since he's the only one even *using* the bedroom."

"I wouldn't say that," Channing taunted.

I side-eyed him. "What's *that* supposed to mean?"

"What's *what* supposed to mean?" Channing batted his eyelashes. They were, I noticed, extravagantly long.

"Oh, come *on*." I glared at him. "You implied—"

"My dear, I would *never* imply that the congressman invited anyone into his bedroom. Or that he didn't." Channing shot back, looking smug.

My face grew hot with a mix of frustration and embarrassment. "Are you implying that *I care* who goes into Oliver's bedroom? I don't.

That was completely not my point at all. I was just saying he should be the final decision-maker on the paint color, since he's—or he *basically is*— the only one going in there. Because I happen to know he doesn't have a girlfriend ..."

"Or a boyfriend?" Channing stifled a giggle.

I recoiled. Goddammit. Oliver told him. I pressed my lips together and waited for Channing's next move.

"Oh, c'mon, Natalie!" Channing threw up his hands. "You're *so* transparent. I walked through the door and you're sitting there like a puppy wagging her tail, waiting for Oliver to come rub your belly and ask, 'Who's a good girl?!'"

I felt the flush in my face go twenty shades redder. I was back at the junior high lunchroom table, cornered by the popular girls, baiting me into admitting who my crush was for their own cruel amusement.

"I don't know what you're talking about," I replied flatly.

Channing cocked his head to the side and shot me a look. "Natalie. You are not the first, and certainly won't be the last, to be spellbound by Oliver Thames. I'm sure you're aware of that."

He paused to let that settle. "That man has unwittingly broken so many hearts by being obsessed with his work. And being scared shitless, of course. I mean, I love the guy, but he does keep an iron grip, God bless him."

I was dying for elaboration, but I wasn't going to give Channing any additional satisfaction at my own expense.

"Personally, I wish Oliver *would* pair up with someone already and get out of my hair for a hot minute. You *do* see what it's done to my hair, don't you?" He pointed at his shiny 8-ball of a head.

The joke was clearly an olive branch, so I let myself ask. "So, it's true then? He doesn't get involved in ... serious relationships?"

Channing looked at me pityingly. "Have you eaten?"

"I had lunch."

He rolled his eyes. "That was ages ago. Join me for an early dinner. My treat."

"I don't know," I replied, still a little stung.

He rolled his eyes. "Oh, come now. What do you have? Three cats and an episode of *Matlock* to get home to?"

"Zero cats, and a lot of work," I retorted. But I also knew the only thing waiting for me at home that night was a frozen Marie Callender Cheesy Chicken & Rice Bowl.

"Have it your way," he sang as he swept toward the front door. Then he paused to look back over his shoulder. "If you really want to miss your chance to pump me for Oliver relationship intel after I've been overserved skinny margaritas."

It was probably just enough rope to hang myself with, but he was making an offer I couldn't refuse. "Where are we going?"

Channing held up a glossy sheet from the junk mail pile, a buy-one-get-one-half-off coupon. "How do you feel about barbecue?"

- -

Hill Country was already jamming when we arrived, a true Washingtonian mishmash: young families and young singles, East Coast accents and Southern charm, Hill suits and cowboy boots. Channing's connection to a manager landed us right across from the stage at a two-top made from a wooden barrel. I wondered what act was performing that night. Whomever it was had really drawn a crowd.

"I never would've imagined you in a place like this," I told Channing over the din, my face illuminated by neon bar signs on every wall. Hickory smoke nestled in my hair and twisted into the fibers of my clothing.

"I'm a North Carolina boy," Channing twanged ostentatiously, "but I *love* me some Texas brisket!"

Our server navigated long rows of family-style tables and dropped off two Modelos. I ordered pulled pork on a bun with coleslaw and a cucumber salad.

Channing hadn't even looked at the menu. "Brisket lean, collards and cornbread. Burnt ends and mac 'n' cheese to share," he told the server, who sped off to the next table.

"It sounds like things have gotten pretty busy this week," I said. "To what do I owe the pleasure of an impromptu meal with you, a Man in High Demand?"

"Sheer coincidence. Hugo and I had a rez at O-Ku, but he got called in for an emergency. He's a thoracic surgeon at GW."

I hadn't known. "So why didn't we just go to O-Ku then?"

Channing gave me a "tsk." "Girl, I'm not spending O-Ku bucks on you, I'm a civil servant. Besides, that rez wasn't until eight."

"Okay ... so why did you bring me *here*?" I crossed my arms.

The tapping of a mic on stage interrupted us. A man in Levi's, a pearl snap shirt, and a ten-gallon hat announced to hoots and hollers that karaoke would begin shortly.

"What will you be singing for us tonight, Ms. Natalie?" Channing inquired.

"I'll wait for the square dancing, thanks," I deadpanned.

"You gotta lighten up, girl."

He shouted to a passing server for a margarita, then made it two, and skinny.

By the time our second margaritas and the food arrived, our warm-up beer was but a distant memory. Channing was keen to hear my origin story, how I wound up in DC from a once-quiet beach town in California. How I'd loved and lost—badly. How I got a golden ticket to the Oliver Thames show courtesy of Dana Krist, and how I hoped—no, planned—to resurrect my career. Along the way my hair came down, my blazer came off, and I even slipped off my shoes.

Then I turned his questions back on him and got a story that he told theatrically, as though it had enjoyed many recitals before.

"Well, as I already mentioned, I grew up in North Carolina. I was the class clown, if you can imagine that. All the girls dreamed of getting my carnation at Cotillion. That is, until I was caught kissing Bobby Beauregard under the bleachers after the homecoming game."

I gave a sympathetic *eek!*

"I don't have to tell you the struggle of coming out as a young, gay, Black man in a small, southern town, especially then. I was a pariah overnight. But all that time I was left out of the fun I was working hard at school. And it paid off when I got accepted to Duke. Even though it took me a long time to come into my own, I did."

"I can't imagine," I said, shaking my head, realizing how simple my straight white female California adolescence was by comparison.

He waved my concern away, licking the salted rim of his margarita. "Since then, it's been gravy. A few years after Duke, a buddy of Oliver's, who was getting his PhD in Durham, asked my bestie Lara to marry him. I met Oliver at their wedding. By the end of the weekend, I was convinced Oliver had the makings of our next inspirational political leader."

I hadn't realized Channing and Oliver went so far back, before Oliver's political beginnings.

"Oliver and I kept in touch. We shared political values and also really just hit it off. A few years later, I stepped down from my position as Chief Comms Officer at Southern Poverty Law Center to raise up the vanguard for Oliver's Congressional candidacy."

As promised, a little liquor released a lot of stories. "So there Oliver is in the Chamber looking out at these tech industry scions in their twenties and thirties, who had never dressed up for work a day in their lives. They're sitting there, sweating bullets and yanking at the collars of their starched dress shirts, testifying about how A.I. works to a Congressional panel of octogenarians who need their diapered grandchildren to show them how to use an iPad!"

He slapped his thigh, erupting in laughter. Between bites, I was rapt. Listening to The Oliver Chronicles made me crave his presence even more.

Channing raised a scrupulously groomed eyebrow. "Natalie, dear, you're salivating, and I don't think it's these burnt ends."

"I am not," I straightened myself in my chair. "You tell an entertaining story. I'm just picturing it all happening."

He shot me a dubious look. "Girlfriend, please. You're picturing Oliver bursting through those saloon doors and two-stepping you across the floor to 'Boot Scootin' Boogie.'"

I scoffed, accidentally inhaling tequila and sour mix. As I coughed,

Channing slammed the last of his margarita and motioned the server for another round.

"So what's your next move?" he asked, point blank.

"My next move?" I coughed.

"It's obvious you got it bad. And you picked the toughest of cookies. That man has not been emotionally available since Camille."

"Camille?" Channing had my full attention.

"His ex-fiancée."

I felt my stomach somersault. I had no idea. So *that* was the detail Oliver had danced around? It was obviously a very sore subject. Equally obviously, I now had to know everything, and I had just enough alcohol in my system to ask.

"Oliver never mentioned anything about dating anyone, let alone nearly *marrying* them," I told Channing, elbows perched on the barrel table, tips of my hair tickling the mac 'n' cheese.

Channing's Cheshire Cat smile overtook his face. "That's because Camille was a childhood friend turned whirlwind romance that burned him. He was still young, just out of college. He and Camille had the long-distance thing going for a while. This is before my time with him, so the details are fuzzy at best. I've pieced this together only from what he shared one night on the campaign trail."

I nodded, riveted.

"Anyway, so Camille. She's a Van der Kamp, total Boston Brahmin. You know, Oliver's breed. Their two families go way back. They basically grew up together. But I suppose little Camille blossomed in college, and their friendship turned into a relationship. Before long, Oliver asks her to marry him."

"Wait," I demanded, "how long are we talking?"

"I don't know, a few months?"

"Oh," I breathed. "That's fast."

"But who knows what that is in socialite years. I think those people would have arranged marriages, if it was still a thing. *Anyways,* for all the pomp and circumstance that wedding would have had, it wasn't meant to be. They were broken up before the year was out."

"Why? What happened?" I was literally perched on the edge of my seat.

"That's the million-dollar question, my dear." Channing rolled the glass stem of his margarita glass between his fingers, making it pirouette like an upside-down ballerina.

"Which one of them broke it off?"

"I got the impression it was Camille by the way Oliver talked about it. But you know he's not the most forthcoming about matters of the heart. Personally? I think the failure of that early relationship, one that everyone thought was a sure thing, made Oliver mistrust his own romantic judgement. It's had a chilling effect from then on. First, he threw himself into law school, and then work. And while I know he had dalliances along the way—you know, you probably saw the internet went crazy for him with my model friends in Paris—he never let anything get serious. In fact, whenever a girl started wanting more, the ocean between them was always the reason he'd cite to end it. Several women even offered to move."

Oliver's redactions when I'd asked him about his past were starting to make sense. But while Channing painted a compelling portrait, it still didn't tell me what Oliver actually thought or felt.

A ripple of relief gave way to a looming fear. Oliver was already in an unattainable class of his own. But whatever emotional baggage he was carrying had stymied even celebrities and socialites. Any fantasy of him I dared entertain was way, way out of reach. Channing might as well have confirmed that Oliver was gay as a box of birds.

Channing lowered his gaze. "Now, now. I've seen that look before, darling. Don't despair. You may not be a runway model or the heiress to a fortune, but you *do* have something working in your favor."

I squinted. "Do tell."

"Quite honestly, nothing specific I can point to about you, *per se*. But there's something undeniable I see in *him* when you two are together."

The assessment made me do a double-take. Was he fucking with me? Or had he really seen what I thought I had only imagined?

Channing closed his eyes meditatively. "I'm not saying it would be an easy row to hoe. In fact, even for a woman used to the public eye, it would be somewhat *torturous*."

"By all means, please elaborate," I entreated him.

He gave me a look as he sipped his drink. "Okay. First, you have the unrelenting media attention that comes part and parcel with being a Thames, let alone *Oliver* Thames, sex symbol and man of the people. Women are either like deer in the constant, flashing lights, or they're annoyed at being upstaged by him. Then you have his tireless work ethic and schedule to match. Trust me, *lots* of missed dinner dates! I have personal experience with workaholic superheroes from being married to a thoracic surgeon."

I wanted to ask for more details about the perils of pairing with Oliver Thames. But onstage, I thought I heard the man in the ten-gallon hat call my name into his microphone.

Channing's Cheshire Cat smile lit up like the neon signs. "I believe that's *you*, darlin'."

I looked at him, then up at the emcee, then frantically back. "And why did they call my name, Channing?"

"That's what happens when I put it on the list, sugar britches."

I stared at him, wide-eyed. "What are you talking about?"

"Let's *Give 'Em* Something to Talk About!" Channing shouted, head tossed back and margarita glass raised to the sky.

Then the man on stage called again, "Natalie, we've got you up next, singing Bonnie Raitt's 'Something to Talk About!'"

To uproarious applause and whistling from the crowd, Channing physically hauled me off my seat and pushed me toward the stage. I floated up the steps on the tequila rush and euphoria of hearing him say he saw something in Oliver when we were together. It had to count for, well, something.

The karaoke machine blared out the intro to the single I used to play as a kid in the early nineties, dancing across the wood floor in my socks. The room was clapping to the rhythm, tapping their feet, and bobbing their heads in anticipation of the first verse.

Maybe it was the margaritas. Maybe it was hearing I *maybe* had some infinitesimal chance with Oliver. But in that swirling moment, something took hold. I pulled the mic from its stand and let the sound from the speakers pulse through me. A voice I didn't know I had found me, as though I were an instrument of the Country Western Gods.

I sang the first sultry lines as if they were my own, invoking this new, illicit gossip from Channing that sent me flying high.

As I sang, Channing let rip a whistle so bawdy it could've torn open the emcee's pearl snap shirt. The room's energy built, and with it, so did a courage that hadn't paid me a visit since my twenties. Bonnie Raitt's lyrics flowed through me as I channeled every brief but flirtatious moment I had shared with Oliver, relishing its forbidden-ness, the delightfully agonizing toggle of "will-we-won't-we—what's-going-on?"

I was swept up in a movie-made moment, singing to the literal rafters. Channing was on his feet, leading the room in belting the chorus along with me.

By the final chorus, I felt like I was riding a wild bull, one arm outstretched, the other hanging on for dear life, spinning around the arena to the roar of the crowd.

The room exploded and I doubled over into what looked like a bow, tears of joy streaking down my cheeks. Channing ran up onstage and bear-hugged me off my feet, then swung me round like a trophy. The room was on its feet. For the first time in a long time, I reveled in the spotlight. It was a room full of strangers. Maybe that's what made it more powerful. I'd gotten so used to seeing my own face in the mirror every day, I was blind to how awesome I might look to other people.

The night got blurrier from there. More drinks. Some friends of Channing arrived. I seemed to recall doing shots. I had a vague recollection of them shipping me home in a rideshare.

I awoke the next morning on my living room floor, propped up against the couch, head lolled back on a seat cushion, one foot in a plate of partially eaten pizza.

Head throbbing, I stumbled to the bathroom mirror to confront a face that looked like the Joker had given me a makeover. The room spun. I slumped down beside the toilet on the cold bathroom tile and retched.

10

FALLING FOR YOU

The week was a busy one. Two meetings with Jake Cohen's office and a bunch of deliveries and contractors at the townhouse were moving both projects further toward completion.

Channing had been scarce, but he checked in on me the morning after our night out to make sure I was still alive. He and Oliver's whole team, he told me, had their hands unexpectedly full due to "increased scrutiny leading into the Convention." I didn't pretend to know what that meant, nor did I feel it was my place to ask. It was just me and the contractors at the townhouse, making everything go.

Late on Friday, after the contractors packed up for the weekend, I heard the door open. I had shrugged off my jacket and was down to a lacy silk camisole over high-waisted linen pants, a bit clammy from moving things around the house in the late afternoon sun. Shoes off, my pale pink pedicure sank into the soft area rug, and I was about to collapse onto the deep, stiff seats of the newly arrived leather sofa. I hadn't expected guests and was feeling irritated by the intrusion when I remembered: it wasn't my house. It was Oliver's. And there he was, the man I'd been trying not to picture every night as I fell asleep.

"There she is. I was hoping to catch you." I felt chills up my spine that I wish I could say were caused by the air conditioning.

"You caught me," I said. Naturally it would have to be in a state of partial undress. I glanced down to make sure no errant nipple was doing something untoward. He glanced too, and let his gaze linger. I crossed my arms, self-conscious.

The sleeves of his white button-down shirt were rolled up to his elbows in classic Oliver fashion, showing off strong, tan forearms. His tie was removed, the neckline of his bright white undershirt showing beneath an unbuttoned collar.

He strolled over to the narrow space where I stood between sofa and coffee table. Our eyes remained fixed on each other's as he came nearer but said nothing. My heartbeat picked up. He was inches away when he began to squeeze past me, face to face, breath brushing my clavicle, the chiseled chest beneath his button-down grazing thin silk. I breathed in faint sandalwood, salty skin, and the smell of a hot summer's night. I was grateful to have the presence of mind not to fling myself into his arms and wrap my legs around him.

He took his time moving across me, then finally took a seat on the sofa, breaking our trance. I sat down beside him, breath returning.

"I wish I'd been able to make it here during the day this past week to spend some time with you," he said. "It's been insane with the whole Conway thing, but never mind, I'm sure you've seen it all over the news. Anyway, I wanted to make sure I wasn't holding up the work on anything. It's really coming together. Like—wow. I can't wait to see it finished."

"Yeah, we got a ton accomplished this week," I said, trying to focus. "It's just a matter of the rest of the furniture arriving and placing all the final touches. I think the last decision I need from you is in the bedroom."

The last word caught in my throat as he raised an amused eyebrow. "The *paint color*, I mean."

"The final step," he said with a languid smile. Then he peeled his eyes away from me, stood up, and headed to the basement door. "We should celebrate."

He reemerged a moment later with a bottle of Barolo and a wine key.

Oh no.

I had noticed bottles of various vintages and provenances had begun populating the wine cellar this week from what I assumed had been Oliver's after-hours visits.

"Where are those red plastic cups?" he asked on his way to the pantry.

Before I could protest, he was setting two Solo cups down in front of us, making easy work of the cork like a seasoned sommelier. He sniffed and handed it to me for my approval, not that I would know what to smell for. Surely a tiny celebratory break from professionalism would be fine. After all, the project was almost done.

Oliver poured a splash into one of the cups and handed it to me.

"Is this all I get?" I joked.

"Based on what Channing told me about your night out this week …*yes.*"

I blushed, scared to know exactly how much Channing had divulged, then gave my attention to swirling and sipping, mimicking a tasting process I had only seen on TV.

Oliver poured one for himself and refilled my cup. And while I knew as little about wine as I did Michelin-starred restaurants, it was easy to tell this one was good.

Oliver took a sip and rolled it across his palate. "I always say that nothing brings out the tar and rose aromas of a Barolo like drinking it from the official cup of beer pong."

"You could squirt this wine into my mouth from a turkey baster, and it would still be better than anything I've tried before," I concurred. "Thanks for sharing it with me."

"Thank *you*, Natalie." He cozied up to me, arm against mine. "I can't believe how you've transformed this place into scenes from my dreams, and in such a short period of time too. Look at this living room! It's like a 1940s Hollywood film set."

I felt warm all over, a combination of his nearness and the wine. I caught him up on the work completed that week and what was left to do upstairs. Oliver refilled our cups.

"Well," he said after a moment, "I guess that means you'd better take me up to the bedroom."

--

I had painted four sample shades on two different walls of the primary suite. Oliver insisted there were only two colors, as far as he could tell, reassuring me that Channing had been right to suggest I narrow it down for him.

"Make sure you look at them closely and then further away on both the sunlit and the shadowed wall to see how the light affects the different shades," I instructed. He took out his glasses and got within nose-distance of the wall, feigning an artist-like seriousness. I placed a hand on my hip and sipped the wine in my cup.

"I think you need to come look at this," he said with some urgency.

"What?" I asked, feeling a tremor of concern.

"I think—yes! I think we have—*a nail pop.*"

"What?! Are you joking?" I rushed up to the wall, barefoot, buzzy and wine-lipped. We stood hunched over, shoulder-to-shoulder, faces pressed to the wall in the dimming light. I searched for a telltale bump poking beneath the paint. The wall was unblemished.

"There's no nail pop here!" I finally exclaimed.

Oliver turned his nose to mine and began cracking up. I could smell the lingering Barolo on his breath. I gave him a playful shove that came out a little harder than intended, a result of the wine muscles I'd apparently grown.

He staggered back a step, heel of his brown leather shoe catching in the drop cloth. Reflexively, he grabbed my wrist for support, but tumbled over backward despite it, bringing me down with him. I yelped in surprise as we crashed onto one of his two beloved beanbag chairs, me and my refilled glass of wine landing on top of the congressman.

My mouth hung open inches from Oliver's face. Our eyes were fixed on one another and somehow his arms were snug around my hips. He wasn't letting go. I felt like the most natural thing would be to press my mouth to his, hot and open and tasting of cherries and earth. Instead, I tried to straighten up, peeling myself off his chest.

Oliver looked like a victim in his own noir film, dark red wine splattered across his crisp, white dress shirt.

"Oh, no," I breathed. "I'm so sorry."

Oliver's face softened. "I should be the one who's sorry. I pulled you down with me."

"Yeah, but I shoved you in the first place." I clambered to my feet. I was spattered with wine, too, though Oliver's chest had taken the brunt of it.

"I have other shirts." Oliver shrugged, unconcerned, unbuttoning it as he got to his feet. The wine had bled through to his undershirt, which he pulled off over his head to reveal a gloriously defined upper body with a peppering of chest stubble.

I glitched for a moment, frozen by the sight. This was the body, or at least half of it, that I had imagined under those well-pressed shirts. So much for maintaining a professional working relationship. Dana would die if she could see me now. I ran a shaky hand through my hair.

"I'm guessing you don't have a change of clothes here," Oliver said, noticing my stained camisole. "That doesn't look machine washable."

"I try to give my dry cleaner a challenge once in a while. The beanbag on the other hand …" I gestured toward the tiny wine pond at the bottom of the vinyl indent our bodies had made.

"What *about* the beanbag?" he asked with dramatic innocence.

"I don't think it's gonna make it," I said with equal gravitas, staring solemnly at the beanbag, avoiding eye contact. "I'm afraid we'll have to trash the other one too, so it won't die of a broken heart."

"But Channing will be *devastated.*" Oliver laughed. "Maybe there's hope for resuscitation. I think vinyl is pretty resilient."

I sighed. I hadn't actually *promised* Channing I'd get rid of them, but I certainly shared the agenda.

I tried to think of something else to say as Oliver wandered into the bathroom. I heard a stream of water pour from the rain shower whose glass door had been hung just a couple days before.

I bolted down the stairs to the kitchen, where I blotted my camisole and the odd droplet of wine on my pants with cold water. My breath was heavy, and I could feel the wine just enough not to trust it. I told myself firmly that I was going to keep it professional, taking a few deep breaths to center myself. But I also wasn't sure what was happening here either, to me, to him, or to us.

The sound of the shower cut off. I climbed the stairs with Windex and a roll of paper towels to clean up the chair. Squatting on my heels, wiping the last bit of wetness from the vinyl, I heard the door to the bathroom slide open. I turned to see a billowing cloud of steam silhouetting Oliver, wrapped from the waist down in a thick white towel. He stood in the doorframe with the stature of a Greek God.

At which point, naturally, I lost my balance and sat down, a gentle but abrupt thud.

"Please feel free to rinse off," Oliver offered, like a dinner host asking if he could take my coat. "I don't have shampoo and conditioner in here yet, but there's another bar of soap under the sink."

Professional. Professional, Natalie. I scrambled to my feet. "I should go, actually."

"Let me at least offer you some dry clothes," he said.

He was terribly sweet, and he wasn't making the whole professionalism thing any easier, either. "I don't think you have any that would fit."

"I actually may. I brought an old T-shirt and sweatpants here last week under the delusion that I was going to paint an accent wall in the study."

"An accent wall?" My head shot up, too surprised to worry about whether or not I was going to get an eyeful of chest.

"Yeah, behind the desk. Like, a bold blue or something."

"Um, well, that's an idea, I guess. Did you want to … talk about that with your interior designer first?"

"Sure, that sounds great. We can pick out the right shade of blue in that swatchy book thing you have there." Oliver twiddled a finger toward the fan deck lying on the ground beside the test wall, near where we'd fallen over.

"Like … now?"

"Yeah. I'll order sushi. No point in you battling rush hour traffic. The way my schedule is looking with this whole Conway shakeup we might as well knock out the rest of the decisions you need from me tonight, so I'm not holding you up next week."

I paused to consider it, feeling electrified and panicked at the same time. But Oliver had already wandered out of the room, leaving wet footprints. Surely it counted as a business dinner, I rationalized.

He returned in a weathered undershirt and sweatpants, handing me a faded Brown University T-shirt, a pair of men's running shorts with a drawstring, and a paper sushi menu.

"You strike me as a Rainbow Roll kind of girl," he said.

"Spicy tuna," I corrected him, taking the menu and the clothes. "And miso soup."

"Split an edamame?" he asked.

"Definitely. And don't forget the ginger salad."

An hour later we were camped out on the hardwood floor of his loft bedroom, squirting soy sauce packets into plastic trays and snapping apart wooden chopsticks. Oliver uncorked a Riesling to complement the meal. At least this bottle wouldn't be on an empty stomach. It also paired nicely with the spicy tuna and the clean cotton scent of the old T-shirt and shorts I had changed into. Being clothed with things that had been up against his body felt deliciously intimate.

He sat across from me on the drop cloth propped up on his side, hair still damp and wavy, light gray sweatpants highlighting sinewy thighs.

We had agreed upon the remaining bedroom details, and even on a color for Oliver's surprise study accent wall, while we waited for the sushi to arrive.

"I guess there's nothing else you need from me now," he said, looking around the room as if searching for something.

"Well, we still have the final walkthrough," I noted with hope in my voice, though I felt a twist in my chest. "Which reminds me, I'd really like to get some pictures for my website, once everything is done. I hope you don't mind. I don't have to identify it as your house."

A huge smile leapt onto Oliver's face. "You're setting up a website? Really? That's fantastic! I can say my home is a Natalie Espinosa original design from when you were still off the map."

"Good angle. We'll play off my prior lack of a website and huge gap in work experience as artistic exclusivity."

"You *did* come highly recommended," he said, dipping his chopsticks into the wasabi.

"You know Dana Krist is my best friend, right?" I asked, popping a piece of maki into my mouth.

Oliver just smiled and raised his red plastic cup in a toast. "Here's to the imminent conclusion of a work of art realized." He clinked my Solo cup. "But also, here's to this maybe not being the end of working together … not just yet, anyway. If you recall, the last time I saw you, you'd expressed an interest in contributing to my campaign."

I looked up at him, remembering saying so as Channing bumped me out of the car seat. I wondered where he was headed with this. "Yes," I said. "I'm just not sure what or how I could possibly contribute."

"Well, that's what I was thinking about since you said it the other day. An idea occurred to me in the car, but I had to check into some things first. You know how Channing hates surprises."

"Surprises like when a random accent wall appears in a house you were hired to decorate?" I needled him.

"That's not a surprise, that's a *delightful enhancement*. I mean a surprise that requires your people to have to change everything around at the last minute."

"Right. No relevance there at all." I tilted my head at him.

"… and then there's a lot of confusion and everyone's secretly complaining …"

I arched an eyebrow. "I can't imagine you're speaking from experience."

"*Anyway,* the good news is, it's all coordinated, and I just need you to say yes."

I froze mid-sip, peering out at him over the Solo cup rim. If he was pausing for effect, it was working.

"Natalie, would you be open to offering your design services as an auction item at my fundraiser gala next weekend?" That classic Oliver smile stretched across his face and dismantled my insides. The glimmer I'd felt burst into a frenetic bundle of electrostatic. I didn't have words yet.

"You're bonded and insured, right?" He threw in the question like a disclaimer speed-read at the end of a political ad.

"Ummm ..."

"Never mind, we'll figure that out next week. Will you do it? And by 'do it,' I mean my team will do everything to showcase the package. In fact, I'm glad you brought up photos, because Channing has a guy coming next week to take some, so we can display examples of what you've done here as it's being auctioned off. I mean, assuming you're up for doing this."

My head was swimming. Oliver and his team had obviously thought this through, and they were no strangers to last-minute pivots of much greater consequence. But I was having a hard time keeping up, especially with a buzz on.

"Based on the other items," Oliver continued, "Channing suggested we start it somewhere between a $20,000 to $50,000 value. Would you be comfortable with that?"

I said something profound along the lines of "um."

"Why don't I just have Channing sit down with you Monday to hammer out all the details? Oh! And I don't know if you already have plans next weekend, but your contribution of course comes with an invite to the gala. Great opportunity to introduce yourself to prospective clients. More than a couple people come to mind, actually, who I already know will want to chat with you."

Oliver seemed to have finally run out of things to say. I popped another piece of sushi in my mouth, chewing and nodding slowly to buy a little more time. If Dana were here, she would be shrieking in my ear to pounce on this incredible opportunity. She might also have volunteered a few pointed thoughts about it being offered while I was wearing my client's clothes.

Chewing through the moment of overwhelm, I washed it down with a gulp of wine. "Absolutely. I'm in."

11

FAIRY GAYMOTHER

Oliver insisted on ordering me a car home, since we'd polished off two bottles of wine by the time we finished sushi. I texted Dana from the back seat. She was out at one of her husband's business friends' soirées. I made it a point to mention that my invite to the gala was not a date, but completely on the professional up-and-up.

The reply was immediate and excited. *OMG, call me tomorrow. We have A LOT to coordinate. Including your dress!*

I wasn't even sure what the dress code was, but I assumed a lot of tuxes and gowns would be involved. I'd confirm with Channing Monday. In the meantime, I browsed inspo pics, well-knowing the timeline was too short to order something online, if it wound up needing alterations. I'd have to shop in person.

I started as soon as I picked up my car at the townhouse the next day, using the rest of my Saturday to scout out all the local department stores to build a gown shortlist to show Dana. By that evening I was patting myself on the back for making serious progress on the dress search, as well as prepping talking points for my meeting with Channing.

I had plenty of other things to worry about besides the dress. In addition to how the whole "contribution" was going to work, how would I get there? Was Oliver flying up that evening? Would I be joining him? Was Oliver taking a date? Maybe some ninety-five-pound Parisian waif fresh off the runway, who he'd fly in for an evening of glamour and casual sex? I rolled my eyes at myself for thinking about it and firmly told myself to focus on the incredible exposure I'd be getting, not what, or whom, Oliver would be doing, at the end of the night.

There was a sea of decisions to make in the span of a week, and the clock was ticking. I fell asleep in the wee hours of the morning consumed with my big plans.

- -

When I awoke, it was midday. A distressing series of calls had finally overridden the Do Not Disturb on my phone, which rang angrily beside my head.

It was Caleb. *"Where the hell are you?"* Caleb barked over what sounded like a crowd in the background. "Aiden's camp bus just pulled up, and he's stepping off any second now."

I felt my chest heave. *Oh fuck!* I had completely forgotten Aiden was coming home from camp today, and now he was going to step off the bus at the local pickup lot and into the arms of Caleb and Victoria without seeing me waiting for him.

"I'm coming right now!" I shouted into the phone before flinging it on the bed and jumping to my feet. I rushed into the bathroom, Caleb's distant voice railing against his fulfilled prediction that I was late and completely unreliable, even on a day like today.

I had, of course, set a calendar reminder for the day before, but in the flurry of trying on dresses and fielding texts from Dana, I must've dismissed the alert without noticing. Obviously, I'd also slept through the reminder for the time I needed to leave.

I had no time to even pee, let alone brush my teeth, look in the mirror, or do anything besides shove my feet into a pair of flip-flops and sprint to my car. I realized at the first red light that I was wearing Oliver's Brown University T-shirt and mesh shorts with the waist rolled up, nineties-gym-class style. Completely out of clean pajamas, I had put them back on the night before.

Tires squealing into the now deserted parking lot where the camp bus had been, I tumbled out of my SUV looking like I was midway through a college Walk of Shame. Even the normally composed Victoria gave a little gasp as I approached her and Caleb, who were waiting patiently with Aiden on a bench.

"Mom!" Aiden ran up and hugged me around the waist.

"I'm *so* sorry I'm late, Aiden! I completely overslept. I came as fast as I could."

"That's okay, Mom. Daddy and Victoria are taking me to lunch at Kneady Dough. Are you coming with us?" he asked hopefully.

Caleb's stare bored holes into my head. "Maybe Mommy would rather do something separate with you tomorrow," he suggested. "When she's dressed for it."

Aiden turned to me, "Can you come, Mom?

I was about to say no. Caleb clearly didn't want me there. Every fiber of me wanted to slink away and hide, but my feet remained rooted to the ground. "Yes! Yes, I can. I'm starving. Let's go."

Caleb shot Victoria a look. She shrugged back.

Caleb's voice was icy. "Aiden, why don't you ride with Mommy so you can catch her up on the camp stories, and we'll meet you there? We've got your bags in the trunk."

Aiden hopped into my back seat and talked a mile a minute. I listened and laughed but also glanced into the visor mirror distractedly to wipe smudged eyeliner from under my eyes, smooth my hair into a ponytail, and fix my appearance as much as I could before having to choke down an egg sandwich in front of The Perfect Couple.

Caleb and Victoria walked up to the counter to order ahead of Aiden and me. Caleb placed Aiden's order and handed him a table number to go with Victoria and pick out a spot. As soon as they were out of earshot, he turned on me.

"I knew there was a fifty-fifty chance that you'd be late today, but seriously? Having to call to *wake you up* in *whoever*'s bed you crawled into last night to remind you that your only son was coming home from camp after weeks of not seeing him?"

"I slept in my *own* bed last night, not that it's any of your fucking business. But that's pretty rich, coming from someone who lived a double life for a year and crawled back into *our* bed, night after night."

Caleb shifted tactics, now cold and condescending. "I'm sorry you're still stuck in this embittered emotional place, Natalie. You should really talk to a professional. I mean, it's pathetic enough that you stalked Victoria's ex for a pity fuck or something—believe me, he couldn't *wait* to leave her *that* drunken voicemail—but now you've lost sight of the most important person you still have left in your life. How long will you go on choosing your own selfish indulgences over your son before he starts to realize what's going on, and I can't cover up for you anymore?"

Caleb shoved the accusation and a separate table number at me, then thrust his chin at my unfamiliar T-shirt. "I hope the Brown grad left enough money on the nightstand to buy your lunch today." He turned and sauntered off to the table.

I wanted to hurl the table number at his head and scream, but I turned in the opposite direction and pushed my way into the women's room. I grasped the sides of the sink and leaned into the mirror, breath fogging up the glass. Hot needles stung my eyes as it occurred to me this was not a safe place to bawl it out: Victoria might wander in.

I sucked in a few more deep breaths. What would Dana say? She'd tell me not to let him gaslight me. She'd say, *"You haven't done anything wrong."* She'd insist on what I already knew, that I was not the deranged whore Caleb was trying to make me believe I was.

The logic was sound, but I still needed to cry. I slunk into a stall, closed the door behind me, sat down on the toilet, and sobbed for a minute. It wasn't going to make my slept-in makeup look any worse. Then I went back to the sink, splashed cold water on my face, and patted myself dry with a paper towel. I exited the bathroom to collect my sandwich and have a deliberately non-reactive lunch with my delightful child and his asshole father.

- -

My Monday meeting with Channing ended up being just a brief phone call and follow-up email from Maryam. The photographer would arrive Thursday to shoot the whole house. I'd complete as much as possible in twenty-four hours, and swap in something from a next-day staging firm for anything that wouldn't make it in time. It would have to do. Thursday night, the photographer would send a photo dump to me and Channing, and we'd select the best shots for rush printing for a poster for the gala. There'd be no time for edits, the photographer cautioned, but it would get the job done.

On Saturday, I'd meet Channing and Oliver at the townhouse. We'd take the car to the jet and get dropped at the gala as cocktail hour got underway. Yes, I needed a gown, not a cocktail dress, and no, I did not need to prepare any remarks or bring anything with me, besides a clutch to match my "doubtlessly gorgeous ensemble."

Channing flinched audibly when I mentioned my plan to show Dana my favorites at the mall. "This is not some *hoi polloi* wedding, Natalie. Women will be in Elie Saab, Tom Ford. Not something off the Macy's sale rack."

I reassured him I wouldn't be caught dead in anything less than red carpet ready. Channing expressed skepticism that such a thing could be found at a mall. "But Godspeed to you, woman. In your design instincts I trust."

- -

I had been so busy finishing the house for the pictures that I didn't notice the string of missed calls and texts from Dana until one lit up under my nose while I unboxed a table lamp.

Scrolling back, I caught up on her events of the day.

9:58 a.m. Andrew's mother fell, and we're at the hospital. She has a broken hip and a few broken ribs. One punctured her lung so they're taking her in for surgery. I'm going to have to keep you posted on tonight—I don't see us getting out of here anytime soon.

12:01 p.m. Did you get my text?

2:35 p.m. Still at the hospital. Andrew and I are taking turns driving the kids where they need to go. Shopping another night?

4:22 p.m. Natalie, I'm so sorry. I'm not going to be able to do tonight. I just tried to call you. Call me?

4:58 p.m. Can you call me? I just left you a VM.

5:24 p.m. I am so sorry I have to bail. It's terrible timing. Send pictures from the dressing room. I'll try my best to weigh in.

"Shit." I sighed just as Channing came up the steps from the study with a box in his arms.

"Oh no, is it the study accent chairs?" he fretted. "I was so hopeful they'd come in time for the pictures."

"No," I said, "those are on their way. I just got cancelled on for dress shopping tonight."

Channing paused mid-stride. "Oh dear …" he crooned sympathetically. "No Macy's then."

"No Macy's, no Nordstrom, no Bloomie's. Not with Dana anyway. I'll have to figure it out on my own."

Channing began to putter around the room. A typically hurried man, it didn't take me long to notice he was stalling.

"Can I help you with something?" I asked pointedly.

"No, darling, but perhaps I can help *you.*"

"Are you waiting for an invite to go dress shopping?" I asked, dubious.

Channing shook his head. "I am not your gay for that. But my dear friend Ezra has always come through marvelously in a pinch. He's dressed AOC, Ivanka, even Michelle."

"And how would I go about getting an appointment with Ez—"

"Well, I'm glad you finally came to your senses! And you are exceedingly fortunate," he said, swirling a finger at me, "because although I have a very dull engagement to attend this evening, I now also have the perfect excuse to miss it. Totally justified to cancel when saving a friend from a career-ending fashion calamity."

"'Career-ending calamity' is a bit of a stretch," I muttered as Channing glided off.

"Oh, no it isn't," he sang over his shoulder. "I'll just make a call, and we will away!"

A couple of hours later, I was taking disjointed directions from him in my passenger seat, weaving through Northwest DC and driving down one-way side streets, at one point in the wrong direction. "I don't know why I can't just put it in the GPS," I complained.

"Because I don't *know* the address, only how to get there!" But get there we did, to Ezra's last after-hours appointment of the day. Channing made sure to let me know what a "small miracle" this was.

We finally parked on a narrow street of elegant townhomes lined with ginkgoes and began walking. I recognized the backside of the park I'd walked by with Dylan. It had only been a month or so, but it seemed like years ago.

I pointed the park out to Channing, recalling Dylan's factoid about his great-great-grandfather. "You know that used to be a Union encampment during the Civil War?"

Channing fluttered his eyelids. "I can dress you to the nines, Natalie Espinosa, but as God is my witness, you're on your own on Saturday when it comes to conversation starters."

We crossed down another one-way street on foot and, just as I thought Channing had no clue where we were, he darted up a set of wrought iron stairs and confidently pushed a doorbell beside a glossy black front door.

An elegantly outfitted woman in her early thirties answered and led us up to the second floor, where every wall had been removed to make a large showroom. Mannequins lined one wall, dressed in everything from smart casual to suit sets, cocktail attire to evening gowns. I was inspecting a stunning red Oscar de la Renta when a gravelly Staten Island accent interrupted my thoughts.

"Channing, darling! It's been a while. You're looking well." A stooped, silver-haired figure embraced the tall, broad-chested Channing in a bony hug.

"Ezra, thank you for making the time. You are, without a doubt, the only man for the job," Channing replied effusively.

Ezra turned to me, and I suddenly felt shy. "This is the job?" Ezra asked Channing, as though I were just another mannequin.

Channing came up beside Ezra to study me. "Ms. Espinosa here will be attending Congressman Thames's fundraising gala this weekend and nearly opted to go in tatters before I, her Fairy Gaymother, benevolently intervened. Hence why we sought you out on this very last-minute, after-hours appointment for which we are both *eternally* grateful, Ezra."

"Ah. I see." Ezra jabbed a thumb in my direction, looking back at Channing. "Is she … attending *with* the congressman?"

My cheeks flushed to match the de la Renta.

"Ms. Espinosa will be *traveling* with the congressman and I, as she's an esteemed contributor to the auction and the congressman's personal interior designer-decorator," Channing clarified.

"Ah. Okay." Ezra clapped his gnarled hands together as though he had heard magic words. For the first time, he addressed me directly. "Miss, uh, Espinosa, was it? Would you kindly step up on the fitting platform here?"

I did as he asked while he paced around me, assessing me like a lump of clay.

"This is a rush job, you said?" he asked Channing.

"Yes, we need it by Friday. Saturday morning at the drop dead latest. We fly up that evening." Channing replied to a frowning Ezra.

Ezra fretted, studying my shape. "We're gonna definitely need to hem something, at the very least …"

"You've worked bigger miracles before," Channing encouraged him.

"True. That Ambassador's wife last year was very poorly proportioned." He paused for a second, then bellowed. "Isabellllll-laaaaaaaaaaaa!"

His assistant appeared as if materializing out of thin air. "Pull the Vera Wang with the plunging neckline, the black de la Renta with the beading …" Channing had taken a front-row seat in an upholstered armchair, legs crossed, facing the three-way mirror I stood in front of.

Ezra rattled off several more options, my eyes growing wider with each one.

I turned on the dais. *I cannot afford these!* I mouthed to Channing with vaudevillian exaggeration.

So put it on Oliver's bill! he mouthed back and rolled his eyes.

Ezra's measuring tape wrapped and unwrapped around various parts of me, Isabella scribbling things in a tiny notebook with a tinier pencil. Eventually they stepped away.

"Oh, sure," I whisper-yelled at Channing. "Oliver will have no problem with a line item for an extravagantly expensive ball gown as part of my interior design services."

"Mark up something else," Channing sniped, dismissing my concern. "Besides, who do you think is the one approving the bills?"

I looked up and away to consider it, but just for a second. "That feels wrong!"

"Darling, trust me." Channing's voice was serious now. "Oliver would prefer you be properly attired and not embarrass yourself on the night he introduces you to his circle of supporters. Think of it this way: He's paying it forward with your contribution to the auction."

Isabella returned, pushing a rack of gowns. With sample heels on, two sizes too large, I felt like I was playing dress-up in Mommy's closet: the gowns were made for those skyscraper models Oliver had flings with, not five-foot-four me. Once properly sucked-and-tucked into the thick, faded shapewear Isabella handed me, I took my place on the fitting platform in front of three inscrutable faces.

Ezra sprang into action, pins between his lips, snatching and cinching dresses here and there and there ... and there. He and Channing exchanged a series of "nos" and "maybes." Isabella was sent to fetch more gowns.

I'd been standing there for an hour, and I was starting to feel both fatigue and despair. Then Isabella brought in something very different. Something *else.* A fitted black silk dress, cut on the bias with a sheer, beaded bodice of gold and crystal that created a starlight effect. Flowing black gossamer sleeves added a retro note and a bewitching allure.

They unzipped the back and lowered the gown over my head. I slid my arms through the armscyes and felt the silk slither down me. Someone zipped me up from tailbone to mid-back where the fabric ended. The black silk hugged my hips gently; the beading molded to me like mermaid scales. All my curves were tastefully accentuated, as though I were Sophia Loren on her way to the Oscars. It took Channing a second to look up, but when he did, the hush that fell over the room was thick, almost reverent.

"Gentlemen," Isabella declared in a resonant alto. "We have a winner."

POLITICAL INSTRUMENTS

On the divan in the townhouse living room, I blotted my matte red lips. A soft tendril from a timeless updo brushed my shoulder. Channing crossed the threshold from the kitchen with two frosty martini glasses and a hammered pewter shaker. He looked even more debonair than usual in a sharp, classic tux.

He placed the glasses down and poured, then held his up in a toast: "To beauty. To love. To the love of beauty … and the beauty of love." Our glasses clinked delicately. "And honestly, to this night going off without a hitch, because I'd like to enjoy myself for once without having to put out multiple fires."

"Amen," I said, tipping my glass. "Thank you, by the way, for all your help with the photographer. The pictures of the rooms look amazing. I can't wait to have Dana's guy help me with the website. I hope the shots printed out well."

"Yes, I heard yesterday that the poster came out perfectly. Between your auction contribution and your stunner of an ensemble here, Natalie," he said as he stepped back to acknowledge my look, "you are going to have a very full calendar."

The front door swung open and Oliver blew into the entryway, adjusting his cuff links. "I tell you what, we're going to want to get off the ground before this storm hits. It's starting to look really bad out there."

I stood from the sofa and took a step toward him as his eyes connected with mine.

He stopped in his tracks. "You look absolutely stunning, Natalie," he said breathlessly. "It's like—"

He shook his head. I raised a brow in anticipation. "You complete the room," he finished, softly.

My whole body began to tingle. "How do you mean?"

He stepped back so he could take me in. Then, almost as if he were talking to himself, "It's not just the dress. Although it's a beautiful dress. You're *different* tonight. You're carrying yourself differently. It's like you walked right out of that noir scene we talked about weeks ago. You're the femme fatale!"

I toasted him gently with the glass still in my hand. "And you're the man of the evening."

Channing crossed the room, handed me my clutch, and took my arm. "Well, kids, what are we waiting for? Our coach is outside. Best not be late for the ball."

- -

The impending summer storm Oliver was worried about had whipped itself into a tantrum by the time we arrived at the airport. The sky was swirling shades of gunmetal. Stepping out of the car, my nostrils flared at the smell of ozone threatening an imminent downpour.

Channing helped steady me in my pointy stilettos. Foreboding gales of wind lapped at my dress, silk clinging to my legs like a frightened child. He walked me toward the jet steps, where Oliver was already several paces ahead, beelining for a word with the pilot. Channing and I made a dash for it, mounting the steps and ducking for cover in the jet cabin just as needles of rain pelted the tarmac. We were breathless, but—thank goodness—not dampened.

The pilot announced we would have to take off now or risk not making it out tonight. A moment later the jet peeled down the slick runway, torrents of rain in its contrail.

Takeoff was harrowing, and while Oliver seemed mostly unfazed, I thought I could hear Channing muttering a prayer to my right.

The flight attendant sat erect in the jump seat, her eyes closed. I didn't dare move, as if doing so could unbalance the delicate equilibrium of this tin can hurtling through a storm-battered sky. The turbulence worsened over minutes that might as well have been hours, jostling us in our seats and creating unnatural noises that made coherent thought almost impossible.

By the time we got above the weather and things evened out, Channing was frantically signaling the flight attendant for a round of drinks. She jumped out of her seat to prepare him a martini.

"For crying out loud, Tammy," Channing finally wailed, "stop fiddling with the vermouth and just bring over the bottle! I just saw my whole life flash before my not-even-middle-aged eyes."

"Not-even-middle-aged, Channing?" Oliver chuckled from his seat. "You have any 110-year-old relatives I don't know about?"

"You say that like you haven't been a Cologuard candidate for years," Channing clapped back. "You know, I throw out those AARP magazines they mail you. You're welcome."

Oliver shook his head, laughing to himself as he pulled out his folio of papers and notes. Still trembling, I accepted a beverage from Tammy—a proper martini I waited for her to prepare—while Channing poured himself Grey Goose into a rocks glass.

Oliver drank nothing but water. I stole glances of him across the aisle as he penned last-minute notes into his printed remarks.

My mind drifted back to our evening of sushi and spilled wine and hideous beanbag chairs, and falling—the all-consuming feeling of falling—followed by an abrupt landing. The awkwardness. But also the sensual shower steam and Oliver wrapped in a towel.

I tried to center myself, to rejoin reality. I was going to come apart before I even got to the gala. It wasn't like I was his date. I'd just let Channing's comments and Oliver's universally friendly personality spin my head around. I was dangerously close to creating a fantasy world, and if I kept it up, it could only lead to pain. I had enough of that already.

I resolved to turn my thoughts to the very real opportunity in front of me. That's what Dana would do. The night was a gateway to a new start. My talent had never left me, it just lay dormant, gathering its strength. Now it had woken, and powerful advocates like Oliver and Channing took notice. I wasn't an insipid puddle of desire for an unattainable man, I was a femme fatale who didn't have to look around to know the whole room was watching. And I was just getting started.

- -

The evening was fair and breezy when we arrived at the Museum of Art at the Rhode Island School of Design. It was as if the storm swirling in Washington were as much a figment of my imagination as I'd told myself the chemistry with Oliver was. The cocktail hour was half over, and we were very fashionably late to Oliver's own party.

Channing took my arm and escorted me in as Oliver walked beside us, entering the foyer to the fragrance of armfuls of hydrangeas and lilies in urns along the walls. The harmony of a harp and violin duo amid mingling partygoers played beyond the antechamber doors.

Channing plucked a cream-colored place card with my name and table number on it from the seating assignment table and handed it to me. There were hardly any cards left, which made one of them jump out at me all the more. Emblazoned in elegant gold calligraphy were the names of Mr. Caleb Weir & Ms. Victoria Demerest, Table 9.

My mouth went dry as paste, limbs numb. I stared at the place card in disbelief. Channing and Oliver turned to see what was keeping me. When feeling returned to my body, I strode toward the doors, where they ushered me across the threshold and past the point of no return.

Oliver was immediately pulled in another direction by his handlers, not to mention throngs of admirers. Panic hit, and I felt like a lost kid in a crowd.

"What was that about back there?" I heard Channing in my ear.

"What? What do you mean?" I asked absently.

"You looked like you'd seen a ghost in the foyer."

But if Channing was going to ask me to explain, he didn't get the chance. He was descended upon by a very fancy elderly couple, both eager to see him. The man sported a top hat and an antique walking stick. The lady wore metallic blue eyeshadow and a gown that resembled a taxidermized peacock.

"And who is this ravishing escort of yours, my dear?" the woman asked.

"This is the radiant Ms. Natalie Espinosa, joining us from DC tonight. She is Oliver's personal interior designer-decorator." Channing turned to me with encouragement, as if fledging his baby bird.

"Natalie," he introduced, "this is the esteemed Herr Gustav Ignatius Constapel—transatlantic shipping magnate by birthright, impeccable haberdasher by the grace of God—and his wife, the unparalleled Ava von Vosges Constapel, champion of the arts and board member here at the museum." Herr Gustav tipped his top hat and Ms. Ava nodded warmly at me.

"Such a pleasure to meet you both," I said, resisting a fleeting impulse to curtsy.

Ava reached and took my hand, holding it between both of her soft, thin-skinned palms. "Natalie, *darling*, what fortuitous timing. I'm in the midst of redecorating our summer home in Antibes—"

"She's always redecorating, Natalie," Herr Gustav chuffed. "It is perpetually 'fortuitous timing' for Ava to meet a talented designer."

"Oh, Gus, stop. Don't listen to him," Ava said, shooing her husband. "We must talk at length. I would love your expertise. There are some tricky spaces I just can't decide on."

Channing had already made a stealthy exit, leaving me to Ava. Just like that, the little bird had been nudged from the nest.

The rest of the cocktail hour was a flurry of activity. If I had worried I'd be ignored in a sea of well-heeled guests, Ava made sure of the opposite, introducing me to every single person who stopped to kiss the proverbial ring and quite a few others she plucked from the crowd.

When I finally made it to one of the bars to order a drink, I was intercepted by a strapping strawberry blond man in his late forties wearing a white dinner jacket with black trim. He gave off a roguish Robert Redford air as he leaned against the bar, sipping what looked like a gimlet.

"I was wondering if you'd make it over here," he said, slyly nonchalant.

"I beg your pardon?" I was dying for a drink.

"To the bar. You looked like you were trying to slip past that last couple Ava Constapel was showing you off to."

"Oh, yes," I agreed. "She's so thoughtful, introducing me around like that."

"Are you a new exhibitor at the museum?" he asked with a raised brow.

"No … I'm just up from DC." I tried to catch the bartender's attention.

"From DC, you say? A political type?"

"No, not at all political." I glanced over at him. "I'm an auction contributor tonight."

"Is that so? And which item should I have my eye on?" I caught his bemused half-smile from the corner of my eye.

"Not an item, actually."

"An experience?"

"A service," I stated. "Interior design and decorating." I couldn't tell if he was flirting or toying with me.

"Ah. I see why Ava took such an interest then. Not to say that you're not quite … interesting." He scanned me, stem to stern.

I succeeded in getting the bartender's attention and ordered a vodka martini.

The man reinserted himself. "Vodka over gin … James Bond would disapprove."

"Actually," I replied, opening my clutch to touch up my lipstick, "James Bond was known to drink both. His drink of choice is the Vesper Martini, which is vodka and gin mixed together, 'shaken, not stirred' as you know, and named after the only woman he ever truly loved."

"Vesper Lynd," the man tacked on. "And a traitor at that. Did you ever notice what name *Vesper Lynd* sounds like, quite intentionally?" He shifted his weight and finished his drink.

I impatiently awaited the answer I knew he was waiting to give.

"West Berlin," he declared with satisfaction, placing his empty glass on the bar. "A land of divided loyalties."

"And what, might I ask, is *your* name?" I said, growing tired of his little game, but also unsure if this was the wrong person in Oliver's orbit to piss off.

"Vance," he said, extending a handshake, then pulling my hand to him for a somewhat creepy back of the hand kiss.

"Vance Delano Oglethorpe the Third. But for you, we can keep it on a first-name basis." He winked.

"Delano?" I asked. "As in Franklin Delano Roosevelt?"

"The very same one," he said smugly. "And he wasn't the only President in the family. We also have Grant and Coolidge. Or maybe you read Laura Ingalls Wilder as a girl? Or remember learning about Alan Shepard, who walked on the moon? They're Delano family as well."

"Goodness. I'm afraid I can't hold a candle to that."

"And yet I'm nonetheless intrigued to learn your name." Vance was practically drooling.

"Natalie Espinosa … The Only," I said, not extending my hand.

"Charmed to meet you, Natalie. I'll be on the lookout for you in the auction. It's a prize that's too good to pass up." Vance gave me the once over once more before taking his leave. I hoped it would be the last time.

Sipping my martini in silence, I had a moment to process how well things were going, aside from Vance the Third. It was almost like Channing had planned it that way. I wouldn't have put it past my self-anointed Fairy Gaymother. Thankfully I hadn't spotted either Caleb or Victoria yet, though the thought that they were on the guest list still unsettled me.

I was just beginning to wonder what was in store for the rest of the night when I caught a flash of Oliver from across the room. It was hard to see who he was talking to through the crowd at first, but then I saw her, a tall, slim woman in an emerald dress with honey-colored hair done up in an elegant chignon. It didn't look like anyone else was part of their conversation.

I drifted a few feet for a better look. Oliver's body language was relaxed and convivial. They both seemed quite familiar with one another, based on how close they were standing. Oliver appeared to stroke the woman's bare arm, and a sinking feeling assailed me. Who was that?

Ducking past a knot of chatting women for a better look, I dodged a server and walked directly into a table I hadn't even noticed was there. A few empty glasses crashed to the floor, guests whipping their heads toward the commotion. Consummately professional, a nearby server was instantly at my elbow, apologizing for the mess.

"Natalie, are you okay?" Suddenly, Oliver was beside me, looking concerned, the mystery woman close behind.

"Yes, yes, I'm fine." I laughed nervously. "So many fascinating people here, I wasn't watching where I was going."

"Natalie is one of our auction contributors," Oliver told the woman. "She's the artistic genius behind my townhouse interior, and she's offering bidders the chance to work with her."

"Oh, how lovely," the woman replied. "It's a pleasure to meet you, Natalie. Every time I talk to Oli, he has been absolutely enthralled with how the townhouse is turning out."

'Oli?' 'Every time she talks to Oli?' I willed her to be his sister or an extremely femme lesbian.

"I'm so glad to hear it," I managed to reply.

"I'm sorry, where are my manners? Natalie, this is Camille," Oliver piped in.

"Camille van der Kamp." She held out a delicate arm, braceleted in emeralds and diamonds, for a handshake that carried the scent of gardenias.

The name struck awe and panic in my heart. This was the Camille Channing told me about, Oliver's Camille!

"Camille is a political columnist for the *Post*," Oliver added. "What am I saying? You probably already know that. Camille is a bit of a household name, at least around the Beltway."

She was definitely a household name in his household, anyway.

"You give me too much credit, Oli." Camille grinned back modestly as I wished I could melt into the floor.

"Natalie's no stranger to the cabal of DC pundits and political journalists," Oliver told her.

"Is that so?" Camille asked, turning to me. "Do you design a lot of their interiors?"

"Not exactly," I demurred.

"Oh, do you write then?"

"No, I—"

"Hmm … NGO work?"

"Nope, I actually—"

"Ugh! I thought for sure I'd guessed it." Camille tilted her head back with a musical laugh. "Ah, well, what *is* your connection?"

"I haven't got one," I finally got out.

"Sorry?" Camille looked at me confused.

"My husband, soon-to-be *ex*-husband, to be precise, is Caleb Weir. That's my political news connection."

"Really? How interesting." I could see several other responses in her expression, but she was far too polite to say them out loud. "I thought I saw him here tonight."

I turned to ice. Oliver's brow furrowed.

"Hmmm … maybe I just saw the place card," Camille pursed her lips. "Either way, good luck with that." The way she looked at me matched her vague remark that felt obnoxiously over-familiar.

Had Caleb slept with Camille at some point too? I wouldn't put it past him, but my circuits were overloaded from meeting the woman Oliver had edited out of his past.

Camille excused herself and Oliver and I stood there alone. I couldn't tell if he felt awkward or if I just thought he *should* feel that way. Careful to not jump to any deli-style conclusions, I opted for the second-most pressing question on my tongue:

"Is Caleb here?" I asked him flatly.

Oliver shrugged his shoulders. "I didn't even know he was invited."

"Bullshit. You vet those lists." *Oh, Natalie, so much for playing it cool ...*

"Natalie, I don't even know half the people here."

I scoffed.

"Seriously," he insisted. "And there are plenty of invites that go out that are just ... perfunctory. Like it or not, your husband—your *ex*-husband—is one of those players in the political news landscape who automatically gets an invitation to things like this."

"Invite, maybe, but you don't get a place card unless you've accepted." I could feel my emotions getting away from me no matter how much my brain pleaded with them to stay calm.

"I can't control if he accepts or not," Oliver replied.

"No, but you could've warned me," I insisted.

"I didn't even know he was invited!" He threw his hands up.

"You just said he's a 'perfunctory invite!'" I held up both hands in a stopping motion. "You know what? I'm going to grab another drink."

Oliver's lips formed a thin, crooked line to match the ones embedded in his forehead. I pivoted toward the bar, just as guests were getting shuffled into the dining room. I fumbled in my clutch for the place card with my table number on it.

God help me if I'm seated with Caleb and Victoria ...

The cocktail stations had closed, so I made my way to Table 1, front-and-center of the ballroom. A woman in her early sixties and a conservative black gown was situating herself in a seat with a square view of the stage.

"I think I have the best view in the house," she proclaimed as I sat beside her.

"I was about to say the same thing," a voice came from behind us as Vance pulled up a seat on the other side of me. "But in my case, the better view isn't of the stage."

"Oh hello, Vance," the woman addressed him. "Is this lovely woman your date?"

I shook my head energetically.

"Not yet," he replied, making himself comfortable in his chair.

The woman rolled her eyes, then turned to me. "Pleased to meet you. Daphne Atwood. Don't let that presumptuous man ruin your night. He's all bark."

"I only bite on request," Vance interjected.

Daphne was clearly accustomed to Vance, because she spoke to him like she would a badly trained dog. "Vance! Stop it."

"It's all in good fun, Aunt Daffy," Vance told her, tilting onto the back legs of his chair.

Daphne looked at me, "Is it 'good fun' for you? I don't even think I got your name."

"Natalie," I replied, happily shaking the hand of a new ally. "And no, that isn't the phrase I would've used."

Herr Gustav and Ms. Ava had made their way over, along with two other couples. "Natalie!" Ava exclaimed. "Such good luck we're seated together. I want your thoughts on what to do about the Antibes upper loggia. I'm sure you'll agree, these seaside indoor-outdoor spaces can be such a challenge to decorate."

"Oh, are you an architect, Natalie?" Daphne asked as I nodded sympathetically to Ava.

"Interior design and decorating," I clarified.

"Natalie is an auction contributor tonight, Aunt Daffy." Vance reasserted his presence.

"Natalie, that's wonderful," Daphne said, refusing to engage her nephew. "I may need to pick your brain myself. I'll be breaking ground in Massachusetts later this year on a state-of-the-art campus for victims of domestic violence, and I just secured an architect."

"Congratulations, what a wonderful project!" I told her, my interest piqued.

"Yes, thank you," Daphne replied with a soft smile. "It's been quite an undertaking. I don't know if you've ever worked on community spaces before, but it's so important to me that this campus feel like a home to the women and children who will live there until they get on their feet. Many times, if there's a place for them to go at all, it's some

sterile government facility that just makes the displacement and alien-
ation worse."

"I would be honored to be consulted," I replied. "It's an important
vision."

Applause ended the conversation as the evening's emcee
approached the podium. The night was about to get properly underway. I hadn't watched Oliver speak in front of a crowd before, but
wasn't surprised that he was a natural, with an easy cadence and
personal warmth that made everyone in the room feel like he was
speaking directly to them from the stage. Between the well-timed
laughter and powerful silences, it was like he was conducting an
orchestra. I couldn't help but watch him in pure admiration. And my
desire bloomed eternal, despite the distractions of Oliver's cadre of
gorgeous women and the specter of Caleb and Victoria.

As the next speaker took over, I scanned the room. Table 9 had
two empty chairs. Good. Caleb was never late to a party, let alone a
professional event. Had the weather in DC grounded them? Whatever
it was, I was grateful.

Exhaling in relief, I listened to the speeches and in between
enjoyed chatting with Daphne, who was, unlike her nephew, a delight
to be seated beside. We chatted about the Atwood Foundation's
campus, the latest in a series of philanthropic initiatives she seemed
born to lead. She reminded me of Oliver, focused on outcomes, effi-
ciency, and giving back to the world from a position of privilege. I
also appreciated her taskmaster personality and her total lack of
pretension.

"I am admittedly not a creative mind, Natalie. I'm a process person
—a doer who does best at keeping the mission central and everyone
working in concert," Daphne explained over the salad course. "My
strength is shepherding the whole circus to successful conclusion. But
I always need help with the details. They truly do make all the difference. And interior design and decorating fall right into that category.
If the place feels institutional, the design becomes one more deterrent
to people getting help. It's a barrier to entry. I want to do better."

I expressed my admiration. Some people wouldn't even think

about how a domestic violence sanctuary might be designed or decorated, assuming that just having one was more than enough. But not Daphne Atwood, whose ethos and vision extended far beyond the basics. She didn't want the campus to feel like a shelter, but a home. I asked questions, tossing out a few ideas as they came to mind.

"I'm thinking about spaces where childcare is baked into the design," I mused. "Rather than a separate playroom, why not build kid-friendly exploration zones into spaces where parents are going to want to be? A play kitchen within eyeshot of the real one, art and reading tables integrated into places where parents will be getting support services?"

Daphne looked delighted as she passed the breadbasket. "You get it. *Exactly* the kind of creative perspective I need, function *with* aesthetics. I can see why Oliver enjoys working with you, Natalie. Are you a mother yourself?"

"I am," I replied, "and there isn't a better hands-on learning program at any design school in the world. My son is ten now, but he could be a handful when he was younger. In fact, sometimes he still is."

"Motherhood is a life path I never embarked upon." She shook her head with a frown. "My nephew there was enough to put me off having children permanently." We giggled at Vance's expense while he blathered about yachting to the man to his left.

I was feeling pretty good by the time the entrées were served. I hadn't thought much about the empty seat at our table. The only two empty chairs that worried me were still vacant, so I was caught off guard when Oliver arrived and sat down with us.

"Are you sure you don't mind sitting next to a politician?" Oliver joked with the man to his right.

The rotund, silver-bearded man let loose the cackle of a lifetime cigar smoker. "On the contrary, I am quite used to being seated next to people asking me for money!"

Ava grasped Oliver's arm. "I, for one, am waiting for Natalie's prize to come up!" she gushed. "I can already tell she is such a talent!"

"I'll second that, Oliver," Daphne chimed. "She is also a delight to talk to, but you already know that."

"I wouldn't mind talking to her more myself," Vance barged in.

I thought I noticed Oliver wince as he stood to reach an arm out in a handshake. "Vance, it's been a while, how've you been?"

"Just put the new boat in the water a couple months ago," Vance replied. "Been taking it back and forth to the Vineyard, mostly shuttling Mother. Are you up here for the rest of the weekend? Come out for a sail!"

Oliver shook his head. "Would if I could. My schedule's about as tight as Tom's cummerbund." He gave Tom a slap on the back. Tom was a good sport, patting his substantial midsection. His wife looked like she thought it was hilarious.

"Another time then," Vance said, saving face. "I think the last time I saw you on the water was at Camille's, two, no, three summers ago."

"The Van der Kamp Fourth of July raft-up, of course," said Oliver.

"Or did it turn into more of a Fourth of July *hook*-up for you and Old C?" Vance said with a leer.

"Vance!" Daphne hissed.

My eyes darted from Vance to Oliver to Daphne and back to Oliver again. The lines in Oliver's forehead were again visible, even across the table.

"Oh, Daff! Oliver knows I just like to stir the pot." Vance leaned back in his chair.

"*No one* ordered the Vance Special," Daphne stated.

To my surprise there was no long awkward silence. The rest of my tablemates, clearly practiced at navigating one another in public, just acted as if Vance weren't there. Herr Gustav turned to Oliver to praise the menu while Ava and Daphne began talking about a mutual acquaintance in the art world. Vance stared at his plate like a sulking schoolboy but said nothing. I listened, fascinated. This was a whole new world.

The emcee announced the start of the auction just as the chocolate mousse and crème brulée were brought around. Bidders oohed and aahed and clapped as people snapped up jewelry, artwork, rare autographed sports memorabilia, a two-week spa and wellness stay in a luxury overwater cabin in the Maldives. My heart pounded as I waited. Then two easels were placed beside the podium, thick four-by-three-foot poster boards of glossy photos from Oliver's townhouse. They looked so professional it took me a moment to remember it was my own work.

Vance sat bolt upright in his chair when the auctioneer announced my name and the item, beginning the bidding at $25,000. He raised his paddle.

"Vance, you have nothing to decorate but a boat!" Daphne chastised.

He looked blasé. "Isn't that enough?"

"Enough to make you delusional, apparently."

Ava's hand shot up next, and a handful of others raised around the ballroom as the bidding ticked upward.

Vance raised bids as others dropped out, enjoying needling his aunt with his game of high-dollar Whack-A-Mole.

Ava held her own until Gus signaled her. She waved to me from across the table, mouthing, *I'll just call you, dear.*

When the bidding hit fifty grand, Vance was silently duking it out with someone from the other side of the room whom I couldn't see from my seat.

My heart was in my mouth at the thought of anyone paying that much for what equated to about a week's worth of work for me, but it didn't help that Vance's bid was the last one standing.

"We have fifty thousand … $50,000 on the table … Do I hear fifty-five?" the auctioneer was goading the final bidders. "Fifty thousand going once … going twice …" Vance was already directing a smug expression my way in what appeared to be a *fait accompli.*

Holding onto my last stale breath, I saw another hand shoot up from the corner of my eye.

"Oliver!" Vance shouted, nearly tipping out of his chair. "You can't bid at your own fundraiser!"

"Rules were made to be bent, old man." Oliver might as well have been Superman emerging from a phone booth.

The auctioneer called out, "Fifty-*five* thousand! Do I hear sixty??"

Not to be outdone, Vance began to raise his hand when Daphne raised hers.

"Sixty," she enunciated, crystal clear, daring her nephew to move so much as a finger.

"Going once, going twice …"

The gavel whacked.

"Sold for sixty thousand dollars!" The applause was mixed with impressed murmurs. "This item is now closed."

13

RIGHT-WING, LEFT WING ... EAST WING

My head was spinning. The night was coming to a close, and I tried to recall all the events that had played out in just a few hours. Guests began filing out, some lingering to chat up Oliver. I said a fond farewell-for-now to Daphne Atwood. She explained she would be out of the country for the next couple weeks but promised to come collect on her winning bid shortly after Labor Day, as there was "much work for us to do."

I gathered my clutch and headed toward the entrance. Vance had slunk out before the auction ended, likely to avoid his aunt. He was probably waving hundred-dollar bills at some poor cocktail waitress to make himself feel better about the night.

For the first time since our arrival, I heard Channing's voice. "Hell's bells, Natalie Espinosa! Talk about a narrow escape from Sex Trafficking Island!"

"No kidding. Where have you been all night?" I asked.

"Whipping up support among Oliver's most loyal contributors," he said. Then he leaned in, continuing in a whisper, "as in pumping them full of booze and playing them against one another in a battle of unfettered hubris to ratchet up those donations."

"Bravo," I trilled. "I hope your efforts were fruitful."

"Naturally." He spiffed his lapel. "But the award for most *dramatic* contribution goes uncontested to you!"

I rolled my eyes. "What is Vance's deal anyway?"

"Boarding school frenemy of Oliver's," Channing explained. "He and Vance just barely play nice in the sandbox. Politics with both the big and little 'P.' Vance is from another monolithic New England family. You already met his aunt."

"Who is lovely. I would've thought Vance fell out of a completely different family tree."

"A rotten apple to the core." Channing scowled.

I wasn't sure what was supposed to happen next. "I suppose we need to get back to the plane?"

"What, you turn into a pumpkin at midnight?" Channing flashed a judgmental look. "We're all going to the after-party."

"You never mentioned an after-party," I said.

He gave me an Elvis-caliber sneer. "What kind of gala would this be without an after-party?"

Oliver popped out of nowhere. "Natalie … wait for me here, if you don't mind? I have to finish a conversation with someone, but I'll be back in a few minutes."

"Well, *I'm* not waiting," Channing interjected. "I'm taking the staff to Marcello's to celebrate a successful night. Natalie, would you like to ride with us?"

I glanced back at Oliver. "No, I'll wait. I'll see you there."

"Mmmm-*hmmm!*" Channing's eyes shifted ostentatiously from me to Oliver and back to me again, then pushed through the foyer doors as Oliver retreated to the grand gallery, leaving me by my lonesome among the empty cocktail lounge chairs.

- -

Time passed. Eventually it was just me and some cleaning staff. I curled my legs into a giant armchair and regretted saying I'd wait. Oliver had probably forgotten he'd even asked me, and I'd have to show up at Marcello's alone. But then my nose was getting booped. By

Oliver's index finger, in fact, and he was softly but tunelessly singing, "Beautiful dreamer, wake unto meeee …"

I sat up with a start. I must've nodded off.

"I'm sorry, Natalie. That took forever. Not easy to get out of a conversation with a long-winded guy who wants to write you a check. Thanks for waiting."

I tried to draw saliva back into my mouth and get my bearings.

"Anyway," Oliver went on, "I wanted to make sure we were good. You seemed upset earlier about the Caleb invite, and I really wanted to apologize for Vance. Vance is kind of … uh …"

"A perfunctory invite?" I offered.

Oliver looked relieved. "Yes. Exactly. You get it."

"I guess every table had at least one," I said, standing. My skirt had gotten creased during my nap in the chair.

"Well, rest assured," he said, trying to make eye contact with me, "you were not one of them."

I shied away. He followed. "I'm so glad you were here. And not just because of that bidding war either. So many people wanted to make your acquaintance, if you couldn't tell. You're going to really hit it off with Daphne. I mean, you already have. If ever there were a woman to be connected to in all of New England, she's the one."

For some reason I felt like a kid getting congratulated for a mediocre ballet recital. I stood there, ill at ease. What could it be besides a door prize? He had women like the breathtaking Camille in his life.

Oliver kept going. "You know, I requested for you to be at my table tonight. Even though we didn't get to talk much, I loved looking up and seeing you there, thriving."

"Well, you did your good deed for the evening. I appreciate it," I told him curtly. "Daphne and Ava and the rest are going to be great leads for future work. And you get the credit for connecting me."

Oliver wrinkled his nose. "Is that what you think? That I brought you up here as some kind of charity case?"

"Isn't that what this is?" I asked, fatigued by the pretense. "I mean, I certainly don't fit into the equation otherwise. I'm not wealthy or glamorous or accomplished or New England. I'm the farthest thing from your friend Camille."

Oliver's look of wounded confusion suddenly morphed into understanding.

"Camille is a family friend," he said quietly, lowering his gaze. "Our families go back four generations. She and I have known each other since time before memory, and she has shown herself to be a genuine confidante through the years. She's *loyal*. She has my back when plenty of others would just as soon stab it. She looks out for me. And as for why I invited you here, beyond any kind of *perfunctory invite* for auction contributors? Well, honestly, I wanted to show you off."

I looked up.

"You and the incredible work you did to make the house something amazing," he said. "To listen to me and be so intuitive in how you made it my *home*. It's impressive. You're impressive. I wanted to show you off to everyone. I'm sorry, I guess that sounds kind of self-absorbed, now that I'm saying it."

"No," I said softly. "Thank you. That's really lovely. That makes me feel good."

"Good," he reached for my hand. "Let's hit the after-party then."

I turned to walk toward the entrance, but Oliver tugged at my hand. "Better if we leave out the back," he suggested. He guided me through darkened rooms and dim corridors toward a glowing red exit sign.

He pressed the door open and ushered me out into the cool night air. A limo was there waiting. But we weren't alone. Camera flashes attacked my pupils in the darkness. A dozen voices began shouting.

"Oliver! Oliver!"

"Where are you going?"

"Who's your friend?"

Oliver didn't even look, just scooped his arm around my back and helped me into the black sedan, scooting in behind me and pulling the door shut. The driver pulled away posthaste.

"Thanks, Danny," Oliver told him from the back seat.

"No problem, sir! Where to?"

"Marcello's!" Oliver called to him jovially. "And try to lose these assholes!"

Danny was happy to do it. The limo wound through the narrow back alleys, making a few deceptive turns.

"Do you get chased by paparazzi often?" I asked, bracing myself as we went around another corner.

"It can be particularly bad at well-publicized events," Oliver admitted. "And up here, I'm a known entity. Less so in Washington, since I'm only one of 435. 535, if you count the Senate. But it does still happen."

"Will our pictures show up on the cover of something tomorrow?" I asked, partly terrified, but kind of exhilarated.

"Nah, just the tabloids up here, which you won't even see. You'll already be back in DC."

Marcello's was on the rooftop of a swanky hotel, a busy terrace of candlelit tables and huge potted plants. Strings of lights formed a canopy above our heads. Contemporary jazz wafted through the elegant scene, competing with clinking glasses and laughter.

We entered a section beneath a wooden pergola twined with grapevines. A wood-burning firepit lent the seating area a glow, and the logs crackled. As if on cue, a server brought Oliver a Dark 'n' Stormy. Then Oliver raised his glass, gathering thirty or so members of his innermost campaign circle around.

"Everyone, you owe yourselves a big hand." I took his drink so he could applaud them. "Tonight would not have been possible without you. Truth be told, *every day* I'm in office would not be possible without you. Because you're here for so much more than these extravagant outings with colleagues and friends and like-minded people. As much as we love good food, better company, and *great* times together, you've made a commitment to American values that leave no one behind. You've made commitments not just to me, but to work hard for the betterment of this country and for the good people of our district, so they have the resources to improve their lives and the lives of those they love."

The applause was intense and sincere each time Oliver paused in his thanks, which were equally intense and sincere. At last he held up a hand and spoke softly, almost intimately, into the hush of the crowd hanging on every word.

"But let the *real* thanks come from the mother who can now earn a living wage to support her family, and the father who doesn't have to see his child suffer from the lack of affordable healthcare. The kids who can go learn and play in safety."

The electricity in the air was tangible as the congressman drove it home. "And let the thanks come this November, when we are asked back to Congress to keep making positive change in people's lives! Channing! What's the running total as of tonight?"

"Eleven point six million and *countinnnnng!*" Channing broadcast from the back of the group, seated regally at the pergola bar, waving an oversized frozen margarita to the tune of the night's campaign donations. The crowd went wild.

As the din died down and people resumed their conversations, Oliver picked up his glass, ordered a drink for me, and steered us both toward a loveseat near the fire. The burning logs popped, and embers twisted upward in an invisible spout before disappearing against the dark sky. We had almost had a chance to talk when a thin, tall woman wrapped in a cream pashmina bustled up to us on legs surrounded by extravagant layers of mauve ballgown. She came in hot, with a relentless stream of campaign finance data.

"Sharon," Oliver finally cut in, "have you met Natalie?"

She looked annoyed to be interrupted. "Ah, yes. The decorator."

"I don't think we've met," I said, turning to shake her hand.

She barely made the effort to smile. "Charmed," she said, turning back to Oliver.

"Hey, Sharon, can we catch up on the campaign figures Monday? I think I'm about shot for the night." Oliver was diplomatic, but Sharon was miffed.

"Sure," she clipped. "I suppose chatting about throw pillows is more important than campaign funding two months out from an election. I'll send you an invite for Monday at seven." And with that, she turned on her heel and left the rest of the oxygen for the fire to feed on.

"Did she mean a.m. or p.m.?" I asked Oliver over the rim of my drink.

"She means a.m.," he said with a sigh, "but I would prefer neither. Sharon can be a handful, but she's a force to be reckoned with. Don't take her rudeness personally."

I settled into the loveseat. "I guess even elected officials can't escape annoying coworkers. Do you ever get a free minute to just be a private citizen?"

"It's a rare and glorious moment, for sure," he said, getting comfortable beside me. "But when I do, I usually prefer spending it by myself."

"Considering you're surrounded by people all day, I can understand that. What do you like to do when you're finally by yourself?" I held my palms toward the firepit, absorbing its warmth on the breezy rooftop.

"Well, you already know a couple of them," he said, elbow on the back of the loveseat, leaning his chin on his hand. "I'm big into jazz. Old movies. Any good movie, really. But other than that, when I get the chance, I like whipping something up in the kitchen or just taking it easy."

"What do you usually 'whip up?' I asked, sipping my drink. "Maybe I can swap you a recipe for my Lazy Lasagna."

He laughed. "If you have a way to make lasagna go quicker, I'm all about it. I usually don't have enough time to cook half the things I want to."

"You don't look like you sit on the couch a whole lot," I noted, recalling a vision of his glistening wet, post-shower body.

He scratched behind his ear bashfully. "Yeah, well, I try to hit the gym a few times a week. Even if I can't fit in a full workout, I'll get on the rower for eight minutes and try to go at least 2,000 meters."

"I have no idea how much that is, but it sounds painful," I said, smoothing back an errant piece of hair the wind whipped into my mouth. "I'm embarrassingly ignorant about anything sports. I was more of a theater kid."

"Theater, huh? Are you a triple threat?" He pulled a knee up onto the seat cushion, turning toward me.

The reference made me smile. "If by 'triple threat' you mean set design, construction and painting, then yes."

"Ahhh, that makes sense. You were born with the visual, three-dimensional art gene. What was your favorite show to work on?"

"*Into the Woods*, by far," I answered, looking past the rooftop ledge at the skyline beyond. "But what stuck with me about it had nothing to do with design. It was the deeper meaning to the show."

Oliver gave a thoughtful nod. "You mean, 'Careful the things you say; children will listen'?"

"That's such a good one, and God, don't I know it?" I thought of Aiden and smiled.

"Or 'Be careful what you wish for—wishes come true'?" Oliver guessed again.

I rubbed my chin. "The one I was thinking of was 'Anything can happen in the woods.'"

As if timed to hit our own scene's downbeat, Efrain and Kylie hung over the back of the loveseat between Oliver and I, completely inebriated and insisting Oliver take a Fireball shot with them and a group of staffers.

"Alright, alright ... what are we toasting to?" he asked, getting up. "Two more years!" was overridden for an emphatic "No sleep till November!" which set the drunk twentysomethings alight. I wondered if they realized they were referencing a Beastie Boys song from their boss's adolescence.

Oliver handed me a shot glass and told me to skip it if I wanted, and then we all slung them back, liquid Red Hots coating our throats like a libertine's cough syrup.

Instantaneously, Sharon's voice cut through the noise. "Oliver, can I talk to you for a moment?"

"Only if by 'a moment' you mean the rest of the night, Sharon," Oliver cracked, as the Chief of the Fun Police pulled him aside.

Sharon didn't look amused. "I think you should just remain cognizant—"

"Of course, Sharon," Oliver interrupted. "They all know to take a cab wherever they go, or to just get a hotel room here tonight from the room block." Just to make the point, he bellowed out a reminder to all and sundry.

Sharon nodded primly. "I was speaking more to the *optics* of ripping *shooters* with staffers born after 9/11."

"No one calls 'em 'shooters' anymore, Sharon," Channing sang out as he rolled past with a drive-by zinger on his way to the bar.

Sharon was undeterred. "And can you please limit your visibility with the decorator? That's all we need is someone sneaking a picture of you two and blowing it out of proportion. What a complete distraction from not only your reelection, but the whole Marques—"

I was weirdly flattered to be on her radar. Oliver reassured her as blandly as possible, then excused himself with a tilt of the head and a nod in my direction to tell me to follow.

Back inside, just past the hostess stand, he stopped, leaning close to my ear. "Would it be a little too presumptuous to steal you away from the party and show you something? Something I could use your professional opinion on? Would that be selfish of me?"

"It's definitely selfish of you, but I should probably earn my keep given the jet fuel," I told him, trying to mask my excitement. He chuckled and gestured toward the elevators. I didn't know where we were going but the idea of going anywhere, just the two of us, was a far better ending to the evening than I had expected.

We exited out the back of the hotel to avoid any unwanted attention, Danny the driver right on time. I slid to the far side of the back seat, and Oliver came in behind me, sliding right up beside me into the middle seat.

My breath tripped over itself. That was an ... unusual seat choice. I felt the urge to lean into the warmth of his body and wondered how many drinks he'd had over the course of the night. After all, Channing had promised me Oliver would "get more fun" as the night went on. But what kind of fun was I in for?

A couple of sweeping turns dipped me toward Oliver's lap. I steadied myself with a hand on his knee, then loosened my grip, but let it remain there. I thought I could feel him shimmy closer. New car smell mingled with Oliver's now familiar, intoxicating aftershave.

"What's been your favorite part of the night so far?" he asked, breathing into my hair.

This. Definitely this, I thought, even as I told him how much I enjoyed meeting Daphne.

"I'm thrilled you two hit it off. You're going to make an incredible difference for her big project," he said. "I knew you'd sparkle tonight."

I blushed and felt him lean closer. "I hope you're having fun," he said softly.

I turned my head to meet his eyes. "Fun?" I asked. "I'm having an absolute ball."

He held my gaze with a bewitching smile. "Good. You hungry at all?"

"I don't know how I could be," I replied. "Dinner was delicious. And dessert, oh my God." I rubbed my belly, which the dress thankfully did a good job of keeping comfortably snatched.

He watched me in extended silence. "I'd like to cook for you sometime," he finally said, as if he'd been mulling the idea. It felt special and private, and my breath hitched.

"I'd love that," I replied, then cast my eyes away, buckling under the heat of the moment. "What do you like to cook?" I asked him, a coil of hair falling into my eyes.

"What do you like to eat?" he replied, sweeping the hair back from my face and tucking it behind my ear.

Heat flooded into my cheeks at the sensation. "Oh, I'm ... not really picky. I do love Italian though," I said, glancing up at him.

"That's my specialty," he flashed a smile. "Maria taught me all her tricks and secret recipes."

"Sounds like I'll be getting my own private chef?"

"Trust me, some days I wish I'd become a chef instead," Oliver replied.

We sped down Interstate 95 and branched off on another highway, chatting as fluidly as the drinks had flowed at Marcello's. When I finally looked up, we were approaching the Claiborne Pell Bridge—the gateway to Newport, as Oliver described it. It was lit up in splendid suspension, lights dotting the inky sky above the matching blackness of the chilly Narragansett Bay. As much as I wanted to know where we were headed, I thought better of asking and let the moment take us there.

We cruised along Ocean Drive. I cracked my window and closed my eyes for a moment to breathe in the sea, pulled in by the undertow of seaside nostalgia. Towering mansions with five, six, or more chimneys stood like sentinels in the night. I'd only seen pictures of Newport's "cottages," but I knew how breathtaking these homes were and, in the vast chasms of dark space between them, could imagine how stunning the drive would be by daylight.

The car finally slowed and an iron gate swung open. A sign on one gatepost read "Pebble Bluff." The tires crunched on gravel drive, winding back through the blackness, no moon to illuminate our path. We stopped in a circular driveway before a massive, completely dark house.

"Thanks, Danny," Oliver told the driver, hopping out of the car and jogging over to my door.

"Be careful," he said, giving me his hand. "It's really dark. Don't want you turning an ankle in those heels."

"Thanks," I said, the warmth of his palm enveloping mine. "I'm sure the Fireball won't help either."

"You and me both, sister," he admitted, guiding me up the front steps.

Oliver punched in a code and then pushed open one of a pair of large doors. Stepping inside, my heels echoed on the marble floor. He closed the door behind us and hit the nearest light switch, suddenly illuminating a grand staircase and a sweeping foyer. "Welcome to my childhood home."

The words left me awestruck. The grandeur would've been enough to take in, but this wasn't just any old Newport mansion, it was *this* one. My mind flashed back to our first flight up to Providence, when he told me about his parents, his sister, their beloved cook Maria, tormenting the nannies. It had all happened here.

"Oh, wow," I breathed, head craned upward as I turned to take it in.

"Let me show you around." He led me through the house, turning on lights room by room. The place had the faint, not unpleasant smell of being shuttered for a while. Some rooms had dust cloths draped over furniture and artwork hanging on the walls. It was a home, but frozen.

Excitement built in Oliver's voice as he led the way, but not about the intricate joinery of the wainscoting or crystal chandeliers bespoke from Waterford. It was a tour through the memories of his youth.

"And here, in my dad's old study—oh, God. I don't know if he ever found out, but when I was about ten, I pried up a floorboard in his atelier, just up that spiral staircase. He had his art supplies up there, and I would play pirate ship while he was downstairs working at his desk. There was this one floorboard against the wall by his easel that always stuck up in a funny way." He started mounting the steps two at a time as I tried to keep up in heels.

"It took me weeks to build up my courage," Oliver was saying, "I was *sure* there was some kind of treasure map hidden under that floorboard. One day, I used an oyster shucker I pocketed from Maria and yanked it up. Of course, there was no treasure map, and I was left with the problem of how to put the board back in place without my father noticing."

"You must've been an adventurous little boy to play with," I mused, reminded of my own son for the second time that night.

"I guess it depends on who you ask," Oliver turned to me, face shifting expression with a sudden thought. "I'm sorry I just dragged you all the way up here. I forgot you had heels on."

I popped them off and dangled them from my index and middle fingers. "Problem solved," I said. "I'm loving this tour. It's like I can see you and your family and the staff bustling around here all those years ago ..."

"Not *that* many years ago," he stressed, running fingers through his hair. Our eyes connected. "Anyway, what I really wanted to show you was the East Wing."

"Are you kidding?" I asked. "We've only seen the West half so far?"

"Yeah, of the main house, anyway."

"The *main* house? There are others?"

"The cabana, the guest house, you know," he said as if I did. "We'll skip those for now."

We made our way down from the atelier and across the house. A door opened to a corridor that was all glass on one side, looking into the starry blackness. It led out into what felt like a separate house.

"This is the East Wing," Oliver announced as we emerged into an empty great room under a cathedral ceiling. "You can't see it now, but it faces the ocean. Madeleine and I used to call this part the Sunny Side. It was a favorite for hiding and playing when we were little. Good spot to do our own thing and stay out from underfoot."

The East Wing had clearly seen better days. The two-story room we stood in was mostly a shell, barren of furniture. I scanned the walls and floor, surprised to see water damage. Some areas were still covered in tarps.

"What happened here?" I asked, my footsteps echoing in the empty chamber.

"A Nor'easter ripped off some roof a few years ago." He came up beside me. "Everyone had already moved out. My mother was ready to be rid of the whole estate, but I convinced her to keep it. Told her I would update it for my own residence and visit more often. Which I sometimes do, but the work in Washington keeps me away more than I'd like. This place deserves a consistent presence. Then again, if I'm not reelected in November, I could come back here and just pick up where I left off. In any case, I'd like to restore this wing to its original glory."

"It could really be magnificent," I said, envisioning the possibilities. My teeth chattered and I folded my arms against the salty chill of a room that had been closed off to life for too long.

Oliver approached quietly from behind, resting his hands on my shoulders, rubbing my upper arms to warm them. I closed my eyes. I wanted to revel in the contact, but Dana's words echoed in my head. *Keep it professional. Even if he is flirting, where do you honestly think it could ever go?*

I wandered away from him through a grand set of French doors into an adjoining room. It was an airy library, with two stories of packed bookshelves and a sliding mahogany library ladder to reach them. The fourth wall had no shelving, just more panoramic windows facing East. The few items of furniture were draped in dust cloths, except for an antique green velvet chaise that probably dated back to the turn of the twentieth century.

Oliver walked over to a shelf in the corner and carefully selected a record, removing it from its cover. He placed it down on an old record player not unlike the one in the shop that afternoon a few weeks ago. He dropped the needle, and a sweet jazz melody began to play as I circled the room.

"This place is absolutely gorgeous," I said, running my fingers along tight rows of book spines.

"You like it?" he asked.

"Like it? I love it. How could I not?"

He walked up beside me again. "Well, if you love it … I'd love it if you'd take the lead in bringing it back to life."

I turned to face him. "The East Wing?" I asked, taken aback. "The Sunny Side?"

"The Sunny Side," he repeated, shifting to face me, arms at our sides.

I felt his fingertips brush mine. My breath shortened, the heels I'd been holding dropped from my hand. His hands gathered mine as he pulled me toward him in a gentle spin. His left hand settled at my waist while his right held onto mine, and we began to dance.

"So will you do it?" he asked softly.

I felt the pull of his gravity.

"I would love that," I whispered, allowing my cheek to rest naturally on his shoulder as he twirled me around the room. It was like we were floating, him holding me close, hand low on my back. I could feel him breathe in my hair.

His fingers alighted on my chin as he pulled my face up toward his, lips parted, eyes aching … and a buzz came from his pocket. We startled apart as he reached in, annoyed, and clicked the phone over to voicemail. He pulled me back into his arms, and the buzzing throbbed in his pocket again.

He sighed and took the phone out, letting out a "tsk." His face hardened as he shifted his weight to one side.

He answered the call. After a long pause, he muted the phone and looked at me with disappointment. "I'm sorry, it's Sharon. Her hair's on fire. Make yourself comfortable. This could take a while."

I nodded silently as he exited the library, heart still thumping in the wee hours of the morning. I paced the room, investigating the books and wondering what it would feel like to leap onto the rolling ladder and ride it across the library. Probably not the best look for him to re-enter to. I took my time scanning the shelves, reading each neatly aligned spine, categorized and alphabetized. I picked up an old hardbound copy of *The Great Gatsby* and opened it, a yellowed notecard dropping to the floor.

I picked it up, glimpsing the messy cursive of a bygone era:

With fond memories of Pebble Bluff behind me. Alas and alack! For Evangeline, a souvenir of a pleasant summer, from one who was almost made to feel like—a guest.

—F. Scott Fitzgerald

Jesus Christ.

I returned the card to the book, and the book to its shelf. My fingers ticked over the other Fitzgeralds, landing on *Tender Is the Night*. I pulled it out, shook it to make sure no letters worthy of gifting to the Smithsonian fell loose, then curled up on the fainting couch in my gown to read.

14

SUNNY SIDE UP

Flat gray light tiptoed into the library, announcing the dawn. I rose up on my elbows upon the firm velvet chaise to discover an afghan had been draped over me while I slept. The library smelled faintly of leather and firewood, but the prevailing aroma was freshly brewed coffee.

I sat up abruptly and looked around. The sweeping ocean view out the wall of windows was stunning, even though the sun had not yet crested the horizon. Turning around, I discovered Oliver seated at the lacquered mahogany bureau in the glow of his laptop, sipping from a white porcelain mug.

"What time is it?" I asked, swinging my legs to the floor and trying to get my bearings.

"Not yet six," he said, looking up from his work. "Do you have somewhere to be?"

I wasn't awake yet. I had to think about it, "No, I don't think so." I relaxed back on the couch, rubbing sleep from my eyes. "Thanks for the blanket. I guess I was asleep when you came back. Were you up all night?"

He pushed back his desk chair to walk over and settle beside me on the couch. He had changed out of his tux into a T-shirt and sweatpants. "I got a couple hours of sleep, then I came back down half an hour ago to get some emails out of the way. You were out cold when I finally got Sharon off the phone last night. I didn't want to wake you, so I went upstairs."

"I'm sorry I fell asleep."

"Don't be." He rested a warm hand on my knee, face silhouetted by soft morning light, his eyes holding mine in suspension. "I'm sorry I took so long to get back to you."

Then he looked down and ran a hand through his hair. "You know, of all the things that could've kept me up last night, the only one that actually did was knowing you were asleep on the couch down here by yourself."

I waited to see if he would say more, but he stood up to head back to his desk. "Feel free to go back to sleep. It's still early."

There was no way I'd be able to close my eyes again. "I think I'm up for the day," I told him, following him to the desk as he took a seat in the high-backed green leather rolling chair.

"I don't want to make you feel rushed," he said, "but Mom and Madeleine are hoping I'll join them for breakfast this morning. They knew I'd be in town for the gala."

My stomach fell. "Ah. So, uh, do you need me to get out of here?"

"What? No." He looked confused. Then a smile stole across his face. "I guess I should have led with, 'How do you like your eggs?'"

I gaped back at him, unblinking. "Oh, you mean … you'd like me to *join you?*"

"Well, you did sleep over." He laughed. "I know a family breakfast invite probably seems weird. No offense taken if you'd rather I have Danny drive you back to the airport and get you home."

"No, no. I'd love to join you. I just …" I looked down at the previous evening's ensemble, now a bit worse for wear. "I'm not sure your mom and sister will get the right idea if I show up in last night's ball gown and smeared makeup."

He chuckled. "That's totally fair. I could go for a shower myself. Why don't I show you to Maddy's old room? See if there isn't something you can dig out of her closet. The bathroom should have every-thing you need. I'll take you up there now."

We passed back through the East Wing and down the solarium corridor. In the daylight, the view was spectacular: a terraced garden leading down to crags overlooking the Atlantic.

"So where will we meet your family for breakfast?" I asked, antici-pation giving way to anxiety. I would've been nervous meeting them under normal circumstances, let alone one where I had no idea what I'd be wearing.

"Mom's house is just down the road. I'll drive us there," he said, arms swinging as we strolled.

"Oh … I thought you said this was your childhood home."

"It is. After the divorce, Mom didn't want to be here anymore. Then my grandmother passed away, right around that time, so Mom decided to move into Sea Thorn when her parents left it to her. She made a bunch of updates and it's been her primary residence ever since."

What a lovely luxury, to leave the reminders of a failed marriage behind, I thought to myself. I was on track to be wrapped up in litigation for a couple years getting Caleb to buy me out of our house.

Oliver and I reentered the foyer. He started up the broad, circular stairs two steps at a time. I trotted after him and down the corridor until we reached the third door on the left.

"This is Maddy's room." He pushed open the door. It had last been occupied with any consistency sometime around her college years, it appeared: floral prints and pastels, posters of nineties icons on the wall. I smiled at Alanis Morrissette.

"Make yourself at home," Oliver told me, leaning up against the doorframe. "I'm gonna hop in the shower and return some calls. Meet back up in two hours or so?"

I nodded and he bowed out, closing Maddy's old bedroom door behind him and leaving me to the sound of nothing but birds chirping outside her windows. I poked around the room a bit, feeling more at home than I would have expected. The untouched decor made it feel almost like time traveling. I rummaged through her wardrobe, which also looked like it had partied like it was 1999. To my disappointment, everything was a size two with a 32-inch inseam. What was it with all these tall, skinny bitches up here? Camille and Maddy's figures were more akin to Oliver's model "acquaintances" than mine. It was not going to be easy to find something that fit.

I dug through bell-bottom jeans and Tommy tube tops, denim jackets and miniskirts. And while floral print maxi dresses were temporarily back in style, the one I discovered in Maddy's closet would drag on the floor if I put it on. On the verge of meeting the women of Oliver's nuclear family, my only choices were to show up as Ally McBeal or Baby Spice.

Locating a colorful Benetton cardigan, a fitted white tee, and a pair of black leggings whose label read "cropped" but reached all the way to my ankles, I told myself that fit would have to trump fashion, given the circumstances. But first, I needed to get cleaned up.

I ran the hot water in the walk-in shower until steam filled the tiled *en suite* bathroom. I got in, hot water dousing my head, relaxing muscles that had slept but a few hours on a stiff couch. I lathered an Herbal Essences shampoo into my hair, a scent I hadn't smelled in decades, steamy botanicals wrapping me up in nostalgia. Suds teemed down my body as I rinsed off a night I could barely believe had happened.

I found a hair dryer and blew out my hair, then rooted through bathroom drawers until I found a dull-pointed brown eye liner and a crusty tube of mascara that I hoped wouldn't give me pink eye. Finishing off my neutral face with some lip balm and a spritz of Elizabeth Arden's *Sunflowers*, a true blast from the past, I was ready for footwear.

Madeleine's Keds were two sizes too big, so I slipped my own pointy black heels back on. While less comfortable than Keds, they still worked with the vintage sweater and leggings. I rolled up the sleeves and gathered my hair into a side ponytail just to make myself laugh. I was ready to guest-star on *Saved by the Bell: The Ancient Years*.

"Oh, *wow*," said Oliver as I came down the stairs, politely masking his chortle with a cough.

"You like my sweater?" I teased, turning left and right to model it.

"I'd like to unbutton it," he muttered through a smirk.

"What?" I asked, sure that I couldn't have heard him correctly.

He blocked my path before I could reach the last step, coming close enough that we were eye to eye. I felt a tug on the sweater, then another. I glanced down to see him undo the three oversized buttons, exposing the fitted white T-shirt beneath.

"There," he declared. "*That's* how you're supposed to wear it."

I stared back, trying to read him.

Oh my God. I am getting a proper eye fucking from the congressman.

I bit my lip, warmth pooling inside me.

"I guess it's been a while since Maddy's cleaned out her closet," he finally said, moving aside so I could pass. "But you *really* pulled off the look, Natalie!"

I blinked a few times, trying to hold on to the moment, but it had already evaporated. I pulled the hair tie out of my gag ponytail and let my tresses fall back to my shoulders. Shaking my head, I confessed, "I can't believe I'm going out in public like this, let alone meeting your family."

"Don't be crazy," he said, flashing a smile. "You remind me of my high school crush."

He took my hand, his palm warm and broad against mine. "Let's get going," he said, walking us back through the living room, the dining room, the kitchen, and out through an anteroom to a porte-cochere big enough to fit four vehicles abreast.

On the other side was what he called the "car barn," which was basically a fancy, two-story garage. An army green G-Wagon, a pearl white Bentley sedan, and a zippy little cherry red Ferrari convertible from the sixties were lined up side by side.

"Decisions, decisions!" I tutted, inspecting the vehicles.

He brushed it off. "My dad is the big car guy. The 1965 Ferrari he left me before moving to Zurich. I got my appreciation for cars from him, but I'm not a fanatic. I just keep these three toys."

These three toys? "Toys," in my world, were what I literally tripped over back at home. But I wasn't about to worry about that now. After all, my chariot awaited.

Oliver opened the passenger door to let me into the Ferrari, which had been impeccably maintained. I slid onto the cool tan leather and ran my fingers along the polished wood dash. The signature horse reared up at the center of the shiny, slender, wood grain steering wheel.

Oliver jumped effortlessly into the convertible's driver's seat like the door didn't open. We backed out onto the crunchy gravel drive, sun warming my face, scent of sea air filling me with the sensation of having just arrived on vacation.

"I'll take you the scenic way," Oliver said, sliding his sunglasses on.

"Isn't all of it 'the scenic way?'" I asked, my head on a swivel.

His smile glinted in the sun. "Pretty much!"

Then we took off with a jolt. Gravel spattered backward and adrenaline flooded my system.

Winding down Ocean Drive, I felt like I was living my own *Ferris Bueller's Day Off*. The scent of algae at low tide sparked memories from my childhood in Pismo. The damp breeze sunk into Maddy's knit sweater, cooling my skin. Glancing over at Oliver in profile, dark sunglasses perched on his cheekbones, hair billowing in the open breeze like the Stars and Stripes itself, I couldn't remember a time that a drive made me feel this revived.

I gawked at the mansions speckling both sides of the road. "Oh my God! How many chimneys are on that thing? Wow, look at that Beaux-Arts facade!"

Oliver smiled over the steering wheel with quiet enjoyment. "I'll have to show you the real mansions after breakfast."

"The *real* mansions?"

"Yeah, The Breakers, Marble House, Rosecliff…"

The names rang a bell from a college lecture hall. "Oh, yes, I learned about them. The opulent summer homes at the turn of the century, before income tax was a thing."

"Yeah, the Golden Age!" he joked.

"You mean the *Gilded* Age!" I called back over the wind. "What was it like growing up in the same neighborhood as the Vanderbilts?"

"Ah, well, you know …" He shrugged. "Anderson was always a good pal. Kind of like an older brother, when we were little."

"You're friends with Anderson Cooper?" I exclaimed. "What am I saying? Of course you are. You're a congressman and you grew up down the road from his mother."

"Yeah, but Gloria and Anderson only summered here once in a while. They were mostly in New York and Paris."

I marveled at how Oliver's childhood intertwined seamlessly with the most glamorous parts of American history. I was resigned to him being far out of my league, but content to enjoy the ride while it lasted.

We approached the wrought iron gate of Sea Thorn, Oliver greeting the security guard familiarly. The gate gave entry to meticulously landscaped, rolling, rocky grounds, the main house overlooking the water in the distance. It was a four-story Victorian mansion with pale gray shakes, two spiraled turrets, a double-arched entryway, and a to-die-for wraparound porch. I didn't have time to count the chimneys, but there were a lot.

We pulled around the back to a view of three tennis courts and the ocean. Oliver led the way up the porch steps, past a row of lazy ceiling fans and an arrangement of tasteful, cream-upholstered aluminum porch furniture. He pulled open the door and led me in.

"Mom! Maddy! We're here," he shouted, hooking his sunglasses through his collar buttonhole and slipping off his loafers. I did the same with my heels, my bare, pedicured feet kissing the chilly wood floor.

Oliver led us into the open, sun-washed Victorian kitchen. My eye caught a row of blue Murano glass pendant lights dangling from the high, and clearly original, tin ceiling.

Oliver's mother was seated at a long French country table, sipping tea from a china cup. She was a petite, well-preserved woman in her late seventies, fully made up with brick-colored lipstick and wearing a navy herringbone pattern St. John knit suit, as if she'd just returned from church. Her white hair was pulled back in a tidy bun, show-casing pearl earrings surrounded by sapphires. They looked weighty enough to stretch her earlobes like Silly Putty.

Beside her stood Oliver's sister Madeleine, a large coffee mug in hand. She was as tall and thin as her high school wardrobe foretold, soft, silver-stroked hair tied back in a low ponytail. Her face bore some resemblance to Oliver's, natural but attractive and creased in the places one might expect of a woman of about fifty. Her outfit was much more casual than her mother's, a beige linen jumpsuit with canvas espadrilles and no jewelry.

His mother stood up stiltedly to hug her son. She seemed fragile, like the normal force with which he returned the hug might've broken her bones. Madeleine hugged him next. Then he introduced me.

"Mom, Maddy, Natalie came up from DC for the gala. She's been a godsend in designing the Capitol Hill house, and she contributed to the auction last night."

"Charmed," said Oliver's mother, extending a dainty white hand.

"Pleasure to meet you, Mrs. Thames," I replied, taking it gingerly.

"Please, call me Agatha."

Madeleine smirked over her coffee mug, stepping forward to size me up. "Such a rare treat of you bringing a friend up, Oli. And what taste! I could swear I loved the same sweater in another life."

I smiled sheepishly, glancing down at the ensemble. "You must be Madeleine. And yes … thank you for involuntarily outfitting me this morning. I'm afraid I wasn't prepared to stay overnight, and I didn't think last night's gown would be quite the right thing for breakfast."

Madeleine shot a look at her brother at the mention of my staying overnight. My spine zippered up as she extended a handshake and a decorous nod. "Lovely to meet you, Natalie."

Based on the reappearance of her old sweater, I knew she'd easily, although inaccurately, assume some level of intimacy between Oliver and me. But she would likely peg it as spur-of-the-moment, at best. A girlfriend would have known to pack a bag. I wanted to give some clue that I wasn't just a fly-by-night floozy who fell into Oliver's bed after a bunch of after-party cocktails.

"Likewise. You know, Oliver's told me stories about the two of you growing up. But then when he asked me to take a look at Pebble Bluff to start thinking about a renovation, it really brought all the stories to life."

"Not sure Oli's the most reliable narrator," Madeleine said, leaning on the *most*. "You'll have to take whatever he says about me with a grain of salt."

Oliver drew an arm around his sister's shoulders, "I have only said flattering things, Maddy."

"Proving my point." Madeleine winked wryly, shaking her head. "Not reliable in the least."

"How was the gala last night, Oliver?" Agatha asked, having reseated herself at the table. "Any old friends?"

"A couple, yes," he told her. "We had Herr Constapel and Ava."

"Ugh," Agatha rolled her eyes and took a sip of tea, "she's such a braggart."

"And we had Tom and Averie Wetherell ..."

"Mmmm, I'm sure he made a show of things," Agatha nodded.

"... and of course Daphne Atwood, who chatted up Natalie all night about her Foundation's new campus for victims of domestic violence. Daphne was the winning bid for Natalie's interior design and decorating consultation."

"Oh?" Intrigued, Agatha looked up from her steaming cup. "Well, that's something new."

"She seems like an impressive woman," I said, though I worried I might say the wrong thing. Agatha obviously had opinions. "I'm really looking forward to working with her."

"Yes, Daphne has always had a good head on her shoulders," Agatha agreed. "About as fun as a paper straw, but the woman knows how to make things happen. Although I have to warn you, she's not known for being the easiest client to please."

"I'm sure I'll have my work cut out for me, compared to the delight it was working with your son." I beamed a smile over at Oliver.

Madeleine arched an eyebrow and almost succeeded in suppressing a smirk. "Did he make you use *the beanbag chairs?*"

I laughed. "Only one of my greatest décor challenges!"

"I can tell when I'm about to get ganged up on." Oliver shook his head, but he was smiling. "So I'll let you all get on with it and I'll start breakfast. What are we in the mood for this morning? Omelets and bruschetta? Apple-walnut mochi pancakes with mascarpone?"

Wait, what? Oliver was making breakfast? I glanced around the room, confused.

"I've been *dying* for your shakshuka, Oli," Madeleine wheedled.

"Not for me," Agatha trilled. "All that tomato will wreak havoc on my esophagus."

"I thought they put you on a proton pump inhibitor, Mom," Oliver said, turning to her.

From behind her mother's chair, Madeleine waved his question away as if to signal, *let's discuss later.*

"My system would not tolerate it," Agatha continued, unbothered, as her daughter cringed. "Such flatulence like I've never experienced!"

Oliver looked like he wished he hadn't mentioned it. I suppressed a giggle. "That's alright, Mom, you and Maddy can catch me up on the doctor's notes after breakfast."

Agatha was undaunted. "And the *diarrhea*! Ugh! One night I barely made it to the toilet. They don't warn you, these doctors."

Oliver changed the subject loudly. "So what can I make you for breakfast, Mom?"

"I know *my* appetite is positively whetted, Mother," Madeleine muttered over her coffee cup.

"I thought Maria made all the meals around here," I finally cut in, trying to help change the subject. I wasn't sure why Oliver was taking over for the family cook.

"Oh, good Lord," said Madeleine, "that poor woman would be a hundred and twenty today."

"Maria, bless her, passed some years ago, dear," Agatha confirmed. "Don't think us total barbarians for eating in the kitchen. It's just on these special occasions when Oliver prepares something for us. We'd be in the breakfast room, but then I'd hardly get to talk to my son."

I wasn't going to say it, but questions about where the meal should properly be eaten hadn't even entered my mind.

"Was Maria the one who taught you to cook?" I asked Oliver.

"She was!" he replied, rummaging through the cabinets. "I have all her old recipes. I guess you could say I kind of carry on in her tradition when I visit here."

"Natalie," Madeleine queried, "did Oliver not tell you about his stint at the CIA?"

Now I was even more confused. "You're a spy too?"

"No, no—" Madeleine clarified, amused. "The *other* CIA: The Culinary Institute of America. Napa, not Langley."

"Oh," I said, unaware it even existed. Honestly, I wasn't sure which version would've made more sense.

"Oli, how have you managed to keep your great talent a secret from Natalie?" Madeleine prodded.

"It didn't come up," came his muffled response from the walk-in pantry.

Madeleine's eyes flickered from Oliver to me. I could see her wondering just how deep our "relationship" went as she changed the subject to her tour of Central America just a couple weeks prior, catching him up on her adventures with a group of friends.

He emerged from the pantry with his hands full. "Oli, I wanted to give you these beans."

"Magic beans?" he teased.

"No, I gave those to my other brother Jack." Apparently, the deadpan thing ran in the family. "*Coffee* beans, from Apaneca. Along the Ruta de las Flores in El Salvador."

"Oh, wonderful," he said, taking the unlabeled, black coffee bag from her. He squeezed it in one hand, holding the degassing valve to his nose and inhaling deeply.

"Oooh, fresh!" he exclaimed, emptying his lungs.

"It should be," Madeleine replied. "They packed it the same day I was there. I bought it before they even put the label on."

Oliver scooped the beans into a hand-cranked grinder he took down from the shelf.

"I have a job for you," he told me, handing me the grinder and pantomiming a circular grinding motion.

Less than a minute into cranking the handle I noted I'd never had to work so hard for a cup of coffee in my life.

"The work is what makes it worth it!" Oliver called over his shoulder from the stove, where he was starting the shakshuka.

When I finally delivered the small glass jar of coarse coffee grounds to him, he poured them into a stainless-steel French press with boiling water and steeped it to full intensity. He frothed the rich, black liquid with heavy cream, vanilla extract, and sugar, adding a dash of cinnamon and nutmeg to the layer of foam.

"You're spoiling me," I said as I watched him work. "How am I ever going to enjoy a regular cup of coffee again?"

"I had my first truly transformative cup of coffee in Athens," he said as he worked.

"That little spot in Psyri with the graffiti?" Madeleine chirped. "The one where the two brothers who owned it made us an amazing freddo?"

"That's the one. The one we found when Mom and Dad left us to explore Athens on our own at thirteen and seventeen."

I looked back at Agatha, who was flipping through the Sunday paper. She looked up momentarily, as if trying to remember. "I didn't know we brought you along to Athens. I suppose we did."

Madeline widened her eyes in Oliver's direction, as he quietly shook his head. He pushed a mug to me and Madeleine across the center island, keeping one for himself.

"Let me know if it needs more sugar," he said, taking a sip.

Seated on one of the island barstools, I put my mouth to the steaming cup. Rich notes of almond, cocoa, and clove blended with the sweet, creamy foam as I rolled it across my palate. I was definitely going to need another.

I watched Oliver bustle about the kitchen, overlaid upon the mental image I'd constructed of Maria in decades past. It wasn't long before the aroma of fresh August tomatoes and bell peppers stewing in garlic, olive oil, and truffle salt enveloped the kitchen.

"I'd love to hear more about your time studying in Napa," I suggested. Madeleine took it as an invitation.

"He was a top student! We all thought he would become a celebrity chef."

"Oh?" I asked, looking at Oliver expectantly. "I guess you meant it literally last night when you told me you sometimes wish you'd become a chef instead. What made you change gears?"

Oliver was busy multitasking between the shakshuka, a spiced banana porridge for his mother, and a chive, mushroom, and goat cheese omelet for me. But Madeleine was happy to fill in. His conscience, she explained, wouldn't let him continue. She let the sentence hang in the air, either for dramatic effect or to give Oliver the chance to tell the story in his own words.

Taking the prompt with a frown, he added, "My time in Napa was brief. I had come back home for a visit and … that's when I found out about Carter."

"Carter?" I asked.

Madeleine picked up the story again, unsatisfied with her brother's lack of detail. "Oli had met this young man, Carter, a couple years earlier while volunteering at the soup kitchen over Thanksgiving weekend. Oli was so good with food and wanted to give back to the community. Carter came from a broken home, you know, no father around, single mother working to support the family, but still struggling with drugs. Carter hanging on by a thread, just trying to make it through high school. Oliver became the big brother he needed."

Oliver cast a stern look at his sister, like she was trying his patience.

She doubled down. "Oli, you did more for Carter than anyone ever had. Your friendship and guidance alone were invaluable to him, and there was nothing you could have done to prevent what happened."

So that had been his name, the friend who died while Oliver was away.

Oliver's jaw tightened, his movements quickened. "I already told her about Carter," he said, without looking up.

"I seriously doubt that," she murmured, taking the seat at the island beside me and forging ahead. "While Oli was away at CIA that year, Carter's mom had relapsed. Carter dropped out of school to take on a couple part-time jobs to take care of her, but he stopped taking care of himself."

Madeleine glanced up at Oliver to gauge his reaction. He seemed to be ignoring her. She turned back to me. "Carter was a juvenile diabetic," she continued, "but when his mother fell on hard times again, the money he would have otherwise used to buy insulin started going to all the other necessities his mother wasn't able to provide. They were like many people at the time. Couldn't afford health insurance, especially with a preexisting condition."

"That sounds awful," I commiserated.

"Yes, and it gets worse," Madeline explained. "Carter collapsed in the street one night, walking home from a double shift at the gas station. A good Samaritan brought him to the ER in a diabetic coma, but he passed away not long after arrival."

Oliver broke in then, pointing a wooden spoon tipped in red sauce to the ceiling, delivering the impassioned rhetoric I'd come to know as part of his DNA: "There were, and continue to be, so many injustices and failure points in our healthcare system."

He returned to the shakshuka and stirred in silence for a moment. "A couple weeks later," he added, "I couldn't stop thinking about it. It's funny, you know. Toiling toward mastery of the culinary arts feels out of touch when your friend literally dies in the street."

Maddy didn't jump in to say anything. I didn't say anything either. I watched Oliver stir the shakshuka with the tip of the wooden spoon until he raised his head to speak again. "I was crafting dishes for people who paid more for a bottle of wine than people like Carter earned in a year. Carter had to choose between insulin and food, while I was choosing between Grand Cru pairings."

"I'm so sorry, Oliver," I said, aware of how tepid it sounded in light of it all.

Madeline smiled at her brother with a protective warmth, then turned to me. "Oli decided to do something with his own position of privilege by fighting for the people who never got a fighting chance.

He applied to law school later that year. He represented economically disadvantaged people in the courtroom, and now he's representing them in Congress."

Oliver decided it was time to lighten the mood again. "And now I just cook for fun. Or whenever these two make me," he said, motioning with the spoon to his mother and sister.

I could've crawled over the countertop and pressed my lips to his. Was there *anything* unattractive about this man?

I noticed Madeleine noticing me looking at him, so I fixed my eyes on the omelet Oliver placed in front of me. Mouth already watering, I cut a bite with my fork, tendrils of melted cheese stretching across the plate.

The soft texture and deep umami flavors combined with creamy, mellow goat cheese and chive had my mouth orgasming. I might need another one of these too. The room fell silent for the first time as everyone dug into their breakfast, Oliver splitting the pan of shak-shuka with his sister.

"*Mmmmph!*" Madeleine savored her first bite. "Your sauce is just something else, Oli. And I love how you did the eggs sunny-side up, instead of poached."

"Speaking of Sunny Side," Oliver told his sister as he flashed me a smile, "it's specifically the East Wing I've asked Natalie to help me renovate. That is, when she's not working on the Atwood Foundation project, of course."

"How wonderful!" Agatha exclaimed from her porridge, coming to life once again. "I should hope that would mean we'll see you more often, Oliver."

"I should hope that too, Mom," he told her. "We'll see how my schedule goes leading into November."

As the four of us enjoyed breakfast, Madeleine regaled me with a couple more stories I wouldn't have heard from Oliver, but none as heavy as the one about Carter.

As we cleaned our plates, Agatha turned to Oliver. "Oliver dear, I'd like to show you the dilemma Duncan and I are dealing with in the garden."

Madeleine rolled her eyes to indicate she was already familiar with the subject as Agatha went on, earnest. "Duncan is insisting we move the hydrangea. Something about not getting enough sunlight since we built the gazebo. But we can't agree *where.*"

"Old Dunc might as well have a PhD in landscape architecture, Mom. You should probably just listen to him on this one," Oliver told her, mopping up his last bite of shakshuka with a piece of bread.

Agatha poo-pooed the comment. "If you'll just indulge me with your honest opinion after breakfast, Oliver."

"That *was* my honest opinion, Mom. Listen to your gardener," Oliver dismissed her. "And for that matter, *she's* the one whose opinion you want. Natalie has an eye for that sort of thing."

I straightened with a start in my chair at the surprise referral, as Oliver continued to gush. "She's seriously transformed the Capitol Hill house into something that should be in *Dwell.*"

"Oh, I like that magazine." Agatha looked at me with approval.

"Natalie sketched out everything by hand and sourced all the furniture and decor from specialty shops," he went on, my cheeks turning rosier by the second. "She even had the idea to finish the wine cellar walls in *azulejos.* Remember when we went to Portugal, Mom?"

Agatha had a faraway look for a second. "Yes … yes of course. Your father and I were inspired by the tiling in the palace in Sintra. Those *azulejos* were spectacular. And the fountain. Remember, I brought back a similar one for the garden?"

Oliver nodded, picking up his empty plate. "And you can show it to Natalie when you take her to look at the hydrangeas."

"Very well, then," she agreed, giving me a determined look. "Natalie, if you wouldn't mind, I'd be much obliged, seeing as my only son is too preoccupied championing the downtrodden to offer an opinion on his mother's garden."

"I would be honored and delighted to stand in for him on the matter." I bowed my head. "I also noticed your beautiful light fixtures here. Are they from Murano?"

"Yes, dear, they are!" Her eyes brightened. "I had them imported from Italy when I moved in here and renovated the house. You have a very good eye."

"That blue, you can't mistake it. You have very good taste," I told her. It was true. Agatha smiled back immodestly.

"Let me just change into my gardening togs. Please excuse me a moment." She rose from her chair. "Natalie, make yourself comfortable in the drawing room. I have a book on New England design on the table there that you may find interesting. Oh, and I believe there's also a photo album from when Oliver and Madeleine were children."

"*Really?* I think I'll have to take a look then." I looked over to see what Oliver's reaction would be, but he was soaping pans and didn't seem to be paying attention.

"I don't know why you won't just let Gloria do her job," Agatha quibbled on her way out of the kitchen.

"I've made it a point to clean up my own messes, Mom, and I'm not gonna quit now. Go show Natalie the garden, and I'll be out soon. It's a gorgeous morning."

Agatha led me into the drawing room on her way upstairs and pointed out the New England design book. I picked it up and thumbed through, half expecting to see Sea Thorn featured.

I could make out Oliver and Madeleine's voices over running water in the sink, and I found myself moseying back through the dining room toward the kitchen as I scanned the pages of the book. I could see them, just barely, without being seen.

Madeleine prompted Oliver with, "So … the Sunny Side …"

Oliver took her empty coffee mug.

"Is that where you both came from this morning?" she asked.

"It is," he said.

"And last night?"

Oliver glanced up from the sink. "Last night we had a lovely conversation."

"Oh, come on now." She cocked her head at him disbelievingly. "Conversation, my foot. My Benetton sweater says otherwise. How did she ever find that old thing, anyway?"

Oh, God. She thinks I'm a whore.

"I'm sorry to disappoint you, Maddy," he turned his head slightly, arms deep in dish suds, "but a conversation and a dance to *King Cole Trio* were the only things we had before I got an important call. Natalie fell asleep on the chaise in the library before I came back, and I went up to bed."

Whew! Not a whore!

Madeleine let out a sigh. "You know, Oli, you don't have to die on the barricades. You deserve to be happy."

"What's that supposed to mean?" he asked, head down, resuming his scrubbing.

"It means that it's OK to put down the phone and give in to romance once in a while. The Revolution will carry on. You're allowed to have more in your life than selfless causes and the occasional fling with a Monégasque heiress."

I heard him exhale, his shoulders drooping over the sink.

"I'm serious!" Madeleine pressed. "Granted, I know almost nothing about this woman, but for you to be bringing her by, even if it *was* incidentally, it must mean something. You must have some feelings toward her ..."

He continued washing dishes, so she walked over to the sink to finish the sentence. "Even if you maybe haven't admitted it to yourself yet."

By this point, I had abandoned pretending to thumb through the book. Eyes wide, I pressed my back against the wall beside the door frame between the dining room and kitchen and strained to hear over the kitchen clean up clamor.

"Yes," I heard him say, "I'm fond of her. Natalie is different."

"Good," Madeleine chirped. "At least we've established that. You know, Mom reacted favorably when I told her you'd be bringing a 'female friend' to brunch."

"Is that so?" Oliver asked flatly.

"She did. She would like nothing more than for you to meet the right person and have happiness."

"That wasn't exactly her reaction the last time, if I recall ..."

"Oh, Oli! You're not twenty-something anymore," Madeleine's

tone switched to exasperated. "You have so much to offer someone, and they you. You never know, you might still have children! Nothing would make Mom happier."

"Ha!" Oliver exclaimed. I peered around the doorframe to catch him snapping a yellow rubber glove into the sink.

Madeleine's brow rippled. "She's changed, Oliver. She's not the same person we grew up with. She's even admitted there's much she wishes she had to do over with us. With you, especially. I've made my peace with her."

"Sorry, Maddy, but the idea of Mother wanting more children around is a bit of a knee-slapper."

"And how much time have you really spent with her in the last decade or two to know?" Madeleine asked pointedly. Oliver thought for a moment. She had him there.

"Besides," Madeleine added, "She knows she's not going to get any grandkids from me."

"You mean your coming out had a mellowing effect on her?" Oliver asked dryly. "Or should I say *humbling* effect?"

"It definitely took the wind out of her sails for a while," Maddy equivocated. "But she's come around. I think she's grown quite fond of Beth."

"Where is Beth, anyway?"

"Leading a group of kayakers through Baja Sur. Back tomorrow."

"Things with you and Beth are good?"

"Couldn't be better. Of course, we spend plenty of time apart, given her work schedule, but it actually suits us. Makes the time together that much more satisfying."

"Time apart is hard for a lot of couples," he said. Their voices grew more distant. I guessed they were looking out onto the patio.

"I know that's been *your* excuse for quite a while," I heard Madeline say. "You owe it to yourself to give whatever this is a chance. Election or not."

An unintelligible grumble from Oliver. Maddy's voice again, more insistent now.

"Look, I don't want to see you so absorbed in fixing your country that you wake up one morning, an old windbag incumbent finally leaving office, with no love in your life. Or worse, scrambling to marry the first thirty-year-old who gets your dick hard again, because you're panicked, staring into the sunset of your political career."

Oliver's response was inaudible. Maddy's wasn't. "Until I met Beth, I didn't know what I was missing. All I ask is that you keep an open mind."

It seemed like a good time to not be caught eavesdropping, so I went back and sat down on the sofa, reopening the New England design book as if I'd never left. Oliver and Maddy made their way in a few minutes later.

I looked up as if surprised. "Oh, hi! You know, they have quite a few of the Newport mansions in here. I can't wait to see them in person."

"You mean you didn't dig out the old family photo album?" Oliver asked, walking over to the shelves to the left of the fireplace, then pulling out a heavy, leather-bound book with gold filigree. "This, this, you need a clearance to view, Natalie."

Madeleine swiped it from him and handed it over. "We'll give you the double polygraph once you get to the bathtub shots."

I took the heavy album from her and flipped the cover open just as Agatha puttered in. She noticed it on my lap and smiled. "Oh, good, you found it!"

Oliver swooped down to snatch the album from my lap. "Why don't we check this out when you get done in the garden?"

"Why don't you join us?" Agatha asked, hopeful.

"I have to return a couple calls I missed over breakfast," he said. "Let's reconvene in half an hour or so?"

"Madeleine?" Agatha turned to her daughter. "Will *you* join us?"

"I only know enough about hydrangeas to agree with Duncan, Mom," Madeleine replied.

"Very well then! It's evident that Natalie and I are the only ones with gardening sensibilities in this group!" Agatha harrumphed, then led the way into the sunroom. Oliver and Madeleine gave me sympathetic looks as I followed her shuffling feet out of the room. She chatted all the way, intent on providing all the fine points of the Great Hydrangea Debate for the previously uninitiated. After a pause to admire several other plants, we exited to the upper portico's 270-degree view of the garden. From there, we descended the deck steps, Agatha gesturing as she walked me through the timeline of garden development, including when elements were constructed, planted, and even buried. Several generations of family pets had been interred in favorite spots, each with a tiny headstone.

The Sea Thorn estate had belonged to Agatha's father Raymond and her mother Evangeline, and Agatha was the eldest of three daughters. She'd taken Sea Thorn over not long after her own children had set out into the world from Pebble Bluff.

"When I moved back to Sea Thorn, Oliver was adamant that I not sell Pebble Bluff," she told me as we strolled. "He promised if I kept it in the family, he'd settle down one day and make it his permanent home. Well, I don't need to tell you that day has not come, but he's always managed to keep one foot in it, thus thwarting my plan to sell it out from under his nose."

Stopping for a moment, she turned to me. "Are you from New England, dear?"

"California," I replied. "But I've lived in the DC area for twenty years now."

"And how did you and Oliver meet?"

"My friend Dana owns the brokerage that sold him the townhouse, and she recommended I finish and decorate the interiors for him," I explained.

"Ah, I see," she nodded, returning to her slow stroll. "So, you and Oliver are recently acquainted."

"Yes." I hoped it wouldn't count against me.

"I can tell he's quite impressed with your work on his new townhouse. And now you'll be restoring Pebble Bluff ..."

"Yes, it looks that way," I replied, hands clasped behind my back as we ambled. "What a fantastic project to be able to work on. I'm really looking forward to helping him restore the East Wing to what it once was."

Agatha paused and looked at me directly. "It would be lovely if the refurbishment had some sticking power, and Oliver settled back in again."

"When I'm done with it, he won't want to leave," I said with a laugh.

Agatha stared back. "Maybe *you* won't want to leave either."

"Um ... I ... pardon?" I asked, brows furrowing.

"A young woman like yourself, who appreciates fine living, may not want the completion of the renovation to mean the end of her time at Pebble Bluff." Cold suspicion in Agatha's eyes betrayed her polite smile.

Message received, Mrs. Thames. I took half a step back.

"Pebble Bluff is truly breathtaking," I said, threading the needle. "But I'm afraid even if I were to visit Oliver after the project is over, I'll always be tethered to Maryland, at least for the next eight years or so."

"Oh?" she raised an eyebrow and resumed walking. "And why is that?"

"My son Aiden lives there with me. He was away at camp for the summer, and now he's spending the rest of the month with my ex-husband." I decided to keep it simple and refer to Caleb in the past tense. No need to complicate matters.

Agatha nodded. "And has Oliver met your son yet?"

I was the one who paused our walk this time. "My relationship with Oliver is purely professional."

She gave me a look that made me feel like a third grader caught in a fib. I fumbled to explain, "I mean of course we've become friendly, and he asked me here for breakfast. But that was unexpected. I thought we'd be flying back to DC last night. But the evening got away from us after he showed me the house, and then I fell asleep in the library while he took a phone call."

Agatha's eyes softened. "You mean you and Oliver aren't in a relationship?"

"No, ma'am. Not at all. I mean, I really enjoy his company, but I'm just his interior designer." I shrugged my shoulders. "And now I suppose his friend."

"Well then. Are you *hoping* you and Oliver might become romantically involved?"

My breath caught in my throat. How was I supposed to answer *that* question?

I let my shoulders fall. "I don't even know how that would be possible, to be honest with you. I just restarted my career after a fifteen-year hiatus, and now I'm trying to juggle that with not failing as a single mother. And I still *feel* like I'm failing. All the time."

Agatha gazed off into the distance as we strolled, twisting the rings on her arthritic fingers, a soft smile on her face. She wore a gumball-sized Tahitian pearl ringed with diamonds on her middle finger and an old-fashioned signet ring on her pinky, but her fourth finger, where a wedding band would go, was bare. "When Charles and I were still married, we spent a lot of time away from Madeleine and Oliver. Of course, we had to. Business and life events and other expectations. If I'm being honest, though, I quite enjoyed the hustle and bustle at the time..."

Her expression clouded over. "But eventually, life quieted down. I wasn't as energetic as I once was. And I realized my window to spend time with my children while they still *were* children had passed me by."

We came to a stone bench along the path, where she seated herself and motioned for me to sit beside her.

"You're right to prioritize your son." She looked at me squarely. "Take it from me. You don't get a second chance."

I nodded, feeling the sting from imagining Victoria stealing the spotlight of Aiden's childhood.

"Yes, well, fortunately for my son, he's very attached to his father and the woman who replaced me, so it's not a terrible hardship for him when we have to be apart."

Like a groundhog, my resentment had poked its head out in that garden, looking for its shadow. But it was met instead by a curious look and compassion.

"Natalie, dear," she said, meeting my eyes, "if there's one thing I've learned from a lifetime of maternal missteps, it's that nothing can replace a mother's love and attention. Not unless you leave a gaping hole that drives your son to seek it elsewhere."

I flinched. I wanted to apologize for taking the conversation here, with a woman I barely knew, who lived multiple socio-economic rungs above me, and who happened to have birthed the man I was falling in love with. But now the floodgates were open, and I couldn't help myself. I had to make it clear to her that this was not my fault. I had been wronged.

"That woman stole my husband without me even knowing, and now she is stealing my son. She stole my life," I whispered, pain threatening to spill over my eyelids.

Agatha's clear blue eyes were steady. "Ah, but that's not *your* life, dear."

The statement sliced straight through me.

"At least," she added, "that's what I had to learn myself over time. Someone else built a life with the people I'd taken for granted. But people and lives can't be 'stolen' without their consent."

She said this as matter-of-factly as she would correct someone who called a pothos plant a philodendron.

I was thankful to already be seated, because I felt a little dizzy. But Agatha just smiled at me, a woman in whom she had spotted a splinter of herself.

"I had to learn that the hard way, but maybe you won't have to." She patted my hands and stood. When I joined her, she took me by the arm and resumed our walk, gesturing to the gazebo in front of us. "Now, *here* are my hydrangeas!"

- -

Oliver emerged from the other side of the gazebo not five minutes later, surprising us.

Agatha was thrilled. "Oliver! You decided to come take a look!"

"Not exactly, Mom," he replied with a hard expression. "I came to steal Natalie from you. I'm unfortunately needed back in Washington earlier than planned."

Oliver hugged his mother and sister goodbye, and I thanked them for a lovely morning. Agatha startled me with a farewell air kiss, both cheeks. "I really enjoyed our conversation in the garden, dear," she said with a nod. I smiled and thanked her.

Madeleine gave me a normal hug and said how glad she was she got to meet me, adding, "But next time, for the love of God, please leave my unfortunate wardrobe choices entombed where they lay!"

I laughed and promised that when I came back up for the renovation, it would be with a suitcase.

On the ride back, Oliver's mind seemed mostly to be elsewhere, but he leaned over to ask what I thought of his mother and sister.

"They were delightful," I replied honestly.

"I'm not buying it!" he cracked back.

"I'm serious!" I said, twisting toward him in the passenger seat, the breeze catching my hair and whipping it into my mouth, forcing me to pull it out again. "They're characters, for sure, but I like them. I'd welcome getting together with them again."

He glanced over at me, one hand on the wheel, the other behind me on the backrest. "Maybe you will."

15

BREAKING NEWS

I sipped a London Fog on my back deck, knees scrunched up on the love seat in an unseasonably chilly dawn. The creamy vanilla mingled with black tea and bergamot, coaxing me from sleep. After the cup of coffee Oliver had made the morning before, I couldn't bring myself to drink the usual K-cup swill.

The brambly morass that my own yard had become after Caleb left made a stark contrast to the view from Sea Thorn's upper portico. I considered doing something about it, calling a landscaper or maybe picking up a trowel myself. Okay, probably not that. I enjoyed landscape design, but not the manual labor part.

I reentered the house and walked upstairs to change. Looking around the bedroom I had shared with Caleb, I could suddenly see it with fresh eyes: the dated bed set and dresser from our wedding registry, the carpeting in dire need of replacement, the bed sheets and comforter that had faded with time.

A spark of motivation ignited. I was ready for a change, and I couldn't wait to pick out whatever I damn well pleased, without compromise.

Dana lit up my phone. She had been texting rapid-fire all day Sunday to hear about the gala. My silence that whole morning must've worried her, until I texted back from the tarmac that afternoon: *I'm going to have to tell you about it tomorrow. I'm still up here.*

Dana probably realized this was going to be a juicier update than she had expected.

"I'm shocked you're awake," she said when I answered on the first ring.

"Then why'd you call?"

"To wake you up to hear all about your weekend! Besides, this is my quiet time before the storm that will be Monday rolls in. Andrew's mom was just released from the hospital, and it's becoming more work for me than when she was *in* the hospital."

I cradled the phone between my ear and shoulder, picking at my cuticle. "I'm sorry, Dane. I know you've probably been going through a bunch of crap, and I've been scarce. If you need a break, come on over. I want to hear how everything is going. And I have a lot to catch you up on too."

"Yes, be there in fifteen minutes. I have less than an hour, but I'm dying to hear."

"Bring good coffee," I added.

"Didn't I give you a whole package of mushroom coffee?"

"Yeah, exactly why we need *good* coffee."

I could almost hear Dana's eyes roll on the other end. "See you soon!" she chirped, then hung up.

- -

She rang the bell right on time, letting herself in simultaneously. In spite of the early morning hour, she already looked picture-perfect in high-end athleisure, her complexion glowing. In her hand was a cardboard tray of paper coffee cups that smelled fantastic.

"You came bearing artisanal coffeehouse beverages!" I sang.

She kicked off her shoes and handed me a cup. "Seriously, Natalie, if you're not going to drink the mushroom coffee, I'll take it back from you. That little pack was sixty bucks!"

She joined me in the kitchen, where I handed her back her nearly unused hologram-bedazzled packet of instant "coffee."

"So, tell me about Andrew's mother," I said. "That sounds like a lot." Dana had always been such a good support to me, it had rarely occurred to me she might need one herself.

She got comfortable on a kitchen bar stool as she caught me up on the frustrations of caring for elderly parents, while still caring for children, balancing a career, and everything else. Any spare time she'd once had was nearly nonexistent.

"Is there anything I can do to help?" I asked Dana.

She gave a comforting smile. "Probably not, but thanks for offering. And for listening. It helps just to get it off my chest." She glanced down at her smartwatch, "I now have only thirty minutes to hear every single detail about your weekend."

I relayed the sequence of events, starting with what Oliver said to me at the townhouse Saturday evening about "completing the room" as the "femme fatale."

"Natalie." She stopped me there. "Why is he saying suggestive things like that to you?"

"I *told* you he's flirtatious, or what I can only interpret as flirtatious. But I actually don't need to interpret anymore …" Dana's eyes widened. "Never mind, I'm getting ahead of myself."

"Oh my God, you can't leave me hanging like that," she declared, leaning over the island on her elbows. I made her wait through each chronological event, starting with the terrifying flight, then the very eventful gala, including Daphne Atwood, meeting Camille, and the whole auction battle between Oliver and Vance.

"That is insane!" Dana gushed, "I wish I could've been there to see it. And then the cherry on top is it shored up your next big *client!* Big, *big* client! That is tremendous. I'm so happy for you."

But by the time I'd recounted my conversation with Oliver at the afterparty, followed by our little dance in the library and unplanned overnight at Pebble Bluff, she was fit to be tied.

"Oh my *God!*" Dana cried, hand shooting up to her mouth. Then her shock transformed into a warning. "Natalie … you have to be careful with that. That man has cycled through models before. You don't want gossip circulating among the people who are going to be your clients. It'll ruin your business before it even gets off the ground."

"I totally hear you," I told her, holding up my hand, "and let me assure you, nothing physical has happened between us."

Dana set her jaw, "I understand, but sometimes just the perception is all it takes …"

"You mean, like, if people found out I got invited to breakfast at his mother's house the next day?" I dangled it airily to see how she'd react.

She gasped. "No fucking way. You met *his mom?*"

"And his sister."

"Holy shit, maybe he *does* have it bad for you. What were they like? What happened??"

I went into detail about the whole morning, including the conversation I overheard between Oliver and Madeleine. "I mean, based on that, am I wrong to think we *could* become a thing? Maybe?"

"Wow, Nat, I'm speechless," Dana said, getting up to throw out her empty coffee cup. "I was not expecting all that. I feel like I'm getting a recap from Andrew's mother on one of her soaps. So, when are you seeing him again?"

"He asked if I wanted to grab dinner when he's back in DC at the end of the week," I said, peeling a banana. "But once we're past Labor Day, his schedule kicks into overdrive."

I took a bite of the banana. "And then I have the kickoff call for the Atwood campus when Daphne gets back that first week of September."

"Well, sounds like *your* dance card certainly filled up fast," Dana teased. "*Ahem*, I can't help but take a little credit for that …"

I swallowed my mouthful. "You get *all* the credit, Dane. You have my eternal gratitude and indebtedness."

"You can write an homage to me on the website my guy is designing for you."

"Oh my God!" I blurted. "I have that first meeting with him this week. Plus another with Jake Cohen to review the forensic accounting. Then Aiden starts school a week from today."

"Tell me about it. Where does all the time go?" She checked her watch again. "Well, let me know how everything goes ... and dinner. Especially dinner."

She slung her purse over her shoulder as she got to her feet, pointing a finger at me. "*Do not* sleep with him."

"That is, like, the *furthest* thing from what could plausibly happen at our next meeting," I insisted.

"I dunno," she said, pausing on the threshold, "the way things have been going with you two, not much would surprise me now."

"Ha ha, Dana. I promise I'll be good." I nudged her out the door and closed it.

Then I flopped down on the sofa, replaying scenes from the weekend in my head. I gave into the temptation to check social media, having posted the only photo I had of the gala: a selfie of me and Channing when I arrived at the townhouse that night. I wondered if the event photographer had captured a few frames of me flitting around.

I scrolled down my feed. Just below a targeted ad for perimenopausal hair growth capsules and what felt like Tricia Melman's thirtieth post about her new Westchester house, I gasped. It was very infrequent that Caleb posted anything, which made me do a doubletake when I saw the photo.

Posed on their front lawn, picture-perfect home behind them, were Caleb, Victoria and Aiden, with someone else: a speckly, chocolate English setter, tongue flopping out of its mouth. Aiden's arms were wrapped around the dog, and Caleb and Victoria squatted behind them in one big, smiling group hug.

"We've adopted!" the caption read, posted one day ago.

That can't be serious, I thought, mind racing. *Caleb has never wanted a dog. Caleb hates dogs!*

But there it was. I hadn't even heard it first from Aiden. I checked my watch and decided to FaceTime his iPad. No answer. I tried again. On the fifth ring, Aiden picked up my call from the kitchen table. I could see him stuffing blueberry waffles with gobs of butter and syrup into his mouth, slurping a glass of chocolate milk.

"Mom! Hi! We got a dog!!" he shouted through unchewed bites.

"*What*? You did?! What's its name?"

Through a mouthful of waffle, he told me, "Affogato."

"You forgotto?" I teased.

"Nooo!" he laughed, swallowing. "Her *name* is Affogato!"

"Oh, as in coffee poured over vanilla ice cream. Clever. I gotto it."

He smiled from one syrup smudge to another. "Look at her!" He tilted the camera down at a wiggly butt and slobbery mouth patiently awaiting fallen waffle bits. I could hear Caleb and Victoria at the table in the background.

"What a cutie!" I told him. "Well, it looks like you're busy …"

"I'm eating breakfast."

"I noticed …"

I heard Caleb whisper, "Tell her you have to finish up before soccer camp."

"I have to go to soccer soon," Aiden repeated.

"Okay, well, give me a call before bedtime and you can tell me all about soccer and the dog," I said.

"Okay, I will. Bye, Mom! Love you!"

He hit the "end" button before I could say it back.

I looked down at my empty cup and decided I needed a refill. I turned on the Keurig, not able to be bothered with making anything fancy again.

"That's not your life," Agatha had said. Hell, it wasn't even my husband. Now he was a dog person?

"People can't be stolen without their consent," Agatha's voice echoed in my mind. Oliver's mother had expressed regret about a mother-son relationship that was lacking, and she had also mentioned having to learn the hard way about taking her family for granted. Had her husband cheated on and left her too? It wasn't exactly something I could've asked her, although she certainly seemed like the open book type, at least in her advancing years.

Still, I couldn't help but wonder how Oliver's parents' relationship had deteriorated until coming to its inevitable end. How had mine, for that matter? According to Agatha, I had consciously or subconsciously let it.

Had I? I recalled a night, maybe three years ago, when Caleb still wanted me. Spooning me in bed, I had felt his erection pressed to my back like a gun.

"Seriously, Caleb. Find someone else to touch your dick," I remembered saying to him. Sure enough, he had.

I took my refilled mug and dumped in cream and stevia, stirring half-heartedly as I peered out the sliding glass door. I pulled out my phone and searched for "landscapers near me," a wealth of options instantly appearing. I scrolled for a moment, then sighed, clicked the screen off, and crawled onto the couch.

As I did, a text appeared on my screen that sent a pulse of electricity to my fingertips. It was a picture of the seascape view from the empty East Wing great room. Below it, *Can't wait to show you the sunset view.*

Heart pattering, I wrote back, *Looking forward to chatting about it at dinner.*

I let the glow linger, then sprung up from the couch, leaving my mug in the sink. Suddenly I wanted to go for a jog before it got too hot out.

- -

Toweling my hair after a shower, excitement bubbled inside me. Maybe it was a runner's high, but I felt like my dinner with Oliver next week couldn't come soon enough.

My phone lit up on the bed. It was a text from Dana:

OMG have you seen this?????

Below it, a link to a *Party Lines* story published that morning, with the headline:

"WHO WORE THE CONGRESSMAN BETTER? HIS DESIGNER OR HIS EX-WIFE?"

I felt like I'd been dropped off a bridge. I reread the headline, petrified. When I finally clicked the link, there in split-screen was a blurry image of Oliver helping me into the SUV in the back alley after the gala. It jockeyed for attention next to a photo of him with his hand on Camille's shoulder captured during the cocktail hour.

Ex-wife?? Camille was Oliver's ex-wife? My eyes scanned the story frantically, every nerve in my body in hyperdrive:

Representative Oliver Thames (RI-1) made the rounds at his fundraiser gala last weekend, held at the Rhode Island School of Design Museum. The event was well-attended by Congressional colleagues, Northeast socialites, and esteemed leaders of industry, all with vested interest in Thames's reelection.

*Perhaps more intriguing than what the Congressman wore at his black-tie affair is who was wearing him. Thames was spotted earlier in the evening, engaged in an intimate conversation with ex-wife and **WaPo** political colum-nist Camille van der Kamp. However, he was later spotted leaving the gala with a woman identified as his personal interior decorator, whose design services were auctioned off at his fundraiser for upward of $50,000.*

The room went wobbly. I had to sit down. Dana was blowing up my texts as I skimmed the rest of the story, stopping as it segued into campaign inside baseball. I picked up the phone the instant Dana called.

"I don't even have words," I began, pacing the living room.

"*What the actual fuck??*" Dana cut me off. "Crazy enough that your picture is in print with the congressman, but *Caleb* must have approved the story before it was published!"

"Well, if you remember, he was supposed to be at the gala that night, but I don't think he and Victoria ever showed."

"*Someone* from *Party Lines* showed," Dana pointed out. "Looks like Caleb, or someone, made a calculated decision not to name you in the article though. Maybe he stopped short of putting your name in print so he wouldn't look like a fool whose soon-to-be ex-wife upgraded for a hot political celebrity."

I could feel my forehead furrowing. "Dana, are you just trying to put a positive spin on it, or are you forgetting everything you warned me about? People's perception and gossip messing with my career?"

"This isn't just gossip, Natalie, it's photo evidence. This is *good publicity!*"

"Are you kidding me? All I look like in this article is Oliver's booty call. I'm not sure it gives the impression that I've 'upgraded' in any respectable way. Nor does it speak to anything about my design talents."

"Maybe *certain* talents …" She giggled.

"Dana!" I resumed pacing the floor again.

"Sorry! Bad timing, bad Dana!"

My mind raced to put everything together. "Caleb was also probably worried if people had my name and tracked me down, it could affect Aiden. I'm sure he's not interested in our son getting pulled into the public eye. Or witnessing his mother be bombarded by paparazzi."

"Totally," Dana said. "I have every confidence Caleb was strategic about it. But can we address the whole ex-wife thing?"

"It was *Camille!*" I pivoted hard on my heel. If I had been in a cartoon I'd have trodden a trench into the living room rug. "She's the woman I met talking to Oliver. Remember? I nearly overturned a cocktail table?"

"Oh, right," murmured Dana, "Yes, I remember."

"Yeah. Not a great first encounter with her. And this is not a great second."

"I thought she was the 'family friend?'"

I threw up my hands. "All news to me as well!"

"*News* being the operative word here," Dana underscored. "You should probably prepare yourself for inquiries."

"Inquiries from who??" I asked, entering a new level of distraught.

"I don't know! Inquiring minds! Tabloids and other political news outlets. This is a *sexy, young, rich* Congressman we're talking about, Natalie."

I thought I might puke. I was scared to look at my phone. "Shit! I have to take down that selfie I just posted."

"Take it down?" Dana asked, bewildered.

"I need to minimize my exposure," I said, pulling my phone from my ear to locate my post.

"Minimize? Are you kidding? This is your chance to pack your schedule with new business consultations. You've just been touted to the whole metropolitan area as the exclusive interior designer to the sexiest Congressman alive. You've gotta juice this exposure for all it's worth!"

"Are you *out of your mind?*" I yelled into the phone, holding it away from my mouth and putting Dana on speaker. "The last thing I need is attention from people looking for an interior designer who presumably gives happy endings. And Dana, hello? Do you remember what Oliver said when I got the wild idea he was gay? He was specifically suspicious of me delivering a scoop to *Party Lines* about his personal life."

"Well, you obviously didn't take that picture of the two of you getting in the limo," she reasoned.

"No, but I could've tipped someone off," I wailed, deleting the photo and all its likes and comments. "Dana, it feels like he's just beginning to let me in. He even texted me this morning about looking forward to showing me the view from the East Wing at sunset. The last thing I need is him pulling away because he thinks I've betrayed his trust. Especially after he introduced me to A-list clients at his gala. The worst possible outcome would be him thinking I'm a social climber."

"I dunno, Natalie. I think you're making a mistake by not playing up your fifteen minutes of fame."

"I don't *want* fifteen minutes of fame." I yelled into the phone. "I want *Oliver.*"

Dana fell uncharacteristically silent, and the implication of what I'd just said sank in. Had this turned into more than a fun distraction? Did I truly want Oliver?

"Natalie—"

"I have to go. I have to let Oliver know I had nothing to do with this story." I hung up on her. I started typing out a text to Oliver, rewriting each sentence, trying to find the right words that didn't make me sound like I was covering something up.

My phone lit up with a call from Channing before I could finish.

"Good morning, Cinderella," his voice rang. "I take it you found your way home from the ball?"

"Channing, have you seen that story Caleb published?" My words tripped over themselves.

"Of *course*, darling. That's why I'm calling." His tone was irreverent. "It appears you left a glass slipper behind."

"Channing, why didn't you tell me?" I moaned.

"*Tell* you? I just *called* you," he replied.

"No, I mean Camille. You played it off like she was only his girl-friend. Why didn't you tell me Oliver *married* her?"

"Girl, I didn't 'play it off' like anything," he rejoined. "I just learned about the annulment today, same as you."

I stopped in my carpet tracks. "Did you say 'annulment?' Like the marriage never happened?"

"That *is* the definition. Would you like me to spell it for you too?"

Why would Oliver get married to Camille, then get it annulled?

Channing went on as I reeled. "We are working through this new development. And Oliver received a refresher on why *not* to lie by omission to the Number One Confidante holding your entire campaign together."

I was shaking. "Well, what should I do now?"

"Do? You?"

"Yeah, like what if the media tries to contact me?" I wove the draw-string to my sweatpants around my finger until it couldn't go any further, then let it unspool and wound it up again.

"*Has* anyone tried to contact you?"

"No."

"Okay, so nothing to worry about," Channing said crisply.

I let a long breath escape. "Not *yet* anyway."

"Here's what we're going to do," he said, sensing my panic. "Any-thing that comes in, you just send it directly to me. Don't answer, don't acknowledge. Nothing. Nada. Just send it to me, and we'll handle it together. Screen your calls. Only accept ones you recognize. Let the rest go to voicemail, then repeat step number one."

Thank God for Channing. He had the sangfroid of an energy conglomerate spokesman after an oil spill. "Got it."

"People are going to try to track you down, but we'll be ready for them. Your gem of an ex-husband was spiteful enough to run the story, but self-motivated enough not to name you in it, so that will buy us some time."

"Thanks, Channing," I said, breathing out slowly.

"This is not a big deal, Natalie. You think Oliver hasn't been photographed leaving places with other women before? It's all been handled. Usually Sharon does this, but I told her I'm in charge of this one. Just stay cool."

"Okay, will do," I said.

"Good. That is all for now," he trilled.

"Channing, wait!"

"Mmmm?"

"I don't want Oliver to think I had anything to do with this story running," I said.

"Don't worry, you didn't strike me as the political media mastermind type."

"Caleb is trying to ruin me," I groaned.

Channing cut me off sharply. "Natalie. This story Caleb ran was just as much about hobbling Oliver's political ascendency as it was about spiting you. You were just conveniently in the frame. Caleb is trying to influence *politics*, dear. Trying to put more scrutiny on Oliver since Marques dropped Compton."

My mouth hung open. "I have no idea what any of that means."

"The scandal?" Channing asked, annoyed by my ignorance. "The news has been all over it for almost three weeks!"

"Not a clue," I shook my head. "I remember you guys mentioning it, of course."

"Natalie," Channing lowered his voice and spoke very deliberately and patronizingly, pausing between every word. "Do you know who the president is?"

"Of course I know who the president is," I snapped.

"Do you know who *our* party has nominated to run *against* the president in November?"

I paused. "Elena Marques?"

"That's right! Elena Fernandez Marques. You're doing great, slugger. Now, have you happened to overhear any news segments or read any articles about who was supposed to be Ms. Marques's choice for VP?"

"Was it the Compton guy?"

"Yes, yes, it was 'the Compton guy,' who, as we just established, has become political hazmat following the story that broke weeks ago about him taking …" He waited in vain for me to finish the sentence.

"*Bribes.* He was taking bribes, Natalie, as uncovered by the Office of Congressional Ethics."

"But what does that have to do with Oliver?" I asked.

"Good Lord," Channing said aloud to himself. "Do I have to teach an AP Government class on it? Here's the best I can do for you: Marques dropped Compton as her running mate. Now she's scrambling to find a replacement, heading into the final stretch of the campaign, with the National Convention next week, which may even get pushed back as a result. Now, would you like to buy a vowel, solve the puzzle, or do I need to spell it out for you? Oliver is on her shortlist for a running mate. As in … vice president!"

Channing paused to give it time to sink in, to be met only by my stunned silence. "That's why Oliver has stayed in DC so much during this recess. That's why we've all been flapping around like chickens with our dicks cut off the past few weeks. Natalie! Were you not *aware* of any of this?"

"I actually wasn't," I admitted, feeling stupider than ever. I had been so caught up in work and my own drama and the gala and flirting with Oliver that I went oblivious to the very public fact that he had been under intense political scrutiny all this time. Looking back, I recalled him referencing it, but he'd always brushed it off in modest Oliver fashion.

Channing let out a heavy sigh. He suddenly sounded very tired.

"Okay, well, consider yourself officially notified. I've got to return six thousand calls now."

"Channing, wait!"

"*What?*"

"Can I still talk to Oliver in the meantime? I mean, he just texted me this morning before we saw the story. We have dinner plans later this week."

"By all means, carry on, but please do your best to keep it out of the public eye for now, until we know what we're dealing with. Let's see what other photos surface or if anyone can verify where you two stayed that night."

"You mean…"

"I certainly do," Channing snipped. "I don't think it's likely anyone trailed the car to the house. But it's possible. But this is how it works: before we say anything, we figure out what they already know."

My panic fluttered anew. I tried to remember if any cars were behind us on Ocean Drive.

"Besides," Channing added tartly, "by the time your little candlelit dinner rolls around, I'm betting you'll be old news, and the media trolls will be fiending for fresh meat."

1 6

———

DINING IN

After hanging up with Channing, I noticed I'd missed a text from Oliver:

Call me when you get this.

My heart began to race. My finger hovered over the call button. I took three deep breaths and let them out slowly—something I'd seen in an ad—reciting the mantra "I am in control of my thoughts and emotions" until I felt as calm as I was probably going to get.

I finally pressed Call.

It rang several times before Oliver picked up. "Natalie, hey," he said.

"Hey," I echoed, drifting around my living room, at a loss for where to begin.

"Did Channing call you?" he asked.

"Yeah." I suddenly felt drained.

"I don't want you to worry about the media. We've got it all under control," he said calmly.

"Yeah. You're good at controlling the flow of information," I countered snidely.

He hesitated. "I know that headline probably came as a shock to you."

"Ya *think?*" I bleated. "Oliver, I can't believe after all the opportunities I gave you to so much as *mention* you'd been married, and to a woman you'd even *introduced* me to, that I had to find out about it next to a picture of my face in Caleb's magazine."

So much for mantras.

"Natalie, I would love to talk about this with you in person."

"You had *every* opportunity to tell me this in person." I bit my lip.

"You're right. I did." Now he sounded defeated. "And I owe you a detailed explanation. But I'd rather do it over dinner than over the phone."

"You're seriously going to make me wait all week to hear about your secret *ex-wife?* After you prodded me to open up to you about everything with Caleb?" I cried, pacing past the sofa.

"I know it's not ideal. But just know that it's not nearly what it sounds like. And I had my reasons for not mentioning it to anyone."

"Well of course you had *a reason*. If you didn't, that would just make you a sociopath."

He took a breath, "Natalie, listen. I will explain fully when I see you again in just a few days. *In person.* And not while I'm rushing between meetings this week. I want to give you and this topic my full attention."

So this was how it was going to be. I slumped onto the couch. I felt nauseous.

"In the meantime," Oliver continued, "Channing and Sharon and the rest of the staff are actively working to snuff out the story. They don't think any more pictures are going to surface, and my driver Danny confirmed there was no way anyone tailed us to the house. So you shouldn't have to worry about any unwanted attention."

Unwanted attention for me, or for him? What was this really about? Was I being swept under the rug? Did he have misgivings about almost taking it to another level with me in the library Saturday night?

Whatever questions were beating on the door of my mind, it was clear there was nothing more he was going to tell me on this call that would make me feel any better. "Great. Well, listen, I have to go," I muttered.

"I'm looking forward to dinner." He added with hope in his voice.

"Sure," I said flatly.

"Speaking of which, do you mind if we take it to your place?"

"My place?" My head shot up. We had planned on a nice dinner out. But now it felt like he wanted to hide. "You mean you'd rather cook?" I asked.

"Nah, I'll pick up takeout."

The words dealt me a final blow. I pulled up my legs onto the sofa and buried my head between my arms.

Sensing my silence, he added, "I don't want to impose, if it's an issue. I just figure it's better to lay low while the news settles down. We don't need more pictures of us hitting the town together right now."

Again, I wondered whether the "we" was really just him. I knew this move was completely prudent. I was also pretty sure that Sharon was puppet-mastering the optics. It felt like the old equivalent of being taken to a hole-in-the-wall Chinese place for dinner because your date is keeping you and your relationship secret from the rest of the world, something Oliver had already expertly done with his annulled marriage.

"Yeah, sure, whatever," I mumbled, hot tears building. "I'll text you the address."

"Great, I'll—"

I hung up the phone before he could say anything more, and let the tears fall.

Why did he even want to get together now? Was he still "fond" of me, like he told his sister? Or was he going to make it uncomfortably professional after all this and talk strictly about remodeling the East Wing? Or was he even going to want to do that with me anymore? Was dinner going to be the "in-person" farewell?

Instead of looking forward to dinner now, I was absolutely dreading it. How could I have ever let myself believe he could have feelings for me? And even if he did, how could I ever trust that he wasn't hiding something that could blindside me one day in the headlines?

Then there was the whole thing of him being considered for a vice-presidential bid. I didn't have to be politically savvy to know that if cameras were chasing him now, his private life would become even more public if Marques picked him to be her running mate. If he didn't want to hide me from the press already, he was going to want to bury me in an unmarked grave if he got the nod.

During the next few days, when I wasn't fixated on Oliver's secret marriage or his ascent to national stardom, I tried to stay focused on the most important things in front of me, like kicking off the website design with Dana's developer and drilling down on the finance piece of my divorce case with Jake Cohen. The handful of "inquiring minds" that tried to contact me I referred directly to Channing as instructed. I was relieved when it looked like my fifteen minutes of fame were up fourteen minutes early, but it was small consolation.

I fed my demons with toxic comparisons of myself to Camille. When I couldn't sleep, I looked up pictures of her, read about her, read articles she'd written, and I swirled down a spiral of insecurity.

By Friday evening, the sky was clotted with black clouds threatening to pour down another summer storm. I nervously applied mascara and lip gloss, then thought about touching up my complexion with bronzer. Then I got carried away applying eyeliner, eye shadow, and shimmery lipstick, all for a simple night in with takeout.

Grabbing the makeup remover and a huge cotton pad, I wiped everything off, down to my bare skin, staring at my face in the mirror. Why was I so anxious about seeing him? I felt more comfortable in his sister's mothballed sweater than I did now in my own house. What had changed?

I crumpled into a sigh, sitting on the ledge of the tub: *Only everything.*

I reapplied a simple coat of mascara to my lashes and nude gloss to my lips. I threw on my favorite leggings and an extra soft hoodie and gave myself a spritz of black rose and oud. If whatever we had was coming to an end before it even began, at least it didn't look like I tried too hard on my "breakup" makeup.

The bell rang. I ran downstairs and answered the door. Oliver stood soaked on the front steps, holding a heavy plastic bag of takeout and a bottle of Sancerre.

"Oh, God, is it raining?" I asked, motioning him inside.

"Just a drizzle," he joked, coming in from the downpour. I took the bag and bottle from him and placed it in the kitchen.

He peeled off his drenched T-shirt, exposing a bare, wet chest. Again. My breath slowed, watching his hair drip on the floor. I'd had every intention of pouncing on the Camille subject as soon as he was on my turf. I was going to hold him accountable, not let him get away with changing the subject, as he was inclined to do, if I had to sit him down and interrogate him at length, like a handcuffed suspect in a room with a two-way mirror. Instead, I ran upstairs to get him a towel.

I returned downstairs to Oliver browsing the pictures in the foyer, mostly of Aiden, me, and my parents. All traces of Caleb had been removed. He took the towel from me and tousled his hair with it. "Aiden's a really cute kid. Looks like he gets it from his mom."

His playful smile cast its spell over me again. No matter how frustrated I was with him, no matter how much time we spent together, I could never manage to keep myself from reacting to it. So much for playing hardball about Camille.

"He's been at Caleb's full-time, going to soccer camp," I said, turning to face the photo wall. "I can't believe he starts fifth grade on Monday."

"Is that when you'll get him back here on a regular basis?" Oliver asked, draping the towel across his bare back like a cape.

"Ideally," I replied, turning to face him, then looked down toward his feet. "Everything's been a whirlwind the last couple weeks. I figured I'd wait for the kickoff call with Daphne to get a better idea of when I'll be needed up there before scheduling with Caleb when Aiden comes back here."

"That's fair. I'm sure it must be hard to be apart from Aiden so much in the meantime. You must miss him a lot." Oliver was close enough that I could feel the heat coming off his damp body as he collected the ends of the towel and pulled it taut across the back of his neck.

"I do," I said, looking up. I so badly wanted Oliver's arms around me. To pretend like the whole Camille story was a lie concocted by the media. To pour out my anxieties and inadequacies to him and have him whisper in my ear not to worry, that everything would work out okay. But I couldn't think of anything less attractive than baring this feeble part of my soul to him. And even if that didn't turn him off, could he really be trusted with it?

I shifted anxiously, "I miss Aiden. I'm just not sure that he misses me."

"What do you mean?" Oliver's brow rippled, eyes fixed on me.

"Well, Caleb got him a dog, he's busy with soccer camp, and Victoria seems to have the whole mothering thing covered, in spite of never having had children of her own."

Then I paused for a moment, unsure if I wanted to take the conversation in that direction, especially while standing in the foyer talking to Oliver's bare chest, but I continued. "I guess I'm worried I may have sat out one too many moments with Aiden in the past to jump in now."

I walked into the living room. Oliver slipped off his shoes and followed me. "Well, that doesn't sound like you."

"I mean, I was always there for him," I said, curling up in the corner of the sofa in my socks, pulling my legs underneath me. "But I deferred a lot of playtime to Caleb. I just needed some time to myself, after all the feeding and carting Aiden around places and keeping him alive."

Oliver sat down beside me, pulling one leg up onto the seat cushion to face me. I watched him anxiously, waiting for him to run for the hills. He didn't have to say anything for me to realize he wasn't going anywhere. The tension in my neck relaxed a little.

"A lot of the time, I just felt so … spent," I admitted. "And Caleb always got to be the fun guy, the dad who played. So, it was like Aiden had everything he needed in that way from his father, and I could finally take a break. But it wasn't until recently that I realized I'd delegated my way out of a role. And anytime I think about stepping back into it, it feels like it's too little, too late."

A sadness came over his face. "You know, Natalie," he said, turning his eyes down, "I didn't get a whole lot of playtime with my mom growing up either."

"She mentioned that, actually," I said.

"Oh, really?" His eyes flashed up at me.

"Yeah, on our walk in the garden. To be honest, she gave me some kind of blunt advice on the topic."

"Oh, yeah?" he asked, bracing his elbow against the backrest and his chin on his hand.

"Yeah," I said. "Somewhat unsolicited. But based on how, uh, *open* she was about her bodily functions at breakfast in the first half hour of meeting her, it sort of tracked."

Oliver threw back his head in a belly laugh. "I'm so sorry you had to experience that!"

"Especially right before breakfast," I smirked, settling into the sofa. "But what she told me later in the garden, well, it was shocking to hear at first. Particularly from someone I had just met, who happened to be your mother. That's probably why her words have kept coming back to me again and again this past week."

"What exactly did she tell you?" Oliver asked, probing me with his eyes.

"Well, a few things. First, that I was fooling myself to think Victoria stole my life. And that Caleb and Aiden's affections couldn't be 'stolen' without their consent. And that she learned 'the hard way' that her dissatisfaction over her relationship with you was her own fault. Also, and I might be reading too much into this, I don't know, but it sounded like she feels like the divorce from your dad was her own fault too, for taking her family for granted for too long."

A look crossed Oliver's face that I hadn't seen before. It was a mix of surprise and sadness and serious thought. I felt him pull away, and instinctively wanted to reel him back in.

"Your mom's words were different from when Dana or anyone else tries to give me advice. I'm used to that. That's easier to ignore. They think they understand, but they've never been in my shoes. Your mom, on the other hand … that was a cold splash of water. I didn't see it coming at all."

He refocused on me, intrigued. "But I couldn't say she didn't know what it was like being in a similar situation, to feel distant from her son. Because it sounds like you both feel like your relationship was … incomplete."

Oliver shifted his eyes again, uncomfortable. I filled in the silence, "Maybe your mom thought the same thing I keep thinking. That you didn't really need her. She figured you had Maria and the nannies and your sister and friends. But she told me something else she finally realized: 'Nothing can replace a mother's love and attention.' I keep coming back to that."

I searched Oliver's face. Had I lost him? Had I rubbed salt in a wound that I wouldn't be able to rinse out? Had I just revealed myself to be what he disliked most about his mother, the reason for their distant relationship?

After a long pause, Oliver looked at me. He spoke slowly, "I should probably make an effort to spend some one-on-one time with her soon."

I exhaled. "I think she'd really like that." I smiled. "In fact, I know it."

He smiled back. It wasn't the butterfly-inducing one, but one that was quiet and resolved.

"And what about you?" he asked, shifting back on the couch, drawing in closer. "If my mother's words made such an impact, why are you still feeling conflicted and left out of Aiden's life? You already know he would welcome spending time with you, if you offered it to him."

I nodded. "I'm getting used to that idea. In fact, I scheduled Aiden to come here for lunch on Sunday and take him back-to-school shopping. We can talk about whatever he wants to talk about or play whatever games he wants to play for the rest of the afternoon."

"I would have loved to have had a day like that with my mom," Oliver said. "Even more than the vacations."

"I just hope it's not too late for me to make space in Aiden's life again," I fretted out loud. "At least Caleb didn't give me any grief when I asked to take him on Sunday. So he seems willing to give me the chance."

"Well, that's encouraging," Oliver said sitting up. "I'm really glad you're making that happen, Natalie."

A feeling of hope trickled through me, one that told me things were maybe going to be okay. I was finding my way again.

I broke from his gaze to look down at the damp shirt he was still holding. "Let me throw that in the dryer for you."

I fetched the Brown T-shirt he had loaned me, so he wasn't sitting around topless any longer while his other shirt dried. Then we opened the sushi and poured the Sancerre.

I didn't realize how hungry I was. During a week of sheer anxiety, my appetite had been nonexistent. Now, with Oliver there, sharing these things that had been bothering me, I felt like some of the pressure had been released. But there was still one big elephant sitting on my chest.

"Oliver," I finally said as we sipped miso soup and arranged maki on our plates. "You'd been waiting to tell me 'in person,' and now you're here. So, why did you hide your marriage to Camille from me? From *everyone*, for that matter?"

He took an audible breath and wiped his mouth with a napkin. "I figured you'd be asking that as soon as the headline broke."

"Uh, *yeah*." My eyes flickered across his face, as if waiting for the punchline. "I know it might not have been any of my business at first. But then you straight-up lied to me. And to Channing, which was even more shocking. You can see how shady that looks, right?"

Oliver bowed his head. "I know. I never wanted to lie to anyone. I just wanted to leave that part of my life in the past. But when the story broke, it became clear I can't do that anymore. So I'll just say it plainly and hope you can understand."

I nodded. "Of course."

"Camille is a family friend," he began.

"Yes, you told me that, before." My heart was pounding.

"Yes, I know, but I want to restate it, because that's how it all started. We had been friends since childhood, and our families were very close. But it wasn't until after Carter died and I came back home from Napa that I really leaned on Camille as a sounding board. She was still getting her degree in journalism and political science from Georgetown."

I listened as patiently as I could, knowing the impact Carter's death had had on Oliver and how hard it was for him to talk about it.

"I was in a bad place," he admitted. "I told you how devoting my time to culinary arts suddenly felt frivolous, selfish even. Most of my family couldn't understand what Carter's death had to do with becoming a chef, but Madeleine and Camille got it. I found myself confiding in them about wanting to rechart the course of my life.

"I visited Camille at Georgetown a lot in that in-between time. We started to feel a closeness that just caught fire, as young love tends to. Being together was just so easy, and other things at that time were so hard. The summer before her final year, we became an official couple, and I was basically moved into her place in DC. She encouraged me to take the LSAT that fall and apply to Georgetown Law. She thought that way I could embrace this humanitarian calling I'd been grappling with in a way that our families could understand and actually get behind."

"But you didn't go to Georgetown," I cut in. "I mean, I can see why you'd turn it down for Harvard ..."

"That's just the thing," he said. "I didn't get in."

"*What?* How do you get into Harvard, but not Georgetown?"

"Everyone was just as stunned as you. I almost didn't even apply to Harvard, but my father was a Harvard grad and felt it would be a snub to both him and the school if I didn't apply. So, I sent in my application, with his understanding that I would choose Georgetown over Harvard to be closer to Camille. By that point, our families knew we were talking about marriage. Camille's career in political journalism was, of course, going to be rooted in DC. And what better place for me to start my law career?"

"But I still don't get how that even happened," I said. "Did you find out why you weren't accepted?"

"Because I probably didn't deserve to be. I just wasn't that good, Natalie." His face fell, almost apologetically. "But my father had a lot more sway at Harvard."

I sat back in my seat, unsure what to say. "So the rest is history. You went to Harvard. But how did Camille react?"

"She knew this wouldn't be great for our relationship, which made her uneasy. But she also knew that waiting to apply to Georgetown again the following year while turning down acceptance from Harvard would be absolutely insane. Besides, my father would never have it. And honestly, I was stoked." The corners of his mouth crept into a smile.

"You both agreed you should go?" I asked, sitting back.

"Yes," he nodded. "We were committed to staying together though. We knew we'd see each other when she visited home a few times a year, since Cambridge is less than two hours from Newport. I told her I was going to be so busy in law school anyway, it wouldn't matter if we were 500 miles apart or twenty feet."

His expression darkened. "But deep down, we both knew that wasn't true. Which only made Camille more anxious as the time got closer. In our last two weeks of the summer before I moved up to Cambridge and before she started her job, we escaped to St. Lucia for a getaway. I could tell Camille wasn't handling my impending departure well. I wanted to give her something before I left to set her mind at ease for the long stretch until the holidays when we would see each other."

Oliver paused there, either to see if I had any questions or to make sure he still had my full attention. I don't think I even blinked for a couple minutes straight.

"Natalie, let me be the first to say: I was young and stupid and had an oversimplified understanding of relationships and the world. A few nights into that vacation, after lots of frozen drinks in front of a tropical ocean view, I proposed to Camille on the spur of the moment. I didn't even have a ring. I thought an engagement would give her some assurance we'd get through the separation."

I imagined him dropping to one knee, a freshly picked hibiscus flower in hand. They were probably perched high in their fantasy suite in the mountainous jungles of St. Lucia, overlooking the Caribbean Sea, while the sun bled into the horizon. I would die for that to be me.

"But it wasn't enough," he continued. "She became almost obsessed with getting married on the island before we left. And I wanted to make her happy, so we did. We said we would have the big family wedding reception once I graduated, and then we could finally move in together in DC, where I'd look for a law firm to join."

"Were your families thrilled?" I asked. I could only assume Camille would be Agatha and Madeleine's number one choice for Oliver.

He laughed to himself, "Not exactly. We thought they'd take the news better than they did. Both sides called it 'impetuous' and 'short-sighted.' They couldn't understand the rush, when it was only a few years until I'd graduate. We'd already spent our whole lives together, in a way."

He moved his sushi around his plate, then continued. "Camille and I thought they were just upset that we weren't taking the traditional engagement path for our parents' social circles. But it became clear after just a few months that we really had made a mistake."

My heart lifted at the way he said "mistake."

"Camille enjoyed her work life right off the bat. And my absence gave her even more time at the news station. But the same level of interest she had in her job? Well, other men had that amount of interest in her. By the time I came home for Thanksgiving break, she was crying to me over turkey and scalloped potatoes that she had feelings for someone she worked with. She had spent a couple months wrapped up in an emotional affair, horrified that we had made a hasty decision."

My jaw dropped. "I'm so sorry."

He shook his head decisively. "Don't be. It was the best thing that could have happened, in the long run. Camille and I were definitely not each other's intendeds. So rather than be branded as divorcés at the ripe old ages of twenty-two and twenty-four, our families suggested we get the marriage annulled on technical grounds that the legal proceedings had been improperly conducted in a foreign country."

So they had, like it had never even happened. Because the whole thing felt like a juvenile embarrassment, it hadn't been publicized at all, and no one even had any pictures of the wedding, their families and friends kept it quiet.

"And that's why no one paid it any mind until your husband dug it all up and smeared it across his magazine last week." Oliver's eyes looked back at me, cool and placid.

I sat there in amazement. Rich people really could make anything go away. I rubbed my face, trying to take it all in.

"But weren't you devastated when you'd found out about Camille and that other guy?"

He let out a breathy laugh. "That would be the first of many of Camille's relationships. I came to learn she's a serial dater, through and through. She'll fall madly in love with a man who needs rescuing, until she either rescues him or the newness wears off. Whichever comes first."

I definitely did not expect his opinion of her to be so brazen, especially after seeing them together at the gala, but it didn't really answer the question of whether he was still secretly in love with her.

"Don't get me wrong," Oliver said, swallowing a piece of salmon avocado roll. "Camille is still a close friend and doggedly loyal. She keeps her ears to the ground for me in this town, which has come in handy a few times. Our friendship has never been a secret. But I guess all it took was motive and some digging to turn up a sensational headline, and it's no coincidence that it's while the Marques campaign has my whole life under a microscope. Your husband is a shrewd bastard, you know that, Natalie?"

I stared back at him with a face that said, *believe me, I know.*

"You never answered my question," I pressed. "Were you devastated when Camille told you she'd met someone else? What was going through your mind?"

He poured another packet of soy sauce into a ramekin and dotted wasabi on a piece of maki before dipping. "It didn't feel great at the time, for sure. I did care deeply about Camille. But what surprised me was how much it *didn't* hurt. In those few months at law school, I had fallen in love with something else."

"Please tell me you didn't find some *other* woman you've been keeping secret?"

He barked a laugh. "Nah. What I found was my purpose. At law school, I finally realized what I wanted to do with my life. That's when Maria gave me the starfish and said, 'Go live what you were put here to do.'"

"The starfish!" I gasped, leaping to my feet. I had nearly forgotten it was still on my desk. I ran to get it, my mind replaying not just what he'd said but *how* he'd said it. Nothing seemed to indicate that he was still pining for Camille after all these years. If anything, clearing the air gave me hope that the door might be open for me.

"I'm so sorry," I said, returning with the shadow box. "I still need to place this in your study. I'm thinking on the built-ins in front of your blue accent wall."

"That sounds perfect," he said, smiling up at me.

"You never told me it was Maria who gave this to you." I placed it in front of us on the table.

"Well, when I gave it to you, I hadn't told you about Maria yet either. She's the one who told me the starfish story. She claimed it happened not far from where she grew up, somewhere on a beach in Sicily."

"Maybe it did."

He shrugged. "Either way is okay, really. We choose whether or not to play out that story every day. We choose how we treat the people we come upon who are stranded. They may not even realize they need help."

Oliver and I gazed at each other for a moment, almost like we were trying to read the other's thoughts. Could he see through me? And if he could, did it turn him off? What was he thinking?

"Was I a starfish to you, Oliver?" I finally asked.

He raised a brow. "Am I to you, Natalie?"

The inversion caught me by surprise. I had never considered that. He obviously felt like a starfish to Camille. Once she'd thrown him back in the sea, she'd moved on to another.

I suddenly felt defensive, tossing my hands up and letting them flop back down into my lap. "Why would *you* possibly need saving? But you were interested in helping me restart my career. Helping with my divorce. Taking me all the way up to Rhode Island on a whim to help me—I don't know—reassert myself in the world or something."

He looked hurt. "You're mad at me for *caring* about you?"

"I'm not mad at you for caring. I'm mad that you're making it sound like my agenda was to save you, like you were a project or something. When in reality, I've always felt like I was *your* project."

"Project?" His stare hardened. "What kind of project would you be for me?"

"A charity case for the Second Chance Whisperer!" I declared. "One that would prove to your circle, your donors, that you live by your credo to help out the little guy."

Oliver sat back a moment looking confused, trying to make sense of what I'd just said. When he spoke, it was quiet and deliberate. "And which of my donors exactly did I tell that I referred you to my buddy because you needed an attorney? Or that we went door-knocking together, because you were blind to your own power? Or, for that matter, whom did I tell that you had no current work experience when I signed the contract to redesign and decorate my house?"

"I don't know who you might've told," I fired back. "Maybe you just needed to do it for your own knowledge. So you wouldn't feel like an all-talk rich guy."

He guffawed. "You can't seriously believe that. That all this time we've spent together has been to pay penance for being born with a silver spoon in my mouth."

"Isn't that what Carter was?" I blurted out, instantly regretting it.

His face made clear I'd struck a nerve. *"Please* don't talk about personal matters you don't fully understand."

I felt embarrassed now, and I was losing ground. "I'm just saying I don't want to be anyone's starfish. I'm not stuck on the sand, and I *don't* need anyone throwing me back in the sea."

"I feel the same way!" he thundered back, standing up suddenly. "Do you have *any* idea how many women have tried to rescue me, or fix me, or tame me, or hurry me along, or tell me what's wrong with me that they have the antidote for? My whole life I've been in other people's crosshairs for one reason or another. And it's always under the guise of being in *my* best interest. You know what that can do to a person, Natalie?"

I stared at him with nothing to fire back.

"Then *you* came along," he said, to my shock, taking a step nearer as I sat paralyzed in my chair. "You weren't trying to change me or tell me what I wanted to hear. You had your own shit going on, and you were just being yourself. And that struck me from the moment we met and only kept gnawing at me every time after. Because you just let me be me. And at the same time, you could still be you without changing everything about yourself to fit in with who I am."

I sat there in disbelief. Was I really hearing that I had some special dynamic with him that no one else had cultivated?

He crouched down beside me, looking into my eyes with both pain and affection. "You bring out the best in me, Natalie," he whispered.

For a moment, I dissolved into his stare. I wanted his mouth to crash into mine, plumb my depths, mix with me until we were one. But he didn't move. My terror of misreading the moment kept me frozen. We were on the precipice of something we might never be able to return from.

"I forgot to get dessert!" I sputtered, dousing the glowing heat between us by pushing back my chair so fast it nearly tipped over.

He stood up and gulped his wine.

I yanked open the freezer door, sticking my head inside like a firebrand into a bucket of water. Trying to catch my breath, I rummaged through freezer-burned bags of veggies, microwave meals, and

Aiden's lunchbox ice packs, trying to find something else to occupy our mouths.

Oliver's hand landed on my shoulder. "Tell you what," he said through escaping plumes of cold air, "let me poke around your pantry and see what I can do."

"What, are you planning to make something?" I asked.

A mischievous smile spread from ear to ear. He opened his arms disarmingly wide. "What else good would my abandoned culinary training be?"

He rummaged through my kitchen, pulling things out and setting them on the countertop. It looked like the setup for a televised cooking competition with random ingredients: whole sweet potatoes, maple syrup, avocado oil, cocoa powder, pecans, a carton of oats, a dark roast K-cup.

"I'm gonna need your help as my sous chef," he said, tying on the never-used apron that had been hanging on the back of the pantry door.

I looked lost in my own kitchen. "I'm not sure how I could possibly help in this situation."

"Just follow my lead," he said, gliding across the floor and taking me by the hand to twirl me around. "It's kind of like dancing."

Caught off guard, I tripped over my own foot, but Oliver caught me gracefully.

"Or maybe just follow my instructions," he winked, setting me back on my feet.

"Yes, Chef!" I replied as he reached for a wooden spoon.

Then he had me pull out a blender, mixing bowls in varying sizes, and some silicone baking pans. I popped the sweet potatoes into the microwave while he set up what he insisted on referring to as "our *mise en place*," measuring out all the ingredients ahead of time. Blindly following his orders on a mystery dessert mission was more fun than I'd ever had in a kitchen. It was possibly more fun than I'd had in other rooms too.

"Nice work, Nat," he told me, peering into my bowl of mashed sweet potato. Apparently, we were on nickname terms now. I wondered if calling him "Oli" would be acceptable.

"Grab that large mixing bowl and combine our wet ingredients, starting with the sweet potato you mashed, and ending with the vanilla. Then run the hand mixer through it all to get it even."

"If everything is being combined, why does it matter what order they go in?" I asked.

"Chemistry!" he exclaimed, stirring dry ingredients in another bowl. I was definitely feeling some of *that*.

"It's easiest if you start with the toughest ingredient to work," he explained, "then blend in the easier ones."

"I dunno, that teaspoon of vanilla at the end might be a real bitch," I wisecracked.

"No, no … LIFO. Last In, First Out. You add the aromatics last to maximize their aroma." I was getting a private culinary masterclass, but I couldn't help wanting to touch the teacher inappropriately.

Bit by bit he sifted his dry ingredients into my wet ones, as he narrated how I was to beat them into an even, rich, smooth chocolate batter. While I did so, he pulled out yet another mixing bowl, a whisk, and the heavy cream I had in the fridge.

"What are you doing now?" I asked.

"Making whipped cream. It tastes better when it takes some effort," he said, glancing up.

"It tastes better when I don't have a million things to clean after eating it," I noted.

"Gotta clean as you go," he advised.

"Now I have to add cleaning to the task of baking?" I asked, pretending to be annoyed. He had already rinsed out everything we'd used so far and placed it in the dishwasher with Tetris-like precision.

Waiting on my next instructions, I dipped my finger in the batter and licked it off my finger, murmuring appreciatively.

"No sampling yet!" he scolded.

"Oh, yeah? What if it accidentally winds up on you?" I said defiantly, dipping another finger in and blooping a glob of chocolate batter right on the tip of his nose.

He looked up, mouth agape and laughter in his eyes. "I can't believe you just did that! You going to lick it off?"

"Be careful what you wish for!" I laughed back, shimmying out of reach.

"Oh, you just wait! You're gonna get it." He whisked faster. "Just wait."

I dipped my finger back into the batter, dangled it in front of his eyes, then put it in my mouth with exaggerated pleasure.

"Oh, so that's how it's gonna be?" he threatened. He set down the whisk, scooped a dollop of softly whipped cream onto his index and middle fingers and wiped it right across my face. I dodged and grabbed my arsenal of brown batter, and he reached for his whipped cream artillery. We'd chased each other halfway around the kitchen island when the oven reached temperature and beeped out a ceasefire.

The chef regained his composure. "All right, you. Let's get these in the pan and then prepare for your punishment for being a naughty sous chef."

"Are you going to make me stand in the corner?" I teased.

"I'm going to make you clean this all up!" he shouted, eyes wide with laughter.

We managed to get the batter in the pan, the pan in the oven, and a timer set for twenty-five minutes, despite my protests that I could've made a Swiss Miss with Reddi Whip an hour ago and had my chocolate fix already.

"This is going to be way better," he insisted. "Have you guessed what we're making?"

"If it's not a chocolate cake or brownies, I'm stumped."

"*Ding ding ding!* It's a fudgy brownie recipe with whipped cream."

I was genuinely impressed. "I never realized I could make my own oat flour before."

"Well, considering you didn't have *any* flour ..." He side-eyed me as he put the oat-dusted blender in the sink.

"Why's there coffee in it?" I asked.

"Makes the chocolate flavor even richer. But you probably won't taste the actual coffee."

Leaning against the counter, I wrinkled my nose and crossed my eyes, spying an errant fleck of whipped cream on my nostril. I tried to stretch my tongue high enough to lick it off.

"Let me get that for you," he said, bringing his face close to mine. I could feel the warmth of his breath on my lips. He wiped up the whipped cream with a finger and popped it in his mouth.

"I thought you said no tasting," I protested.

"Then. *Now* we can taste."

I used my finger to wipe away a splat of batter on his cheek. I offered it to him. His green eyes met mine and he opened his mouth. I placed my finger gently inside its warmth and wetness as he sucked on it, pulling back until my finger came out. I felt an intense urge to grind against his body.

He plucked a small fluff of whipped cream from my hairline and extended it on a finger. I sucked hard, letting him know with my tongue what I wanted to do to the rest of him. He pulled his finger out of my mouth with the sound of a lollipop breaking the barrier between my lips.

Then the distance between us collapsed. He took my hips between his hands and hoisted me up on the countertop effortlessly, leaning into me and I into him. His face dipped down to mine, our lips only grazing at first as if giving me the chance to pull away. I pressed my mouth into his in a collision that consumed us both, tongues entwined, bodies heaving for air. His hands clasped my face and tangled in my hair. I threw my legs around him and squeezed, palms clapped to the sides of his face as we kissed each other. My fingers climbed upward, grasping fistfuls of soft hair.

He pressed into me until I could feel the hard cylinder like a rolling pin in his apron pocket. His hands were all over my face, shoving handfuls of me into his mouth. He made his way down my neck, kissing and sucking as we groped one another, then back up to my ear, breathing, "I need you, Natalie." Legs still wrapped around his waist, I pulsed against him.

If this was anything like the rush heroin addicts feel when it hits their bloodstream, I got it now. I could never quit this.

I had already pulled the apron off him and reached for his belt buckle when he pulled my sweatshirt over my head, my hair a careless mess of sugar and desire. He stopped to take me in for a second, panting and disheveled, then returned to my mouth with soft, penetrating kisses as we slowly worked to undo one another.

A jolt came from within my leggings pocket, my phone vibrating hard against the countertop, startling us both apart.

I fumbled, yanked it out from the stretchy fabric, and saw Aiden was trying to reach me on FaceTime.

"It's my son," I said, holding my phone out in front of me, breathless and confused.

Oliver backed away, running a hand through his hair. I placed the phone down just long enough to comb my fingers through my own hair before answering. Oliver leaned up against the far end of the island.

"Heya, Buddy! What're ya doin'?" Aiden was in his jammies, tucked into a sleeping bag on a carpeted floor somewhere, excited little voices in the background.

"I'm at a sleepover at Hudson's!" he exclaimed via his iPad. He panned around the room to show me everyone.

"Oh wow, how fun!" I said, breathless and lightheaded.

Aiden resettled the camera on his face. "I just wanted to say goodnight."

My heart skipped a beat. "Oh, I love that! I'm so glad you called," I gushed. I was, too, despite the timing. "Have so much fun tonight, and don't stay up too late."

"I won't, Mom," he assured me. I smiled to myself, knowing perfectly well he would stay up too late regardless.

"Goodnight ... *love you!*" I called, blowing kisses.

"Goodnight, Mom!" he said, waving, before the call cut out.

Happy tears formed in the corners of my eyes as Oliver rested his hand on mine. "I'm so happy for you," he whispered. "It's all gonna work out."

I nodded, flushed with emotion.

Then he pulled his hand away. "I'd better get going," he said, glancing at his watch.

My heart felt like a hot sweet potato landing on the floor. "What? Why? You're not even going to stay for the brownies?"

"I got to enjoy a better dessert," he said, looking back at me with a soft smile. "Let me help you clean up though."

I was flustered, "That's okay. You already helped. I can get the rest."

"I insist," he said.

"You mean you have time to clean up, but not to wait for the brownies?" I asked, confused.

He looked like he was wrestling with something. After a moment he shook his head. "Nah, you enjoy them. Pull them out of the pan by the parchment paper and let them cool on the rack for ten minutes or so, then roll this pizza cutter through them to cut the squares. The whipped cream's chilling in the fridge."

He turned to leave, but I put myself between him and the door. "Wait. Did something upset you? I don't understand what just happened."

He took a deep breath. "Nothing happened, Natalie. You didn't do anything wrong. I probably did though. Impulse finally got the better of me. I shouldn't have overstepped."

"You didn't," I insisted. "We both … wanted that."

"I know, but at what cost?" he asked, rubbing his forehead. "I got to see with my own eyes that you're building your relationship with Aiden. I wish my mother had done the same with me as a kid. You and me becoming an 'us' could only get in the way of that."

"Why would me having you in my life get in the way of my relationship with Aiden? He certainly didn't have a problem when Caleb brought Victoria into his life."

"Yeah, but Victoria isn't in the headlines as a VP candidate," Oliver replied, looking tired. "Natalie, you're finally creating the life you want. With your career. With your son. Do you understand what comes with being with me?"

"So, you have cameras on you sometimes."

"God, if only it were that simple!" He searched me for a glimmer of understanding. "Do you have any idea the gauntlet you'd be running with me as vice-presidential nominee? If Marques selects me, there are a lot of matters I immediately cede control over, especially around optics, professional or personal. If the headline in Caleb's magazine was enough to scare you, just imagine what it would feel like with national news outlets fixating on every detail about the potential Second Lady of the United States."

His words shook me. I don't know why I hadn't thought more about how Oliver's future could affect me. Maybe because I never believed I could be more to him than his interior designer.

"But you haven't even been selected yet." My argument sounded flimsy, even to me.

He looked pained. "Natalie, listen to me. Do you really want to take this plunge? Because, unfair as the choice is, once you make it, there's no going back. Once the media knows that we're in a relation-ship, the attention it will bring down upon you—*and* on Aiden, as unfortunate and unnecessary as that is—will not go away. Not even if you change your mind and we stop seeing each other. In fact, if they smell blood in the water, it gets worse."

Oliver's words hit like a rogue wave, forcing me under and not letting me up for air.

"I let myself get carried away tonight, Natalie," he continued softly in my silence. "And that was selfish. I'm glad Aiden called you. It gave me the wake-up call I needed. I wish he'd called a little earlier, if I'm honest."

"You wish we'd … are you saying you regret what just happened now between us?" I was gutted.

His eyes and forehead furrowed. "I regret that I overstepped with you, when I can't possibly promise to keep you, or your son, or this new life you're building, safe. Not on this journey with me."

He touched my face tenderly, then pulled away. I was suffocating, heart and mind racing as he started to walk past me toward the door.

"Isn't it my decision though?" My question stopped him. "Because you're treating it like I already made my choice."

He turned to face me, shaking his head, arms at his sides. "Don't you want to do what's best for you and your son?"

"Of course I do, but I don't want to give up on this. Not yet." A tear streaked down my face. "You've told me what we're up against. It's fair warning. Nothing has changed outside these walls here, Oliver. No one has to know about us, least of all the news media. Don't we owe it to ourselves to see if Marques even *selects* you? I'd have to imagine that being your girlfriend, if you're passed over, can't be nearly as stressful. I'd sign my name to that deal tonight, if I had to."

"And if I *do* get selected?"

"Can't we just take that as it comes? I mean, how long could it be before she finally makes her pick? We'll keep it quiet until then. But I'm not letting you walk out of here thinking I give up this easy."

"We both risk this getting a lot harder, if we let this go on," he warned.

"It's a risk I'm willing to take," I insisted. "If the alternative is I lose you now? I'd rather double down."

He glanced away, then looked at me again. "As long as we have our eyes wide open."

"I've never felt more awake," I told him, staring into his eyes, fighting to hold my hands steady in the adrenaline surge.

Buzzing from the countertop made us turn in surprise. My phone was ringing again.

I shot Oliver a look to say "don't move," then scurried over.

It was Aiden again. "Hi baby, what's wrong?"

"Hi Mom. Do you think you could bring Mr. Bear to Hudson's house?"

"Mr. Bear? Are you missing him?" I was surprised. Aiden's once-favorite bedtime stuffed animal had been collecting dust at my house since before he left for camp. He didn't want to "look like a baby" to his bunkmates.

"Umm … maybe a little," he confessed. "Everyone brought their own plushies tonight."

"Aha, I see." My eyes were fixed on Oliver, still halfway to the door.

"I'll make sure Mr. Bear didn't make other plans, and then I'll bring him over in like ten minutes or so. Does that work?"

"Yeah, thanks, Mom!" he exclaimed, and hung up.

I breathed out slowly. Oliver's smile was bittersweet. He reached out to rub my shoulders. "Sounds like you have an emergency transport to make tonight."

"Yes, a Very Important Bear needs to get to a rager of a slumber party."

He nodded slowly, kissing me on the cheek. We looked at each other for a while, unwilling to break away.

"Goodnight, Natalie," he finally whispered. Then he left, a piece of my heart leaving with him.

I watched him drive off, vapor rising from the wet pavement in the cool night air, the storm now gone. Inside, the timer went off.

REFLECTIONS

 I had trouble sleeping that night. But I wasn't the only one. Oliver texted at five in the morning to ask if I was awake. I was.

Are you sure about everything you said last night?

More than ever. There would only be more sleepless nights if I changed my mind now.

We agreed to meet up on the National Mall for a walk. I hadn't been there in a long time, but the weather was mild after the storm, and the sun had only just risen.

Oliver wanted to take me to visit a couple of his favorite three-letter leaders: MLK and FDR.

"What about JFK?" I asked.

"He's all the way in Arlington, so we'll have to save him for another day," he said, swinging my hand in his.

At each monument, Oliver couldn't help but give a little history lesson. It didn't even bother me today. We blended into the quiet morning, anonymous among the trickle of early risers.

By the time we'd walked around to the Lincoln Memorial and strolled past the Reflecting Pool, the sun was higher in the sky. The Mall would only get busier. It was unlikely that tourists or passersby would recognize Oliver or have any questions about my being with him, but we knew our time in public for the day was growing short.

"We should probably head to the house," he said, looking around.

I nodded. It wasn't ideal, but we had to play it safe. "Want to take one loop around the Reflecting Pool and head back to our cars?" I asked.

He hesitated. "Sure," he said, lowering his sunglasses over his face.

Being with him made me feel like skipping. But knowing he wanted as badly as I did to make it work in the face of every potential consequence made me feel indestructible.

"What are the top three things you want to accomplish if you're running the country?" I asked him, never having gotten the opportunity to ask someone with an actual chance at doing it.

"You mean you haven't heard enough policy tirades yet?" he asked, wrapping his arm around my shoulders.

"Maybe I should rethink the question," I teased, "but seriously, how will the world be different if you're in office?"

"Well, everything I've talked about being important to me and my constituents, for starters, would have a much better chance at becoming law," he said, eyes dancing. "That's of course after months or even years of hard work, barring all the usual obstacles and partisan politics. But having a national stage and, if we're lucky, an undivided legislature would mean so many more people could benefit from a commonsense agenda."

"And I'm assuming that agenda is something you've already been working on?" I asked. A little boy and his mother caught my attention as they tossed bread to the ducks.

Oliver shot me a look. "Are you kidding? I've spent *years* thinking about it. And not only the agenda, but how I'd go about it. How I'd get buy-in across party lines."

He detailed an example for me about his favorite topic, making America's healthcare system more efficient and equitable. But somewhere between policy points two and three, where his plan tied into an omnibus bill, I fell a couple steps behind as the mother scooped up her toddler in the nick of time before he splashed into the Reflecting Pool after the ducks.

Oliver turned around mid-sentence, realizing I'd disappeared. I nodded at the knee-deep water. "You just missed a close one," I said.

"But you didn't," he said, hugging me from behind with a kiss on my head. We watched the mother explain to the little boy "why we don't go swimming with ducks."

"You've got that mother's instinct," Oliver said into my ear.

"I'd love for you to meet Aiden," I blurted, then wished I could take it back.

"And I'd love to meet him," Oliver replied, pulling away to resume our walk, hands in his pockets. "But you know, Natalie …"

I nodded. I knew. The looming weight of life-changing news hung heavy above my head. I had not only agreed to this limbo, but I'd created it for both of us, even though I felt about as patient as a wind-up toy waiting to be set on the floor and let go. But the only place Oliver and I could go was in circles around the Reflecting Pool.

"Did you still want to place the starfish?" I asked, changing the subject.

He looked pleased and surprised. "You brought it with you?"

"I did," I said, threading my arm around his waist. "Along with your dry T-shirt from last night and almost the whole batch of brownies."

"You think of everything!" he said, squeezing me to his side as we strolled to our cars.

"Don't worry." I winked. "I'm billing for that too."

- -

Down in Oliver's study, the room felt nearly complete, all his belongings and memorabilia in a space I'd only conceived on paper a few weeks earlier. I took the starfish from my bag, and I pushed aside his rolling chair to give us more room behind the desk to identify a suitable place for it.

"Do you think over here, next to the Willie Mays baseball?" he asked, trying it out.

"You know what?" I said, airlifting it to the top of his desk. "Maybe instead of putting it *behind* you, where only other people can see it, we let it live on your desk, where you can be reminded of the power of 'one regular person' every day."

I leaned a hip against the edge of his desk, tilting my head up at him with a smile.

"Natalie," he said, coming in for a kiss, "you were always the perfect person for this job."

1 8

CONVENTIONAL WISDOM

I left the townhouse a little while later. The day after was my day with Aiden, and I wanted to be ready. Oliver printed out a few of his favorite recipes for me, including a simple shrimp and pesto penne I knew Aiden would love. I hit the store to get the ingredients on the way home, then cleaned and organized Aiden's room, making sure all his clothes were washed, folded and put away. After that I cooked, since reheating the dish at lunch would give us more time to spend together. When I portioned out a bowl for myself for a late dinner, I had to admit that not only was it good, but I was also pretty impressed with my work.

When I slipped into bed at ten and set my alarm, I was excited. I was picking Aiden up in exactly twelve hours and couldn't wait to hear about everything he'd been doing at Caleb's since he got home from camp. That admittedly wasn't *my* life. But this was. And Aiden was. And we had our own new, exciting life to build together.

- -

I rang Caleb's bell at exactly 9:59 on Sunday morning, setting off a cascade of woofing inside the house. My thoughts flashed to the side door code. I took a breath, held it … and let it go.

The door opened, and Victoria stood there in her robe, holding the dog back by its collar. I had never seen what she looked like before she'd gotten ready for the day. She had no makeup on, her hair wasn't styled. She almost had that "neighbor next door" kind of look.

"Oh, hey, Natalie. Come on in," she said, shooing the dog into its crate. "Aiden will be right down."

I handed her the morning paper from their front porch. "Thanks," she said. "Can I get you a cup of coffee?"

"I'm okay, thanks," I replied, entering the foyer I had secretly explored weeks earlier.

Caleb jogged down the stairs looking like he was headed to the gym. "Aiden's just finishing something up and will be down in a second," he said, checking his smartwatch.

"I'm gonna hop in the shower, Caleb," Victoria told him, then turned to me. "Hope you and Aiden have a great day together." She climbed the stairs, leaving me alone with Caleb, who immediately shoved a list under my nose.

"That's everything we already got for back-to-school," Caleb said, not making eye contact.

"Thanks," I said.

He started to move past me. "Caleb," I called. He turned, glaring silently.

"Fuck you very much for that headline the other day," I said. "As I'm sure you intended, you made things harder for Oliver, who may, thankfully, still be our next vice president."

A nefarious smile curled across Caleb's lips. He relished every bit of this.

I stepped toward him until I was in his face. "But let's be clear, Caleb. Unlike you, Oliver isn't just a vulture pecking apart what's happening in Washington—he's *making it happen.* And he's not trying to tip the scale in favor of his own jealousies by dredging up bullshit from the past. He's rising above it. And I'm choosing to rise above it too. All of it."

Caleb threw back his head in a cackle. "*You*, Natalie? *You?* Rising above it? God, I can't think of anything more hilarious! You couldn't even rise above couch level most days to take care of your own son. *I* had to do everything. *I* had to rise above it. *I* had to be the daddy *and* the mommy while you got a free ride for ten years."

His reddened face bore down on me, voice continuing to rise. "I tried *everything* to motivate you, looked for every opportunity to get you back on your feet. Asked you over and over to please seek professional help. I got stuck in that fucking quicksand pit of a marriage with you for *sixteen years*. Then *I* rose above it. Up and *out*."

"You have no idea who I even am," I spat. My lip quivered but I didn't back away.

He leaned into my face and spoke with such force I could taste his mouthwash, his voice rising with every phrase. "Oh, I know who you are. You are a fucking leech on my soul. And the state of Maryland entitles you to be a leech on my finances, until you're old enough to retire from the workforce that you only spent three fucking years in. You are lazy. You are selfish. You are an embarrassingly mediocre mother and a person I wish every day I'd never *wasted* all those years with. But you know what, Natalie? *I'm rising above it!*"

Caleb's spittle flecked my face like venom.

I blinked hard, refusing to believe I was shaking. "Sure, Caleb. Sure *sounds* like you've risen above it."

Caleb's lip curled through an unbroken stare as he bellowed up the staircase. "Aiden! Come down. Mommy's waiting!"

A moment later, Aiden appeared at the top of the steps. He hesitated, holding something in his hand, then tiptoed down.

He definitely overheard us fighting. The realization opened a pit in my stomach.

"I had to finish up my card for Mommy," he told Caleb sheepishly. Aiden handed me a messy cluster of construction paper glued together in the rough shape of a heart, showered with glitter. Written in near illegible red marker were the words *Best Mom Ever. Love, Aiden.*

The tears I wasn't about to give Caleb flowed down my face as I hugged our son. "Thank you, honey," I said in his ear, "I love this *so much.*"

Over Aiden's shoulder I could see Caleb stepping out the side door. He could shoot his arrows. I had everything I needed.

- -

Later that night, after a full day with Aiden, I was curled up in bed, doing research on facilities for victims of domestic abuse ahead of the September kickoff meeting for the Atwood campus. I had the kind of fatigue that felt rewarding. Not the one I had come to know as chronic and crippling, even after doing a lot of nothing all day. I knew I would sleep well tonight.

How did it go with Aiden? Oliver's text lit up my heart.

Amazing. Your pesto was a hit, Aiden and I had a blast. He showed me how to play Super Tic-Tac-Toe. Did you know you could play nine Tic-Tac-Toe boards as one giant board?

I didn't, but I know what our next activity will be when you come over. What did you wind up doing tonight?

Aiden's sleeping over. He wanted to leave from here for his first day of school, and Caleb actually let him. I'm looking forward to taking one of those doorstep pictures of him holding a "1st Day of 5th Grade" sign tomorrow. I just finished bribing him to go to bed on time with one of your brownies.

Oh, yeah? How'd he like it?

He said, 'Needs salt.' I added a crying laughing emoji.

Everyone's a critic! Oliver typed his emojis by hand, winking in semicolon plus close parenthesis. *OK, I'll let you go. I know you both have a big, early morning. Would you wanna come over here tomorrow night and we can whip up dinner together?*

I would love that, I wrote, grinning at my phone.

- -

Oliver's kitchen looked like a tiny farmer's market when I arrived

Monday evening. He had all the ingredients staged for a five-course meal.

"If you didn't like Indian before, you're gonna love it now," he said, moving deftly about the kitchen, apron on and sleeves rolled up. "But if we want to eat before eight, we're going to have to move at a pretty quick clip."

I put on the other apron and followed his instructions, feeling like the girl who was late to flash mob practice. Luckily, Oliver was wonderfully patient. By the time we finished making the samosas, the beet and cucumber raita, saffron rice, chicken tikka masala, and kheer for dessert, I was absolutely ravenous. I was also ready to collapse in my chair. I had filled Oliver in on my day with Aiden and our morning before school, struggling to cook and talk at the same time.

Sitting down in the candlelight to eat, aromas of Eastern spices filling the room, we dug in, and I got to hear about Oliver's day. "So, when is Elena Marques supposed to make her pick?"

"Should be any day now. The party pushed back the Convention to a week from tomorrow, just to give her team enough time. But that means it won't be long."

"Are you nervous?" I asked, a bundle of nerves myself thinking about it.

"Of course I'm nervous!" Oliver laughed. "It would be a tremendous honor to be selected, especially as someone so new to politics."

"But I thought someone once said the Vice Presidency wasn't worth a bag of piss?" I ribbed him, biting into another samosa.

"It was *technically* a 'bucket of warm piss,' but I won't even bore you with who said it and why." He spooned saffron rice and chicken tikka masala onto my plate. "The point is, in spite of that 'conventional wisdom,' if it weren't a coveted position, the competition wouldn't be this stiff."

"How are they making you compete?" I asked.

"Oh, you know, standardized testing and the like." I shot him an impatient look, and he laughed. "I'm not kidding! There was an extensive, rather invasive questionnaire as a first step. Then there's a ton of

Marques's people crawling into my past and personal life as part of their due diligence."

My face tightened, but he kept going. "The final piece of it is really subjective, though, as any job interview would be. Basically, who does she like more?"

"I saw on the news it's down to you and that other guy." I took a bite of chicken and rice, trying not to let my anxieties spiral as I pictured a bunch of black suits scouring documents and surveilling recent interactions I'd had with Oliver.

He nodded, tearing a piece of naan and wiping up sauce. "Channing told me you, uh, hadn't been following along in the news or anything."

"Yeah, well," I said, tucking my hair behind my ears, "I'm making a point of it now."

The candles were burning low by the time we got to dessert. In spite of feeling quite full, I couldn't pass up the creamy cardamom rice pudding topped with pistachios, cinnamon, and dried rose petals. I rolled the kheer over my palate, like an edible potpourri.

Oliver brewed us a pot of ginger tea to help us digest. It was also a delicious way to get all the garlic out of my mouth before he moved in any closer.

He poured us two glass mugs and gestured me into the living room. He put on some relaxed jazz as I popped off my shoes and curled up on the sofa. Then he sat down beside me and began massaging my feet.

"Mondays just keep getting better for me," I laughed, eyes closed, carried away on the notes of the song.

I decided I wasn't going to let this night be ruined by worry. After all, I was the one who said we needed to just "take it as it comes" until we knew for sure. In my mind, Oliver had roughly a fifty percent chance of even being selected. The news media certainly didn't seem to know more than that, and while the pundits could speculate, all bets were off until Marques made that call. The adage "worry and suffer twice" came to mind. I couldn't recall if it was from the Dalai Lama or J.K. Rowling, and it didn't matter. What mattered were Oliver's magical hands, soothing every muscle they touched. He was slow and methodical as he worked his way up from my toes and feet to my calves, inching higher until he reached my skirt hem.

"Why'd you stop?" I asked, opening my eyes.

He shook his head thoughtfully, my legs draped across his lap. "I think to do an adequate job, I'm going to need to ask you to …"

"To what?"

He ran a hand behind his neck and rubbed it, looking at me from the corner of his eye. "To remove some layers."

"We may need to take this elsewhere then." I winked.

"Oh, yeah?" His eyes widened.

"Oh, yeah." I took him by the hand and led him up the floating staircase, then up another level to the primary suite. I hadn't seen it in a bit. All his things were there. It made everything feel very real all of a sudden. Somehow even the beanbag chairs were just right.

The moon shone through the huge Palladian window as I pulled the drapes across.

"If I'm going to take off some layers, it's only fair if you take some off too. Here, I'll help you." I approached and began slowly unbuttoning his dress shirt until he let it fall off his shoulders to the floor. I reached for his belt.

"I may need that later," he said, laying a hand on mine.

"What, are you going to whip me with it?" I goaded him.

"Only if you misbehave …"

Now he pulled me into him by my hips, laying a warm, spicy, ginger-flavored kiss on my mouth. Then he scooped me up in his arms and carried me to the bed, throwing me down upon the feathery duvet. He knelt atop the bed in his undershirt and pants, my legs between his knees.

"Now, you'll have to do as I say," he told me, raising an eyebrow.

"Yes, Chef," I whispered.

"First things first: the top has to go."

I crisscrossed my arms at the hem of my top, lifting it over my head slowly, making him watch as I pulled it off to reveal my white and gold pushup bra with its dusting of tiny rhinestones.

I could hear him inhale.

"Now your turn," I said.

He unbuckled his belt, then unbuttoned his blue dress pants, the zipper of his fly chattering with expectation all the way down. He let them fall to where his knees met the bed. The bulge in his snug black boxer briefs pointed almost straight up, as if about to toll the witching hour.

I stared at his package. "And here I was thinking you leaned left," I teased.

He glanced down and readjusted to midnight. "You're gonna get it," he muttered, kicking his pants off the rest of the way.

"I'd better!" I proclaimed.

"What happened to 'Yes, Chef?'" he asked, pinning my arms down at my sides. "The skirt goes next!"

He released my arms so he could shimmy my skirt down my legs, leaving me in my pushup bra and matching underwear.

He pulled off his undershirt as I sat up to stroke his erection through the fitted cotton. He tilted his head back, eyes rolling into his head as he exhaled audibly, then pulled himself back to center. "Not yet. I promised you a massage."

He took me by the shoulders and flipped me onto my stomach, climbing on top of me. He began massaging my upper back and shoulders with slow, pulsing pressure, unlocking nooks and crannies I didn't realize were clamped shut.

I felt him climb off me for a moment. Then a wet kiss of lotion landed between my shoulder blades. It smelled like him, subtle sandalwood and musk.

"I'm going to need to take this off," he whispered, unhooking my bra and pushing aside the straps. His thumbs massaged the velvety lotion into muscles up and down my spine, until he reached the waist of my underwear. I felt one finger slip under the center of the waistline, poised to ride the notch of my tailbone down to pull them off me, but then he changed his mind. His hands shifted to caress my glutes, pressing down in all the right places, then moving lower to cup the backs of my thighs, squeezing, rubbing my legs all the way down and back up again.

I was trembling with anticipation as his fingers slid their way back up my inner thigh, grazing my folds through my underwear. He began stroking, petting me over my panties, wetness beginning to seep through.

Then he turned me over, flat on the bed. My bra slid to the side, nipples hard and exposed as his hands moved up my arms, massaging until they reached my breasts. He drew himself down on top of me, pushing my shoulders against the bed, his mouth crushing mine, kissing me deeply, making his way down my neck, taking his time to sample everything, kissing, licking, then lightly sucking my nipples as he hovered there, kneeling above me.

My chest heaved. I reached for his waistband. "Not yet," he whispered, gently pulling my hands away.

He turned me over again on my stomach, massaging me downward, hooking his fingers on the waistband of my underwear again. He leaned forward behind me, so his mouth was close to my ear.

"It's time for these too," he said softly, wiggling his fingers underneath. I nodded eagerly, and he slid them down my legs and off my ankles. I was completely exposed and face down. Still behind me, he ran his hands up my legs and parted them, massaging my thighs again, his caress inching ever closer. I hungered for it, needed it.

"Yes," I breathed, "yes, yes ..."

"You're impatient, aren't you?" he murmured, finally giving me what I wanted, reaching between my legs and parting my lips, running his fingers front to back over and over, then sliding his other two fingers inside as I laid there, legs splayed, still face-down on the bed. I nearly climaxed in his hands.

I turned myself over to face him, pulling him onto me and kissing him hard on the mouth before he traveled back down again. He tasted me delicately, circling with his tongue, sucking and then enveloping me with his lips, playing me like an instrument, a rising crescendo.

I pulled him up again, insistently. "Now," I rasped in his ear. "It's time now."

He let me slide his boxer briefs off, and the reveal did not disappoint. I stroked along his hipbones, finally cupping his manhood in my hand. I locked my eyes on his as I traced a throbbing blue vein with the tip of my tongue.

A guttural noise escaped his lips as I began sucking, then stopped just long enough to steer him down on the bed. I climbed on top, my mouth poised just above his. He took me by the hips and pulled me down, a single slow, deep penetration that filled me completely and then some. I arched my back, the sensation overtaking me.

He began to thrust gently, his pubic bone rubbing against my clit, as I regulated the rhythm. Our naked bodies glided against one another on commingled sweat and fluid with every thrust. He bent me backward, holding me there in his arms, syncing up with my cues until able to bring us both to simultaneous climax.

We collapsed upon the bed, feet facing the headboard. He drew me into him, and I rested my head on his solid, reassuring chest, the swells of our breath moving together.

- -

I was still curled up under the duvet with my eyes closed when the aroma of freshly brewed coffee roused me. Oliver crawled back into bed with two mugs as I sat up, holding mine beneath my nose.

I took it from him, sheets wrapped around my naked body in the early morning light. I laced my fingers around the warm mug, holding it to my face to breathe in. Oliver put an arm around me, sipping his coffee.

"What time is it?" I asked.

"A little after seven. I have about twenty minutes before I have to hit the shower and head into the office. But they'll be twenty minutes very well spent."

He leaned over to kiss me. "How did you sleep?" he asked.

"Like the dead. This might be the most comfortable bed ever."

"All credit goes to you for ordering it." He smiled. "You might be the most comfortable person to sleep next to. I was out cold too."

His phone buzzed on the nightstand, the ongoing kind announcing a call. He was slow to pick it up to see who it was. He answered. By the look on Oliver's face, it was not a call to be missed. He sat up straight, listening intently, brows furrowed.

"You're damn right we're going to do it," he nodded, voice rock-ribbed with conviction. "Thanks, Elena. And thanks for the call. We're ready to hit the ground running. See you at ten."

The call ended. I watched him in profile, sitting directly beside me, the moment frozen in time. He stared off into space for a long, slow while, then turned to face me in bed.

"That was the call. I'm her guy."

My heart was already pounding like a bass drum; I could feel the throbbing in my ears. I threw my arms around him. "You're going to run for vice president!"

He squeezed me back hard, face buried in untamed locks of hair between my neck and shoulder. I breathed his aftershave into my lungs and let it circulate through my bloodstream. How long would I have him?

He broke away, looking at me with earnest eyes, still holding onto my shoulders. "We have to celebrate tonight. I don't know how late my day's gonna go, but I would love to come home to you tonight if you can be here."

"Yes, of course," I said, mind fluttering everywhere at once.

Oliver's look turned somber. "Natalie, take the day to really think about this. To think about what this means for you in the public eye, your son, your career. No rose-colored glasses. If you're ready to do this with me, I want you to be fully prepared for what may come."

I nodded with my mouth open, expecting words to come, but nothing did.

"Things are going to get pretty hectic from here on," he added. "If you think I was busy before, multiply it by a thousand. There'll be times I might not be able to call or text you back right away but just know I can't wait to get home to you each night. In *this* home. The one we created together."

He looked at me with what seemed like so much love in his eyes, then kissed me passionately, hands cradling the back of my head, fingers weaving through my hair. But that was all the time there was for this mixed moment of exhilaration and trepidation. Oliver had to dash. He told me to use the house all day if I wanted. Whatever would make it easier for me to be here when he got home.

A dream scenario was unfolding at lightning speed. But I knew this was the calm before the storm. I wasn't sure exactly what *kind* of storm. But just like the pilot who flew us to the gala, I had to decide *now* if this plane was taking off ... or staying grounded.

- -

I knew Oliver would be late to get home that night, but it wasn't just by a little. Not even by an hour. I had been waiting to heat up last night's leftovers and hear all about his day.

By nine thirty, I'd given up hope of him returning anytime soon. He had texted me a couple hours earlier that he was delayed but wasn't sure for how long. I heated myself a plate and ate, then retired to the sofa with *A Tale of Two Cities* from his shelf to wait it out.

When he entered the house at 11:17 p.m., I had never seen him in such a state, dead on his feet, rubbing his face like a zombie as he trudged into the living room. He stopped and pivoted before he remembered he didn't have to double-check that he hadn't left his keys in the door.

"Oh my God, you're finally home," I said, jumping up from the couch. "You must be starving and exhausted. Can I reheat the leftovers for you?"

"That is the understatement of the year, and yes please," he said, heaving a sigh and crumpling into the leather sofa.

"I can't promise it'll be very good ..."

"I can't promise that I won't fall asleep in it."

He perked up a bit while eating and asked me how my day was, but all I could think about was his. "That's probably the last thing you want to talk about right now though," I observed, "and you probably can't even say much about it anyway."

"Well," he said, through heaping mouthfuls of chicken and rice, "I spent sixteen straight hours with the Marques team and my own, preparing for next Tuesday's Convention. If we could fit a twenty-fifth hour into each of the next seven days for every person on our team scrambling right now, it still wouldn't be enough."

"How's your team handling the shift?" I asked beside him.

"Channing and Sharon are in rare form, for sure. There's a ton of coordination between our team and Marques's that needs to happen, and a lot that just can't be accomplished in such a short time. Which means there are bound to be missteps, but it's the hand we've been dealt."

He shoveled more food into his mouth and kept talking, listing a thousand things he and his team were having to consider, right down to Oliver's wardrobe for Tuesday. Oliver was the most upbeat and energetic person I knew, but I could already see the rigors of running on the presidential ticket were going to take a toll on him. And that wasn't even considering what it'd be like if they won. I'd seen some "before and after" pictures of presidents from when they started their term to when they finished. The amount of aging that happened over four or certainly eight years was always arresting.

I felt like I'd been touched by a live wire and might never sleep again, but I tried to be empathetic. By the time Oliver wiped up the last remnants of his food with a piece of naan, I asked whether he wanted to go straight to bed, and he nodded. The dishes could wait.

We climbed both sets of stairs to the bedroom, where he shed his suit and tie and stiff, leather shoes. I changed into a cute, white tank top and a pair of stretchy boy shorts I'd snagged from home during the day along with a few other things.

He barely finished brushing his teeth before tumbling into bed in his undershirt and boxer-briefs. I clambered in after him.

Turning to me on the pillow, inches from my face, he said, "I take it since you're still here, that you've decided you want to jump in the deep end with me?"

"There's nothing that's made me want to walk away yet," I replied, nuzzling up to him. I felt him hold his breath.

"What?" I asked, pulling my head back to look at him.

"There *may* be *one* thing," he said with a don't-kill-me smile. I looked at him expectantly.

"I know she's not your favorite, but I'd like you to meet with Sharon tomorrow. She's the best person to run you through what to expect and what they're going to ask of you. Think of it as the final gate before you walk into the arena, the one where you can still turn around and run if you need to, once Sharon gives you a better idea of what's on the other side."

"I don't want to run, Oliver," I insisted, pressed into the pillow.

He stroked my face, "I know you don't. But I wouldn't think any less of you if you did. You have to do what's best for you and your family."

I sighed. There was no avoiding this if I was going to prove my commitment. "Where should I meet Sharon tomorrow?"

"I gave her your number. She'll call you in the morning to set a time and place, likely at the House Office Buildings."

"Okay," I said, "Will you be there?"

"Highly unlikely. But I'll poke my head in if I'm in the vicinity. Don't expect to see Channing either. He's been working at warp speed." Oliver shook his head to himself, then mumbled, "I gotta make sure he's not on pills."

I turned out the light and stared into the dark, worrying about this meeting with Mean Sharon tomorrow. I could hear deep breathing from his side of the bed in the darkness half a minute later. Falling asleep instantaneously appeared to be one of Oliver's superpowers. I smiled softly as I realized this was the first time I got to appreciate that about him. Maybe, one day, I would even get to find it annoying.

I couldn't nod off as easily. I told myself not to toss and turn all night worrying. I'd have a lot more information in the morning. I knew I could count on Sharon to not hold back. In fact, the more I thought about it, the more confident I felt that I would have a much better picture of the future in a few short hours. Besides, it wasn't like I had to do this all on my own; I'd have Oliver's team to guide me through. It would all work out. How mean could Mean Sharon be?

- -

The next morning, I woke up to a handwritten note beside the bed, apologizing for having to leave so early. It let me know there was coffee waiting in the kitchen that just needed reheating, and to make myself at home today, even if he wouldn't be back until very late again tonight.

When I checked my phone, I already had three missed calls from the same 202 number. I listened to the voicemail, legs still akimbo in the covers:

The voice was humorless. "Natalie, this is Sharon Glazer from Oliver's office. Please call me back immediately. I'd like to get you on the calendar for eight o'clock this morning."

I checked my watch. It was already 8:10.

"Sharon, *damn ...*" I said aloud, rubbing my eyes and sitting up in bed.

I took a breath, exhaled, and called back. The voice on the other end was already annoyed.

"Hi, Sharon," I cooed, holding out hope I could win her over.

"You're already ten minutes late."

"Yeah ... I'm just getting your message now."

"Can you get here at nine?" She cut me off, unapologetic.

My eyes widened. I wasn't even sure where "here" was. "Where am I meeting you?"

"Rayburn!" she barked. Then sighed. "45 Independence Southwest!"

"Got it!" I exclaimed, tripping out of bed. "Do I need to bring anything?"

"Don't be late!" she snapped, then the call cut out.

After the fastest shower of my life, including a second's appreciation for how gorgeous the bathroom I designed really was, I was whipping my wet hair into a bun and throwing on a less than professional floral sundress from my overnight bag. Had I known about this meeting before midnight, I would've planned my outfit better. Oh well. I was in a rideshare flying down Independence Avenue by eight forty-five, pulling up in front of the Rayburn Building with minutes to spare.

Sharon was already waiting on the stone steps of the pillared building. She looked me up and down as I got out of the car, then turned on her heel to escort me up the steps.

"I really appreciate you skipping mi-mo's at the baby shower for our little briefing today," she deadpanned.

I took a moment to realize it was a dig at my outfit, then forced a laugh. "I didn't have any suits with me, unfortunately," I apologized.

"You don't own a suit?" She scowled, her face as stony as the steps. "Never mind, you'll blend right in with the tour groups."

I bristled. I mean, I hadn't been the one calling before the sun was up, demanding an eight a.m. meeting. "I'm just glad I didn't have anything else scheduled."

Sharon never broke stride. "We *all* had something else scheduled. I hope you're a fast walker. Since you couldn't make it at eight, we have a schlep ahead of us. I have a meeting in Cannon at nine thirty, so I reserved a conference room there."

I hardly had time to regret my choice of wedge espadrilles. Sharon was already off to the races, trotting down a set of marble steps without appearing to care whether I could keep up. Down in the sub-basement I followed her through what seemed like miles of wide, spartan corridor with eggshell white walls, pendant fluorescent lighting, and painted-over piping and conduit lines running as far as the eye could see.

"How long until we get there?" I asked, disoriented.

"A few blocks," she replied. "Long ones."

"Blocks" told me nothing. These tunnels weren't city streets where you could see the next intersection. They were a municipal nightmare of unending sight lines.

"Let's start with you telling me about your politics," Sharon said, without so much as looking at me, heels clacking down the polished concrete.

"Umm ..." I wasn't sure how to answer that. "I don't really have any."

"That explains the almost complete lack of voting history," she replied icily, holding her hand up. "No need to elaborate. I have that information. Where do you stand now on the main issues?"

"Which ones?"

"The economy. Taxes. Immigration. Healthcare. Abortion. Gun control." She fired off topics like rounds from an AK-47, then stopped, giving me a condescending look. "Actually, you know what? We'll just tell you where you stand. We'll save that for the next meeting."

The next meeting? How many of these were there going to be? Sharon didn't pause for a breath. "Let's start with something you can handle. Like HMW."

I jogged a few steps to catch up with her pole vaulter's stride. "You've lost me again."

"Hair. Makeup. Wardrobe. You can't be dressed for a lawn party at the National Convention."

"Am I going to the Convention?" I asked, a wave of butterflies pouring into my extremities.

"Not at this rate," Sharon clipped.

We passed an "exit" for the Longworth Building, but Sharon kept right on truckin'.

"Since you're clearly not already working with a stylist, we'll select one for you that will rebuild your wardrobe with timeless, elegant ensembles for all occasions. Nothing trendy, nothing too tight or too baggy, nothing flashy, brash, busy ..." Sharon halted for the first time in about a mile, and I skidded to a stop.

"And *NO* words, slogans, or sayings on clothing whatsoever." She glowered into my eyes. "You *are* aware of the 2018 debacle to which I'm referring, *right?*"

I nodded without having a clue, wide-eyed and petrified.

Sharon resumed her people-mover pace as if she'd never stopped. "No unauthorized use of the color pink, no colonial-reminiscent headwear." Without slowing, her head swiveled toward me like something out of *The Exorcist*, "You don't own a pith helmet, do you?"

Sharon hadn't even gotten to hair and makeup yet, and my head was spinning. When we finally arrived at the Cannon Office Building, we exited the endless underground highway of trampled dreams and rode the elevator up to a floor of Congressional offices. Sharon led us into an empty meeting room with a long, glossy conference table and a standing American flag large enough for an elementary school assembly. I took a seat, quickly checking a spot on my left ankle where the canvas of my espadrille had rubbed the skin over my Achilles tendon raw. Blood seeped through the canvas.

Sharon sat opposite me on the short side of the table and checked her watch in a crisp motion. "We have about twelve minutes before I have to liaise with the Marques campaign manager. I think our time would be best utilized reviewing the details of your divorce from Caleb Weir and what you can and absolutely *cannot* say to the media or the public. Or really, let's just be safe: things you can't say *at all.*"

"Do you happen to have a Band-Aid?" I asked, rubbing my injured foot.

She was nonplussed. "What do I look like? The school nurse? Oh! Speaking of schools, I understand you have a son. Where does he go?"

"John Muir Elementary."

"John Muir? Is that a special school for environmentally inclined children? Like a fellowship for stewards of the Earth?" For a moment I thought it was a joke. Then I remembered that Sharon didn't joke.

"Do you have children, Sharon?" I asked with a wry smile.

"Of course not," she replied, matter-of-fact as ever.

"You didn't seem like you did. John Muir is a public school," I said.

She didn't react, so I repeated myself. "My son attends a public school, Sharon."

"*Public* school?" her eyes went wide.

"Is that a problem?" I asked dryly.

She looked baffled that I would even ask. "I just don't think the public school system is equipped to handle high-profile children. I'll get you a list of DC private schools that are up to the task."

Sharon scribbled in her notebook.

"But we live in Maryland," I protested.

Sharon didn't look up. "Okay, Maryland, fine. Sidwell is top of the list, and their lower school is in Bethesda."

Sharon went on scrawling, not bothering to ask whether I could afford a private school or had any desire to pull my child out of the one he already went to.

"Oliver tells me his friend Jake Cohen is representing you in your divorce?" Sharon looked up from her notes.

I raised an eyebrow. "Isn't that privileged information?"

She gave a half smile and cocked her head. "Not to us. Not if you're sleeping with the vice president."

"He's not the vice president yet," I said through gritted teeth.

Sharon's eyes bored into mine. "Which is exactly why we're doing our due diligence now. It's my job to uncover any and every piece of potentially salacious or troublesome material that could be used against him and Ms. Marques in their presidential bid. Anything that could be deliberately misinterpreted by some jackass journalist or idiot publisher with an axe to grind. The last thing our party needs is for Oliver to end up like Jim Compton because of some fly-by-night girlfriend *mishigas* that could single-handedly sink our chances at the White House."

Oliver's comment Friday night about having to cede control on personal matters ricocheted in my skull. Sharon was awful. But she wasn't wrong. Everything Sharon was investigating—in fact, everything she was tasked to do, was 100 percent nonnegotiable. No one connected to Oliver would be spared some version of this very special treatment, least of all me. This was exactly what Oliver meant, and it was just the beginning.

"I'm going to schedule you with a private instructor for media training," Sharon was saying. "In fact, Oliver suggested using Camille van der Kamp."

I blinked. Surely not. "He recommended *who? For what??*"

Sharon looked back at me from under heavy eyelids, unmoved. "Camille. The *Post* columnist. She'll be the perfect person to train you on how to handle difficult questions from the media. You'll share with her every article of your dirty laundry, and she'll tell you how to obfuscate, steer conversations, and, if you must, lie convincingly."

A look of horror must've spread across my face. By the look on

Sharon's, she relished it. "I believe you and Camille recently shared a headline together in your ex-husband's—excuse me—your *almost-ex-husband's* little political vanity rag." Sharon flashed me a sardonic smile. "So you're *already family!*"

I seethed. Oliver was scheduling some off-the-record session for me, taught by his ex-wife? *She* was going to tell *me* how to behave and talk in front of the media? I'd rather impale myself on the White House fence.

Sharon leaned an elbow on the conference table, twiddling her pen beside her ear and going over her notes. "So, moving on: custody over your son Aiden and your post-divorce financial vulnerabilities. We'll need to know everything there."

I cracked the knuckles of my balled-up fist. "I think we're done here, Sharon."

One side of her mouth curled upward cruelly as she raised a single eyebrow. "Probably best, given the time. I'd say we've accomplished what we set out to do."

- -

It was nine fifteen that night, and I was still waiting for Oliver at a little Italian place on The Wharf called Dolce Far Niente. I had gotten us a table for two, tucked away on the back patio under a canopy of fairy lights. A server refilled my water glass and brought over a second basket of garlic knots. I had stress-eaten the entire first one.

Earlier that day, Oliver had called me as he ducked into the men's room to get a rare moment to himself. He asked me to meet him at the restaurant for dinner.

"Don't you care if people see us together and recognize you?" I asked, surprised.

"They're going to be seeing a lot of us together in the coming weeks anyway," he reasoned. "Might as well have a nice dinner out before we really start having to hide from the cameras."

I didn't have time to reply before he said, "I gotta run to my next meeting, but let's plan to meet up there at nine."

I was still fuming about being booked for a course at Madame Camille's finishing school, but I didn't want to start that conversation without time to end it. I would tell him tonight about my delightful morning with Sharon and see if getting Camille involved was actually his idea. I had hopes that he'd tell me Sharon was going off the deep end again, and to ignore most of it.

Oliver entered the restaurant patio with a spring in his step, sleeves rolled up as usual, a winning smile plastered all over his face. He ducked down to give me a kiss on the head.

"I can't wait to hear all about your day," he said, grabbing a garlic knot from the basket and tearing into it with his teeth. He pulled back the chair opposite me and took a seat. He had such presence. It filled every room with an energy that made me glad he was there, even when I had a bone to pick with him.

"Well, I started my morning with a 5K race against Sharon on the Capitol Autobahn ..."

Oliver looked confused. "The tunnels? What'd she take you down there for?"

"To haze me in my wedges on her way to the Cannon Office Building, I suspect."

He reached for another garlic knot. "And how'd your meeting go?"

Leaning into sarcasm helped me feel a little more in control. "She was already peeved that I didn't make it in time to watch the sunrise with her from the Rayburn Building steps, so that really set a tone. But we knew she hated me already, from that moment she referred to my work as 'placing throw pillows,' right?"

Oliver sighed. "Yeah," he said through a mouthful of bread. "Sharon is a tough nut to crack."

"Tough nut? More like she got her career start with the Gestapo," I said, spreading my napkin across my lap.

We ordered dinner but decided against wine. It was a late night and was going to be an early morning.

"So anyway," I resumed, "after Sharon fired off 'the easy stuff,' which included a laundry list of no-nos for what I should look and dress like, I got the unfunded mandate that Aiden should be enrolled in *private* school."

"Unfunded mandate!" he laughed into his water glass.

I leaned over the table. My voice and temperature were rising. "Oliver, doesn't it concern you that she basically told me to pull my son out of the public school he's gone to for five years and fork over college-sized tuition for Sidwell? Assuming they'll even take him?"

He shrugged, dialing my anxiety up another notch. Why was he taking this so lightly? "I mean," he replied casually, "you'll want Aiden to be at a school that's accustomed to educating VIPs' children. Not just because it's a superior education, but because they'll know how to handle Aiden being there *discreetly*. They'll protect him."

I should've guessed he'd defend it. I mean, the guy grew up in an elite boarding school. "You know, Oliver, *I* went to public school."

"Yes, but you weren't under threat of being hounded by the press when you got off the bus."

I felt my breath quickening. "And how do you propose, in the midst of a contentious divorce, that I convince Caleb to pay for private school, when Aiden has been excelling where he is for free?"

Oliver opened his arms, guileless. "It's for his own son's benefit."

It surprised me that he could be so clueless. "Speaking of Caleb, Sharon minced no words about getting up close and personal in the details of my divorce, custody arrangements, and financial vulnerabilities and the like."

Oliver's face transformed into one of concern. He put down the bread. I awaited his agreement on how unnecessary all that was.

"Natalie," he said in a low voice, "these are *exactly* the things we talked about being out of my hands from the moment I said yes to Marques and you said you wanted to 'take things as they come.' If I could shield you from them, I would."

I was stunned. "So you're condoning the invasion of my private life?"

"I wouldn't say '*condoning.*'" He wiped the garlic sheen from his lips with his napkin. "It's simply not my decision. We have to be prepared for anything that could blow up in our faces and derail the campaign.

This is standard protocol when you're running on the presidential ticket."

"But *I'm* not running for office!" I cried out, heat radiating from my face.

His face grew stern, his eyes two glassy ice cubes. "I know it doesn't feel fair, Natalie, but it's the way it is."

"So next you're gonna tell me it was *your* idea to get me media training from the ex-wife you hid from me." I was going to lose it, I could tell.

Oliver sighed. "Natalie. Sharon and Channing's workloads are both beyond maxed out, and the whole team agrees that Camille is the most capable and trustworthy person to help us with that."

"Help us, or help *you?*" I fired back at him.

His eyes widened. He looked like he was about to yell, but then became very, very still, his voice quiet. "Natalie. When I tried walking out your front door a few nights ago, specifically to spare you this whole arduous, invasive process—after spelling out for you what was to come—do you think that was for my own benefit?"

I stared him down across the table, lips pursed. I felt overwhelmed and frustrated and just wanted him to comfort me. He was only giving me a stiff shot of reality, and I knew it, but I couldn't stop myself. I didn't even believe the words as they came out of my mouth, but I was like a toddler, hours past her bedtime.

"Of course it was for your own benefit. You didn't want a loose cannon smashing your chances at political stardom. That's why you want me to take media training with your ex-wife. So she and all your henchmen can teach me how to be with you in public!"

His nostrils flared. "If *this* is how it's going to be 'in public,' then you need the training even more than I realized."

His retort was a slap in the face. Mouth agape, my face froze in shock.

Then Oliver let out his breath slowly and deliberately. "Do you remember what I said last night, Natalie? About this meeting with Sharon being the last gate before you're officially thrown in the ring? If the heat is too hot, the time to speak up is *now*. Because it's just a matter of days before the press catches wind that I'm having sleep-overs with the woman who we insisted a little over a week ago was 'just my interior designer.' And once that news is out, well, then we've crossed the Rubicon."

"I don't get it." My throat was tight. "Why is it such a point of no return? Why can't we go back after that?"

"Because once they know we've been intimate they'll never leave you alone. Not even if we broke up. Let me be completely clear: this is not something that will just go away. The fallout will continue, at least until something bigger catches their attention." His expression hardened again here. "And I'm *not* just referring to campaign fallout. I'm specifically talking about you and your personal life."

Tears were welling up in my eyes. I wanted to suck them back in. Everything he said was true. I just didn't want it to be. And now I'd made him angry, disappointed. My only ally in a sea of ill-wishers was growing impatient with me.

"Sharon just made everything so painful," I wailed. "It was like her whole purpose was to scare me away from you."

"I hate to say it, Natalie," he said, leaning back in his chair, "but that means she's doing her job. If Sharon made you scared and angry today …" He looked down and shook his head.

"What?" I breathed, my heart racing, already knowing how the sentence ended. But I needed to hear it from him.

He raised his eyes to meet mine, deeply hurt. "If Sharon was too much for you today, then you should just go now."

The tears finally fell. I wanted to shove my chair back and run, flee from this horrible reality closing in. But if I left, Oliver would likely never let me back in.

Steadying my gaze and my trembling bottom lip, I fought through my pain, wiping streaks from my cheeks. "It's gonna take a lot more than Mean Sharon to scare me away from you," I said, voice quivering.

Oliver stared at me a moment, searching my face. Then he opened the wine list and called out to our server. "*Signore, grazie.* We changed our minds. A bottle of the Barbaresco, *per favore.*"

- -

Over dinner we somehow managed to get back to a somewhat normal cadence, despite our first real fight. Conversation flowed like it always did, but the ghost of what had come before it pulled up a chair and waited.

After dinner, Oliver walked me to my car. With both hope and hesitation, he asked, "Are you coming back to the house?"

I desperately wanted to. I had what I needed back at the house to get me to tomorrow, barring any more unforeseen meetings on the Hill. I wanted to catch all the thoughts swirling in my mind like moths in a net, tie it up, and light it on fire. I wanted to unleash the desire I felt for Oliver, just go back to the townhouse and maul him under the covers.

But the specter that had joined us for dinner kept tapping its watch. If I ignored it long enough, would it go away?

"Yes," I told Oliver, against all misgivings. "I'll meet you back there."

"Good." A reassured smile connected his ears. "And if you beat me there, you can let yourself in."

I knew plenty of women would have swooned to hear that sentence, but now it tied me in knots. This was my chance to finally be happy again, I told myself. Push through. Don't blow it.

I forced a smile. "See you back there."

As my fingers wrapped around the car door handle, he leaned in for a kiss.

Out of the corner of my eye, I spotted a twentysomething couple on the sidewalk not twenty feet away. The man had his phone out, pointed at us, while the woman watched in awe.

I broke from Oliver's incoming embrace.

"Are you taking our picture?" I called out to them. The man dropped his phone to his side, caught in the act. I marched toward them. "Are you *videoing* us?"

The woman stepped back in alarm. The man's eyes grew wide as he shook his head vigorously. "N–no! No! I just—"

I held out my hand. "Let me see your phone."

He looked terrified, pulling away. "I–I'm sorry. I can delete it."

"So you *did* take a video!" I got in his face. I had turned into someone else.

Oliver was suddenly beside me, hand on my back as if he could radiate calm directly into me. He was unruffled. "What's going on here?"

"Congressman Thames!" the guy exclaimed, almost with relief. "My name is Simon Archuletto. Can I just say I am *such* a fan?"

"Pleased to meet you, Simon," Oliver replied politely, shaking Simon's eagerly extended hand.

"I'm from East Greenwich. My whole family voted for you!" Simon was beaming.

"An East Greenwich guy? I always love running into constituents down here." He placed a hand on Simon's shoulder.

Embarrassment tore through me. I was about to take the guy's head off, when his photo op had nothing to do with me. The whole situation was making me paranoid already.

The lamb cavatappi sat heavy in my gut as I listened to them glad-hand a bit. Simon congratulated Oliver on the VP nomination and wished him luck. Then he asked me if I'd take a picture of the three of them together, Oliver between him and his girlfriend. Snapping the shutter a few times, I handed Simon back his phone.

Oliver walked me back to my car but left out the kiss I had interrupted earlier.

"See you back there," he said, closing the door and giving it a pat instead.

- -

The living room light was on when I'd finally found street parking and I let myself in. "Oliver?" I called, placing my bag on the sofa.

"I'm down here," his voice beckoned from the floor below.

I descended the stairs to his study. Oliver was seated at his desk, absorbed in something at his computer, illuminated by the glow of the screen. He didn't look up.

I waited a bit, feeling my heart fall. Something felt off. "Did something happen?" I asked nervously, wondering if that something was me.

He didn't answer right away. "No … I'm just responding to something." He clacked away at his keyboard.

"I'm going to get ready for bed." I turned to leave.

"Not yet," he said, continuing to type. After a moment he looked up. "Natalie, I do need you to take the media training with Camille."

My heart sank. I looked away, barely nodding.

He craned his neck toward me. "Is that a yes?"

I looked him in the eye, cramming down my discomfort. "That's a 'yes.'"

He rose from his chair. "Good."

He came around the desk and got behind me, placing a hand at the base of the back of my neck, massaging the muscles deeply. "I know this has already been stressful for you. It's going to get worse. A lot worse. But my team and I are going to give you every tool we have to help you through it as much as possible. If you have the will, we have the skill. But that first part is up to you."

Oliver turned me around to look me in the eyes, holding me in his arms. I nodded in understanding.

He pulled me in slowly, his lips meeting mine. His mouth opened, hot and sweet, a faint taste of red wine on his tongue. His hands on my bare shoulders squeezed tight, lips making their way down my jawline to neck and chest.

I backed up onto the edge of his desk. The rock-solid rod in his pants rubbed up against me in just the right spot, a throb of excitement pulsing between my thighs. Bracing myself backward upon the desk, I spread my legs further as he kissed me hard, reaching for my hemline with one hand, gathering the fabric and moving it away.

His other hand traveled down, down, as he kissed me, petting me over my underwear. I pressed back toward his fingers willingly, head tipped backward as his lips nestled in my cleavage. I shrugged the spaghetti straps off my shoulders, the top half of my dress falling away to meet the bottom half he'd gathered up to my waist.

His mouth moved down to my nipples, gently sucking the salt residue of the day. I unbuckled his belt and unbuttoned his pants, and he grabbed my hips, settling me firmly on the desktop. His pants fell to his ankles and he pressed harder into me, his bulge fettered only by the fabric of his boxer briefs.

I hooked my thumbs under the elastic band of his underwear and pulled down as he did the same to mine. Then, pulling my hips across the desk toward him, he entered me in one hard thrust, like a puppeteer taking control of his puppet. My every move was animated entirely by him.

His mouth connected again with mine as he slid in and out, my legs on his shoulders as I arched back onto the desk blotter. Papers went everywhere. Neither of us cared.

He moved his lips to my ear and whispered, "Are you going to be a good girl for me? Are you going to do what I say?"

I nodded breathlessly.

"Or are you going to be naughty?" he asked. "And need a punishment?"

Enraptured by each thrust, I didn't know which I wanted more.

He crawled on top of me on the desk, my legs wrapping around his waist. His unrelenting thrusts pinned me down until I gave into the euphoria of climax.

"That was for good girls," he whispered, a single bead of sweat from his brow trickling off his nose and onto mine as I lay there, chest heaving.

"But I think you still need a punishment." He slid backward off the desk and stood me up, my dress falling to my ankles. He spun me around, then pushed my hands down onto the disarrayed desk blotter holding them down with his own broad palms. His hard, sweat-dampened body pressed against my back as he entered me from behind. He thrust harder and deeper than before, panting rough against my ear.

Buckling under his force, I spread my legs wider, letting him in as deep as he could go. "Do you promise to be a good girl from now on?" he breathed, reaching around to stroke me in rhythm with his thrusts.

I lolled my head back against him as I mouthed my *yes ... yes ...*

He kept going until I climaxed again. Biting the back of my neck, he thrust a few final times as he came inside me and lay there, heavy, with me pinned to his desk.

- -

I'm not sure when I fell asleep that night. I only knew I had slept because of the anxiety dreams: on stage at the National Convention, naked in the lights, searching for Oliver among a laughing audience, not being able to find him anywhere.

Oliver was gone when I woke, coffee and another note beside the bed.

Can't wait to see you later. Set up a time with Camille.

Her number was below. I held it in my hand for a long time as I sipped tepid coffee. Was I going to be a "good girl" now?

I put the mug down and dialed. It rang several times, Camille answered, businesslike. For some reason it took me by surprise.

"Camille, this is Natalie. Oliver asked me to reach out to you." I wound the drawstring of my night shorts around my finger.

"Natalie! Oh ... yes, Oli mentioned you might reach out. What can I do for you?" Her voice sparkled. She was evidently a morning person.

"I'm not sure what Oliver mentioned to you already, but he thought it would be a good idea if you helped me with some media training."

"Yes, of course. Would tonight around six work for you? I'm kind of tied up the next few days, but I know that time is of the essence here. I can meet you at Oli's."

I swallowed hard and agreed. The idea of having Camille come to Oliver's home, a home we had made together, rankled. But it was the only private space that made sense, short of making her drive all the way up 270 to my house.

"That works fine. Do you need the address?" I asked, holding my breath.

"Yes, please! He might've mentioned it when he bought the house, but I never wrote it down."

For some reason, that came as a relief. We said our goodbyes and I let the phone drop to my side. I sat in silence for a moment, then my phone buzzed. It was a text from Channing, telling me to check my email.

My heart skipped a beat at the thought of what I might find. There had been a lot of surprises lately. When I saw what it was, I just sighed. Channing and Sharon had sent a compilation of Marques-Thames platform points to familiarize myself with, as well as a follow-up to all the dos and don'ts Sharon mentioned the day before. I began scrolling the list of action items I was to complete ASAP. The scroll went on and on.

Aiden would be coming back to me this weekend. When exactly was I going to have time to read, let alone *do,* all this? My kickoff call with Daphne would be next week as well. My schedule was about to get a whole lot busier. In the bathroom a few minutes later, I stared myself down in the mirror and questioned whether I had the stamina.

Then I thought of Oliver and how jam-packed his own days were. I suddenly felt like I was wasting time. I splashed some water on my face and brushed my teeth, then gathered my few things into my overnight bag to head home. I had to be back here by six, and there was a lot to do.

- -

Four o'clock found me on Dana's couch for the first time since that day in July when she strong-armed me into this surreal situation. Nero the cat looked like he had never moved from his spot. Dana changed into after-work loungewear with her day's makeup still looking fresh on her face.

I had gone home from Oliver's that morning to restock my overnight bag with a variety of outfits for nearly any occasion, not knowing what could be coming at me next. Then I sat down at my computer to put real time and attention into the mass of details Channing and Sharon had sent. I figured it could only help me ahead of my session with Camille. In between bits of political prepping, I readied the house for Aiden's arrival. By midafternoon, I needed a break. I invited myself over to Dana's. There was an awful lot to catch her up on, including the seemingly endless list in my email.

"You can do this," Dana assured me as I relayed some of the platform points I'd studied earlier. "You're doing your homework. If you want it bad enough that you're willing to put in the effort and endure the scrutiny, you've got this."

I turned to face her on the couch, my hand propping my head up from the backrest. Dana sipped a bottle of kombucha whose strong ginger scent brought back the memory of the ginger tea before my first night with Oliver. But now the effervescence and spice stung my nostrils and made me sneeze.

"I'm in over my head. There are so many things coming at me right now, and I have no way of knowing what's next. The last few days have felt like a nonstop fire drill."

"This is going to be the hardest part, leading up to the election. If you can get through this, you're probably in the clear," she said, floppy bun nodding along with her.

"But what if they get elected?" I asked.

"Then it's probably a whole new round of scrutiny," she conceded. "But that's what he and his team are prepping you for." Dana pulled her legs up into a crisscross, her bright, glossy orange lips turned down in a pensive frown.

"I *hate* the idea of his ex-wife coaching me."

"Of course you do. It's a shitty spot to be in. But it does make sense. It might not be as bad as you're expecting, and she *is* the media, so it's bound to be helpful. Besides, you could probably get some good intel from her. I'm sure you have questions you're dying to ask." She nodded at me encouragingly, intrigued by her own idea.

I scrunched up my face. "About the behind-the-scenes of politics?"

Dana shook her head. "No, about Oliver!"

I looked back at her blankly.

"Or about the Speaker of the House, if you're so inclined." She threw up her hands. "You do you."

I hadn't actually thought about asking Camille anything about Oliver. I wondered if she'd even be open to talking about him. Maybe she'd be just as elusive as he had been.

I chewed on the idea when Dana spoke up again. "Just make sure in all of this craziness that you're checking in with yourself. Make sure that you're doing it because it's worth it, not because you're obligated."

I cocked my head. "What do you mean?"

"Like, I get what he's saying about passing a point of no return. It's better to decide in or out before you're halfway over the threshold getting your ass hit by the door. But that shouldn't also mean that you let yourself get locked into a room you don't want to be in anymore. You'll never have to wonder 'what if,' now that you've committed to moving forward. But if what's behind Door #2 isn't all you thought it would be?"

Dana let the question hang, then finished it. "Then you let yourself out."

I let Dana's words sink in a moment, then stood up from the couch, to Nero's disapproval. "It's time. I gotta go. I want to get there before she does."

"You've got this, Nat!" Dana cheered, slapping me on the ass. "Have fun with it."

- -

Pacing the floor in my blue suit pants and cap sleeved blouse, my tan heels tapped out a countdown on Oliver's hardwood floor. When the knock came a couple of minutes after six, I jumped. Camille came in with a warm smile, wearing wide-legged gray dress pants and a silk blouse accented by a long strand of chunky pearls she'd loosely draped double around her neck. Her honey-colored hair was tied back elegantly, a few strands framing her porcelain face.

"Oh, Natalie … the house is just gorgeous!" Camille gushed, crossing from the entryway into the living room. "I love all the choices in here. Perfectly sums up Oli." She took a look around, walking back into the kitchen, remarking on how much she liked the place. It settled my nerves a bit.

"Thank you," I said, watching her from across the room, "I appreciate you saying so. I know you know Oliver so well."

Camille's head turned from the cabinetry to meet my gaze, then glanced down with a sad, half-smile before saying, "We never got to talk after Caleb ran that ghastly headline."

She looked up. I took a step back, arms crossed behind my back.

"Oliver told me everything." I winced at my own graceless phrasing. "Or rather, he explained how you two came to be married for a little while. It's all water under the bridge now anyway."

Camille looked thoughtful, then took another step toward me. "Well, maybe not quite."

My eyes darted to her face.

"I mean, our brief relationship, of course, is a distant memory. But with Oli on the ticket, we have to be prepared for the media to resuscitate all sorts of long-dead storylines." She looked me hard in the eye. "As well as create as much drama as they can around new ones."

"I know," I replied. "That's why we're here tonight."

"Yes," she said, stepping into the living room. I followed her there as she took a seat in the armchair, placing her green leather messenger bag at her feet.

I sat down opposite her, perched on the edge of the sofa, my spine as straight as the fire poker hanging between us beside the hearth.

Camille was relaxed but leaned forward. "Natalie, I know you started this process with Sharon, and it may have felt a bit off-putting. But if I'm to prepare you properly for questions you could be asked in a brutally public way, I'm afraid I'll have to ask you some very personal ones."

"Yes, well, there really isn't anything exciting to tell," I said, twisting my fingers in my lap. I began to regret my decision to act adult about it and go along with Oliver's campaign team on this whole ridiculous meeting.

She gave a waxy smile. "Sometimes we don't realize what could be used against us. Or in this case, against the central political figure we're attached to. Are you familiar with some of Oliver and Elena Marques's platforms and policy positions?"

"Yes, I actually am," I said, my face brightening. "I just read the backgrounder on that today."

"That's great." Camille nodded encouragingly. "One of my jobs is to make sure that any views you express publicly don't diverge noticeably from that path."

She proceeded to quiz me on several hot-button issues, then showed me how to rephrase my answers to be as brief, innocuous, and on-message as possible. "When in doubt, say less," she instructed. "No one actually cares what you think, they just want to catch you fucking up."

"Noted," I replied, staring straight ahead.

"Now this next part could get a little dicey. It's where we talk about your personal life." She took out a notebook.

I shook my head at her. "Like I said, I'm extremely boring."

"Not when you're fucking the playboy Congressman who's on track to become VP, you aren't," she countered coolly. "And also not when the man you're divorcing has a news platform to publish endless reams of your dirty laundry, dating back to college."

I cringed, pointlessly arguing that nothing I'd ever done would be newsworthy.

"You're kidding me, right?" she asked with an incredulous smile. "What you ate for breakfast becomes newsworthy at this level. And all of it reflects on Oli, good, bad or otherwise. The added challenge in your case? Your ex has free rein to publish any of it. Or *all of it.*"

I felt the color drain from my face. Everything I had ever worried Caleb might say to a judge could now appear as front-page news.

"What about libel and slander laws?" I asked, panic rising.

"What about them?" Camille replied, flippant. "You're a public figure now. You'd have to prove defamatory statements to be untrue to be libelous or slanderous."

A wave of nausea seized me, thoughts spinning out every nasty thing Caleb would want to tell the world about me.

"Listen, Natalie." Camille put her pen down. "Caleb had no reservations about what he printed just a couple weeks ago. Consider that a warning shot. I don't know your husband well, but I've seen what he's capable of. He likes putting his thumb on the scale. He's big on power trips. I guess it gets him off or something. And I don't presume to guess what your relationship is with him now, but my money's on him being pretty butthurt. He did try to humiliate you on the cover of his magazine, in front of the whole DC metro region."

My mouth went dry. I squirmed in my seat. Would Caleb really do something like that? Would he let his own poison circulate among people we knew? Aiden's friends' parents? Would it potentially even get back to Aiden?

In my head, I could hear Aiden's classmates peppering him with questions from dinner table gossip:

"I heard you have a terrible mom."

"I heard she didn't take care of you."

"Did your mom abandon you to be with that guy running for vice president?"

Even if Caleb never printed those things, I'd have to live in fear of the headlines every morning. Not to mention the disastrous consequences it could have for Oliver.

Camille's voice yanked me back to the present. "The media loves distractions, Natalie. I know, because I watch them being created. So even if your marital bullshit seems petty and unnewsworthy to you, let me be the first to break it to you: they don't care."

"So what am I supposed to do about it?" I whimpered. This was beginning to feel absolutely hopeless.

Camille picked up her pen again and straightened up in the chair. "The first thing we do is write down absolutely everything he could use against you and create a sympathetic narrative around it. Then we come up with our own attacks on him, which shouldn't be too hard, considering he left the depressed mother of his child for the employee he was having an affair with."

"What did you just say?" My eyes narrowed.

She looked at me, confused. "The employee he was having an affair with?"

"Not that part," I snapped. "The other part."

"About the depression?" she asked.

"Where did you hear that?" I asked, leaning forward in my seat.

Camille looked like she realized she'd triggered a landmine. "Okay, so, Natalie, this is exactly the kind of reaction you can't have. Especially on camera. Some of these cable news outlets will eat you alive."

I stood up. "Just tell me who told you, Camille," I said icily.

She pursed her lips, her gaze drifted away. "Oliver may have mentioned—"

And that was all I heard. I walked back into the kitchen and poured myself a glass of water. Bracing myself over the sink, I guzzled from the glass. I had never used that word with Oliver, never explained my malaise to him that way, yet he had pegged me for a sick woman and told his professional gal-pal ex-wife all about it. And here she was, ready to help me either whitewash my shame or leverage it.

I felt a thin-fingered hand on my shoulder and spun around. Camille's face was soft and sympathetic.

"Natalie, I'm sorry if I spoke out of turn or hit a nerve."

"Sounds like Oliver spoke out of turn first." I snorted.

She opened her mouth like she was about to say something, then thought the better of it. "I'll leave that between the two of you. But I have to ask: have you given *real* consideration to the implications of being with Oliver at this high-stakes time?"

Her eyes were genuinely worried. I pressed my lips into a pale, thin line and looked away.

She went on, quite serious. "Oliver telling me details like this, or speculations, or whatever they may be, is really the least of your worries. I'm here to red team the shit out of you—"

"And it's not going well," I finished her sentence.

She shook her head slowly without looking away. "I'd love to sugarcoat it for you, but it's not."

"Then what do you recommend I do, Camille?" I threw up my hands. "Of all people, you should be able to give me advice. You were *married* to him, for Christ's sake, and you both managed to keep that under wraps for twenty years."

Camille straightened and looked at me like the hardened political journalist she was. "You want my *real* advice, Natalie?" she asked with a steely gaze.

I nodded reluctantly.

She raised her eyebrows. "Run," she said.

I'd already guessed her answer. It was still a punch in the gut.

"I hardly know you," she went on, "but just based on our time here tonight, on what Caleb has already proven himself willing to do and how you feel about that, I honestly don't know why you would put yourself through a world of hurt that could take ages to fully go away."

I walked away. I had to sit down. I slunk into one of the kitchen barstools.

I couldn't look at her. My words came out barely audible. "You really loved him at one point. You felt desperate to keep him once too."

She nodded slowly and sat down on the stool beside mine. "Which is why this may be the most relevant advice you're going to get. I don't know what he told you about our relationship and its inevitable end, but I didn't just fall out of love with Oliver while he was at law school."

"What do you mean?" I asked, turning to face her. "He said you met someone at work and asked to dissolve the marriage at Thanksgiving."

She shook her head slowly. "Did he tell you how little we talked in the months in between? Or how I visited him—twice—and he was completely absorbed in his classes and everything going on at Harvard?"

She waited for me to say something, but I was thrown for a loop.

"Our marriage was dead on arrival," she declared. "And the relationship leading up to it was as flimsy as a wish on a dandelion. I had to learn, after fighting my better judgment for nearly a year, that Oliver is a workaholic who's married to his political ideology. He's got a messiah complex, to boot."

I laughed breathily. "He said *you* were the one in love with rescuing *him.*"

"Maybe I was. But you see where that got me." Her expression was stark.

Camille looked at her watch, then went to retrieve her bag. Slinging it over her shoulder, she stood for a moment looking back at me as her expression turned to one of quiet pity. "You have a lovely design business, Natalie. You have a young son you need to protect, and a divorce from a challenging man that will take a lot of time and energy. I deeply understand your desire to be with Oli, and I can tell you're willing to try at all costs. But as someone who can see the writing on the wall, and who has personal experience, don't turn your whole life inside out on a quest for the Holy Grail. Because if you let it, it will destroy you."

Camille waited for me to say something, but I had gone numb several minutes prior. I sat there speechless as she walked to the door and let herself out.

- -

Oliver returned home very late that night. Pensive after my evening with Camille, I had taken a hot shower and fallen asleep early, plied by anxious dreams. Sometime around midnight Oliver crawled into bed beside me, wrapping his arms around me from behind and kissing my neck and face.

"Go back to sleep," he whispered through the kisses. "It's late. I just couldn't keep my hands to myself."

I breathed him in, the warmth of his bare-chested body against my skin, soothing and sweet. But the conversation with Camille still turned my stomach. I curled into the fetal position as he settled to sleep beside me.

I closed my eyes again in the darkness, eventually drifting back into oblivion.

- -

I awoke the next morning before the sun, the space next to me in bed still warm and smelling of his skin. I could hear muted sounds of Oliver in the shower and closed my eyes again, unwilling to face the day. When he emerged from the bathroom though, I opened them.

"You're awake!" he chirped, toweling off his armpits in the half morning light.

"Barely," I mumbled.

"How'd it go with Camille last night?" he asked, raking his fingers through his wet hair.

I picked up my head slightly. "She didn't tell you?"

"Tell me what?" he asked blankly.

"Did you tell her I had depression?" I asked, focusing my sleep-crusted eyes.

He slowed his toweling, as if he were thinking—or realizing something. "Why would I tell her something like that?" he asked, deflecting my question with one of his own.

"She didn't tell you anything about the session last night?" I asked again, sitting up, scanning his face for the least bit of insincerity.

"She texted me that you two met and suggested we talk about it when I had time, but the way you're asking about it, I'm starting to wonder if we should make it a priority."

I shook my head with a frown. "No. This isn't a good time. You're in a rush, and I have to get back home to be ready to pick up Aiden from school today."

"Oh, that's right," Oliver pulled on his undershirt. "You have him this afternoon through when?"

"The weekend, until Wednesday morning," I said. "Then he goes back to Caleb after school on Wednesday until the following Monday, when I pick him up again."

Oliver nodded as he pulled on his pants. "Sounds like you guys are settling into a good schedule."

"Yes," I said, locked on him, "but I'm telling you because I'm going to have him through the Convention."

He looked at me, not comprehending, as he buttoned his shirt.

"I mean, if that was in the plan, I can't go with you to the Convention." I stated flatly.

His smile came off as patronizing, even though I knew it wasn't meant to be. "That's okay, Nat. Not even necessary. The National Convention is a glorified pep rally. You're better off watching on TV."

I slouched back against the headboard with a mix of relief and embarrassment. Oliver knotted his tie in a half Windsor and pulled his buffed leather shoes from the walk-in closet.

"What if they ask you about me?" I asked him.

He chuckled under his breath as he shoehorned his feet into tight leather soles. "No one asks questions on that stage. It's speeches and roll calls and flashy stage production. Pomp and circumstance, as they say."

"But what would you say if some cable news reporter mobs you on the street when you're getting into the car or something? What will you tell them?" My anxiety rose into my throat.

Oliver shrugged. "Depends on the question, I guess. I wouldn't worry about it if I were you though. You know, it's Labor Day weekend. What do you have on tap for the kiddo?"

I hadn't even thought about it.

"Stop by the Congressional Lawn Party?" he suggested. "All the families and staffers get together on the Ellipse behind the White House. It marks the end of the August recess and Congress returning to session the next day. The staff and I fly out that night to Minneapolis to get situated ahead of the Convention Tuesday, but I'd love to see you, and I'd get to meet Aiden before I go."

The thought of Aiden meeting Oliver filled me with joy. But Camille's warning to *"run"* still rang in my head.

"I'd love that," I told him, "and I know Aiden would too." My words tasted bittersweet.

Oliver picked up his shoulder bag from the beanbag chair and slung it across his body. "Great! That's probably when I'll see you next then. We're gonna have our heads down all weekend, and you'll have Aiden the next few nights. I can't wait to meet him!"

I smiled as he rushed down the stairs. I whispered after him, "I can't wait for you to meet him too."

- -

The weekend was washed out by remnants of Hurricane Ophelia, which had broken up over North Carolina.

By the time the sun peeked through on Labor Day morning, Aiden had been cooped up inside the house with me for two days straight and couldn't wait to get outside. Wrestling with whether or not to introduce him to the perilous world of Oliver Thames, I finally convinced myself it would be a harmless day of sun and lawn games.

"How did we get invited here, Mom?" Aiden asked, holding my hand as we walked from the car to the Ellipse.

"Well, the man whose house I just remodeled is a congressman," I replied, swinging his arm in step with our walk.

"You know a *congressman?*" Aiden asked, looking up at me in awe. "We learned in school what Congress and the Senate do."

"Oh, yeah? What do they do?" I prompted.

"They make the laws that make our country better and safer for everyone. It's an important job."

"It sure is," I said.

Aiden thought for a moment. "Are we going to see him today?"

"That's the plan!" I smiled, trying to conceal my bundle of nerves.

"Oh, cool! Can we get a picture with him?" Aiden asked as he sprung across the crosswalk striping, like stepping stones across a river.

"I'm sure that can be arranged," I said, looking down the block. I swallowed hard. "There will be lots of people taking pictures today."

Reaching the other side, our feet met the close-cut grass of the Ellipse. The White House columns towered in the distance like sentries. Once we gave our names at the checkpoint along the perimeter, I could feel Aiden's anticipation pulling at my arm. Then he broke away to run full tilt across President's Park South.

A large crowd of people had already formed under the tents in the middle, and pop music reverberated through the speakers. Banquet-style tables and chairs were set up in rows, covered in red, white, and blue tablecloths, festooned with patriotic balloons. The muggy air smelled like cut grass and charcoal grills: the smell of late summer in Washington.

We wove through the crowd, searching for the spot where Oliver said he and his staff would be.

"Can I get a soda, Mom?" Aiden tugged on my hand toward the beverage tent with a long table of ice-packed coolers. Waiting to pick a can out of a cooler, I felt someone bump into my back. We both turned around, surprised.

"Whoa! Sorry about that!" A tall, bespectacled Latino man with a cyclist's physique exclaimed. He held up his hand apologetically, a dewy drink in the other. He was dressed in slim white pants and a chic, short-sleeved collared shirt. Behind him stood Channing, also smartly attired for the occasion.

"Natalie!" Channing called out, holding what I presumed to be an adult beverage in a plastic glass. "I was just telling Hugo it's the last day of the year he can wear those white pants. Leave it to him to bump into you and nearly spill his drink all over them."

"Channing!" I said with deep relief. "I'm glad I literally bumped into you guys. Hugo, such a pleasure to finally meet you!"

"Likewise!" Hugo chirruped, shaking my hand. "You must be the Natalie who took my dinner rezzie and got Channing all sauced up at barbecue karaoke."

"Is *that* how he described the night?" I laughed.

"Yes, you evil woman," Channing cut in, "you pumped me full of tequila and made me play Jon Secada's 'Just Another Day' on repeat until Hugo got home at one in the morning."

"I love Jon Secada," Hugo held up a hand as if taking an oath, "but I had just completed a six-hour emergency surgery and needed some rest."

"Totally defensible," I replied as Aiden returned beside me with a canned lemonade.

"And who's this little sprout?" Channing asked, crouching down to Aiden's height.

"This is my son Aiden." I smiled down at him. "Aiden, this is Channing. He works with Congressman Thames and has been extremely helpful to me." Channing shot me a knowing glance.

"What do you do for a living, young man?" Channing teased, hands on his knees and swaying slightly.

"I go to school," Aiden replied.

"School!" Channing cried, standing up, "Well, I guess that's a start. Call me when you need a job licking envelopes. I've got the perfect opportunity for you."

At that moment, I felt a hand on my shoulder. I turned to see Oliver standing beside me, grinning broadly. "My favorite people!" he exclaimed.

I had to stop myself from throwing my arms around him. "And who do we have here?" he asked, looking at Aiden.

"I'm Aiden," he introduced himself, reaching out his hand in a handshake.

Oliver looked at me with delight. "He's a natural!" Then to Aiden, "Are you running for office, young man?"

Aiden laughed. "Maybe someday!"

"Well, take my card then," Oliver said as he pulled out his wallet. "I may be out of a job by that point."

Aiden took the card and looked at it. "Are you the famous congressman my mom knows?"

Oliver jammed his hands in his pockets and rocked back on his heels. "Who? This lady?" he asked, smiling at me. Aiden nodded.

"*She's* the famous one," Oliver told him. "I'm lucky I know *her*."

Aiden looked up at me skeptically, then turned back to Oliver. "I've seen you on TV," he said. "You're going to be president!"

"*Vice* president," I corrected. "And we don't know that yet. He and Ms. Marques still need to win the election."

"Oh, yeah," Aiden said, "we learned about that. Once we're old enough, it's our patriotic duty to vote."

Oliver shot me a look like, *ya see, even your son knows that.* I grinned back, shaking my head.

"Can we take a picture with you?" Aiden asked Oliver.

"I would love that!" Oliver said, opening his wingspan for us to huddle beneath. "I get to have my picture taken with this famous designer and her son who's running for office one day."

I handed Channing my phone. Oliver squeezed me tight in his left arm, his right hand on Aiden's shoulder, as Channing snapped shots every which way.

Can't it stay this way forever? I wondered, frozen in the shutter.

Channing handed me back my phone. I took a look. Oliver, Aiden and I had come out picture perfect.

"Hey, Aiden, do you like to play cornhole?" Oliver was asking him.

"I love cornhole!" Aiden replied.

"Would you wanna toss a few beanbags with this old guy before I have to hop on a plane to the National Convention?"

"Yeah!" Aiden was enthusiastic. "I'm *really* good at it!"

Oliver high-fived him, looking up at me with laughing eyes. "Who will we play against?"

"Mom, will you play us?" Aiden asked excitedly.

I was a little surprised. "Who will my partner be?" I asked.

Hugo shoved Channing forward. "Let's see if this guy can get it in the hole after a few sparkling beverages."

Channing flashed him a naughty smirk. "You *know* I can ..."

"*Alriiiight!*" Oliver clapped his hands together to hype up Aiden. "We have a game!"

The four of us walked over to a set of cornhole boards painted with an American flag pattern. My sundress billowed in the breeze as I stood beside Aiden, tossing a blue beanbag to the matching board across from us, where Channing was having trouble maintaining his footing in doubtlessly very expensive shoes.

Aiden and Oliver were beating us handily when I made my first one in. I cried out "Cornhole!" as if it were Uno, arms raised in a cheer pose above my head.

"Mom. You don't need to say 'Cornhole!' when you get it in," Aiden told me, rolling his eyes.

"Hugo, I'm doing terribly!" Channing waved his arm in the air like a drowning diva. "Please fetch me another Red White & Blue Razzmatazz!"

"I don't believe a lack of alcohol is what's impairing your shot, my love," Hugo teased, but sauntered off to do Channing's bidding.

The day was perfect. I soaked it in through every pore.

Oliver congratulated Aiden on their win, and they took another picture together holding the beanbags in muscle men poses in front of the board.

"I have to head out now, pal, but that was a riveting game," Oliver told him.

"It wasn't *that* exciting," Aiden told him seriously. "Mom and Channing were pretty bad."

Channing rolled his eyes over the rim of his glass.

Oliver gave Aiden a fist bump goodbye, then gave me a long hug, rubbing my back.

"Good luck tomorrow," I whispered in his ear. "I'll be cheering for you."

"I know you will," he whispered back. "I'm so glad I got to meet Aiden."

Then he let go, and the moment was gone. He and Channing took off in one direction, and Aiden and I in the other.

19

WATCHING FROM THE WINGS

The following evening, Aiden and I made Lazy Lasagna for dinner, dumping ingredients into the pressure cooker. It was no Chef Thames five-course meal, but we laughed a lot and filled our bellies with noodles, meat sauce, and loads of cheese, then chased it with a pint of cookie dough ice cream.

Aiden was excited to see Oliver on TV to be able to tell his friends he "played cornhole with the next vice president." We turned on the broadcast of the National Convention at six thirty and snuggled up on the couch. Aiden was already in his jammies so he wouldn't have to miss anything to go get ready before bedtime.

The focus was on Elena Marques, of course, but Oliver had his time to shine. And shine he did, just like when he gave that impassioned speech to me on our way to knocking doors. Or talking to six-figure supporters at his gala or his staffers before the Fireball shots started flowing. I watched him from the comfort of my couch with my son as he delivered the concept of MAWO: "Make America Whole Again." I felt the hairs on my arms stand up. My desire for him still ran hot and deep. But the specter sat beside me too, a silent reminder of a steep price.

A 617 number rang on my phone. Who could be calling now? I

picked up to the sound of Daphne's voice, wanting to know if we were watching the Convention. Right, it was already the week after Labor Day.

"Daphne, hi!" I sat up on the couch so fast that Aiden's head toppled off my chest. "I'm watching on TV too. I just saw that incredible speech he gave."

"*Absolutely* impassioned!" Daphne trilled.

"Are you back from abroad?" I asked.

"I am, dear," she cooed. "And I was going to wait until tomorrow morning to call, but the broadcast got me thinking of you. Are you free Friday morning to chat with me and some of my team ahead of our kickoff call next week? I can send you the invite. We'll all be remote to start."

"Friday works great," I said with a flutter of excitement. "I've been doing some research and can't wait to run a few ideas by you."

"Oh, wonderful! I can't wait to hear them. I think you'll really like this architect I'm working with. Well, I won't keep you. I'm sure you want to watch the rest of the Convention coverage. Enjoy your evening, and I'll see you virtually next week."

When I put down the phone, Aiden glanced up from his bowl of ice cream. "Who was that?"

I snuggled my arm back around him. "That was Daphne Atwood, the woman from Boston whose campus I'm designing. She paid a lot of money at Oliver's fundraiser for me to work for her."

"Oooh, another big client," Aiden murmured, jamming a heaping spoonful of ice cream into his mouth. He smacked his lips together in delight. "I guess you really *are* famous, Mom."

- -

By the next morning, it was clear I had stepped back through the looking glass from the glamorous world I'd been posing in that summer. I slipped on a sock discarded on the hardwood floor, but caught myself on the banister, preventing a tumble down the stairs.

"*Aiden!* I nearly broke my neck on your soccer sock!" I shouted down the hall. "Please clean your things up before we leave for school."

As I waited for him to come downstairs, I scrolled through the news on my phone, curious to see what the pundits were saying the morning after the Convention.

Among the standard headlines, one glared back at me from a more sensational news outlet:

"TWO-TIMING THE TICKET: VEEP HOPEFUL CAN'T KEEP IT IN HIS ... BINDER"

I clicked on the link, jugular vein thrumming like a bass guitar string. Sure enough, a series of pictures of me with Oliver were plastered across the page like a photo collage: one of us hugging tightly at the lawn party, then a grainy one at the Italian place a few days before, and even shots of us entering the townhouse together after dinner that same night.

Oh, fuck, here we go again. I felt dizzy and had to sit down, nausea overtaking me. I held my head between both hands as I read the article from my phone in my lap:

With his National Convention debut behind him and just weeks to go before Election Day, Vice Presidential nominee Oliver Thames on the "Make America Whole Again" ticket is facing a firestorm of questions—not about policy, but passion.

Photos of the charismatic VP hopeful have revealed him "campaigning" after hours with someone decidedly not on the ballot: his interior decorator turned apparent love interest, Natalie Espinosa Weir. The woman is reported to be in the process of divorcing husband Caleb Weir, founder of the political news publication Party Lines.

While his Presidential running mate, Senator Elena Marques, stumps across swing states with laser focus, her newly anointed second-in-command seems more distracted by candlelit dinners than campaign strategy. Critics say Thames isn't just straying from the campaign, he's putting lust before country ...

This was not good. It wasn't just exposing our relationship, it was an attempt to cast aspersions on Oliver's fitness to serve. Sure, it was only one headline so far and it was off in the less credible realm of the opposition. But the dominos could fall fast now that these pictures were public.

I copied the link and texted it to Oliver and Channing, who were on their way back from Minneapolis. Channing replied right away. They were already on it. I wasn't to talk to anyone, for any reason.

Aiden trundled down the steps, ready for school. I did my best to put my panic on mute and bustle him into the car. I sped down our neighborhood streets with the music off, casting a paranoid eye at pedestrians as I pulled up to Aiden's school.

"Are you picking me up here after school, Mom?" he asked, hopping out of the car, backpack strapped to him like a parachute.

"I am, honey," I said, a quiver in my voice. "I'll meet you *right here* at 3:25. Don't talk to anyone you don't know, okay?"

"Mom," he said, giving me a bored look of reproach, "we learned Stranger Danger in, like, pre-K. I'll be fine."

"I know, honey, it's just that strangers may be interested that you met Oliver. If anyone asks, you shouldn't talk to them at all."

He shrugged his shoulders. "Okay, Mom. See you later!"

- -

I spent the remainder of the day riding a wave of worry, compulsively checking the major news sites and aggregators for more stories on us. Dana agreed to come over as soon as she could tonight, if only to comfort me.

Channing texted at 2:10 p.m., asking for a conference call. We settled on four p.m., after I picked up Aiden and before I took him to Caleb's.

Channing's last words were *I'll call you on this number. Don't talk to anyone until we talk.*

Before I left to pick up Aiden, two more stories from partisan publications hit the press, mostly bandwagoning off of the first. They had throwaway quotes from the opposition party on their moral high horse, proclaiming what a distraction, at best, Oliver's "selfish love affair" was while "the soul of the country hangs in the balance." At worst, they intimated, I could be a national security threat.

The accusations made me burn, coming at Oliver like that. As a man who I personally knew had every good intention for the people of this country and worked himself to the bone to serve, was he not allowed to have a personal life? I felt violated by the ugly coverage, but also completely helpless to do anything about it.

I glanced at my watch. It was already 3:24. I normally wouldn't have worried about being a few minutes late to pick up Aiden, except now I had to worry who else might get to him first. I grabbed my keys and ran.

When I pulled up to John Muir Elementary five minutes later, a deluge of children had poured out onto the front lawn and sidewalks. Car traffic kept me from even getting near where I told Aiden I'd pick him up. I'd have to park on a side street and get him on foot. Leaving my car wedged into a parallel parking space beneath a cherry tree, I sprinted out of the driver's seat, dodging little ones left and right, my head on a swivel in search of my son.

Finally I spotted him through the crowd, just standing there, anime keychains hanging listless from his backpack. A woman I didn't recognize was crouched down in front of him.

"Aiden!" I shouted. "Aiden, I'm here!"

Their heads swung toward me, and the woman stood up.

"Who are you?" I asked out of breath when I got to them. "Why are you talking to my son?"

The woman's expression shifted from surprised to smug. "Natalie Weir?" She stepped toward me, tilting her phone's camera lens up at me.

"Aiden, let's go," I muttered, grabbing him by the hand and pulling him away from her. I tried to use my other hand to block my face.

The woman followed us, shoving her phone at me. "Are you in a relationship with Oliver Thames?"

I started to jog with Aiden, who was squeezing my hand tightly. She tracked right along, firing questions as we went. "Has he divulged sensitive information to you about the presidential campaign or legislative affairs?"

I could feel Aiden's terror racing down his arm and into mine. We started to run.

"When was the first time you were intimate with the Congressman and how frequently do you see him?" She was shouting at me now as we ran into traffic, ignoring the crossing guard, whose whistle pierced the air with a long, shrill signal.

Cars jammed on their brakes. Heads snapped our way. Passersby gasped. I yanked Aiden to the other side of the street, the crossing guard now screaming at us. Our pursuer was weaving between two stopped cars to catch up with us.

Still running, Aiden clasping my right hand, we reached the car and flung ourselves inside. My hand slammed the door lock button as soon as we were in, the woman pressing herself and her phone's lens up to the driver's-side window.

Through the door, I could hear her questions growing more absurd. "How many times have you been intimate with the Congressman? What secrets has he told you about Elena Marques?"

I started the car and spun the wheel round, trying not to hit the other vehicles—or run her over. I tore out of there, giving her a great shot of my license plate to conclude her video.

Blood throbbed in my ears, my throat, my gut, all the way down to my fingertips. I could barely catch my breath, less so from the physical exertion of the run and more from sheer panic.

Aiden was still trying to get himself buckled in the backseat. "Who *was* that, Mom? Why did she chase us? Why was she asking about Oliver?" He fired off questions as I watched him through the rearview mirror, his sweet face flushed, mouth hanging slightly ajar to reveal two missing baby teeth.

"What did she say to you?" I questioned back. "How long was she talking to you when I got there?"

"I don't know. A few minutes? I was waiting where you said—"

"I know, baby, I know. You did exactly what I said," I reassured him, needing some reassurance myself.

"She was asking if I liked the lawn party and meeting Oliver. I said, 'Yeah, he's really nice,' and then she asked me if he comes over to the house and how many times I've seen him. I remembered you'd said not to say anything, so I didn't know what to tell her."

"What did you say after that? Anything?" My voice betrayed my attempt to stay calm.

"I don't know! I think I said, 'I don't know'!" He looked like he was about to cry.

"That's okay! That's exactly right. 'I don't know' is a perfect answer. She's probably a reporter and she's not supposed to be asking kids questions without permission from their parents." I actually wasn't sure what the legal requirement was for journalists when talking to minors. I realized I didn't know that woman, whoever she was, or if she was even a legit journalist.

My head darted back and forth on our brief trip from the school to home, looking for anyone else who might be tailing us or lurking around the corner. We pulled into the garage, and I closed the door behind us so fast, it nearly hit my liftgate.

We sat there in the dim garage for a moment, the only trace of sound coming from our heavy breaths.

"That was really scary, Mommy." The way he said it pulled a loose thread in my heart. I couldn't remember the last time he called me "Mommy." It had been the more grown-up "Mom" for a while now.

My thoughts raced. *How am I going to protect him? How can I be by his side or have someone I trust be with him every moment of the day while this is going on?*

"You did great, honey. If that ever happens again, you keep telling them, 'I don't know,' just like you did." I rubbed my face hard, energy draining from me. I sat motionless in the driver's seat.

"Mom?" he finally asked, still buckled into the backseat.

"Yeah, honey?"

"Can we go inside now?"

- -

It wasn't like I hadn't been warned. But living through that invasion of privacy, seeing my son standing there scared and uncertain, hit way different than anything I could have imagined. People were ruthless, and nothing was sacred. When my phone buzzed in my pocket for the conference call, I almost jumped across my office.

"Channing," I answered shakily. "Some woman just chased me and Aiden back to my car, video recording us on her phone. She didn't even give her credentials."

There was a beat on the other end. I could picture Channing and Oliver and whomever else was with them casting serious looks at each other across the conference table.

"Yes, my love," Channing finally replied, a hint of worry in his voice. "I'm here with Oliver and Sharon and a couple folks you haven't met yet from Ms. Marques's team. We expected this might start happening. Could've been our favorite fake news network. Could've been some wingnut influencer or random wacko. We'll know when the video surfaces tonight."

I felt sick. I crawled into an armchair and balled up, like a frightened armadillo. "She was trying to get Aiden to tell her what he thought of Oliver and when they first met and if Oliver visited the house and whatnot."

"Mmmm-hmmm," Channing hummed, "all to be expected. Did Aiden say anything to her?"

I rocked gently in the chair, arms wrapped around my legs. "He told her Oliver was 'really nice,' but then he just kept saying, 'I don't know' to her other questions."

"Spoken like a true politician," Oliver's voice rang over the line.

I exhaled a long, stale breath, but there was still more pressure inside me.

"I saw more headlines this afternoon—" I added.

"We're tracking it all," Channing assured me.

I twisted a strand of hair around my finger. "Is it—is this causing problems for the campaign?" I asked.

There was another uncomfortable silence until Oliver jumped in,

"Problems? No. A couple headaches, sure. But nothing we can't handle. This is a team of pros."

I let out another breath, but an uneasy feeling took root. Oliver was downplaying this for my benefit. There is no way this wasn't creating damage control work, and the staff was already stretched.

"Here's what we're going to do, Natalie." Channing took over the line. "Things are going to evolve rapidly, in all likelihood. We'll know soon enough how the major news networks are going to respond to the photos that ran on the fringe today. Since this story might start taking on a life of its own, we're going to schedule you for an on-camera readiness intensive with Sharon and her counterpart on the Marques team."

"I'm sorry, a—what?" A shiver ran through me.

"An intensive," Sharon's voice sounded through the microphone. "A multi-hour, on-camera drill to prepare and mock grill you on everything, from your relationship with Oliver to your personal values and political beliefs. We will help you with these. And a heavy primer on the national issues of the day and, of course, how you see your potential role as the romantic partner to the candidate, should he get elected."

I sucked in air. "I need to go on camera?"

"You *may*, honey." Channing nudged Sharon aside. "But, like I said, this whole thing could develop very quickly. If the news networks want to hear from you, we can't put it off. If we put it off, the more seedy speculation seeps in, and the more speculation seeps in, the worse it reflects on Oliver, and the deeper the hole we have to dig out of to win hearts and minds by November."

"When do I need to be ready for this?" I felt dizzy again. Things had spun straight out of control in the span of just a few hours.

"Friday, ideally," Channing replied. "Can you meet us at the office again? Say around eight or nine that morning?"

"Yes," I said. "No—wait. I have a call with Daphne Atwood."

"Darling," Sharon's words pierced through the phone with conde-scension, "if that's some other mommy from the PTA, would you be a dear and reschedule? You know ... in the interest of our little campaign and *the American public?"*

Oliver's silence spoke volumes.

I shrank further into my chair. "Y—yes. Yes, of course. I'll call her as soon as I hang up."

"Thanks, Nat!" Channing sang. "See you at Rayburn, eight a.m. sharp!"

"Natalie—" Oliver's voice rang out, *"thank you."*

"She should be thanking *you*," I could hear Sharon murmur in the background.

Channing's voice rose above it, chorusing cheerful good-byes. Then I was alone in my office, battered by the crashing tide of anxiety.

- -

Not an hour later, I was pulling up to Caleb's house with Aiden for our midweek transfer. I grimaced at my timing. Caleb looked up from the dog, who was mid-squat. His eyes squinted as I drove up the driveway.

Aiden tumbled out the back door, tangled in the backpack and overnight bag that contained the few items that couldn't be duplicated and had to shuttle back and forth between houses. Mr. Bear spilled out of the unzipped bag as Aiden ran over to Caleb and Affogato for a hug.

"Dad! I might be on the news tonight!" he blurted as he clumsily approached.

"The news!" Caleb exclaimed, with a chilly glance at me. "Why would you be on the news, kiddo?"

"Because a reporter interviewed me at school, and then she chased me and Mommy to the car."

"You're kidding," Caleb said. "Hey, bud, why don't you take the dog down the street so she can finish doing her business? I'll take your bags in."

Aiden took up the leash and bumbled down the sidewalk with the setter, as Caleb picked up his bags on the lawn and strolled over to my window. I considered backing out of the driveway, but hesitantly rolled the window down.

"A reporter, Natalie? Really?" Caleb crossed his arms.

I set my jaw. "I got Aiden out of there almost immediately—"

"*Almost* immediately? Did you get there late again?"

"The whole thing was out of my control, Caleb! I can't keep Aiden in a bubble all day!" Heat rushed to my face, body bracing for a fight.

"It's out of your control *now*, Natalie, because you were too selfish to control it while you still could. You let this ridiculous fling go on way too long. In fact, I'm shocked the Marques campaign hasn't put the kibosh on it already. You're a fucking wrecking ball!" Caleb raised his arms in exasperation and let them smack against his sides.

"Don't worry about the campaign, Caleb. They have it under control." My hands were clenched in my lap.

"Right now, I'm just worried about our *son*. How long are you going to let this absurdity go on?" he demanded, hands gripping my window frame. He narrowed his eyes at me, "Couldn't you have just learned your lesson a couple weeks ago?"

"My *lesson?*" I hissed. "Is that what your lovely photo spread and story were supposed to be? A lesson?"

He pushed off from the car frame. "Obviously one you were too dense to learn. Listen, Natalie. I don't know if you actually realize this yet, *but I can't help you.* The national media has grabbed hold of this story and will eat you both alive. I'm the only one looking out for Aiden in all of this."

"Yeah, looking out for him so much that you put me in the crosshairs in the first place!" I shouted. I was furious enough to run his foot over, but he was already backing up from the driveway toward the house.

"Hate me all you want, Natalie," he called, arms outstretched like he was being crucified, "but I'm not gonna make our son pay the price. Aiden belongs in a stable household with responsible adults. And the way things are already going, a judge is gonna agree with me, even if you don't."

"Is that a threat?" I yelled out the window.

"It's a reality, Natalie!" he bellowed back. "So buckle up!"

I fumed, grasping for a zinger to shout back at him, as he turned and entered the house. I gripped the steering wheel and backed out onto the otherwise quiet cul-de-sac, then peeled away.

- -

I didn't want to be in my own house that night. I had already paced tracks back and forth into the carpet, like an elephant at the zoo.

I walked to Dana's, trying to burn this nervous energy, ringing the bell and glancing around as though a camera lens were pointed at me from the tree line.

She yanked open the door. "Hi," she said softly, drawing me in.

"Dana, I'm a mess," I broke down upon entry. "I feel like this whole thing has taken on a life of its own. Even Oliver can't do anything about it."

Her face crumpled with concern. And while her next words could have been, "I told you so—we all told you so," they weren't.

"Come sit," she said, gesturing toward the living room where it all started.

The setting sun left an evening glow in the room, and the house was uncannily quiet. Not even Nero stuck around.

I sank into the sofa between two overstuffed pillows. The room smelled like it had just been vacuumed.

Dana crawled onto the sofa beside me, barefoot but still dressed from the workday.

"Okay," she said in the soothing tone of a guidance counselor, "start from when you last left here."

I spilled into the Camille media training, which had started out much better than expected, but ended with that stomach-turning warning. I told Dana about the lawn party that was perfect in every way. Then watching the Convention and things kicking off with Daphne had me riding high until the headlines smacked me across the face the next morning, followed by Aiden and I getting chased by that joke of a reporter. Honestly, the latest standoff with Caleb had paled in comparison to the conference call with Oliver and his team. Things were already an uphill battle for the campaign. Now Oliver and Elena Marques were mired in what the opposition was trying to paint as a scandal.

Running Dana through what was happening left me feeling more helpless and hopeless than I had in weeks. She rested a hand over mine on the couch cushion. "How about we take stock of what's going *right?*" she suggested.

She counted on the fingers of her hand: "You and Aiden are closer than ever. Your first project that restarted your career couldn't have been a bigger success. Your next project, which is massively high-profile, starts tomorrow and will lead to other lucrative, high-visibility jobs. You have a stellar lawyer in your corner for the divorce. And I *think* it's safe to say you are light years happier than you've been in a long time."

She held her five unfurled fingers up to my face in the shape of a starfish.

It was true. In two short months, I had turned my whole life around into one I never dared dream of. If only I could keep Oliver on the list.

But that sixth limb wasn't going to fit.

"Everything with Oliver would be perfect, if he just hadn't been selected to run as VP," I groaned, flopping against the sofa backrest.

"I know, honey. And it's okay to grieve that." She gave me a tight hug.

When I finally pulled away, her face was full of empathy. "One of the things I find helps with grief is gratitude. That's not just some yoga bullshit. When I make a point of listing all the things I'm grateful for, things I've worked hard for, and others that came to me with a bit of luck, it really puts in perspective any losses that come with them."

"So you're saying to be happy for what I have? And stop crying over a relationship I never deserved in the first place?" I asked between sniffles.

"No," she replied. "I never said you didn't deserve this relationship. What I *am* saying is to look back down the mountain at how far you've climbed so quickly and take pride in that. If Oliver weren't Oliver, but some gross old man who just happened to be a great client who introduced you to people and all that, you'd be celebrating all the amazing things you've accomplished to rebuild your life. You'd be so much happier than you are today, instead of crying over what was probably always out of reach. Don't let the illusion of a life with Oliver erase all those accomplishments you would otherwise be thrilled about."

Dana looked at me with an intensity matched by the setting sun streaming through the window. "Isn't that wild? Isn't that reason to feel gratitude for all the wonderful things you've added to your life?"

She wasn't wrong. In fact, she made a lot of sense. I hadn't thought about it that way before. I was so wrapped around the axel with Oliver that I didn't even appreciate the much bigger challenges I had crawled out from under along the way.

"Thanks, Dane," I said, sinking back on the couch. "I guess I lost sight of those things. I *should* appreciate them more. But it doesn't take away how I feel about Oliver or how hard riding this out is going to be."

Dana raised an eyebrow. "Is riding it out really your only choice, Natalie?"

I held my head in my hands. "I don't want to let him go," I pleaded.

"I can accept that," she said, crossing her arms. "But at what cost do *you* accept it?"

I looked away.

Dana leaned in. "Ask yourself: are the things you fought so hard for over the past two months worth jeopardizing in pursuit of Oliver?"

A wrench tightened my innards. But I wasn't going to get upset at her. I wasn't going to defend my feelings or complain that she couldn't understand because it wasn't happening to her personally.

I went limp. I felt like I'd been swimming upstream and finally let the current sweep me along. "What are you suggesting then?"

Dana drew a long breath and looked out the window, then returned to my face. "You can do with this what you will. It's only my opinion. But from someone who has known you all these years and really, *truly* wants to see you happy?"

She hesitated. I nodded. "Go on."

A gentle smile crept across her face. She lowered her gaze at me. "Then here is my advice to you: Love yourself first, Natalie. And when you do, when you *really* do, and when you prioritize the things in your life that need to come first, instead of contorting to fit into someone else's story, you'll be able to love the right person sustainably. And the right person will be able to love you back in the way you need, too."

- -

I didn't sleep much that night, but when I did, the dreams tortured me. Oliver's silhouette against the setting sun searched for me along the beach, calling my name. But I was underwater, unable to breathe air anymore, too far away for him to hear me.

I woke up gasping in the darkness, the relief of waking overtaken by reality. I sat up rubbing my eyes. There was no going back to sleep.

I got up and got dressed in the moonlight, a little after four. But the day was coming.

I closed my car door and hit the start button, a little electric choir drowning out a chorus of crickets in the predawn light. Silence stifled the cabin of my car as I drove down the highway to the GW Parkway. On the other side of the Potomac, all of Washington was dark and still.

I entered through the front door quietly, took off my sneakers, and climbed two flights in my socks up to where Oliver slept in the hazy gray of morning. I crawled in. He stirred ... then startled ... then realized it was me. The both of us under the covers, he wrapped his arms around, nuzzling his sleep-weary head into the crook of my neck.

I kissed his temple.

We stayed like that for a while. I wasn't sure how long. The softness of the bedding and warmth of our bodies engulfed me. I breathed in the oils of his skin and the lingering scent of sandalwood. It was so quiet I could hear our hearts beating, at first in sync, then drifting out of rhythm with one another.

"I wanted to tell you in person," I whispered.

He opened a tired eye to look at me.

"I wanted to tell you that you were right." My voice cracked, as I forced myself to continue. "That it may not be what we want, but it's for the best."

I felt his body shift abruptly in my arms. He sat up and looked at me with a sadness that made it hard for me to take in air.

"You're so strong," I said, "and now I have to summon my own strength to do what's right for both of us. Because even though the situation isn't kind to me, forcing you, and both of us, through it this way is really not fair to you."

"What are you saying, Natalie?" he croaked, groggy.

I sat up to face him. "I'm saying I don't want either of us to risk ruining how far we've come. True love starts with yourself."

He said nothing, just probed my soul with his pale green eyes, then took me in his arms and held me tight.

"I wish …" my voice cracked, tears trickling onto his shoulder, "I wish you *so* much success and happiness."

He exhaled, stroking my hair, and breathing me in again. The light began to filter in through the large loft window. We could have stayed there holding each other until the sun set back below the Earth, but I broke away. I got out of the bed and he looked up at me, a subdued version of the man I'd come to know.

I paused for a moment. There was nothing more to say. "Good luck, Oliver," I said, and exited down the stairs.

RETURN TO SENDER

September never seems to deliver the crisp autumn weather we all believe it will in DC. We turn the page on Labor Day, packing away our white pants in exchange for boots and sweaters, eager to greet the new season before the equinox. Chalk it up to our cyclical longing for beginnings to become endings so new beginnings can take shape.

Standing on a picnic bench in a park in Arlington, Virginia, on one such unseasonably warm September day, I was thankful to be dressed in the appropriate footwear, even as sweat collected down my back. A crowd of volunteers clustered near as I handed out address packets and a colleague explained key campaign talking points and possible objections from voters.

"This is a battleground state!" My colleague concluded her rallying cry, "So get out there and knock some doors for Marques-Thames! Let's Make America Whole Again, people!" The crowd cheered and splintered off to get out the vote.

"Will you be my buddy?" I asked the guy next to me. Aiden laughed and accepted a stack of flyers, thrilled just to be outside doing something with his mom. It was a bonus it was also something so official for "our friend Oliver, the next vice president."

"We won't make it to every door," I told him. "Even the ones we do get to, plenty of people won't answer. But each person we speak to can make that much more of a difference."

Aiden agreed, then asked if we were going to get candy at each house.

I wrapped an arm around his shoulder as we made our way down the street. "Not till next month, buddy, but that's coming up, too."

- -

The pundits were calling it a dead heat, and it was nearly midnight. Would the Blue Wall hold? Would the early vote go the way the statisticians were predicting?

The "Magic Wall" electoral map tracking the path to 270 votes was making my head spin. It didn't help that I was running on little sleep. The previous couple of weeks had included several Amtrak rides to Boston for the Atwood project.

Aiden had long ago fallen asleep in my bed as we watched the returns together in my freshly redecorated bedroom. I'd carried him into his own bed, out cold, and went downstairs to watch the rest of the coverage, surrounded by my election night console of TV screen, phone screen, and laptop screen, trying to take it all in.

Around seven a.m., Aiden had pitter-pattered downstairs, eager to know who'd won. He found me asleep and drooling under a throw on the couch.

"Did he win, Mom? Did Oliver win?"

I sat up with a start. The TV was still on, volume muted. But the result was as clear as the chyron:

"MARQUES UNSEATS MAYBERRY IN HISTORIC UPSET"

"Oh my God! Oh my God!!" I jumped up on the sofa.

In the excitement of the moment, Aiden jumped up on the couch with me like a forbidden trampoline.

"They did it, Aiden! They did it!!" I shouted, wiping tears from my cheeks.

"I can't believe I know the vice president!" Aiden shouted back.

When we finally calmed down enough, I whipped up a celebratory batch of berry pancakes, placing blueberries like stars and strawberries like stripes against the purple batter backdrop. I shared a glass of chocolate milk with Aiden before shuffling him out to the bus.

Back inside, I stared at a blank text message for a long time, contemplating what to write. What was the etiquette for congratulating your recent ex-lover, one you hadn't spoken to in two months, but still had feelings for, on winning the vice presidency of the United States?

I finally settled on something short and sweet that echoed the phrase his dear cook Maria had told him at the beginning of it all, when she'd handed him the starfish:

Congratulations, Oliver ... Go live what you were put here to do. <3

I put my phone away and promised myself I wouldn't wait for a response. I knew he'd be endlessly busy in the coming days.

But I'd be lying if I said I wasn't troubled by the silence that followed. Not a call, not a text, not even an emoji thumbs-up.

The days turned into weeks, and I put it out of my mind. He was on another level now, farther from reach than ever before. I would have to content myself with the memory of what we shared one cosmic August, that strange, in-between time for us both, two starfish caught up in the tide, then spirited back to sea.

- -

Snow had begun to stick to the front lawn and driveway as I pulled back into the garage with Aiden. The news anchor on WTOP finished rattling off early school closures spanning the entire metro area before switching over to the traffic reporter's matter-of-fact announcement that, between the typical inauguration road closures and the incoming winter storm, Tuesday's commute was going to be brutal.

I turned off the car and crunched down the driveway in my boots to check the mail. Aiden bolted inside to put on his snow gear and make the most of the fresh dusting before sunset.

Back in the house, I shed my jacket and sifted through the handful of envelopes: a coupon pack. A save-the-date. A credit card offer. The latest edition of *GRAY Magazine*. Last, a small envelope with hand-written address and a return address at the Naval Observatory.

My breath caught in disbelief. I zipped my finger across the envelope flap, giving myself a paper cut in the process. I removed a pale green note card, official stationery.

I know it's a little early to be sending a note with this return address, so don't write me back here until after January 20th, okay? I'm looking for a real top-notch interior decorator, because this place I'm moving into is plagued by '80s bachelor pad style, if you know what I mean. My colleague down the street has some unique design challenges too. For one, her new office is shaped like an oval ...

My hand shook as I read the note. Then read it again.

Aiden clunked downstairs in his new snow boots and jacket, attempting to pull on his mittens.

"Mom, are you—Hey! Why are you crying?"

"Oh," I said, wiping away a tear. "I just got a letter from Oliver."

"You did?!" he exclaimed, dropping his hat and running over, hand shoved backward into a mitten. "Are we invited to the White House?"

A messy smile I couldn't hold back took over my face. "Possibly," I told him, "but maybe just *his* house, to start."

"Yes!" Aiden threw his arms in the air, mitten flying off. I scooped it from the floor and handed it back.

Picking up his red knit hat, I pulled it down over his ears. "Mom, are you still coming outside to build the snowman?"

"You bet I am," I replied, nuzzling up to his button nose. "Race you outside."

AUTHOR'S NOTE

Hey there, reader.

If you made it this far, I just want to say thank you. Writing *August Recess* let me fulfill a passion, and knowing it resonated with you means the world.

If you loved this book, I think you'll really enjoy what I'm working on next. I've got more relatable heroines, more steamy encounters, and more pageturning storylines coming your way, so I'd love to keep you in the loop.

Join me on Substack for sneak peeks, behind-the-scenes updates, and exclusive content: https://alexandrakleinauthor.substack.com/

As an independent author, I don't have a big marketing machine behind me—just readers like you. So if you're eager for more books in this world (or from me in general), the single most impactful thing you can do?

Leave a review.

Even just a few quick words on your favorite platform helps more readers discover *August Recess* and supports my work in a major way.

Leave a review here:

Amazon: August Recess

Goodreads: August Recess

Thank you for being part of this journey. I write for readers like you—and I'm so glad we found each other.

ACKNOWLEDGMENTS

No book is written alone, and *August Recess* is no exception.

First and foremost, thank you to Amy Suto, my book sherpa: *I could not have gotten to the summit without you.* (And maybe not even basecamp.) You wore many hats and bestowed expert guidance the entire way—on process, editorial, design, marketing, and much more. You were the primary force helping me take *August Recess* from a tickle in my brain to the published page and its promotion. We did it!

To my line editor, Dr. Hanne Blank Boyd, who was the perfect choice for tightening up my prose. Your edits read seamlessly, like a more talented version of myself. I'm equally grateful for your eclectic knowledge and experiences, which helped authenticate even the most niche of story details.

To Ashley Munson, my graphic designer: I *hope* people judge this book by its cover. Your striking artwork and ability to bring to life the hazy vision in my head produced a cover that's truly emblematic of *August Recess.*

To my proofreader, Kate Underwood: Your thoroughness and deep editorial knowledge brought peace of mind to this tortured perfectionist! Thank you for being that final set of eyes when mine had glazed over so many re-reads ago.

To the beta readers who provided detailed and thoughtful feedback on earlier iterations of this manuscript: I appreciate the ideas and critiques you gave me to chew on and the thumbs up where I needed it. You helped shape this book.

To Jeffrey, my self-dubbed #1 Fan—I know it's the truth! My self-esteem would sometimes falter if it weren't for your unabating love, admiration, encouragement, and support. How lucky am I to have met someone who believes in me even more than I believe in myself? Thank you for riding the rollercoaster of emotions with me and being my "steady heart." Thank you also for being my sounding board for this book and for absolutely everything—even when I keep you up all night.

To my mom, who read me books in the womb and helped me write "The Wayward Pigeon" at six years old. I'm not sure what first grade teacher believed "wayward" was my vocab choice, but I'm glad you put such an early emphasis on reading and writing. It contributed to getting me here.

To Mary Hassenplug, my most influential Language & Comp teacher: You and your curriculum had a tremendous impact on my writing. And for all the times I wanted to go off-script in class to write about some romantic encounter du jour, writing romance is finally the assignment!

To Jaci, whose friendship and reassurance in my moments of self-doubt are invaluable. Thank you for fielding the random panic call for 25 years and counting. And for not minding when I needed to knock out a chapter or so while visiting you.

To the romance writing community I've just joined, thank you for the inspiration, the camaraderie … the spicy Pinterest boards. To quote one of the most iconic political romances: "I think this is the beginning of a beautiful friendship…"

And finally, to you, dear reader: thank you for choosing this book, for spending time with these characters, and for making space for stories like this one in your life.

ABOUT THE AUTHOR

August Recess marks Alexandra Klein's debut romance novel. Drawing on her twenty years in Washington, Klein brings an authentic perspective to her storytelling from holding roles in news media, government contracting, commercial real estate, and nonprofit communications. When she's not exploring other pockets of the world with her #1 Fan, Jeffrey, they're enjoying time with his three energetic sons and a grumpy hedgehog named Salinger.

www.ingramcontent.com/pod-product-compliance
Lightning Source LLC
Chambersburg PA
CBHW020244010826
48973CB00006B/1650